Victorian Dress in Contemporary Historical Fiction

Victorian Dress in Contemporary Historical Fiction

Materiality, Agency and Narrative

Danielle Mariann Dove

BLOOMSBURY ACADEMIC
LONDON • NEW YORK • OXFORD • NEW DELHI • SYDNEY

BLOOMSBURY ACADEMIC
Bloomsbury Publishing Plc, 50 Bedford Square, London, WC1B 3DP, UK
Bloomsbury Publishing Inc, 1385 Broadway, New York, NY 10018, USA
Bloomsbury Publishing Ireland, 29 Earlsfort Terrace, Dublin 2, D02 AY28, Ireland

BLOOMSBURY, BLOOMSBURY ACADEMIC and the Diana logo are
trademarks of Bloomsbury Publishing Plc

First published in Great Britain 2023
Paperback edition published in 2025

Copyright © Danielle Mariann Dove, 2023

Danielle Mariann Dove has asserted her right under the Copyright, Designs and Patents Act, 1988, to be identified as Author of this work.

For legal purposes the Acknowledgements on p. viii constitute an extension of this copyright page.

Cover image: Paris fashions in Victorian London, February 1848 © Historical Images Archive/Alamy Stock Photo

All rights reserved. No part of this publication may be: i) reproduced or transmitted in any form, electronic or mechanical, including photocopying, recording or by means of any information storage or retrieval system without prior permission in writing from the publishers; or ii) used or reproduced in any way for the training, development or operation of artificial intelligence (AI) technologies, including generative AI technologies. The rights holders expressly reserve this publication from the text and data mining exception as per Article 4(3) of the Digital Single Market Directive (EU) 2019/790.

Bloomsbury Publishing Plc does not have any control over, or responsibility to any third-party websites referred to or in this book. All internet addresses given in this book were correct at the time of going to press. The author and publisher regret any inconvenience caused if addresses have changed or sites have ceased to exist, but can accept no responsibility for any such changes.

The author and publisher gratefully acknowledge the permission granted to reproduce copyright material in this book. The third-party copyrighted material displayed in the pages of this book is done so on the basis of fair use for the purposes of teaching, criticism, scholarship or research only in accordance with international copyright laws, and is not intended to infringe upon the ownership rights of the original owners.

A catalogue record for this book is available from the British Library.

Library of Congress Cataloging-in-Publication Data
Names: Dove, Danielle Mariann, author.
Title: Victorian dress in contemporary historical fiction : materiality, agency and narrative / Danielle Mariann Dove.
Description: London ; New York : Bloomsbury Academic, 2023. | Originally presented as author's thesis (doctoral). | Includes bibliographical references and index.
Identifiers: LCCN 2023019774 (print) | LCCN 2023019775 (ebook) | ISBN 9781350294684 (hardback) | ISBN 9781350294721 (paperback) | ISBN 9781350294691 (pdf) | ISBN 9781350294707 (epub)
Subjects: LCSH: Historical fiction–History and criticism. | Clothing and dress in literature. | Fashion in literature. | Women in literature. | LCGFT: Literary criticism.
Classification: LCC PN3441 .D68 2023 (print) | LCC PN3441 (ebook) | DDC 809.3/81–dc23/eng/20230530
LC record available at https://lccn.loc.gov/2023019774
LC ebook record available at https://lccn.loc.gov/2023019775

ISBN: HB: 978-1-3502-9468-4
PB: 978-1-3502-9472-1
ePDF: 978-1-3502-9469-1
eBook: 978-1-3502-9470-7

Typeset by Newgen KnowledgeWorks Pvt. Ltd., Chennai, India

For product safety related questions contact productsafety@bloomsbury.com.

To find out more about our authors and books visit www.bloomsbury.com and sign up for our newsletters.

Contents

List of Illustrations		vii
Acknowledgements		viii
1	Introduction: Re-fashioning the Victorians	1
	Re-fashioning the past	7
	Reading and writing dress: Texts and textiles	12
	(Neo-)Victorian sartorial and material culture	16
	Neo-Victorian fashions: Chapter outlines	25
2	Gowns	29
	New materialism and neo-Victorianism	32
	Dynamic dresses in *The Master*	39
	Sartorial entanglements in *Alias Grace*	49
3	Gloves	65
	Fashioning identity, agency and desire in Waters's neo-Victorian trilogy	67
	'The impress of her hand': Victorian gloves	78
	Neo-Victorian gloves: Touch, materiality and queer desire	85
	Material traces of the past	91
4	Veils	99
	Victorian veils	100
	Neo-Victorian veils	108
	Veils and canvases in *The Ghost Writer*: Revealing the past	111
	Veils, bindings, skin: Concealing bodies and books in *The Journal of Dora Damage*	122
5	Jewellery	135
	Ornamenting the Victorian woman	140
	Heirlooms and afterlives: Jewellery in *Great Expectations* and *Havisham*	146

'Talisman' turquoises and 'poisoned' diamonds in *Daniel Deronda*
and *Gwendolen* 158

6   Conclusion 171

References 179
Index 197

Illustrations

1.1	Punch cartoon: Victorian women's fashion – the wide hoop skirt (private collection).	6
1.2	The newest fashions for spring and summer mantles. Illustration for the *Englishwoman's Domestic Magazine*, 1860s.	18
2.1	Dress *c.* 1875 © Brooklyn Museum Costume Collection at the Metropolitan Museum of Art.	39
2.2	*Godey's Unrivalled Colored Fashions*, 1856.	54
3.1	Pair of gloves, made by C. Courvoisier. France, *c.* 1887.	79
4.1	Advertisement for Jay's General Mourning Warehouse in *The Graphic*, Mourning Dress, 1888.	103
5.1	Victorian mourning brooch containing the hair of a deceased relative.	143
5.2	Jewellery at the Loan Exhibition, South Kensington Museum, 1872.	144

Acknowledgements

This book first materialized, in an early form, as a doctoral thesis, and I am indebted to the following people and institutions who have supported and guided me during the course of its (re-)fashioning. A first and special word of thanks goes to my family and friends for their constant love and support. My especial thanks must go to my mum, Rachel, for inspiring me with her creativity and for teaching me to love books and beautiful clothes. To my fiancé, Frankie, I can't begin to express how much I appreciate your love and encouragement – this book is dedicated to you. Deepest thanks to Patricia Pulham for her invaluable advice and generous mentorship; this book would not exist were it not for her belief in the project. I am also indebted to my anonymous reader and reviewers, and to Beth Palmer, Ann Heilmann and Lucy Ella Rose, whose kind and generous feedback at earlier stages in the project has played an important role in the shaping of this study. Thank you to the School of Literature and Languages at the University of Surrey for funding my doctoral research and the Pasold Research Fund for funding image acquisitions and permissions for the images/illustrations acquired from the V&A and the Mary Evans Picture Library. I would also like to thank the curators and archivists at the V&A, Bath Fashion Museum and Leeds Museum who responded to my queries and assisted me in my research. Finally, thanks are due to Lucy Brown and Aanchal Vij at Bloomsbury for their much-appreciated patience and guidance.

 I am grateful for permission to reprint revised and expanded versions of previously published work in this book. Parts of Chapter 2 appeared as '"Wilful Phantoms": Haunted Dress, Memory, and Agentic Materiality in Colm Tóibín's *The Master*' in *Neo-Victorian Things: Re-Imagining Nineteenth-Century Material Cultures in Literature and Film* (2022), copyright Palgrave Macmillan. Chapter 3 is based on an earlier and shorter essay entitled 'Ghostly Gloves, Haunted Hands: The Material Trace in Sarah Waters' *Affinity* and *Fingersmith*', in *Victoriographies* (2019), copyright Edinburgh University Press.

1

Introduction: Re-fashioning the Victorians

In the final pages of Sarah Waters's neo-Victorian novel *Affinity* (1999), Margaret Prior travels to 'a great shop on Oxford Street, to walk among the rows of ready-made-up gowns' (2000: 305). Her shopping expedition and subsequent sartorial consumption are borne not out of mere feminine leisure but out of an urgent, practical need. Margaret and her lover, the imprisoned spiritualist Selina Dawes, plan to enact a daring escape from the patriarchal Victorian institutions that confine them; namely, the stifling heteronormative domesticity represented by Margaret's mother's house, and Millbank Prison in which Selina is incarcerated for her role in performing fraudulent and sexually transgressive seances. Before the two can elope, Margaret must first purchase for Selina an array of 'coats and hats, and shoes, and underthings' with which to 'fashion a place for her in the ordinary world' (305). Such practical, material considerations soon give way, however, to an intensely sensual and phenomenological scene, in which Margaret, unable to fully appreciate 'dyes and cuts and fabrics' when shopping for herself, experiences a kind of sartorial awakening. Recording this moment in her journal, she writes that when 'buying dresses for Selina, I grew light':

> I chose, first, a plain wine-coloured travelling-gown. I thought, Well, that will do for now, and we shall buy her other things when we reach France. But as I held that dress, I saw another – a gown of pearl-gray cashmere, with an underskirt of some thick kind of greenish silk. The green, I thought, would match her eyes. The cashmere would be warm enough, for an Italian winter. I bought both dresses – and then another, a dress of white, with velvet trim, and a narrow, narrow waist. It is a dress to bring out all the girlishness they have subdued at Millbank. Then, since she will not be able to wear a dress without a petticoat, I bought her petticoats, and also stays, and also chemises and stockings of black. And since stockings will be useless without shoes, I bought her shoes – black shoes; and buff-coloured boots; and slippers of white velvet, to match the girlish dress. I bought her hats – large hats with veils, to cover her poor hair until it

grows again. I bought her a coat, and a mantle for the cashmere dress, and a dolman with a fringe of yellow silk, that will swing as she walks beside me in the Italian sun, and flash with light. (2000: 305–6)

Transported by the multisensorial modalities embodied in the soft, downy cashmere, the sensuous sweep of velvet and the flutter of the silk fringe, Margaret's narrative segues from her present moment into an imagined and ideal future. These speculative sartorial scenarios reinscribe Selina's body, working to bridge the gap between Margaret and the object of her desire, while proleptically rehearsing the longed-for moment in which Selina claims she will later 'materialize' with the help of the spirit world. The reciprocal exchange and transfer of vitality enacted between subject and object intensifies when Margaret returns home and imagines that the garments have come to life: 'I seem to hear the silk and cashmere breathing', she writes, 'I seem to feel the slow pulse of the cloth. Then I know that they are waiting, like me, for Selina to assume them – to make them quick, to make them real, to make them palpitate with lustre and with life' (306). Imbued with a kind of latent energy, the garments, though not necessarily pivotal to the plotting of the tale, have a key narratorial resonance: they bespeak Margaret's passivity and prefigure Selina's manipulations. Arresting the flow of the narrative, these garments compel readerly attention. They are suffused with metafictional and creative potential and act as potent sites of imaginative congress. Gathering together the various skeins of this study, these passages thus reveal the surprising intersubjective entanglements to which clothes in neo-Victorian fictions are frequently subject. These vestimentary interludes and the many others like them proffer significant, additional narrative strands in which the affective, agentive and surprisingly uncanny range of Victorian garments is recovered and revived in the present. It is around such sartorial moments that *Victorian Dress in Contemporary Historical Fiction: Materiality, Agency and Narrative* pivots.

This interdisciplinary study traces the imaginative and narrative projections of Victorian women's dress from the nineteenth century to the present day. The first full-length study to examine the remediation of Victorian clothes in the neo-Victorian novel, it investigates and attends to the deeply suggestive and highly symbolic iterations of Victorian dress in the contemporary cultural imagination. In the neo-Victorian novels I closely examine here, garments have complex and layered narratives; their histories, stories and narrative arcs, like those of their human counterparts, are multiple, intricate and ever evolving. More than simply adding to the '*reality effect*' (Barthes [1968] 1986: 148; original emphasis) of contemporary historical novels, dress functions as an interpretative tool through which key textual, material and affective information can be accessed and experienced. Dress is not merely a representational and chronometric marker in neo-Victorianism; its role is not simply to historicize, to add colour and texture to the reimagined material past, although it achieves all these things, but it also provides a dynamic, symbolic device with which to actively re-fashion that past. This book thus foregrounds the sartorial as a fundamental tool for accessing and rethinking the neo-Victorian genre's relationship to the nineteenth century. In what follows, I explore how neo-Victorian writers deal with the creative possibilities afforded by dress and fashion as gendered sites of agency and affect. Drawing on the resonances between texts and textiles, I argue that dress exemplifies the fabricated and fragmentary process of writing, reading and re-imagining the nineteenth-century material past. In so doing, this book seeks to add fresh perspectives to (neo-)Victorian studies and historical dress and fashion theory, respectively. It also seeks to expand critical perspectives on the 'material turn' in neo-Victorian studies by considering the theoretical potentiality of the term 're-fashioning' as a critical-conceptual framework within which to analyse the fabrication and re-patterning of the past in the present. Bringing dress history perspectives into dialogue with Material Culture Studies, thing theory and more recent work on new materialism, it examines the narrative trajectories, affective entanglements and lively vitalities of neo-Victorian clothes.

In the chapters that follow, I aim to cast a spotlight on the textual extensions of Victorian women's dress in a number of 'canonical' and lesser-studied neo-Victorian novels. The rewriting of women's lives, as well as a compulsive interest in gender, sexuality and the re-articulation of the female body, are among the genre's main preoccupations.[1] An exploration of women's clothing thus complements, extends and enhances critical discussions around the recasting of female identity and agency in contemporary historical fiction. Just as it does in Victorian realist and sensation modes, the neo-Victorian novel displays a particular sensitivity to matters of female dress and fashion. Consequently, garments that were predominantly worn by Victorian women, or which proliferate in the contemporary cultural imaginary as being most often associated with female wearers – gowns, gloves, veils and jewellery – recur throughout the novels that form the core focus of this book, reflecting the profusion of female fashions during the nineteenth century.

---

[1] See, for instance, Kontou (2009), Primorac (2018), Renk (2020) and Wallace (2005).

While historians of dress have worked to reassert the significance of Victorian men's sartorial consumption (Breward 1999; Shannon 2006), male fashions experienced comparatively little alteration in the period, a phenomenon famously termed 'The Great Masculine Renunciation' by J. C Flugel (1940: 110). As an 1847 article on 'The Art of Dress' claimed, unlike women's dress, nineteenth-century male fashions were widely considered 'unpicturesque': 'Not a single item is left in his wardrobe with which he can even make what is called an impression – a conquest is out of the question' (Rigby 1847: 373–4).[2] Women's clothing, by contrast, was striking. It underwent considerable and dramatic change during the period. Shifting sartorial structures, increasingly complex constructions and an array of newly manufactured textures, fabrics and colours drew attention to the female form, as well as both demarcating and later blurring prescribed gender roles. Women's dress thus signalled their changing place within society. Whereas men's clothing tended to signify utility, practicality and position, women's dress was often highly decorative, aesthetic and ornamental. A vehicle for female agency, autonomy and creative expression, female apparel signalled, and even concealed, wealth and status, individual taste and sexual availability. Engaging in fashionable display therefore offered women material sites within which to formulate, perform and communicate a strong sense of individuated identity.

The Victorians themselves recognized the gendered specificity of dress. Acknowledging the key differences between men's and women's clothing, an anonymous article published in *Blackwood's Edinburgh Magazine* in 1865 notes the centrality of female apparel in the collective consciousness:

> All general considerations on dress … converge towards feminine costume. When we think of dress in the abstract, we mean women's dress; whatever has been in the world's youth, in our time, her costume represents the art. It is, above all, through the female toilet that fashion transacts its weighty part in the world, and by its ebbs and flows keeps the world at work. ('Dress' 1865: 433)

It is no surprise, then, that women's dress tends to form the primary focus of our contemporary engagements with nineteenth-century sartorial culture. Enthralled by Victorian women's clothing and their material lives more generally, neo-Victorian fictions deploy dress as a key visual and material device with which to reinscribe the female body. Closely connected to

---

[2] 'The Art of Dress' was first published anonymously in *The Quarterly Review* before its republication with another of Rigby's articles in 1852.

notions of embodied subjectivity, dress and fashion proffer apposite tools with which to re-imagine nineteenth-century female subjects and their negotiations of identity, gender and sexuality. Since women's rapidly changing silhouettes functioned as barometers of social change in the Victorian period, mapping such sartorial developments also provides a kind of shorthand for contemporary authors, enabling them to draw upon and efficiently rehearse the complex gendered and sociocultural implications of dress. Beyond such issues of gender, legibility and embodiment, however, clothes also function variously in the fictive worlds of neo-Victorian novels. They are credited with dynamic, affective and narrative significance. They are prominent and central plot points; material nodes from which narrative originates, coalesces and congeals; they take on surprisingly agentive, interactive and independent roles within their fictional diegeses; they signal temporality and historicity and play a key part in the construction of character identity. The historic past unfolds through dress in these narratives.

This is not to say, of course, that other neo-Victorian modes do not proffer equally interesting insights into the remediation of Victorian dress. Yet filmic and televisual adaptations appear to have seized upon, and buttressed, specific cultural mythologies about certain garments that tend to pervade our contemporary cultural consciousness. In older and more recent cinematic returns alike, items of female dress such as the corset and crinoline have been continuously cast and recast as sartorial symbols of female oppression. Mocked by the nineteenth-century press (Figure 1.1), demonized by dress reformers and the male medical establishment in the 1880s, and later re-positioned by Helene E. Roberts in her influential twentieth-century essay as gendered instruments of enslavement (1977), corsets and crinolines provide rich fodder for contemporary period dramas, preoccupied as they often are with highlighting restricted feminine roles. Although dress historians such as Valerie Steele (2001) have done much to recuperate and reorient the corset's cultural significance by identifying its practical functions and separating it from the practice of tight-lacing, modern-day visual recreations tend to portray such nineteenth-century garments as restrictive tools of literal and metaphorical restraint. In *Neo-Victorianism on Screen: Postfeminism and Contemporary Adaptations of Victorian Women*, Antonija Primorac pays close attention to the confluence of corsets and crinolines with birdcages in neo-Victorian films and confirms that contemporary screen adaptations regularly perpetuate these long-held assumptions (2018: 103). In these visual returns to the past, the corset and crinoline often indicate a certain type of fragile femininity. In

Chair Proprietor. "Would you please to pay for the Chairs, Mum?"
Lady. "How much?"
Chair Proprietor. "Well, Mum—How many might you be a sittin' on?"

Figure 1.1 Punch cartoon: Victorian women's fashion – the wide hoop skirt (private collection). © Look and Learn/George Collection/Bridgeman Images.

addition, Victorian corsets and crinolines are regularly shown to be ludicrous and used to induce laughter in modern audiences, as Margaret Stetz has shown (2017: 155). As elements of nineteenth-century sartorial culture that most clearly signal periodicity, such garments are also routinely exploited by neo-Victorian visual productions, which use them as sartorial substitutes to signal an entire era of clothing, often collapsing the significant variations of nineteenth-century women's dress into these two recognizable garments. As handy visible signifiers of both historicity and women's apparently circumscribed roles within the period, it is unsurprising that such items should recur in screen adaptations and costume dramas. Attempting to move beyond these two well-studied and often fetishized or satirized items of Victorian female dress, this study looks to encompass other equally iconic, though comparatively overlooked, garments and their contemporary remediations in literary fiction as a means of producing a politics and poetics of dress in the neo-Victorian novel. Before doing so, however, I would like to begin by outlining a framework through which to understand the theoretical potential of dress and fashion for analysing neo-Victorian fiction.

Re-fashioning the past

The contemporary novels that predominate in this study can be categorized as neo-Victorian: they each enact a critical and creative engagement with the nineteenth-century past and its textual, material and visual traces in the present. Sharing Ann Heilmann and Mark Llewellyn's foundational understanding of neo-Victorianism as '*more than* historical fiction set in the nineteenth century', the texts at play within the present study are all, to a greater or lesser extent, '*self-consciously engaged with the act of (re)interpretation, (re)discovery and (re)vision concerning the Victorians*' (2010: 4; original emphases). As this oft-quoted critical formulation demonstrates, neo-Victorian fictions are characterized by dynamic, intentional interactions with the Victorian past. Adopting and adapting Victorian formal, generic and literary conventions, tropes and motifs, they embrace a variety of narrative strategies such as self-reflexivity, metafiction, pastiche and intertextuality. A similar self-consciousness extends to neo-Victorianism's commitment to the present moment: such works respond to and interrogate contemporary as well as historic concerns. Neo-Victorian fictions ostensibly operate by 'adopt[ing] a dual approach which combines a concern with the past and a concern with the present' (Hadley 2010: 6). By openly questioning and contesting nineteenth-century ideologies, neo-Victorian fictions offer themselves up as imaginative proxies through which current sociocultural issues might also be examined and explored. Speculating on the genre's ethical, political and ideological impulses, the founding editor of *Neo-Victorian Studies*, Marie-Luise Kohlke, argued in the introduction to the journal's inaugural issue that 'much as we read Victorian texts as highly revealing cultural products of their age, neo-Victorian texts will one day be read for the insights they afford into twentieth- and twenty-first-century cultural history and socio-political concerns' (2008b: 13). In a further drive towards introspection, much neo-Victorian fiction also seeks to re-imagine the nineteenth century from alternative perspectives, re-writing overlooked histories of gender, sexuality, class and race as a means of foregrounding suppressed, forgotten or disregarded voices (Kaplan 2007; Llewellyn 2008). This process of historical recovery has been conceived of as a 'spectral' encounter between the nineteenth century and the present day, in which neo-Victorian fictions are figured as probing the porous boundaries between past and present, life and death (Arias and Pulham 2010); in mediumistic or ventriloquial terms (Davies 2012; Kontou 2009); or in ways that call upon trauma, cultural memory and ethics in global and local frameworks (Kohlke and Gutleben 2010).

Emerging in the context of postmodern literature and culture, the neo-Victorian genre's inception is often traced to the publication of two important 'originary' works, Jean Rhys's *Wide Sargasso Sea* (1966) and John Fowles's *The French Lieutenant's Woman* (1969). Since then, neo-Victorianism has flourished, representing both a popular literary and cultural phenomenon, as well as a burgeoning site of academic enquiry. In one of the earliest essays on the topic, written at a time in which neo-Victorianism was experiencing increased prominence, Dana Shiller coined the term 'neo-Victorian novel', defining it as a specific category of contemporary fiction that is 'at once characteristic of postmodernism and imbued with a historicity reminiscent of the nineteenth-century novel' (1997: 538). Such texts 'take a revisionist approach to the past, borrowing from postmodern historiography to explore how present circumstances shape historical narrative' (540). Shiller's argument, which attempts to mitigate Frederic Jameson's critique of postmodern representations of history,[3] is largely underpinned by Linda Hutcheon's assessment of the postmodern historical novel. In her foundational work *A Poetics of Postmodernism: History, Theory, Fiction* (1988), Hutcheon proposes 'historiographic metafiction' as a crucial term with which to theorize 'those well-known and popular novels which are both intensely self-reflexive and yet paradoxically also lay claim to historical events and personages' (5). These texts work to 'install and then blur the line between fiction and history', and in doing so, seek to problematize attempts to recall and represent the past (113). Although, as Hutcheon contends, 'the past really did exist. The question is: *how* can we know that past today – and what can we know of it?' (92; original emphasis). Underscoring the narrativization and fictionalization of history, she therefore privileges 'textual traces' in order to argue that the past can only ever be accessed and understood in the present via its remaining documentary forms. Similarly, for Shiller, who identifies neo-Victorianism as a subcategory of historiographic metafiction, neo-Victorian novels are likewise 'acutely aware of both history and fiction as human constructs, and use this awareness to rethink the forms and contents of the past' (1997: 540). The novels under study in this book demonstrate a shared fixation with the dynamical interplay between past and present, history and fiction.

---

[3] Jameson argues that 'producers of culture have nowhere to turn but to the past: the imitation of dead styles, speech through all the masks and voices stored up in the imaginary museum of a now global culture' and refers to this as a 'cannibalization of all the styles of the past' (1991: 17–18). He also criticizes postmodern historical fiction, claiming that the 'historical novel can no longer set out to represent the historical past; it can only "represent" our ideas and stereotypes about that past' (25).

Focusing on the re-fashioning of the Victorian period, this study is interested in examining the construction of the material past in the neo-Victorian novel. Beyond textualized traces, I am concerned with analysing the productive intersections that emerge between texts and textiles. If much neo-Victorian fiction is concerned with processes of reading, interrogation and interpretation, then dress and fashion provide additional, readable traces through which to explore and examine the construction of history, memory and narrative in neo-Victorian fictions. Rather than only illuminating the difficulties of retrieving the past, however, dress, fashion and textiles offer alternative modes of access. Not only do they proffer supplementary 'textualized' skeins that can be read by intra- and extra-textual readers, but they also offer us a richer reading experience. The literary representation of dress and its sensual and material properties engenders a sense of proximity, however illusory, between reader and reimagined Victorian 'other'. Paying attention to the sartorial plots within neo-Victorian novels therefore offers a more affective, embodied and immersive readerly experience in which the material past might be recuperated and re-encountered in the present. This study therefore proposes a reading of the material traces of the lost Victorian age as significant and revelatory. In so doing, it builds upon recent calls by scholars such as Kate Mitchell (2010), Nadine Boehm-Schnitker and Susanne Gruss (2011; 2014), Rosario Arias (2015; 2017) and Arias and Patricia Pulham (2019) for a form of neo-Victorian literary criticism that foregrounds memory, materiality and phenomenological and sensory matters.

As a literary mode engaged in the imaginative process of re-materializing the past, the criticism on neo-Victorian fiction is rich with references to 'fashioning'. Employed to refer to the genre's creative, critical and aesthetic returns to the nineteenth century, the term has been used, albeit cursorily, with reference to the 're-fashioned/re-furbished' past (Kohlke 2014: 23) and to account for the process by which the re-imagining of that past 'entails a self-fashioning' in the present (Boehm-Schnitker and Gruss 2014: 1). What has not yet been explored but which is ripe for consideration are the term's sartorial implications. 'Fashion/ing' serves as a meaningful metaphor for understanding the purposeful urge to re-pattern the past in the present. Deriving from the Latin *facere* meaning 'to make', the word 'fashion' refers to creative processes of formation, as well as to attire and style (*OED*). Fashion also refers to a recursive industry system in which styles of dress are sequentially and cyclically disseminated according to shifting aesthetic and cultural trends. As Elizabeth Wilson defines it, 'Fashion is dress in which the key feature is rapid and continual changing of styles. Fashion, in a sense *is* change' (2003: 3; original emphasis). While Wilson here describes fashionable dress, her words might equally apply to the neo-Victorian phenomenon which has been described as 'something of a fashion both in academic institutions and on the market' (Boehm-Schnitker and Gruss 2014: 4). In its self-reflexivity, non-linearity and facility for repetition, neo-Victorianism shares a number of striking similarities with fashion. Both are cultural systems that signify temporal distance, and which mark a change, or break, from their literary, historical and sartorial antecedents. Fashion, like the neo-Victorian novel, is also recurrent, representing a recycling and revision of old styles. Both enact a tension between past and present, while drawing attention, however implicitly, to their novelty and construction.

A shared cultural impulse to refashion the nineteenth-century past is evident in fashion brands and on the catwalk. High-end fashion designers Alexander McQueen, Erdem Moralıoğlu, Yves Saint Laurent and Dries Van Noten, among others, have frequently mined nineteenth-century literature and visual and material culture for inspiration.[4] Delineating a similar fascination with the Victorian period and also tacitly acknowledging its contemporary appeal as a lucrative marketing tool, the high street brand H&M collaborated with Morris & Co in 2018, producing clothing printed with William Morris's designs, while their 2020 Autumn/Winter collection 'The Refined Rebel' was partly inspired by the nineteenth-century writer Vernon Lee. Characterized by a self-conscious derivativeness, the production of such styles of dress, like neo-Victorianism itself, pays homage to the past but also sets about remixing, revisioning and reimagining it to accord with modern sensibilities. Dress historian Caroline Evans aptly explains in her study on contemporary dress that 'fashion, while ostensibly a paradigm of novelty and innovation, is in fact trammelled by the very historical conditions that produce it' (2003: 20). The inherently referential and metahistorical nature of fashionable dress thus aligns with the self-conscious reconstruction of the material past in neo-Victorian literature. Consequently, 're-fashioning' becomes a paradigmatic term that both encapsulates the neo-Victorian novel's conscious drive to remake and reformulate and which lends itself to critical interventions into the genre.

---

[4] McQueen's earliest work, presented in his 1992 MA graduation collection 'Jack the Ripper Stalks His Victims', drew on the infamous Whitechapel murders of the late 1880s. Moralıoğlu's Spring 2019 collection drew inspiration from the nineteenth-century cross-dressers and music hall performers Fanny and Stella, or Ernest Boulton and Frederick Park as they were also known. The inspiration for Dries van Noten's Spring/Summer 2015 collection was credited to John Everett Millais's *Ophelia* (1851–2), while the creative designer for Yves Saint Lauren purportedly incorporated Victorian elements into the spring 2022 menswear line.

Neo-Victorian dress, as this discussion suggests, sits at the nexus of time, history, memory and narrative. Past and present inhere in contemporary reconfigurations of nineteenth-century garments, forming a kind of sartorial strata. Current re-imaginings of Victorian dress are freighted with the iterations of past Victorian fashions, as well as with our own cultural assumptions about what the Victorians wore, mediated to us through idealized and fictionalized nineteenth-century fashion plates, extant garments and various popular, though often anachronistic, television adaptations and filmic recreations. This overlap is typical of the appropriative and adaptive tendencies of all neo-Victorian cultural products which work to open up a 'dialogue between new text and old' but which are also informed by 'the intertexts and interplays between different adaptations' (Heilmann and Llewellyn 2010: 212). Critics have usefully employed the palimpsest as a conceptual framework for analysing this re-inscription of past (inter-)texts (see Jones and Mitchell 2016), but in the context of dress, fashion and textiles, such entanglements might be more productively understood in relation to Michel Serres's notion of time and history which he develops in conversation with Bruno Latour in *Conversations on Science, Culture, and Time* (1990). 'Every historical era' Serres asserts, is 'multitemporal, simultaneously drawing from the obsolete, the contemporary and the futuristic. An object, a circumstance, is thus polychronic, multitemporal and reveals a time that is gathered together, with multiple pleats' (1995: 60). In his rejection of the linearity of time, Serres employs the critical-conceptual metaphor of a handkerchief, explaining that 'if you take a handkerchief and spread it out in order to iron it, you can see in it certain fixed distances and proximities … Then take the same handkerchief and crumple it, by putting it in your pocket. Two distant points suddenly are close, even superimposed' (60). The crumpling of the past into readable, tangible layers accessed in the present is analogous to the neo-Victorian enterprise and speaks to the role of the remediated sartorial object in re-materializing the past. The transhistoric task of writing across spatio-temporal boundaries that is so central to the neo-Victorian novel enfolds the Victorian and the present moments, bringing them into intimate dialogue with one another. Hence, Serres's emphasis speaks to the overlapping, or doubling, of time and history, both of which are central to fashion and to neo-Victorianism. His haptically informed approach to understanding the imbrication of distal temporalities also draws attention to the dual practices of folding and unfolding, which might proffer suitable metaphors for the ways in which neo-Victorian works are simultaneously produced, interpreted and accessed: 'folding' resonates with the intersections between past and present and underlines the practice of moulding or adapting existing stories, while 'unfolding' hints at the 'revelatory' nature of contemporary historical fiction as it seeks to uncover hidden histories and re-centre traditionally marginalized narratives.

Reading and writing dress: Texts and textiles

That dress itself has narrative properties is a critical commonplace in dress and fashion theory, and one that is rooted in the nineteenth century. Then, as now, dress constituted a crucial means of non-verbal communication: garments permitted a dialogue of sorts, expressing and narrating clues about identity to those well-versed in reading the social, aesthetic and political significance of sartorial signs. As one article of 1847 states, women's 'dress becomes a sort of symbolical language – a kind of personal glossary' in the period (Rigby 1847: 375). Revealing a rising awareness of sartorial literacy, the article illuminates Leigh Summers's assertion that in the Victorian era 'costume could be read as easily as any text' (2001: 19). This nineteenth-century impulse to decipher clothes can be read as part of that period's wider observation of and adherence to strict social and cultural codes. Dress and dressed bodies were especially potent sites around which such codes coalesced. Underwritten by the expansion of commodity culture, the rise of conspicuous consumption, and shifting class relations and gender roles, the clothing of the nineteenth-century middle and upper classes was replete with decodable signs. Reading dress and manipulating its 'readable' properties therefore proffered nineteenth-century individuals a convenient material means with which to navigate, challenge or subvert social relations during the period.

An ability to 'read' dress, to decipher its shifting structures, shapes and silhouettes, likewise informs contemporary object-oriented approaches to analysing Victorian garments in fashion history and museology. In *The Dress Detective* (2015), Ingrid Mida and Alexandra Kim build upon Jules David Prown's museological study of material culture (1982) to propose a methodology of sartorial interpretation, whereby 'evidence from a garment can be used in identifying the narratives and cultural beliefs that are embodied in dress artifacts' (2015: 79). Analysing historical garments from the nineteenth century onwards, they go on to suggest that collective and personal stories are deeply embedded within items of dress, and that 'in performing a close analysis of a garment' it is possible to 'reveal the stories locked therein' (62). Their interpretation of dress objects in this way dialogizes with the interpretation of texts. Mida and Kim propose a process of close reading clothes that echoes literary practices in which the reader must also 'find patterns, make conjectures, and draw conclusions' (76). Through close textual analyses I aim, in a similar manner, to unravel the stories encoded within neo-Victorian literary garments. Clothes, whether actual or mediated through language, accumulate, contain and evoke narrative. Deeply encoded with symbolic and material meaning, clothes tell stories to others and to ourselves about our identities, tastes, places and roles within society.

The communicative power of dress continues and is accentuated at a textual level. Roland Barthes affirms the importance of attending to 'written dress' in his semiotic study of fashion in *The Fashion System* (1983).[5] Employing the fashion magazine as an example, although his theory might be easily mapped onto other literary genres, Barthes differentiates between three distinct garments – written dress, image clothing and the real garment – all of which, he claims, have their own unique structural features. In his linguistic conceptualization, the 'written garment' is that which is 'described, transformed into language' (1990: 3); unlike real clothing or the other representational mode, image clothing, written dress is the most useful type of garment to study Barthes claims, because it is purely symbolic, 'unencumbered by any parasitic function and entails no vague temporality' (8). Following Barthes, several literary critics and historians of dress have since concerned themselves with the many and varied connections between literature and fashion. Lou Taylor acknowledges the importance of literary approaches to fashion in *The Study of Dress History* (2002), citing novelistic depictions of clothing as central to social and emotional understandings of historical dress (92). Clair Hughes's *Dressed in Fiction* ([2005] 2006) examines the significance of clothing, its colours and styles, in fictional texts published between 1724 and 1984. She argues that reading dress offers an alternative, supplementary plot, one in which the '*different* pleasures of reading a text' might be revealed (3; original emphasis). Beyond the pleasures of attending to written garments, she also aims 'to show how an exploration of the author's employment of dress and its accessories can illuminate the structure of that text, its values, its meanings or its symbolic pattern' (6). Cynthia Kuhn and Cindy Carlson's edited volume *Styling Texts: Dress and Fashion in Literature* (2007) extends the parameters of Hughes's study, providing a comprehensive overview of the function of dress and fashion in fiction from the medieval period to the twenty-first century. In the brief introduction to their study, they draw on the linguistic connections

---

[5] First published in 1967 as *Système de la Mode*.

between literature and fashion when they point out that 'commentators may discuss the "lines" or "statement" of an outfit, designers describe their collections as "telling a story" or "having a voice," and the ubiquitous concept of "style" underwrites them both' (2). Contributors to Katherine Joslin and Daneen Wardrop's collection *Crossings in Text and Textile* (2015) likewise pick up on the interplay between texts and textiles – which share the same Latin root, *texere* – in order to interrogate the transatlantic movement of clothing as represented in nineteenth and early-twentieth-century literature, while Gerald Egan's edited volume *Fashion and Authorship: Literary Production and Cultural Style from the Eighteenth to the Twenty-First Century* (2020), aligns dress and fashion with issues of authoriality and writerly production.

Focusing specifically on the nineteenth century, Christine Bayles Kortsch and Madeleine C. Seys pay close attention to the gendered dimensions of sartorial literacy in their respective studies on *Dress Culture in Late Victorian Women's Fiction: Literacy, Textiles, and Activism* (2009) and *Fashion and Narrative in Victorian Popular Literature: Double Threads* (2018). In different ways, both suggest that proficiency in interpreting the discursive elements of dress was necessary for the negotiation of nineteenth-century gender politics in literature and culture. Bayles Kortsch argues that Victorian women developed a '"dual literacy"' in the period, characterized by a skilful ability to read both paper and fabric, to write in ink and thread, and to interpret clothing, textiles and decorative furnishings as correlatives to other more textual forms (4). Focusing upon the way in which women writers of the late Victorian period negotiated 'the language of print and the language of cloth' she shows how women's participation within 'dress culture' engendered a sense of community, autonomy and authority that was distinct from more male-centred and patriarchal cultural practices (183). Seys likewise advances the notion that Victorian writers recognized the narrative potential of sartorial codes. She argues that the relationship between the sartorial and nineteenth-century popular fiction can be figured as intersecting threads, through which notions of femininity, sexuality and agency might be analysed and explored (5). Reading colour and texture, as well as the historical origins of cloth, into her analyses of Victorian women and the way in which dress informs and encapsulates their narrative trajectories, Seys contends that dress can be 'made to stand in for the techniques of storytelling' in popular literature of the period (17).

These studies provide a rich framework within which to situate my own interrogation of Victorian dress in neo-Victorian novels. As these examples attest, dress is a story-telling device. It imparts key information to readers both inside and outside of the textual diegesis. Clothes take on an active role in all fictions; they communicate unspoken narratives and provide additional information about protagonists, the intricacies of plot, setting, style and societal situations. Examining clothing in the literature of the nineteenth century, for instance, aids contemporary audiences' understanding of the past, enriching our perspective of cultural, social and emotional practices. The same was true for the Victorians, for whom dress reflected and was therefore expressive of human histories. Anticipating the ideological aims of dress history, nineteenth-century literature on historical garments regularly emphasized their role in illuminating the past; as one cultural commentator eloquently argued, dress 'illustrates the long buried past, and holds a candle to History' ('Dress' 1862: 395). Contributing to and expanding these conversations, *Victorian Dress in Contemporary Historical Fiction* explores the implications of neo-Victorian literary garments. In drawing on the interwoven intersections between texts and textiles, I am concerned with the representation of Victorian dress, its literary and figural mediations in contemporary cultural memory. I am interested in the nuanced and multifarious meanings assigned to vestimentary vestiges in neo-Victorian novels. Examining the form, function and symbolic, connotative and literal meaning of garments, I seek to uncover how dress and fashion aid in the reimagining of the past. As simulacral objects, the sartorial items under study here are represented through a doubled timestream. Placed in dialogue with historical reality, they are (re-)imagined copies of nineteenth-century clothes, mediated through words and across time. As in Victorian novels, dress is rendered in often meticulous terms in neo-Victorian fiction: contemporary authors depict nineteenth-century garments in strikingly accurate detail lending a sense of verisimilitude and authenticity to textual proceedings. Yet one of this book's contentions is that dress's significance in neo-Victorianism extends beyond its capacity to signal a recognizably nineteenth-century diegesis; rather, dress encourages an imaginative and affective engagement with issues of memory, narrative and history. Dress in the contemporary historical fictions at play within this study thus proffers additional narrative strands that can be read in tandem with the overarching plots, but which also become metaphors for the re-construction of the past in the present. Dress, whether real or imagined, is indexical. It is imbued with memory and narrative and is enlivened with affective and agentive power. It proffers a means of engaging creatively and experientially with history, and of thinking through the process of rewriting and re-fashioning the past through its physical remains. In neo-Victorian novels, clothes betoken our contemporary desire to re-fashion the Victorian material past.

(Neo-)Victorian sartorial and material culture

An interest in remediating Victorian dress in contemporary literature and culture appears to replicate a similar nineteenth-century fixation with sartorial matters. As many historians of dress recognize, the period is notable for its distinctive and dynamic dress and fashion cultures. Developments in technology, including the invention of the home sewing machine, the distribution of paper patterns, the rise of the ready-to-wear industry and the production of aniline dyes, revolutionized and democratized the fashion industry in Britain from the 1840s onwards. The expansion of commodity culture and the advent of the department store further contributed to the emergence of the modern fashion industry. Alongside these innovations, writers and cultural commentators paid increasing attention to dress, its role and function in society, and its psychological, economic and cultural consequences. *Sartor Resartus: The Life and Times of Herr Teufelsdröckh* (1836), discussed at length in Chapter 2, is Thomas Carlyle's quasi-satirical yet philosophical exposition on the significance of clothes in nineteenth-century society.[6] Widely considered to be one of dress history's earliest progenitors, it identifies and interrogates the perceived analogies between early-Victorian society and dress. Presented as edited fragments of a proposed volume on '*Clothes, their Origin and Influence*' (2002: xxxiii; original emphasis) by a fictional German professor named Diogenes Teufelsdröckh, the book propounds the notion that dress and fashion are useful metaphors for humanity and its institutions. Accordingly, Carlyle's fictional narrator declares the scientific, symbolic and social significance of clothes, asking why, despite 'our present advanced state of culture', the 'grand Tissue of all Tissues, the only real *Tissue*, should have been quite overlooked by Science – the vestural Tissue, namely, of woollen or other Cloth; which Man's Soul wears as its outermost wrappage and overall; wherein his whole other Tissues are included and screened, his whole Faculties work, his whole Self lives, moves, and has its being?' (5–6; original emphasis). Several other philosophical, sociological and economic tracts likewise recognized the implications of dress in nineteenth-century culture. For Thorstein Veblen (1899), dress was purely pecuniary, significant for its role in conspicuous and vicarious consumption. It also strongly demarcated class and gender distinctions: the role of women in the leisure class, Veblen argued, was 'to consume vicariously

---

[6] A Scottish philosopher and historian, Thomas Carlyle (1795–1881) published *Sartor Resartus* in book form in 1836; before that, it was published serially in *Fraser Magazine* between November 1833 and August 1834.

for the [male] head of the household; and her apparel is contrived with this object in view' (2007: 118). In other (con)texts, dress and fashion took on increasingly gendered significances too. Fashion and ladies' magazines like *The Englishwoman's Domestic Magazine* (1852–79), *The Queen* (1861–1922), *The Young Englishwoman* (1864–9) and *Myra's Journal of Dress and Fashion* (1875–1912) documented changing female fashions and disseminated hand-painted fashion plates alongside patterns for gowns and other articles of dress in Britain. *Godey's Lady's Book* (1830–78) and *Harper's Bazaar* (1867–present), among others, dominated the American market. Numerous other periodicals, journals and magazines whose scope extended beyond sartorial concerns, shared a similar commercial interest in fashion, publishing advertisements featuring the latest trends along with opinion pieces on dress and sartorial etiquette.

Though commercially motivated, these publications contributed to the fashioning of ideal femininity. Such was the importance of dressing correctly, and so entrenched was the notion that women experienced an 'ineradicable love of dress', that Caroline Stephen called for dress to 'be made not only a part, but an instrument of education' for Victorian women (1868: 297, 282). The ideal Victorian woman was a well-dressed arbiter of good taste according to Stephen, a sentiment popularly used to reinforce the notion that clothes were intimately aligned with the perceived moral fabric of Victorian society. Since it was widely purported that outward appearance could convey a sense of interiority, clothes, especially those worn by women, were popularly conceived of as indices of morality. As Sarah Stickney Ellis, one of the most prominent authors of Victorian conduct literature, writes, 'the soiled hem, the tattered frill, or even the coarse garment ... naturally carries the observer to [a woman's] dressing-room, her private habits, and even to her inner mind, where, it is impossible to believe the same want of order and purity does not prevail' (1839: 96). If unkempt and unclean clothing signified 'moral degradation' (99), then extravagant, ostentatious or expensive dress that did not align with the wearer's social status, gestured to a similarly impure moral consciousness. Stickney Ellis cautions her female readers therefore against 'artificial wants as the great evil of the present times', encouraging them to instead adopt dress that 'is neat, becoming, or in good taste' (97). Since nineteenth-century middle- and upper-class women walked a thin line between sartorial suitability and improper excess, various publications, whether book or periodical, took up the twinned topics of taste and appropriate style. Fashion plates and illustrations accompanied textual depictions of dress in these publications, offering women a visual, if somewhat idealized and unattainable, touchstone for beauty and fashionability (Figure 1.2).

Figure 1.2 The newest fashions for spring and summer mantles. Illustration for the *Englishwoman's Domestic Magazine*, 1860s © Getty Images.

From among the surviving textual and visual sources that evidence the Victorians' preoccupation with women's clothing and its sociocultural, political and economic ramifications, the Victorian novel is one particular mode in which the significance of female fashion is repeatedly underscored. In Thomas Hardy's *The Mayor of Casterbridge* (1886), the importance of dress in the formation of nineteenth-century subjectivities is particularly evident. When attempting to decide between two gowns, 'one of a deep cherry colour, the other lighter', Lucetta Templeman marks the synergistic relationship that exists between clothing and identity, explaining to her companion Elizabeth that ' "You are that person" (pointing to one of the arrangements), "or you are *that* totally different person" (pointing to the other), "for the whole of the coming spring: and one of the two, you don't know which, may turn out to be very objectionable." ' (2012: 201; original emphasis). Published several years earlier, the eponymous heroine of Margaret Oliphant's *Phoebe Junior* (1876) similarly discerns the power of dress in forming, negotiating and manipulating social identity: ' "I have never undervalued dress," she said, "as some girls do; I think it is a very important social influence' (2002: 75). Novels such as these particularize the connections between sartoriality, society and self-expression, issues which have fed into and helped form the foci of several recent academic texts which chart the multiple ways in which dress is framed in nineteenth-century literature (Aindow 2010; Gatrell 2011; Hughes 2001).

Correspondingly, an emergent interest in the textual, visual and cultural remediation of Victorian fashions can be traced in several book chapters and journal articles on neo-Victorianism and Steampunk. In the earliest essay on the topic, Stetz proposes an interdisciplinary approach to examining neo-Victorian literature and culture 'through the seductive prospect of thinking about dress' (2009a: para. 25). Examining Fowles's *The French Lieutenant's Woman* she asserts that this neo-Victorian novel may have precipitated the consuming public's interest in Victorian things by delineating nineteenth-century dress in rich detail, and concludes by insightfully asking whether 'fashion studies and more traditional sorts of text-based Victorian research might be inextricably linked?' (para. 27). Providing a patchwork of different possible answers to this enquiry, essays on veils, umbrellas and corsets in Steampunk and neo-Victorian young adult fiction have emerged in addition to articles and book chapters dealing with male and female costumes both on and off screen (Feldman-Barrett 2013; Montz 2011, 2019; Primorac 2018). Cross-dressing forms another sartorially focussed branch of neo-Victorian study. Since gender performance and the construction of queer identities are established and recurrent thematic concerns in texts such as Waters's *Tipping the Velvet* (1998) (discussed in Chapter 3), Patricia Duncker's *James Miranda Barry* (1999) and Barbara Ewing's *The Petticoat Men* (2014), critics have called upon novels such as these and their sartorial engagements with historical and fictional cross-dressed individuals (see Heilmann 2018; Neal 2011).

Particularly fruitful connections have been made in recent years between neo-Victorianism and Material Culture Studies more generally. Taking their cue from the Victorian 'material turn',[7] neo-Victorian scholars have highlighted the multiple ways in which the physical, tactile traces of the lost Victorian age continue to have an impact on the contemporary cultural consciousness, generating new or revised ranges of meaning (Arias and Pulham 2019; Boehm-Schnitker and Gruss 2011; Brindle 2013; Dove and Maier 2022; Kaplan 2007). Yet despite this widespread scholarly engagement with neo-Victorian materiality, to date no book-length study has addressed the considerable role of dress in neo-Victorian textual representations. *Victorian Dress in Contemporary Historical Fiction* seeks to fill this critical gap, bringing dress history approaches into dialogue with neo-Victorianism in fresh and innovative ways. Grounded in a number of key critical approaches to dress, fashion and materiality, this study is primarily informed by recent scholarly work in Material Culture Studies,

---

[7] See Pykett (2003).

thing theory and new materialism, but aims to open up and expand upon these discourses by analysing them in relation to the remediation of dress in neo-Victorian fiction.

Although neo-Victorianism is arguably implicated in two periods equally dominated by economic and capitalist exchange, this book moves beyond the consumerist implications of dress and fashion in order to analyse garments' affective economies. Many of the clothes under study here are dislocated from consumer culture in that they are routinely cast-off, lost, bequeathed, borrowed or stolen. Diverging from studies in which clothes are analysed in Marxist terms of use and exchange, labour and alienation, this study focuses instead upon the emotional, affective and sensory impact of clothes in fiction, as well as the capacity of garments to reconstruct the past and to contain, sustain and convey narrative. This engagement with historical things might be seen to expand upon the Victorians' own 'complex relationship to the goods by which they were surrounded and intrigued' (Freedgood 2006: 142). In *The Ideas in Things: Fugitive Meaning in the Victorian Novel*, Elaine Freedgood argues that in critical commentary there is a '"tendency"' to reductively read objects in Victorian fiction as 'symptomatic' of commodity culture (2006: 140). Although she does not consider the metaphoric and symbolic role of objects, preferring instead to advance 'strong metonymic readings' of the things that litter Victorian novels (4), Freedgood likewise moves beyond Marxist understandings of fictional and fictionalized consumer goods. She pays attention to seemingly insignificant things, material objects and items that are mentioned fleetingly in the Victorian novels she examines, and which remain 'largely inconsequential in the rhetorical hierarchy of the text' proving only of value when considered in light of their extratextual 'imperial and industrial histories' (2). The sartorial things I examine here, by contrast, are accorded metaphorical and symbolic resonance *within* the parameters of the neo-Victorian novels, yet a consideration of their nineteenth-century cultural and literary histories in accordance with Freedgood's method of analysis, illuminates their contemporary uses and misuses.

Freedgood's approach to what she calls 'Victorian "thing culture"' (8) intervenes in both Material Culture Studies which encourage 'a scholarly approach to artifacts that can be utilized by investigators in a variety of fields' (Prown 1982: 1), and the more literary field of 'thing theory', which is concerned with charting the shifting human-object dialectic. In his 2001 essay, 'Thing Theory', Bill Brown made a compelling case for examining things, as well as the reciprocal interactions between humans and things, in art and literature. Beginning, significantly, with A. S. Byatt's neo-Victorian novel, *The Biographer's Tale* (2000) (although he does not identify the text as 'neo-Victorian'), Brown examines a specific material moment in the text in which Byatt's main protagonist looks '*at*' a dusty window rather than through it (4; original emphasis). This interaction poses, for Brown, a means of differentiating between objects and things. The dirty window in Byatt's novel becomes a thing as opposed to an object precisely because it operates beyond its normative use-function: 'The story of objects asserting themselves as things … is the story of a changed relation to the human subject' (4). For Brown, things are those objects that lie beyond linguistic and epistemological apprehension. Things are also significantly understood 'as what is excessive in objects, as what exceeds their mere materialization as objects or their mere utilization as objects – their force as a sensuous presence or as a metaphysical presence, the magic by which objects become values, fetishes, idols, and totems' (5). My analyses of written dress dialogize with thing theory; they encompass the peculiar interactions that take place between garments and bodies and explore the agency, animation and 'sensuous presence' of clothes in neo-Victorian texts.

In its focus upon the liveliness of matter, this study also shares some of the assumptions of new materialism. For new materialist thinkers such as Karen Barad (2007), Jane Bennett (2010a) and Diana Coole and Samantha Frost (2010), the human body in contemporary culture is one material thing among a constellation of others. Emerging at the turn of the millennium, new materialist theories underscore the affective, agentive and sensory significance of things in present-day society. Concerned with tracing the entanglement of bodies and things, new materialism works to disrupt the dualistic conceptions of subject and object, nature and culture, and in so doing, seeks to reorient and re-establish the primacy of matter. Rising to prominence at a similar point in time, neo-Victorian fictions are sites within which human and non-human matter repeatedly converges and aligns. The vocabulary of new materialism, its theorization of the imbrication of subject and object, human and non-human elements ('assemblages', in Bennett's formulation [2010a]), and its insistence upon the agency of things, therefore proffers a useful critical-conceptual framework within which to consider the lively matter of clothes in neo-Victorian fiction. Just as new materialism aims to reinvigorate conceptualizations of matter by addressing the vibrant energy inherent in all objects, neo-Victorianism likewise evinces a notable preoccupation with the resurrection and revivification of material things.

The idea that things might contain a certain agency of their own seems to have originated not, as the term 'new materialism' would appear to imply, in contemporary culture, but rather in early nineteenth-century scientific discourse, when '"life"' was thought to 'lurk in numerous, previously unexpected places: in electricity, in magnetic "force"'; though 'not itself actually and actively alive, inorganic matter seemed pregnant with life potential' (Gallagher and Greenblatt 2000: 189–90). As the period progressed, interest in the vitality of things intensified, while perceived notions about the demarcation between the human and nonhuman worlds were 'fundamentally reconfigured through rapidly advancing industrialization, the unprecedented growth of consumer culture, and the rise of evolutionary theories' (Boehm 2012: 3). These innovations and emerging discourses made it possible for the Victorians to understand and express 'the dynamic modes in which subjects and objects merge, exchange positions, and materially transform one another' in nineteenth-century culture (Boehm 2012: 2). A corresponding fascination with vitality can be traced in numerous fictional texts of the period. Charles Dickens evinces a notable interest in the animation and reification of matter, and his works have been repeatedly mined for their curious intersubjective portrayals of people and the objects and things that make up their material environments. That the Victorians anticipated new materialist discourse is the central topic of debate in Jo Carruthers, Nour Dakkak and Rebecca Spence's *Anticipatory Materialisms in Literature and Philosophy, 1790–1930* (2019), which traces the origins of materialist thought in Romantic, Victorian and Modernist literature and culture. In a similar vein Ariane de Waal and Ursula Kluwick posit that 'Victorian interrogations of the boundaries between human and nonhuman as well as active and passive matter pave the way for contemporary conceptualizations of materiality' (2022: 3). Indeed, new materialism has proven to be a particularly fruitful theoretical framing for scholars wishing to examine the active lives of things in contemporary culture, American fiction and Modernist short stories (Bärbel Tischleder 2014; Boscagli 2014; Oulanne 2021). Yet to be explored, however, is the way in which neo-Victorianism adopts and adapts new materialist discourse in its resurrection and revivification of sartorial things from the nineteenth century. Following in the wake of their nineteenth-century counterpoints, neo-Victorian novels imbue clothes with distinct energies. Through means of metaphor, prosopopoeia, personification and anthropomorphism, clothes are depicted as dynamic, vital and vibrant. In the chapters that follow they appear as sentient things, imbued with memory, emotion and narrative. They contain and transmit stories, enliven the trace of past histories and synecdochally reveal submerged narratives. Freighted with the emotional, affective and somatic imprints of past wearers, garments, whether real or imagined, thrill with residual life. The lively energy with which these clothes are suffused bespeaks, this study contends, a contemporary fascination with the aura of Victorian material traces.

That these garments are literary does not alter their theoretical framing. Rather, as Bennett explains, 'texts are bodies that can light up, by rendering human perception more acute, those bodies whose favored vehicle of affectivity is less wordy: plants, animals, blades of grass, household objects, trash ... Poetry can help us feel more of the liveliness hidden in such things and reveal more of the threads of connection binding our fate to theirs' (2012: 232). Her words underscore the affective, agentive and sensory work of clothes in texts. Garments make us feel, both emotionally and sensorily, in neo-Victorian fictions. Whether or not they are physically present and palpable does not necessarily affect the way in which they operate in the fictional diegeses of such texts; rather, their textual presence informs perceptual and affective imagination. Dress in the neo-Victorian novel is a material medium existing in an immaterial space; but while it borders on the virtual, written dress is always a lively and insistent force in any text. It punctuates the narrative of the novels that I examine here with its sensuous materiality and lively vitality. As is made clear in the paragraphs from Sarah Waters's *Affinity* with which I began this introduction, clothes arrest the flow of the narrative. Made present and palpable via phantasmatic agency, they impel readerly attention; further, dress incites emotional and affective engagements and promises a more immersive, material encounter with the reimagined Victorian past.

Clothes' capacity to affect us is one specific way in which their agency is made manifest in the neo-Victorian novel.[8] Affect, as a concept, tends to occupy a relatively nebulous and unstable definitional space in literary studies. Capturing its fluidity and indefinability in a way that renders it suitable for a consideration of the lively function of clothes in neo-Victorianism, Gregory J. Seigworth and Melissa Gregg describe it as 'visceral forces beneath, alongside, or generally other than conscious knowing, vital forces insisting beyond emotion, – that can serve to drive us toward movement, toward thought and extension that can likewise suspend us (as if in neutral) across a barely registering accretion of force-relations, or that can leave us overwhelmed by the world's apparent intractability' (2010: 1). The term 'affect' therefore implicitly recognizes the 'visceral forces' at work within dress, as well as the complex range of feelings and forces they incite within human protagonists and the contemporary reader. It marks the vital flows and reciprocal encounters between bodies and sartorial things in the pages of the neo-Victorian novel and accounts for our emotional,

---

[8] Many critics have connected dress, affect and agency. See, for example, Sampson's recent object-centred approach to footwear (2021).

sensorial and occasionally libidinal investments in and interactions with these remediated garments. Depicted as lively, recalcitrant and uncanny, clothes operate in tandem with and often in opposition to their human counterparts in neo-Victorian fictions as the following chapters will show.

Written dress is envisioned and consumed in the neo-Victorian novel through a range of tactual, visual and olfactory literary devices. These imagined and imaginative encounters with clothes on the page often serve to collapse the distinction not only between subject and object but between past and present. In recent years, sensorial, phenomenological and affective approaches to neo-Victorian literature and culture have highlighted the various ways in which recourse to the senses and emotions can dissolve the boundaries between the contemporary reader and the nineteenth century. Cora Kaplan identifies the 'high degree of affect involved in reading and writing about the Victorian past' (2007: 5), while Rosario Arias has insightfully shown how 'paying attention to the overflow of the Victorian past into the present through sensorial engagement, from the point of view of phenomenology and tactility, illustrates the affective interaction between the Victorian past and today's culture, in which a reassessment of materiality is deemed necessary in the light of the relevance of social media and virtual human interaction' (2017: 52). Fashion theory has also turned to embodied and affective modes of study, analysing garments, real and imagined, through frameworks of touch, materiality, memory and mourning (Hunt 2014; Sampson 2021; Stallybrass 1999). These studies profess that wearing, making, collecting and otherwise interacting with clothes are fundamentally corporeal engagements. A multisensorial phenomenon, dress, even written dress, is therefore closely connected to issues of embodiment, sensoriality and phenomenology. Along with other 'material forms', it is 'encountered through the multiple sensuous and socialized subjective apparatus of our bodies (sight, sound, touch, smell, taste): the manner in which we comprehend both things and persons through our embodied being in a lived world which we share with others' (Tilley 2006: 8). Dress also signifies and substitutes the bodies that it has previously adorned, and clothes often retain the physical imprints of past wearers embedded within their fibres. Acting as material conduits, allowing feelings and memories from the past to be carried through to the present, they work to bring distant bodies into close proximity with one another and to particularize historical and cultural events. Specific items of dress can even provide an indexical record of our own lives; as Lynda Nead has persuasively argued, clothes can 'be the prompts for remembering moments in our past; we recollect our history through what we were wearing. Time, history and memory are all folded into the meaning of clothes' (2013: 502). Such notions are easily translatable onto written garments which, due to their fluidity and fictionality, tend to function in more sensuous and metaphysical terms than their real-life analogues.

At the conclusion of Rhys's *Wide Sargasso Sea*, for instance, when Antoinette (Bertha) is imprisoned with her warder Grace Poole in Thornfield Hall, a red dress worn in her youth vividly embodies the sensorial and memorializing power of fabric. The touch, sight and smell of the cloth anchors Antoinette to the past, evoking distant memories, and enfolding distal temporalities. The gown appears to transcend time, working to connect past and present: 'Time has no meaning', Antoinette explains to Grace, 'but something you can touch and hold like my red dress, that has a meaning' (2000: 151). The mediatory potential of the dress is fully realized when its lush vibrancy and potent scent conjure Antoinette's Caribbean birthplace. 'The colour of fire and sunset. The colour of flamboyant flowers' (151), the red dress evokes both the beauties and dangers of post-Emancipation Coulibri which is riven with tensions between the previously enslaved plantation workers, the white colonizers and the Creole people. The scent which emanates from the red dress re-enacts such conflicts and, at the same time, transports Antoinette back in time to the West Indies by recalling its rich intersensorial landscape: 'The scent that came from the dress was very faint at first, then it grew stronger. The smell of vertivert and frangipanni, of cinnamon and dust and lime trees when they are flowering. The smell of the sun and the smell of the rain' (151). Acting as a visual and olfactory memory prompt, the red dress is imbued with and proffers a sense of agency. Besides its linkage with past events, it provokes Antoinette to future actions. Dropping it to the floor, she is struck once again by the red dress's fiery properties, stating, 'I looked at the dress on the floor and it was as if the fire had spread across the room. It was beautiful and it reminded me of something I must do. I will remember I thought. I will remember quite soon' (153). Here, the garment, like Serres's handkerchief, precipitates a connection between past, present and future: for Antoinette it acts as a marker of her past identity while simultaneously holding out the possibility of future change and liberation.

Neo-Victorian fashions: Chapter outlines

This book explores the creative, textual and material potentialities of dress in the neo-Victorian novel. In the four chapters that follow I aim to re-fashion and reinscribe the Victorian female body through four specific dress elements: gowns, gloves, veils and jewellery.[9] Drawing upon a range of cultural texts, including neo-Victorian novels published between 1990 and 2014, their Victorian counterparts, nineteenth-century fashion magazines, illustrative material and extant Victorian garments, this study aims to advance critical discussion of (neo-)Victorian literature through the lens of sartorial culture. It offers new readings of contemporary historical novels which represent well-trodden critical ground, such as Margaret Atwood's *Alias Grace* (1996) and Sarah Waters's *Fingersmith* (2002), while also interrogating less well-known texts like Diana Souhami's *Gwendolen: A Novel* (2014). It aims to show how these twentieth- and twenty-first-century novels' engagements with Victorian dress and fashion open up new interpretational avenues for exploration. Studying literary representations of historic dress in present-day literature and culture proffers a means of imaginatively engaging with the past. It also provides a lens through which to examine the construction of historical narrative as interwoven skeins that might be gathered, unpicked and re-entwined.

Each of this book's chapters offers a detailed discussion of the neo-Victorian garment under study, while working simultaneously to situate the item of dress historically and culturally. By tracking the garments back to the nineteenth century and tracing their forward trajectories, this study aims to illuminate their re-appropriations in contemporary cultural productions, showing how neo-Victorian authors often concurrently employ yet subvert and challenge inherited sartorial codes. Chapter 2 'Gowns' examines cast-off dresses as sites of ghostly agency in two neo-Victorian biofictions. It begins by examining the ghostly force represented by old and empty clothes in the nineteenth-century imaginary, before exploring the manifold ways in which Colm Tóibín's *The Master* (2004) and Margaret Atwood's *Alias Grace* (1996) adopt new materialist discourse in their deployment of lively gowns. In staging the importance of animate objects in contemporary historical fiction, novels such as Tóibín's and Atwood's show how material things, especially clothes, are central to the narrativization and (re-)formulation of the past. Chapter 3, 'Gloves', continues this exploration by considering the symbolic and sensory work of gloves in three neo-Victorian novels that are themselves deeply concerned with issues of touch, traces and interiority. In Sarah Waters's *Tipping the Velvet* (1998), *Affinity* (1999) and *Fingersmith* (2002), gloves thrill with residual life. They foreground issues pertaining to female homoeroticism and dramatize the tensions within the texts

---

[9] Here I follow Gatrell's useful understanding of a 'dress-element' as any material item that adorns the body (2011: 2, 79).

between issues of absence and presence and interiority and exteriority. Situating the glove as an explicitly Victorian item, this chapter demonstrates how cast-off gloves, whether stolen or given as keepsakes, were popularly gendered feminine in nineteenth-century print culture. Re-imagining gloves in her neo-Victorian fictions, Sarah Waters adopts but ultimately subverts nineteenth-century heteronormative codes of glove wearing and giving. Through their movements between and amongst hands, the gloves record the intimate stories and desires of the female protagonists.

Iterations of the Victorian veil in neo-Victorian fiction form the sartorial foci of Chapter 4. Considering John Harwood's *The Ghost Writer* (2004) alongside Belinda Starling's *The Journal of Dora Damage* (2007), this chapter shows how neo-Victorian fictions engage the idea of the veil as a site of tension. A deeply complex material, symbolic and discursive construct, the Victorian veil was a literary invention, distinct from social and sartorial realities in which it was worn as a protective and practical garment. Drawing upon the garment's malleability to promote the notion of revelation, neo-Victorian authors deploy the veil strategically so as to prompt a consideration of the mechanics of rewriting the past. Chapter 5 is linked to this discussion in its own exploration of the way in which sartorial objects are aligned with issues of revision. 'Jewellery', begins with an extended analysis of A. S Byatt's *Possession: A Romance* (1990). In this reading, I identify a nascent material plot that emerges in the novel with the (re)discovery of a jet jewellery brooch and a hair bracelet and which runs counter to the novel's more literary strand. Typically, the epigraphic poems, embedded letters and diary entries that dominate *Possession* have been accorded special status in neo-Victorian criticism. Yet a reading of jewellery in this novel, I suggest, grants a richer, more immediate form of engagement with the historical past. The issues raised in *Possession* proffer a suitable point of departure for a consideration of jewellery in the more recently published *Havisham: A Novel* (2012) by Ronald Frame and Diana Souhami's *Gwendolen: A Novel* (2014). Yet to receive sustained literary criticism, both novels are engaged in a feminist process of rewriting in which they return to and challenge the primacy of canonical nineteenth-century novels, while actively centring issues of female identity and agency. Jewels and jewellery come to play pivotal roles in the negotiation of such themes. This chapter therefore explores the reprisal of the jewellery motif across the primary nineteenth-century novels and their two neo-Victorian rewritings. As sartorial items that have an intercessorial capacity, jewellery links the protagonists and plots both intra- and extra-textually, while also working to re-materialize memories, events and actions from the past. Finally, the book's conclusion extends some of these readings in its focus on Richard Flanagan's *Wanting* (2008). It interrogates how sartorial objects, a shell necklace and a red dress in particular, are the material means by which the author exposes and critiques empire and Britain's colonial rule in Australia. This chapter broadens the focus of the book by considering the influence of Victorian fashion in a more globalized context. The power of clothes to both represent and disrupt not only individual but collective identity is the central focus of this concluding chapter and works to bring the study to a close.

Victorian Dress in Contemporary Historical Fiction: Materiality, Agency and Narrative is the first full-length study to examine the vestural remains of the nineteenth century in neo-Victorian literature. Collectively, each of this book's chapters consider the ways in which Victorian dress and fashion find expression in neo-Victorian fiction, asking how they contribute to and alter established ideas about writing, reading and re-imagining the material past. Victorian garments emerge in these contemporary narratives as key material sites that evoke the memory of past wearers. They become significant material things through which the emotional, physical and psychological connections with the nineteenth-century dead might be recovered and re-experienced. Inscribed with psychical and somatic traces, garments draw the desired Victorian 'other' closer, while promising to immerse us in the material past.

2

Gowns

Fashionable dress possessed and exerted a powerful social, cultural and economic force during the Victorian period. Ever-changing sartorial styles reflected gender and class relations, dictated consumer practices and impacted commercial trade, while the political dimensions of clothes, as well as their symbolic, spiritual and metaphysical resonances, were being widely debated in the literature of the period. As discussed in the introduction, Thomas Carlyle's foundational text, *Sartor Resartus* (1836), was the first nineteenth-century philosophical treatise to consider the power of dress in society. Although it was originally met with an indifferent critical response, Catherine Spooner affirms that 'after the publication in 1837 of Carlyle's more instantly successful *The French Revolution*, *Sartor Resartus* found general acceptance and eventually became one of the bestsellers of the Victorian age' (2004: 49). Framed as a review of the fictional German professor, Diogenes Teufelsdröckh's book, *Philosophy of Clothes*, by an unnamed English editor, *Sartor Resartus* examines the symbolism of garments and is largely predicated on the conceit that cloth and human life are analogous. Essentially, Teufelsdröckh posits that the material world, particularly dress, signifies the spiritual: 'all Emblematic things are properly Clothes, thought-woven or hand-woven: must not the Imagination weave Garments, visible Bodies, wherein the else invisible creations and inspirations of our Reason are, like Spirits, revealed' (Carlyle 2002: 83). The connection that Carlyle draws between the phenomenal and the noumenal becomes an important motif in *Sartor Resartus*, and one that is later developed when Teufelsdröckh contends that bodies and clothes are intimately entangled; if man is 'A Soul, a Spirit, and divine Apparition' then the human body, he argues, is a kind of garment too: 'Round his mysterious ME, there lies, under all those wool-rags, a Garment of Flesh (or of Senses), contexured in the Loom of Heaven' (75). This affinity between garment and body troubles the subject-object dialectic and consequently forges a link between the animate and inanimate, a theme that is borne out in his chapter entitled, 'Old

Clothes'. In the latter, Teufelsdröckh recounts his thoughts on walking through what was then London's second-hand clothes market, Monmouth Street, and remarks on the forceful vitality of old clothes:

> With awe-struck heart I walk through that Monmouth Street, with its empty Suits, as through a Sanhedrim of stainless Ghosts. Silent are they, but expressive in their silence: the past witnesses and instruments of Woe and Joy, of Passions, Virtues, Crimes, and all the fathomless tumult of Good and Evil in 'the Prison called Life.' Friends! trust not the heart of that man for whom Old Clothes are not venerable. (2002: 247)

Though mute and ostensibly lifeless, the discarded garments exhibit something of a ghostly force for Carlyle. Not only are they sartorial effigies of the bodies that they once adorned, but they are also rendered lifelike as 'expressive' and active 'witnesses and instruments' of human life. Cast as a metaphorical space upon which the uncanny trace of past emotions can be read, Teufelsdröckh attempts to decipher the clothes as a means of recalling the past. In this vein, he contends that old clothes exhibit a 'ghastly affectation of Life' (222) and become readable texts that express and exert a certain uncanny agency.

Evidently indebted to Carlyle's *Sartor Resartus*, Charles Dickens's short sketch, 'Meditations in Monmouth Street' (1836–7) in *Sketches by Boz*, likewise contemplates the lively but haunting potential of old clothes.[1] Following Carlyle, Dickens depicts Monmouth Street as a ghostly space when he refers to it through secular imagery as 'the burial-place of the fashions' (1995: 98). The perceived spectrality of old clothes is intensified when Dickens's narrator, Boz, similarly acknowledges the capacity of discarded clothes to resurrect the bodies of those that they once adorned. Commenting on a suit of clothes hanging in a shop window, Boz interprets the garments as a kind of sartorial narrative: 'There was the man's whole life written as legibly on those clothes, as if we had his autobiography engrossed on parchment before us' (99). His biographical reading of the old clothes discloses their communicative power and capacity to act as memory prompts, as well as staging what Elizabeth Wilson has referred to as the haunting distinction between corporeal bodily decay and clothes' durability (2003: 2). Crucially though, as in Carlyle's *Sartor Resartus*, the clothes exhibit a powerful force of their own:

---

[1] Catherine Spooner argues that 'Dickens's comical-grotesque sketch, "Meditations in Monmouth Street" ... strongly recalls Carlyle's own description of Monmouth Street ... in *Sartor Resartus*'. She also acknowledges the agency of the old clothes but does not examine them in light of new materialism (2004: 50).

We love to walk among these extensive groves of the illustrious dead, and to indulge in the speculations to which they give rise; now fitting a deceased coat, then a dead pair of trousers, and anon the mortal remains of a gaudy waistcoat, upon some being of our own conjuring up, and endeavouring, from the shape and fashion of the garment itself, to bring its former owner before our mind's eye. We have gone on speculating in this way, until whole rows of coats have started from their pegs, and buttoned up, of their own accord, round the waists of imaginary wearers; lines of trousers have jumped down to meet them; waistcoats have almost burst with anxiety to put themselves on; and half an acre of shoes have suddenly found feet to fit them, and gone stumping down the street with a noise which has fairly awakened us from our pleasant reverie. (2002: 98)

Boz's fanciful desire to conjure clothes' 'former owner[s]' by considering the 'shape and fashion of the garment' dramatically prefigures object-oriented dress study, as well as anticipating the neo-Victorian novel, whose recreation of the past is often figured through an evocation of its material traces. It also lends the clothes an active presence: while it is the narrator's imagination that initially enlivens the garments as a means of accessing the past, they eventually exert their own independence and begin to move 'of their own accord'. Enacting a transition from inanimate to active matter, the clothes' liveliness disrupts both the narrative and the narrator, who is awakened from his contemplation as they demonstrate their unruly material presence.

Carlyle and Dickens's respective works proffer a suitable point of departure for this chapter, which examines the nexus between dress, agency and memory in fiction about old clothes. As these examples attest, cast-off garments in the Victorian literary imagination were frequently inflected with notions about death and dying. Old clothes functioned poetically; they were the imagined evocations of the profound ephemerality and instability of human life. In her illuminating study on the material culture of death in the nineteenth century, Deborah Lutz finds that 'bodies left behind traces of themselves, shreds that could then become material memories. Such vestiges might be found in objects the body had touched as it advanced through existence: clothing worn, letters written, utensils handled' (2015a: 1). Bearing the significant and intimate traces of wear, old clothes, whether real or imagined, were thus frequently figured as the material conduits to the dead, drawing particular attention to and communicating wider nineteenth-century anxieties around mortality and materiality.[2] Intimating

---

[2] Curiously, if clothes were the mechanisms by which ghostly re-encounters could take place in the Victorian literary imagination, then they also offered an epistemological challenge to non-materialist and spectral occurrences too. See McCorristine (2010).

a similar cultural tension between im/materiality, the neo-Victorian novel likewise figures old, worn or cast-off clothes as sites of imaginative recuperation and vehicles for ghostly returns.[3] Rather than demonstrating an explicit concern with death and dying, however, the contemporary texts under study in the present chapter deploy Victorian dress and fashion as a means of analysing the fabric(ation) of the past.

Drawing on and developing the threads of new materialist thought introduced in Chapter 1, this chapter reads the textual representations of dress in neo-Victorian fiction as active, yet ghostly, agents. In its focus on dresses and gowns in two neo-Victorian novels, it explores the presentation of cast-off clothes as haunted sites that disturb the central storylines. The novels under study here, Colm Tóibín's *The Master* (2004) and Margaret Atwood's *Alias Grace* (1996), are both populated with discarded clothes that become ascribed with agentic vitality. Focusing on material garments which exude strange energies in Tóibín's and Atwood's novels, this chapter proposes that the animation of gowns in these texts highlights the narrative potential of dress to relate the stories of the past. Clothes augment intra- and extra-textual readers' understanding in neo-Victorian novels by conveying important unspoken signals about characterization, as well as highlighting key aspects of narrative, setting, and plot. This agentic ability to recall and reanimate past events has close links with sensorial experience and affective remembrance that dialogizes with the neo-Victorian genre's propensity to re-fashion the past through its material traces.

New materialism and neo-Victorianism

If old and empty clothes were often inscribed with peculiar energies in the literature of the nineteenth century, then the fashion system was itself subject to similar animations. Often personified as 'the tyrannous Dame Fashion, whose arbitrary decrees a trembling population had to obey', Victorian fashions, especially those followed by women, were regularly codified as frivolous, ephemeral and illogical (Schaffer 2000: 103). According to one article in *Bow Bells*, 'Fashion is tyrannical! The laws with which she governs the world are arbitrary, and most generally irrational' ('Fashion', 1869: 246). In a similar vein, 'Foolish Fashions', a short piece published in Charles Dickens's *All the Year Round*, declared the dangers

---

[3] As mentioned in the introduction to this book, neo-Victorianism itself is frequently figured in terms of haunting and spectrality (see Arias and Pulham 2010).

posed by fashionable dress in terms that resonate with hyperbole: 'Fashion is a tyrant; always has been, and apparently has no intention of ever being anything else; a cruel and oppressive tyrant, delighting in nothing so much as in bodily torture and general inconvenience' (1868: 65). Beyond its ostensibly repressive control at both individual and collective levels, 'Dame Fashion' fomented further anxieties precisely because it appeared to function independently of human involvement and according to its own principles. Commenting on its 'awful power', Rigby warned in 'The Art of Dress' that 'Fashion, like the animal, or vegetable, or mineral kingdom, has laws and boundaries of her own, deep seated in the nature of things' (1847: 76). Such sentiments manifest the Victorians' acute preoccupation with the subject-object binary, while the connotations of animation and agency resonate with and anticipate new materialist ontologies, the central tenet of which is that things, whether human or nonhuman, possess surprisingly agentic capacities of their own.

New materialism, occasionally referred to in its plural form 'new materialisms', is the term for the renewed focus on and reconceptualization of matter in the humanities and political and social sciences.[4] Originating in the field of Gender Studies, the phrase was first coined by Rosi Braidotti in her 1994 text *Nomadic Subjects: Embodiment and Sexual Difference in Contemporary Feminist Theory*; for Braidotti and other feminist critics such as Karen Barad and Donna Haraway, new materialism proffers a critical rethinking of the cultural turn (Schouwenburg 2015: 63). Closely related to and deriving from Material Culture Studies and thing theory, new materialism essentially presents a new ontological approach to understanding objects and challenging conceptualizations of matter in contemporary culture. It poses new questions about our interactions with the material world and seeks to confront, challenge and contest anthropocentrism and the rise of human exceptionalism. New materialism does not seek to entirely decentre the human, however, which is a strategy adopted by object-oriented ontology; rather, key proponents of new materialist thought such as Jane Bennett, Manuel DeLanda, Iris van der Tuin and Rick Dolphijn, and Samantha Coole and Diana Frost, among others, seek to reconsider our cultural,

---

[4] Coole and Frost insist on the plural 'new materialisms' to indicate their acknowledgement of the various initiatives in new materialist scholarship that rely on and reflect different levels of materialization (2010: 4). Ahmed (writing in the same volume) prefers the term 'critical materialism' because she finds that the earlier feminist engagements with phenomenology that her own work draws on, 'belie the claim made by some recent materialist critics to the effect that, during this period [the period of the "cultural turn"], matter was the only thing that did not matter' (2010: 234). I use the term 'new materialism' in conjunction with most other critics but acknowledge these points when defining new materialism as drawing on, not rejecting, the work of previous feminist and materialist scholars.

political and ethical implication in the world of things. They urge us to attend in more nuanced ways to our material environments, to the reciprocal flows and relational connectivities that arise between us and the material things with which we are entangled.

That matter constitutes a vital and vibrant force is one of the central features of new materialist thought.[5] In order to describe the energies and intensities that accrue to and originate from material objects, Jane Bennett coins the term 'thing-power' in her essay 'The Force of Things: Steps Toward an Ecology of Matter', in which she attempts to 'promote acknowledgement, respect, and sometimes fear of the materiality of the thing and to articulate ways in which human being and thinghood overlap' (2004: 349). Building upon this notion of 'thing-power' in her book *Vibrant Matter: A Political Ecology of Things*, Bennett goes on to explore the force, or what she calls the 'vitality', of material objects. Here, she clarifies her use of the term 'vitality' as referring to 'the capacity of things – edibles, commodities, storms, metals – not only to impede and block the will and design of humans but also to act as quasi agents or forces with trajectories, propensities, or tendencies of their own' (2010a: viii). In doing so, Bennett encourages us to take seriously the material world and to pay close attention to the vital materialism inherent in all things, whether we perceive objects to be animate or inanimate. Returning to the concept of 'thing-power', she argues that this phrase is key to developing a 'vital materialist vocabulary', claiming that the term 'gestures toward the strange ability of ordinary, man-made items to exceed their status as objects and to manifest traces of independence or aliveness' (2010a: xvi). 'Thing-power' thus aptly names the strange tensions that arise between bodies and garments in neo-Victorian fiction. Clothes demonstrate vigorous and vital tendencies in the neo-Victorian novels examined here; they proffer additional 'readable' traces and act alongside and in opposition to the other protagonists in the novels' diegetic worlds.

On this point, Bennett acknowledges the way in which agency is distributed and distributive. With particular reference to the works of Spinoza and

---

[5] The renewed focus on the agency of things in new materialism (as well as the entangled ontologies of subjects and objects) owes much to the work of Bruno Latour and actor-network theory (ANT), which recognizes the agency of things and the interactions that occur between humans and nonhumans. Borrowing the term 'actant' from narratology, Latour claims that all matter has agency; he defines an actant as being anything (whether human or non-human) provided it is considered to be the source of the action (1996: 373). In *Vibrant Matter*, Bennett appropriates the term 'actant' in relation to new materialist thought in an attempt to further elide the distinction between humans and objects (2010a: ix).

Deleuze and Guattari she conceives of agency as occurring within networks, or 'assemblages', in which human and nonhuman elements coincide. In this vein, she aptly reminds us that 'while the smallest or simplest body or bit may indeed express a vital impetus ... an actant never really acts alone. Its efficacy or agency always depends on the collaboration, cooperation, or interactive interference of many bodies or forces' (2010a: 21). The entanglement of garment and body in the production and formation of identity, emotion and affect might be seen as an assemblage, and Bennett's reasoning might therefore aptly explain the generative potential that exists between bodies and clothes.

Likewise highlighting the way in which new materialist ontologies 'are abandoning the terminology of matter as an inert substance', Coole and Frost explain that new materialists are strongly 'attracted to forms of vitalism ... They often discern emergent, generative powers (or agentic capacities) even within inorganic matter, and they generally eschew the distinction between organic and inorganic, or animate and inanimate, at the ontological level' (2010: 9). Appearing to echo Bill Brown, they contend that materiality 'is always something more than "mere" matter: an excess, force, vitality, relationality, or difference that renders matter active, self-creative, productive, unpredictable' (9). One of the key reasons for this (re)turn to matter is the current ecological crisis and the growing conviction that we must rise to the challenge of practicing sustainability in contemporary society. For Coole and Frost, as for Bennett, paying increased attention to lively things has an overtly ethico-political dimension in that it aims to encourage more sustainable, considerate and environmentally aware engagements with the world of things.

Although new materialist thinkers such as Coole and Frost and Bennett refer primarily to physical objects in real world settings, their arguments can be extended to include literary representations of things too. The same vitality and vibrancy with which material objects are suffused in life is reflected and enhanced in literature. Babette Bärbel Tischleder convincingly argues that because 'narrative fiction depicts human subjects in the concrete circumstances of everyday life, it is a medium that grants us particular access to a material world that can become fully animate. The worlds conjured up in and by narrative are usually configured as a tangible universe' (2014: 17). Literary representations of dress are fluid and multiple; they are metaphysical and, at the same time, represent solidity and tangibility. Through the medium of language, dress is enlivened and made animate. Hence, the agency and vitality of written garments have already been the focus of important scholarly work by Casey Sloan and Rachel A. Ernst. In their respective essays on dress as a disguise in Victorian novels, both Sloan and Ernst adopt new materialist language in order to argue that dress subsumes female characters' identities. For Sloan, in Wilkie Collins's *The Woman in White* (1860) garments are granted 'a great deal of narrative agency or, to use Jane Bennett's terminology, "thing power,"' in that they have the capacity 'to completely overwhelm and transform their characters' (2016: 812). Similarly, Ernst argues that in Charles Dickens's *Bleak House* (1853), Lady Dedlock's dresses are active members of the narrative that revolt against their wearers in an attempt to exert their own independence and establish their own separate identities (2018: 502). Ernst concludes by suggesting that the 'agentic dress' in this novel 'anticipates similarly active dresses and disguises in other nineteenth-century novels, emphasizing the role active matter plays within Victorian literature' (515). Departing from literary representations of dress and instead focusing on agency in relation to haute couture that incorporates technology into its design, Anneke Smelik also foregrounds new materialism as a suitable theoretical tool for examining the interactive relationship that exists between technology, materiality and the body (2018). While the theoretical concept of new materialism has been thus employed to examine physical garments in real world settings and the deceptive nature of costume in Victorian novels, it has not yet been considered in relation to the power of neo-Victorian dress. This is surprising, given that neo-Victorian literature and culture is populated with all manner of Victorian things that have important and active narratorial roles. Indeed, the neo-Victorian novels which I discuss in this chapter (and in the study as a whole) imagine a highly intentional, vitally interactive relationship between human agents and objects – especially clothes – in which the imaginative ability to interact with the things of the past and to have them interact with us in return is overtly linked to notions of agency, affect and the entanglement of humans and objects. As such, new materialism emerges as a suitable theoretical framework for thinking about the active power of garments in neo-Victorian literature.

In the two contemporary novels studied in this chapter, disembodied Victorian clothes populate each narrative with subversive agency and vibrant energy. In their strange and lively returns in these texts, ghostly clothes typify what Jane Bennett refers to as 'materialism in which matter is an active principle and, though it inhabits us and our inventions, also acts as an outside or alien power' (2010b: 47). One of the key ways in which dress exhibits this agentic power is in its capacity to produce emotional and affective responses in its human counterparts: 'the power of things to affect us is one facet of their potential agency' (Oulanne 2021: 26). The interaction of things and their affective ties are, for László Munteán, Liedeke Plate and Anneke Smelik, central components in taking a new materialist approach to understanding memory and materiality. In the introduction to their edited volume, *Materializing Memory in Art and Popular Culture*, the authors maintain that memory and materiality are intimately entangled; they affirm that 'the practice of remembering endows a thing with affect and hence with psychological importance. The thing, however, may also have agency on its own not only in precipitating remembrance, but also, potentially in remembering on its own' (2017: 15). As a result, they contend that 'memory is thus no longer conceived of as a sole privilege of human beings who use objects to remember but rather as an activity deeply entangled with nonhuman things and processes' (15). Examining materiality, memory and techno-fashion in their essay in the same volume, Lianne Toussaint and Anneke Smelik note that 'many scholars have pointed to the particularly close, yet ambivalent, connection between dress, fashion, and memory' (2017: 92). They draw on the work of Ann Rosalind Jones and Peter Stallybrass who, anticipating these discussions in relation to Renaissance dress, have already argued that clothing is a powerful memory prompt: 'we need to understand the animatedness of clothes, their ability to "pick up" subjects, to mold and shape them both physically and socially, to constitute subjects through their power as material memories' (2000: 2). This theorizing is applicable to the neo-Victorian novel also, in which fictional dress functions as a key element in practices of remembering and recalling the past.

Exploring the relationship between history, narrative and practices of remembering, Atwood's *Alias Grace* and Tóibín's *The Master* are suitable texts for exploring the ideas outlined above. These novels, which take as their narrative impetus the lives of real nineteenth-century figures, each present fictional versions of their eponymous protagonists: *Alias Grace* is based on the life and story of the 'celebrated murderess' Grace Marks (Atwood 1997: 25), while *The Master* is about the author, Henry James, who was often referred to as 'The Master' by his contemporaries. Both are examples of neo-Victorian biofiction. Defined by Marie-Luise Kohlke as 'the literary, dramatic, or filmic re-imaginings of the lives of actual individuals who lived during the nineteenth century, in which said individuals provide the sole or joint major textual foci' (2013: 4), this subset of historical life-writing sits at the uneasy juncture between fact and fiction, authenticity and fabrication. Atwood's and Tóibín's novels are thus engaged in a process of adaptation and appropriation that blurs the lines between fact and fiction to create alternative narrative accounts of these two historical figures.

Because of their self-reflexive and postmodern inflections, both texts can also be read in light of Linda Hutcheon's theorization on historiographic metafiction. As has been discussed in the introduction, in *A Poetics of Postmodernism* Hutcheon argues that the postmodern historical novel, or 'historiographic metafiction' – of which neo-Victorianism is a subgenre – 'asks both epistemological and ontological questions. How do we know the past (or the present)? What is the ontological status of that past? Of its documents? Of our narratives?' (1988: 50). For Hutcheon, 'historiographic metafiction plays upon the truth and lies of the historical record' and 'acknowledges the paradox of the *reality* of the past but its textualized accessibility to us today' (1988: 114; original emphasis). While not entirely metafictional, the repeated references to James's writing processes in *The Master* and the epistemological uncertainty surrounding Grace Marks's narrative, as well as her polysemic portrayals in *Alias Grace*, draw attention to the construction and composition of each novel, while simultaneously problematizing contemporary attempts to retrieve and re-present the past. Both novels draw on official historical records and piece together their tales from information available in traceable documents. In his acknowledgements, Tóibín lists the factual works (including Leon Edel's five-volume biography) that he drew on to write *The Master*, and notes that he has 'peppered the text with phrases and sentences from the writings of Henry James and his family' (2004: 360). *Alias Grace* also demonstrates a 'theoretical self-awareness through the undissimulated piecing together of information from historical documents' (Murray 2001: 66). Atwood writes in the 'Author's Afterword' that '*Alias Grace* is a work of fiction, although it is based on reality. Its central figure, Grace Marks, was one of the most notorious Canadian women of the 1840s, having been convicted of murder at the age of sixteen' (1997: 537). Relatedly, both texts employ alternative modes of representation to tell their particular stories; they each play with the use of different 'texts', such as dress and fabric, in order to facilitate their historical narratives. In *Alias Grace* and *The Master*, the reconstruction of the Victorian past is inherently material. Both are populated with cast-off clothes and, in each of the novels, these discarded dresses function as discursive emblems that interact with and disrupt the central plotlines, as well as becoming decipherable agents of emotion, memory and narrative. In the following sections, I explore how dress takes on a haunting life of its own in first *The Master* and then *Alias Grace*, showing how it shapes the social worlds of the novels, producing affective and emotional responses and recalling the historical past.

Figure 2.1 Dress *c*. 1875 © Brooklyn Museum Costume Collection at the Metropolitan Museum of Art, Gift of the Brooklyn Museum, 2009; Gift of Jim McAnena, 1968.

Dynamic dresses in *The Master*

Writing of the American-born novelist Henry James, and the impact of his friend and fellow-author Constance Fenimore Woolson's suicide in 1894,[6] Lyndall Gordon introduces her biography, *A Private Life of Henry James: Two Women and His Art* (1998), by describing James's disposal of Woolson's gowns in the Venetian lagoon. Her opening chapter is prefaced with the following vignette:

> In April 1894, a middle-aged gentleman, bearing a load of dresses, was rowed to the deepest part of the Venetian lagoon. A strange scene followed: he began to drown the dresses, one by one. There were a good many, well-made, tasteful, and all dark, suggesting a lady of quiet habits and some reserve. The gondolier's pole would have been useful for pushing them under the still water. But the dresses

---

[6] Constance Fenimore Woolson (1840–94) was a renowned nineteenth-century American writer.

refused to drown. One by one they rose to the surface, their busts and sleeves swelling like black balloons. Purposefully, the gentleman pushed them under, but silent, reproachful, they rose before his eyes. (1)

Gordon later explains how the story originated from the BBC Third Programme in memory of Henry James. The radio programme aired in 1956, exactly forty years after his death, and featured an interview with an elderly American woman named Mercede Huntington, who claimed that Henry James had imparted the '"strange story"' to her many years before (1999: 288). For Gordon, this pivotal tale provides a potentially significant clue about James's close relationship with Woolson: 'Sinking her dresses at that time was not, I believe, a casual act, but sign of a strange bond which James guarded with discretion, and which suicide almost exposed' (5). Gordon also reads James's culpability in Woolson's suicide through the strange burial of her clothes and depicts his apparent guilt metaphorically by explaining how, despite James's efforts, the black dresses came up in the water around him 'like wilful phantoms he could not dispel' (1999: 289).

Just as the black dresses could not, apparently, be suppressed, neither can the tale itself, which has since attained mythic status and has taken on a life of its own. While some critics (including Gordon herself) note that the account, let alone the event, is highly unlikely, many scholars, such as Hazel Hutchison and Fred Kaplan, and writers of contemporary fiction like Emma Tennant, David Lodge and Colm Tóibín, include this highly symbolic scene in their works.[7] Typically read as an uncanny manifestation of James's repressed guilt over Woolson's death, the dresses' return from the depths of the lagoon might also be read in light of new materialist views on agentic materiality. That Woolson's dresses have been portrayed as 'wilful phantoms', both in Gordon's account and in several popular contemporary reimaginings of James's life, lends a mysterious liveliness and haunting power to these fictional old clothes, which this section aims to tease out.

A similar link between agency, haunting and dress occurs in Henry James's own fiction. The tale of the drowned dresses resonates with one of James's early ghost stories, 'The Romance of Certain Old Clothes', which features a woman's dresses that have an unsettling haunting power.[8] Published in *The Atlantic Monthly* in February 1868, the short story centres on the rivalry between two eighteenth-century sisters, Viola and Perdita Willoughby.[9]

---

[7] Sheldon M. Novick also regards the story as 'improbable', but includes it in his book, *Henry James: The Mature Master* because it has 'become canonical' (2007: 554).
[8] Yoder is the first to point out this connection (2014: 478).
[9] In his 1885 revision of the tale, James changed Viola's name to Rosalind and the sisters' surname to Wingrave. I refer to the original version of the story in this chapter.

After both women fall in love with the same man, a bitter competition for his affection ensues. The suitor, Mr Arthur Lloyd, eventually chooses to marry the youngest of the sisters (Perdita), and Viola's jealousy is depicted sartorially. After she discovers her sister's triumph, Viola insists on dressing Perdita in a 'stern silence' and 'forced upon her acceptance a bit of lace of her own' to wear (1868: 213), thus setting in motion what Clair Hughes has accurately termed 'the substitution of herself for Perdita' (2001: 171). This imagery intensifies later on in the tale, when, in a highly symbolic scene which occurs shortly after the wedding has taken place, the extradiegetic narrator observes Viola dressing herself in her sister's 'cast-off wedding veil and wreath' (215). Focalized through the perspective of Perdita, who witnesses the strange act, the narrator observes that:

> on her neck she had hung the heavy string of pearls which the young girl had received from her husband as a wedding-gift. These things had been hastily laid aside, to await their possessor's disposal on her return from the country. Bedizened in this unnatural garb, Viola stood at the mirror, plunging a long look into its depths and reading Heaven knows what audacious visions. Perdita was shocked and pained. It was a hideous image of their old rivalry come to life again. (1868: 215)

In this dramatic moment, Viola's transgressive act troubles the boundaries between self and other. By dressing in her sister's cast-off wedding clothes and jewels, Viola is depicted as Perdita's uncanny double, and indeed, when Perdita dies, Viola will appropriate her role as Arthur's new wife. Though beautiful on the bride, the garments are rendered 'unnatural' on Viola and actively bring to life the 'hideous' rivalry that exists between the sisters. This materialization of the sisters' enmity in sartorial form foreshadows the conclusion of the short story, when Perdita's clothes come to life on her behalf and exert her ghostly vengeance. Weakened after childbirth and fearful of her sister's avaricious nature, Perdita entreats Arthur to seal her gowns in a chest and place them in the attic for her infant daughter. As soon as Perdita is dead, however, Viola marries Arthur and blackmails him into giving her the key to the chest. When unearthed by Viola, the clothes, which are inscribed with Perdita's agency, unleash her curse. In the tale's concluding paragraphs, Arthur discovers his new wife dead beside the chest which exposes, 'amid their perfumed napkins, its treasure of stuffs and jewels'; the final lines of the short story linger over a description of Viola who bears 'the marks of ten hideous wounds from two vengeful ghostly hands' (1868: 220). Jennifer Bann has drawn attention to the agency of the ghostly hands at the conclusion of James's 'The Romance of Certain Old Clothes' (2009: 676), but crucially it is Perdita's dresses that recall and convey the ghostly force of their wearer and thus become powerful agents in their own right.

Commenting on the often-overlooked importance of clothes in several of Henry James's other texts, Clair Hughes argues that dress plays a surprisingly central role in the depiction of his ghosts (2001: 170). In his neo-Victorian novel, *The Master*, Colm Tóibín capitalizes on this Jamesian interest in fictional dress and ghostly figures; he pays especial attention to themes of materiality and spectrality in the novel before dedicating several pages to describing the lagoon scene and the disposal of Woolson's dresses in detail.[10] Published in 2004 along with David Lodge's *Author, Author* (in which Henry James is the novel's main protagonist), and Alan Hollinghurst's Man-Booker Prize winner, *The Line of Beauty* (in which the novel's protagonist, Nick, is a postgraduate student writing his doctoral thesis on Henry James and literary style), Tóibín's *The Master*, which was shortlisted for the same Man-Booker prize that Hollinghurst's novel won, forms part of what Lodge has since called 'The Year of Henry James' (2006: 2). Writing of the coincidence that saw three books on James published in the same year, Lodge also refers to Emma Tennant's novel *Felony* (2002), which was re-issued in paperback form in 2004, and Michiel Heyns's novel *The Typewriter's Tale*, which was initially rejected by publishers in 2004 due to the sudden abundance of novels on the subject of James (2006: 1). For Ann Heilmann, what these novels represent is an attempt to 'retrace, recreate, and refract the multiple personae of a writer whose experimentation with issues of authorship, identity, and subjectivity reflects central literary and critical preoccupations of the turn of the millennium' (2010a: 111). It is no surprise, then, that in positioning Henry James as its main protagonist, Tóibín's *The Master* plays with notions of narrative, identity and memory throughout.

Opening in January 1895 with the failure of James's unsuccessful play *Guy Domville*, the novel, offering only a snapshot of the author's life, spans a four-year period and draws to a close in October 1899. Highlighting its investment in memory and haunting, however, the novel is interspersed with analeptic passages which provide James's backstory. Through a sequence of flashbacks, the extradiegetic narrator recounts James's American upbringing before

---

[10] Dennis Kersten points out that while it is only a paragraph long, Emma Tennant's *Felony* 'ends with the lagoon scene, thereby giving it the same prominence it has in Gordon's biography and confirming its status as a key scene in James' life story', whereas Lodge's version of the scene in *Author, Author* 'reads like a page from Gordon ... [and] is less ambiguous than Tóibín's text' (2013: 228). Because of the brevity of both Lodge's and Tennant's depictions of the lagoon scene, however, I refer to *The Master* in this chapter.

revealing the tragic deaths of his sister, Alice, his young cousin Minny Temple and his close friend, the writer Constance Fenimore Woolson, whose dresses he disposes of after she has died by suicide. Filtered through the lens of queer theory, *The Master* also implies James's repressed homosexuality by underlining his tentative, homoerotic friendships with several other men, including Oliver Wendell Holmes, with whom he shares a bed as a young man; Corporal Hammond, who acts as his manservant in Ireland; and the sculptor Hendrik Christian Andersen, with whom he develops a close homosocial relationship towards the close of the novel. Daniel Hannah writes that 'while scenes exposing James' intense, unconsummated desire for men punctuate Tóibín's novel, homoeroticism remains shrouded in an ambiguous silence of potentiality' (2007: 74). For Hannah, James's undeclared sexuality is closely connected to his aversion to publicity (73), and on this point Karen Scherzinger concurs when she posits that in *The Master* 'James is often preoccupied with the indignities attached to publicity and being on show. In each case the indignity is attached to sexual uneasiness, and not only with reference to himself. He is appalled by the "unsuitable nature of the attention" (45) bestowed upon the child, Mona, at the Wolseleys' fancy dress party' (2008: 189).

Here and elsewhere in the novel clothing, or the absence of it, is the root cause of the fictional James's uneasiness. It is the precocity of the young girl, Mona, dressed as 'the Infanta from Velázquez, wearing a dress five times larger than she was' (Tóibín, 2004: 45) that provokes his initial disquiet at the Wolseleys' fancy dress ball in Ireland. Specifically, it is the spectacle of Mona's sexuality staged through her provocative costume that troubles the fictional author. As the omniscient narrator observes, 'Henry was disturbed by her, the flaunting of her female self, and her own poised alertness to her allure' (2004: 45). The artificiality of the fancy dress ball also unsettles James, who fails to recognize one of the guests in her disguise, and whose description of his hostess, Lady Wolseley, centres on the materialistic ostentation and excess of her costume:

> A mixture of peacock blue and a deep red, her silk dress had an enormous sash, and was full of tucks and flourishes and bulges. It was low-cut to a degree that none of the other ladies had risked. Lady Wolseley was not wearing a wig, merely her natural hair with ringlets added, the connection between the real and the false hair seamless. (45)

While the invaginated 'tucks and flourishes and bulges' in Lady Wolseley's lowcut silk dress reflect the form of her body and provoke feelings of discomfort in

James, it is not only the public display of both her and Mona's sexualized female bodies that trouble him but also the 'seamless' dissimulation involved in their respective costumes and performances that prompt his increasingly anxious response. The insincerity and depravity represented by both the ball and the excessive costumes are given further significance when James's distaste for the event is aligned with his growing unease at British colonial rule in Ireland. Upon 'observing the dancing, the candles slowly burning down, the gowns and wigs increasingly tawdry in their appearance' (46), James ironically notes that 'these were the English in Ireland. This building was an oasis with chaos and squalor all around. The Wolseleys had imported their silver as they had their guests and manners' (46–7). Although the Victorians generally favoured fancy dress balls and saw them as a fun and harmless pastime, the fictional James's response situates dress as both an active means of and metaphor for deception, while the wild dancing and gaudy gowns invoke associations of the carnivalesque.

Later in the novel, dress is aligned more closely with James's own sexual identity. Since they are often in contact with the body, clothes function as indicators of sexuality and desire and become appropriate alternative narrative sites in *The Master* for playing out the protagonist's uncertain sexual orientation. Early-on in the text, the dramatic moment in which James's friend, Oliver Wendell Holmes, undresses in front of him and the two share a bed is one of the most implicitly erotic scenes in the novel (97). This homoerotic tension is enacted again towards the novel's conclusion, when James imagines his friend, the sculptor Hendrik Andersen, undressing in the bedroom above him:

> As the floorboards creaked under Andersen's feet, Henry imagined his friend undressing, removing his jacket and his tie. And then he heard only silence as perhaps Andersen sat on the bed to remove his shoes and his socks. Henry waited, listening. And now after an interval came further creaks as, Henry surmised, he must have been removing his shirt; he dreamed of him standing bare-chested in the room, and then reaching to find his night attire. Henry did not know what Andersen would do now. He wondered if he would not remove his trousers and his underwear and stand naked studying himself in the mirror … not making a sound … Henry, as he lay on his back with the book he was reading left to one side, his own lamp still switched on and shining, closed his eyes and envisioned his guest now, naked in lamplight, his body powerful and perfect, his skin smooth and soft to the touch. (2004: 310–11)

James's unspoken desire for Andersen is revealed through a series of imaginative 'visions' which are both highly sensual and phenomenological. Denied the opportunity of gazing upon Andersen while he undresses, James's imagination fills in the blanks. He pictures his friend removing items of dress in an erotic and unintentional strip-show and, like the statues that Andersen sculpts, James visualizes his naked body as an art object within the frame of the mirror. The tactile quality of the garments and Andersen's 'smooth' skin which is revealed with the removal of his clothing to be 'soft to the touch', mediates an imagined tactual encounter between James and the object of his desire. The erotically charged scene is further manifested through the sequence of intimate creaks; connecting the sounds of Andersen's movements to the removal of different items of clothes, James is able to conjure Andersen's presence through aural imagery and the scene thus becomes the closest Tóibín comes to unveiling James's homoerotic desire. Despite this promised unveiling, however, the physical distance between the two men and the silences that permeate this passage reinforce James's marginalized sexuality, positioning him as an outsider in both his own home and Tóibín's novel. Ostensibly it is the silences and gaps in the text, along with the moments of sartorial anxiety, which narrate James's repressed sexuality.

For Patricia Pulham, who discusses Tóibín's novel at length in her illuminating essay, 'Neo-Victorian Gothic and Spectral Sexuality in Colm Tóibín's *The Master*', the unspoken homoeroticism and silences in the text are precisely what haunt the narrative. Examining the uncanny portrayal of repressed homosexuality in *The Master*, she posits that the novel is 'on the surface ... a fictional biography of Henry James, shadowed by covert and haunting expressions of homoerotic desire' (2012: 149). The theme of haunting pervades the novel, which begins with a dream 'about the dead – familiar faces and the others, half-forgotten ones, fleetingly summoned up' (Tóibín 2004: 1). The ghosts that return to Henry James are those of his mother and aunt Kate, and they set the tone for the rest of the novel which is populated by ghostly figures that return to haunt both James and the novels that he crafts. This sense of haunting is not only reserved for James's dead friends and relatives, however, but extends to the author himself, whom Pulham argues 'functions as a "double" caught between fact and fiction; he is an animated "corpse", a dead author brought back to life, and yet retains a death-like, ghostly quality' (2012: 151). The same might be said of the resurrection of Constance Fenimore Woolson's dresses in chapter nine, which can be read as material metaphors for Tóibín's own attempt to resurrect Henry James. Although Pulham refers to Woolson's haunting presence and persuasively argues that the passage in which James 'buries' her dresses is 'a visual representation of Freud's the uncanny' (155), she is not concerned with the agency and vitality of

Woolson's gowns and thus leaves space for a reassessment of the novel in terms of materiality.

Significantly, Woolson's ghostly returns in the novel are depicted along specifically material lines. Shortly after James hears of her death, the narrator reveals that 'some part of her spirit brushed through his rooms' (2004: 256). Seemingly, it is James's thoughts that conjure Woolson's material presence, and the aural imagery of her gowns brushing through his rooms aligns her spectral proximity with physical materiality. Speaking of her haunting presence, James acknowledges that 'she came to him forcefully, palpably', as 'a phantom he dreamed about' (257). He also refers to her in more corporeal terms when the narrator observes, 'now he thought about her dead body, and the rooms she had filled with the passion of her aura, her books, her mementoes, her clothes, her papers' (257). This theme is later developed when the objects that Woolson has touched, used and handled during her lifetime, appear to retain her trace. Such is the importance of matter in *The Master* that Woolson's sister and niece, Clara and Clare Benedict, imagine that Woolson's personal things share an inextricable commonality with her absent body. Focalized through James's perspective, the narrative reads:

> Her sister and her niece remained helpless in the face of the practical. At first they did not wish to disturb Constance's papers and seemed happy to leave everything in situ. They appeared not to believe that she was dead; and touching her things, they thought, would be a way of consigning the woman who had possessed them to oblivion. (2004: 259)

Following Bärbel Tischleder's assertion that 'literary texts in particular reflect the intimate entanglement between people and things' (21), Woolson is here presented as being closely entwined with the objects that were linked to her in her lifetime. In the following chapter, I suggest that the sense of touch conjures the presence of the absent other through their sartorial objects. However, during this moment in the text, the handling of Woolson's things, which are imbued with her memory, does not bring the women closer to her absent body; rather, Woolson's very life force appears to be contained within the things that bear her trace and their presence recalls her own. By removing and disposing of these personal objects, the Benedicts seem to suggest that Woolson's death will be enacted again, but this time the process will be complete. That Woolson's vitality is somehow contained within her personal things is further staged when Clare Benedict remarks to James that 'we have not been able to find a will, it may be buried among her papers' (261). Acknowledging the power of material objects to contain and evoke identity and memory, the women and Henry James locate Woolson's last will and testament, which is the physical document that sets out her desires and agency after death, as being suggestively 'buried' among her material things. Woolson's vitality is thus diffused among the objects that make up her material environment and which remain as potent traces of her past life.

The superstitious fear that Woolson's life force is entangled with and contained within the objects associated with her, anticipates the climactic scene in which her dresses are 'buried' in the Venetian lagoon. After they discover that Woolson's family has departed Venice 'leaving wardrobes full of dresses and cupboards full of shoes, underclothes and other items, that appeared not to have been disturbed' (266), James and Woolson's gondolier, Tito, are left to dispose of the garments. Because the clothes retain something of her physical and psychical trace, however, they are pervaded with a sense of the spectral: 'Henry suggested that perhaps one of the convents might be interested in old clothes. Not the clothes of the dead, Tito told him, no one will want the clothes of the dead' (266). Finally, the two men decide to 'bury' the garments in the lagoon, but the removal of Constance's personal effects from her rooms conjures her phantom-like presence:

> As soon as he held the dresses in his arms, Henry caught a powerful smell, which sharply evoked the memory of his mother and his Aunt Kate. It was a smell so redolent of them, their busy lives around their dressing rooms and wardrobes, their preparations for travel, the folding and protecting and packing which they did themselves no matter where they were. And then as he crossed the room carrying the bundle he caught another smell which belonged to Constance only, some perfume of hers, something she had used in all the years when he knew her, which mixed in now with the other smell as he carried the dresses down the stairs and deposited them in the waiting gondola. … The smell had brought her so close to him that he would not have been surprised if, at that moment, he had found her standing in the bare room. (268)

The interweaving of sensory modalities in this instance reflects the dynamic connection that exists between dress, memory, and the human sensorium. Here, the tactility of Constance's material garments and the smells their fibres contain and emit recall both her presence and, strangely, that of James's dead female relatives. This unexpected correlation exemplifies what Yannis Hamilakis refers to as the unpredictability of sensorial flows. Commenting on the relationship between matter, memory and the senses, especially olfaction, he acknowledges that 'memories can be unpredictable; they can spring up involuntarily and disrupt and upset the consensual order' (2013: 117). Elusive and intangible, odours have an especially intimate association with emotion, memory and temporality.[11] They elicit strong affectual responses and operate by disrupting the perceived distinction between past and present. Transformed into potent olfactory stimuli, Woolson's gowns thus facilitate James's ghostly re-encounters with the women he has lost. In much the same way that the neo-Victorian novel re-materializes the past via recourse to the material world, James's intimate and sensual engagements with the material garments of the dead might be said to bring them to life again.

The connection that James draws between Woolson and her clothes in the above passage is amplified when he later imagines the garments to be doubles of her body: 'They might as well have been carrying her body, he thought, to lift her and drop her from the boat, let her sink into the water' (269). Like the secular imagery set forth by both Carlyle and Dickens, the empty dresses are reflections of Woolson's corpse and the disposal of them is analogous to a second burial. The solemnity of the occasion is marked by Tito who 'blessed himself' before 'tenderly' placing the garments 'on the water, and then continued, working with a slow set of peaceful gestures shaking his head as floated away each time, and moving his lips at intervals in prayer' (270). If the disposal of the clothes is thus engineered through human agency, the dresses' subsequent return from the depths of the lagoon stages matter as agentic. At the climax of the lagoon scene, Woolson's dresses seem to partake of Jane Bennett's notion of '*Thing-Power*: the curious ability of inanimate things to animate, to act, to produce effects dramatic and subtle' (2010a: 6; original emphasis), when they float upwards causing both James and Tito to react with guilt and horror. In a scene that closely mirrors Lyndall Gordon's own description of the same event, Tóibín writes:

> It was only when Tito reached to lift the [gondolier] pole that both of them at the same time caught sight of a black shape in the water less than ten yards away and Tito cried out. In the gathering dusk it appeared as though a seal or some dark, rounded object from the deep had appeared on the surface of the water. Tito took the pole in both hands as if to defend himself. And then Henry saw what it was. Some of the dresses had floated to the surface again like black balloons, evidence of the strange sea burial they had just enacted, their arms and bellies bloated with water. (2004: 270)

---

[11] Silvana Colella analyses the sense of smell in neo-Victorianism, arguing that in addition to invoking memories odours 'have an intangible and spectral quality that defies the power of language to represent reality' (2010: 90).

The image of the dresses rising to the surface of the lagoon 'like black balloons' stages a double resurrection of both Woolson and her old clothes. To read the passage in line with Gordon's claims, the cast-off dresses signify James's denial and rejection of Constance in life and manifest his complicity in and guilt over her death; however, in their wilful return, Woolson's dresses function as more than just the material embodiment of James's repressed guilt. As they break through the surface of the lagoon, they disrupt and trouble the protagonists in the same way that their historical presence haunts the contemporary narrative. Their unruly movements make their recalcitrant agency visible and tangible and, like the discarded garments in Carlyle's *Sartor Resartus*, Woolson's enlivened dresses display a 'ghastly affectation of Life' (2002: 222).

What also occurs in this moment is a metaphorical slippage between body and garment as the discarded dresses transition into animate but ghostly doubles of Woolson's physical self. As the dresses take on an uncanny corporeal existence, their bloated and ballooning shapes at first mimic then disproportionately distort the contours of her body. This imitation and subsequent misrepresentation of the absent body both amplifies the sense that the gowns are horribly alive and serves as an example of the entangled ontology of human and object. The twisting and 'swelling' of the gowns also reflect the emotional turmoil purportedly experienced by Woolson in her lifetime and provides the clothes with a kind of twinned consciousness that reinforces her supposedly suicidal emotions. In this way, Tóibín ostensibly reimagines Gordon's claim that Woolson's dresses are 'wilful phantoms' (289). The co-entanglement of body and dress, human and nonhuman, also surfaces in *Alias Grace* as the following section will demonstrate.

Sartorial Entanglements in *Alias Grace*

Margaret Atwood's 1996 novel, *Alias Grace*, marks something of a new direction for the author, according to Sharon R. Wilson, since it is based on actual historical events and 'appears to take seriously topics and genres, including double personalities, sex scandals, and murder mysteries, previously exposed to parody' (2003: 121). In spite of this, Wilson observes, *Alias Grace* appears to make 'use of genres in which Atwood has written before, including the Jamesian ghost story, detective thriller, Gothic tale, autobiography, and Scheherazade story' (121). Like the various genres from which it borrows, the novel consists of multiple layers or fragments that are stitched together in a mimetic adaptation of the novel's central patchwork quilt motif.[12] At the centre of the patchwork is the narrative of the Irish immigrant, Grace Marks, imprisoned at the age of sixteen for the murders of Nancy Montgomery and Thomas Kinnear in 1843 at Richmond Hill, Ontario. Based on fragments of the British-Canadian author Susanna Moodie's autobiography, *Life in the Clearings Versus the Bush* (1853), in which Moodie dedicates an entire chapter to her visit to the penitentiary to 'look at the celebrated murderess, Grace Marks' (qtd. in Atwood 1997: 4), *Alias Grace* is a fictional retelling of Grace's life in prison during the period 1851 to 1872. Her story emerges through the yarn she tells a fictional character, the proto-psychiatrist, Dr Simon Jordan, who has been employed by Grace's supporters to cure her amnesia and prove her innocence. It is Jordan's job in the novel to sort fact from fiction; he aims to disentangle the web of Grace's words, as well as those spoken and written about her. In this, Jordan's role ostensibly parallels the authorial task undertaken by Atwood in her construction of the novel. Drawn from official prison records, Moodie's third-hand accounts, and contemporary, sensationalized press reports, Atwood's *Alias Grace* is an assemblage of fragmented documentary traces. Noting the difficulties of attaining historical truth from such sources, she admits in the 'Author's Afterword' that 'I have of course fictionalized historical events (as did many commentators on this case who claimed to be writing history). I have not changed any known facts, although the written accounts are so contradictory that few facts emerge as unequivocally "known"' (1997: 541). Like Tóibín's *The Master*, Atwood's biofictional novel is thus preoccupied with the recollection and reconstruction of history.

Segueing between Grace's past and the novel's present, *Alias Grace*'s non-linear progression provides an appropriate structure to set up and explore, not only the fallibility of memory, but the difficulties of remembering and re-presenting the past. For Rosario Arias, the novel's blurring of boundaries between historical fact and fiction, past and present, can be aligned with Grace's own status as a marginalized person. She suggests that 'the liminal position that Grace occupies in the novel, between animal and human, between angel and demon, mirrors … the ambiguous position that women held in the Victorian period as well as the in-betweenness of ghosts and spirits' (2005: 93). As Arias shows, *Alias Grace*, like Tóibín's novel, addresses notions of haunting and spectrality. Atwood's book might even be termed a 'spectral novel' because it is a text in which 'the haunting spirit of the Victorian past and the occult manifests itself, and where

---

[12] Several critics have already drawn attention to the metaphorical significance of the patchwork quilt in *Alias Grace*. See Ingersoll (2001), Murray (2001), Rogerson (1998), and S. R. Wilson (2003).

the writer fulfils the role of a materialisation medium' (2005: 91). Grace herself is also frequently presented as having a close association with death and the supernatural: she witnesses the death and subsequent burial of her mother at sea; sees her only friend and fellow-servant, Mary Whitney, die of a botched abortion; witnesses, and perhaps participates in, the killings of Nancy Montgomery and Thomas Kinnear and imagines that she is haunted by each of their ghosts in turn during the remainder of the tale.

The 'in-betweenness' that is so central to Grace's character is further exemplified through her various 'afterlives': the many literary and cultural reassessments to which she is subject and which she references in the metafictional passage below:

> I think of all the things that have been written about me – that I am an inhuman female demon, that I am an innocent victim of a blackguard forced against my will and in danger of my own life, that I was too ignorant to know how to act and that to hang me would be judicial murder, …that I am well and decently dressed, that I robbed a dead woman to appear so … that I have the appearance of a person rather above my station, that I am a good girl with a pliable nature and no harm is told of me, that I am cunning and devious … And I wonder, how can I be all of these different things at once? (1997: 25)

This self-reflexive statement ruminates on both the processes and problematics of rewriting figures from the past and, at the same time, recalls the various patriarchal permutations of women – angel, whore, muse or monster – that pervade Victorian literature and culture. The indeterminacy that characterizes Grace, who embodies these multiple mythologies, is manifested most strongly through dress in the novel, which troubles the boundaries between self and other, subject and object, and the real and inauthentic. The various labels and aliases that Grace is assigned by her contemporaries are aligned with sartorial disguises or costumes throughout the tale. Reflecting on the label 'murderess', for instance, Grace refers to it in sartorial terms when she explains that '*Murderess* is a strong word to have attached to you. … Sometimes at night I whisper it over to myself: *Murderess, Murderess*. It rustles, like a taffeta skirt across the floor' (25; original emphases). Dress, as a material means of expression and transformation, is employed by Atwood in the novel as a way of allowing individuals to intimate who they are and, at the same time, to conceal and re-fashion their identities. In this way, the dresses and gowns that adorn the pages of *Alias Grace* are performative; they invite interpretation, can be 'read' like texts and on a literal level help to both divulge and submerge key aspects of character, identity and plot.

In her monograph *Self-Fashioning in Margaret Atwood's Fiction* (2005), Cynthia Kuhn examines the role and representation of dress in Margaret Atwood's literary oeuvre. Summarizing the cultural and symbolic significance of garments in *Alias Grace*, she posits that 'clothing provides an accurate historical element highlighting issues of class, gender and power. The main female characters are linked by the lending, borrowing, and wearing of each other's clothing, and Atwood positions clothing as a crucial metaphor for spiritual possession' (89). Indeed, the narrative enfolds and unfolds through items of dress. The opening chapter of *Alias Grace* signals its interest in the sartorial through a number of references to dress and fabric, from the blood-red 'satin' pansies made of 'cloth' that Grace imagines she can see in the prison courtyard (4–5), and which she repeatedly sees throughout the remainder of the text, to her fleeting, but detailed, recollection of Nancy Montgomery's 'pale dress with pink rosebuds and a triple-flounced skirt' (5). Nancy's pale pink and white morning gown, Mary Whitney's petticoat and Grace's striped prison gown each play a vital role in the tale and in the formation of the patchwork quilt that Grace will later construct. Her dress even becomes an important clue in the case against her when it comes to light that she is wearing one of Nancy's gowns during the murder trial (419). Clothing also plays a significant part in the staging and perception of each of the protagonists, offering a means through which Grace can come to understand herself and those around her. Indeed Grace, who has 'remarkable abilities as a dressmaker' (99), is an avid 'reader' and translator of others' garments, being acutely aware of and attuned to their symbolic and social resonances.

Wearing a plain, serviceable prison dress for much of the narrative, Grace openly deplores her own lack of fine clothes. At the beginning of the novel when she is working at the Governor's house as an unpaid servant, a dubious reward for her good behaviour in the penitentiary, Grace recognizes the unsuitability of her attire while sat in the Governor's wife's parlour. She draws attention to her ungloved and therefore socially unacceptable hands, stating: 'I have my hands folded in my lap the proper way although I have no gloves. The gloves I would wish to have would be smooth and white, and would fit without a wrinkle' (23). She also pays marked attention to the gowns that the Governor's wife and daughters wear and therefore 'provides commentary on dress as reflective of class, from the servant's point of view' (Kuhn 2005: 96). Later, Grace notices that the Governor's wife and her female visitors all 'wear afternoon dresses with rows of buttons up their fronts, and stiff wire crinolines beneath' (1997: 23–4). She goes on to say that:

It's a wonder they can sit down at all, and when they walk, nothing touches their legs under the billowing skirts, except their shifts and stockings. They are like swans, drifting along on unseen feet; or else like the jellyfish in the waters of the rocky harbour near our house, when I was little, before I ever made the long sad journey across the ocean. They were bell-shaped and ruffled, gracefully waving and lovely under the sea; but if they washed up on the beach and dried out in the sun there was nothing left of them. And that is what the ladies are like: mostly water. (1997: 24)

The precise allusion to crinolines authenticates the historical narrative, serving as a chronometric marker in the novel and demarking the period of time spent by Grace in the penitentiary. She notes in a revealing aside that 'there were no wire crinolines when I was first brought here [to Kingston Prison]. They were horsehair then, as the wire ones were not thought of' (24). Grace's perceptive sartorial observations not only ground the novel in the historic past but they also reveal her avid desire to participate in and perform fashionable femininity. As a prisoner, much like the women incarcerated in the Insane Asylum and Millbank Prison in Sarah Waters's *Affinity* (1999) and *Fingersmith* (2002) (discussed in Chapter 3), Grace is denied the possibilities and pleasures of self-fashioning. The 'conventional dress of the Penitentiary' which consists of 'a striped blue and white skirt' (68) is used as a disciplinary tool, encouraging bodily and behavioural reform and curbing creativity, individuality and self-expression.

Without a sartorial identity beyond this plain prison costume, Grace's interest in fashionable matters is acutely rendered in the novel. Her overt fascination with dress serves to highlight Victorian, and by extension, contemporary concerns pertaining to gender, class and power, issues with which Atwood's novel appears to be deeply preoccupied. Linking the crinoline with naturalistic imagery in the above quotation, Grace envisions the female visitors as insubstantial women, soft like jellyfish or innocuous as water. In her objectification of these women, Grace is filled with a sense of her own superiority, but the imagery is subverted when it becomes clear that the women are not spectacles to be observed, but rather, have come to observe *her*. As Grace herself admits, 'the reason they want to see me is that I am a celebrated murderess' (25). Here, and elsewhere in the novel, Grace is assigned a startling sense of objecthood. She is placed on display for the women to peruse along with the Governor's wife's scrapbook which is left open on the table, covered by a silk shawl 'sent from India by her eldest daughter' (27). Grace, the exotic Indian shawl, and the macabre scrapbook which has 'all the famous criminals in it – the ones that have been hanged, or else brought here to be penitent' are arrayed to amuse, excite and 'horrify' the Governor's wife's acquaintances (29). Exhibited alongside these treasures, we learn, 'is the stack of Godey's Ladies' Books with the fashions that come up from the States, and also the Keepsake Albums of the two younger daughters' into which they 'put all kinds of things ... little scraps of cloth from their dresses, little snippets of ribbon, pictures cut from magazines' (27) (Figure 2.2). Together, the pile of Godey's fashion magazines, the keepsake albums and Grace herself, are all subject to the enquiring female gaze. Positioning nineteenth-century fashion as a female-centric phenomenon, Sharon Marcus has persuasively shown 'that Victorian women as well as men enjoyed objectifying women and entertained active, aggressive impulses towards femininity. Victorian commodity culture incited an erotic appetite for femininity in women, framed spectacular images of women for a female gaze, and prompted women's fantasies about dominating a woman or submitting to one' (2009: 112). Aside from pointing to the centrality of dress, fashion and textiles in the lives of nineteenth-century women, Atwood appears to comment here on the complicity of the female protagonists who collude in and contribute to Grace's subjugation. Although Grace assumes that Jordan is 'a collector' intent on cataloguing and medically classifying her for his own professional advancement (45), it is the Governor's wife and the female visitors who 'stare without appearing to, out from under their bonnets'

Figure 2.2 *Godey's Unrivalled Colored Fashions*, 1856. Photograph © Library of Congress.

(25), that are the agents of patriarchy. While much has been made of the novel's condemnation of the misogynistic male medical establishment, then, a reading of this moment in terms of material culture highlights the role of the female protagonists who also seek to objectify and consume Grace.

Dress and its associated implications of self-/re-fashioning is also closely associated with storytelling in the novel. Grace herself, as Atwood explains elsewhere, is 'a storyteller, with strong motives to narrate but also strong motives to withhold; the only power left to her as a convicted and imprisoned criminal comes from a blend of these two motives' (1998: 1515). The modes and methods by which she tells her story are consistently aligned in the text with the culturally feminized practices of stitching, sewing, making and mending. When Grace recounts her story to Jordan, for instance, she is often portrayed industriously sewing. Indeed, her story and the garments that she makes develop in tandem across the novel. Not only can Grace accurately 'read' others' dress, then, but she is also a proficient dressmaker. Her skill is so advanced that for the other protagonists it proves somewhat difficult to reconcile her prowess in this domestic occupation with her status as a prisoner and condemned murderer. In her report of Grace's character, the Governor's wife tells Jordan that 'she is a wonderful seamstress, quite deft and accomplished, she is a great help with the girls' frocks, she has an eye for trimmings, and under happier circumstances she could have made an excellent milliner's assistant' (26). The creative ingenuity that underpins Grace's skill in this profession not only connotes a sense of permissible femininity but also undoubtedly informs the construction of her narrative. Just as Grace 'has an eye for trimmings', she also has a particular flair for storytelling. As the novel progresses, her dressmaking abilities are thus repeatedly interwoven with the fictional re-construction of her past. Choosing her words carefully in one of her dialogic exchanges with Jordan, Grace turns to metaphors of sewing and sartorial making to facilitate and fabricate her narrative. She wonders:

> What should I tell him when he comes back? He will want to know about the arrest, and the trial, and what was said. Some of it is all jumbled in my mind, but I could pick out this or that for him, some bits of whole cloth you might say, as when you go through the rag bag looking for something that will do, to supply a touch of colour. (410)

The potent imagery invoked by Atwood aligns the practice of historiography with processes of sartorial making. Like the historian or storyteller who 'picks out the facts he or she chooses to find significant' (Atwood 1998: 1516),

Grace mines her past as though it is a 'rag bag'. Needlework and sewing, often dismissed and trivialized as 'women's work', and therefore overlooked both intra- and extra-textually, here assume significance as sartorially inflected forms of narratorial control and creative expression. Fictional fabulation and literary fabrication are aligned within the very fabric that Grace works and handles. As a skilled dressmaker and the mender of the household, she is equally figured as a producer, or crafter, of narrative. And while Grace literally patchworks and sews throughout the course of the novel, she is also busy at work, figuratively fashioning a story that will satisfy Jordan's curiosity.

Notably, it is Jordan himself who assists Grace in these creative endeavours: it is he who encourages and enables the synergic process by which she assembles both garment and narrative. As she sews, Jordan is responsible for cutting Grace's thread because she is not allowed to handle scissors: 'if I want to cut a thread or trim a seam' Grace explains, 'I have to ask Dr. Jordan, who takes them out of his vest pocket and returns them to it when I have finished' (71); in addition, he offers her verbal prompts and presents her with physical objects in his attempts to draw out her tale. Despite this, Jordan fails to discern what Kuhn has called the 'intricate' interrelationship between 'dressing, sewing, and storytelling' in *Alias Grace* (2005: 121). This is perhaps typical of the complicated status of historical women's needlework and domestic crafts more generally. Bayles Kortsch recognizes the ambiguities that characterize the act of sewing in the nineteenth century, arguing that 'the needle may allow women to express their creativity and ambition, but it creates a type of writing the masculine world cannot decipher, and most often ignores' (2009: 1). Grace's sewing, her creation of garments and patchwork quilts, speak to her capacity for creativity, invention and fabrication, qualities that inform her unreliable narrative and which Jordan, unable to fully understand or appreciate the implications of her sartorial activities, grapples with throughout.

Beyond acting as containers and vehicles of narrative, the dresses in *Alias Grace* possess other dynamic energies of their own. They produce material, sensorial and spectral nodes that trouble the central protagonists, and which resist the distinction between humans and things. In many of Atwood's novels, as Kuhn points out, 'clothing takes on supernatural qualities or is related to supernatural activity' (2005: 41). In her neo-Victorian biofiction, clothing is seen to be especially alive with subversive, lively potential. Just as it is in Tóibín's *The Master*, clothing is figured as a medium for ghostly returns and is suffused with nineteenth-century superstitions about death and the otherworld. In the novel's early section, for instance, Grace recounts the story of her family's crossing from the North of Ireland to Canada. During the voyage, Grace's mother falls ill and dies of a mysterious ailment that the ship's doctor says might be 'a tumour, or a cyst, or else a burst appendix' (1997: 138). On wrapping her mother's body in an old white sheet for burial, Grace is confronted with a practical dilemma and recalls that 'it seemed like disrespect to use an old one, but if I used the new one it would go to waste as far as the living were concerned; and all my grief became concentrated, so to speak, on the matter of the sheets' (139). Eventually Grace decides upon the old sheet because it is 'more or less clean' and she wraps her mother in it before she is buried at sea (139–40). Unlike Tóibín's text, this water burial does not result in the return of agentive garments, but rather, the burial garments become a catalyst for a material haunting. When her mother's prized teapot later falls and breaks despite the ship being becalmed, Grace imagines that it is her mother's spirit, trapped in the ship and 'angry at me because of the second-best sheet' (141). In this instance 'clothing seems to take on the vibrations of the wearer or to provide a gateway for the return of the dead' (Kuhn 2005: 104). Draped about her body and imbued with her physical trace, the burial garments apparently channel Grace's mother's anger and work to facilitate her ghostly return in the present.

Evincing a similar superstitious dread of empty and cast-off clothes, Grace later informs the reader that it is 'bad luck to wear the clothes of the dead' (313). She goes on to recall, in a similar vein, that although she had taken Nancy's clothes to wear after her murder, she 'left the dress that [Nancy had] been sewing, because it seemed too close to her altogether, as it was not finished; and I'd heard that the dead would come back to complete what they had left undone, and I didn't want her missing it, and following me' (1997: 387). Representing another potential medium of return, Nancy's unfinished dress is presented here as a material link between the dead and the living. Infused with Nancy's creative touch, Grace's suggestion that the dress seems 'too close' to its maker, also notably personifies and enlivens it, opening up the possibility of reciprocal exchange. Just as Nancy might miss the dress she had been sewing and return from the dead to follow Grace, so might the dress remember Nancy and attempt to stage an agentic return of its own.

By carefully eschewing the dichotomy between matter that is alive and animate, and matter that is inert, the dresses in *Alias Grace* are frequently depicted as lively entities beyond human control. At the point in Grace's story when she is working as a servant in Mrs Alderman Parkinson's house, she claims that laundered garments seem 'like pale ghosts of themselves hovering and shimmering there in the gloom; and the look of them, so silent and bodiless, made me afraid' (1997: 184). Depicted as phantom-like, these ghostly clothes substantiate Bärbel Tischleder's provocative suggestion that 'objects are no longer dead' (2014: 17) and indicate their 'thing-power' by producing in Grace an uneasy affectual response. The latent energy emanating from these empty clothes also foreshadows the dream sequence that Grace will have when she is a maid at the Kinnear residence. Becoming increasingly wary of James McDermott and his alleged plans to kill both Nancy and Mr Kinnear, Grace dreams that the house is surrounded by angels 'whose white robes were washed in blood, as it says at the end of the Bible; and they were sitting in judgement upon Mr Kinnear's house, and on all within it. And then I saw that they had no heads' (327). When she wakes, Grace dresses and goes about her daily chores as normal. However, upon stepping outside she sees the laundry that she had washed the night before 'blown into the trees by the tempest in the night' and she explains that:

> I'd forgotten to bring it in; it was very unlike me to forget a thing like that, especially a white laundry, which I'd worked so hard at, getting out the spots; and this was another cause of foreboding to me. And the nightdresses and shirts which were stuck in the trees did indeed look like angels without heads; and it was as if our own clothing was sitting in judgment upon us. (1997: 327)

The peculiar symmetry between Grace's dream and the clothes blown into the hedge presages the fates of both Nancy and Mr Kinnear and tacitly communicates Grace's downfall. The displaced dresses also provoke a response of fear in Grace precisely because their 'thing-power' is made manifest. Blown into hedges, the clothes are 'not entirely reducible to the contexts in which (human) subjects set them' (Bennett 2004: 351) and, as they 'sit in judgement' upon the inhabitants of the house, they therefore reveal an independent life and purpose of their own.

If the gowns reveal a kind of agentic materiality in these instances, then they also double as bodies throughout the remainder of the text. Just as Woolson's dresses substitute her physical form in Tóibín's *The Master*, in *Alias Grace* gowns act as corporeal correlatives. In so doing, the dresses elide the ontological distinction between humans and things, even as they exert their independence. Rendering the 'thing-power' of dresses manifest, Grace recalls that after the murders of Nancy and Mr Kinnear had taken place

> The last thing I did was to take off my clothes I'd been wearing that day; and I put on one of Nancy's dresses, the pale one with the white ground and the small floral print, which was the same one she had on the first day I came to Mr. Kinnear's. And I put on her petticoat with the lace edging... and Nancy's summer shoes

of light-coloured leather, which I had so often admired ... Then I put on a clean apron, and stirred up the fire in the summer kitchen stove, which still had some embers left in it, and burnt my own clothes; I didn't like the thought of wearing them ever again, as they would remind me of things I wished to forget. It may have been my fancy, but a smell went up from them like scorching meat; and it was like my own dirtied and cast-off skin that I was burning. (388)

By removing her own clothes and replacing them with Nancy's, Grace enacts a symbolic swapping of identities that will be rehearsed again, albeit with a slight variation, towards the novel's climax. In substituting her dress for the housekeeper's, Grace here suggestively displaces and replaces Nancy. The detailed description of Nancy's dress 'with the white ground and the small floral print' as well as the 'light-coloured' shoes that Grace covets, underlines her acquisitive nature, perhaps implying her guilt. A further clue to Grace's culpability appears to lie in her own tangled and discarded clothes, which are agents of memory, or as Carlyle finds, are the discerning 'witnesses and instruments' of human life (Carlyle 2002: 247). Disposing of the clothes so that she can 'forget' the events to which they are privy, Grace figures her old gown as a material record of the past. In her burning of this gown, which metaphorically transitions into her 'own dirtied and cast-off skin', she destroys any evidence of her involvement in the murder even as she apparently erases and effaces herself. Troubling the boundaries between self and other, the gown as skin/body is both a site of recollection and forgetting and reinforces Grace's own objectified, liminal and circumscribed position within the narrative.

The novel's pivotal scene in which Grace is hypnotized by her old friend Jeremiah – who is masquerading as the mesmerist, Dr DuPont – explicitly closes the gap between subject and object. When asked if Grace had anything to do with the deaths of Nancy and Mr Kinnear, the spirit of Mary Whitney ostensibly speaking through Grace, admits: ' "She knew nothing! I only borrowed her clothing for a time". "Her clothing?" says Simon. "Her earthly shell. Her fleshly garment" ' (468). Here, Atwood dramatizes Carlyle's assertion in *Sartor Resartus* that the human body is a 'Garment of Flesh (or of Senses)' (2002: 75).[13] In doing so she highlights what Jane Bennett has referred to as the 'extent to which human being and thinghood overlap, the extent to which the us and the it slip-slide into each other. One moral of the story is that we are also nonhuman and that things, too, are vital players in the world' (2010a: 4). In this dramatic moment, human being and dress overlap, presenting garments as important material and

---

[13] Kuhn likewise acknowledges this link (2005: 6).

narratorial actants within the novel's story world. While Cynthia Kuhn refers to the 'body as flesh dress' as a supernatural site of 'border crossing' (105) in that it allows Mary and Grace to swap places, I suggest that the real border crossing that takes place in the novel is between subject and object.

The slippage between garment and body, human and nonhuman, and the energies and intensities that ensue from such exchanges can be figured here in Bennett's terms as an 'assemblage' or in relation to Karen Barad's view of agential matter as entangled: a network of entities that inter- and 'intra-act', a phrase coined by Barad to refer to the circulation of agencies and forces between and amongst subjects and objects (2007: 141). At the conclusion of *Alias Grace*, Atwood figures patchworking as a process of sartorial entanglement: an 'assemblage', in which scraps of fabric cut from the gowns of the female protagonists form a constellation of intertwined narratorial, material and memorializing actants that 'intra-act' with one another. In the final part of her narrative which she addresses directly to Jordan in an imagined epistle, Grace, who is freed from the penitentiary and now married, sews a 'Tree of Paradise' quilt. Describing the swatches of fabric that will constitute the quilt's central sections, she explains that

> three of the triangles in my Tree will be different. One will be white, from the petticoat I still have that was Mary Whitney's; one will be faded yellowish, from the prison night-dress I begged as a keepsake when I left there. And the third will be a pale cotton, a pink and white floral, cut from the dress of Nancy's that she had on the first day I was at Mr. Kinnear's, and that I wore on the ferry to Lewiston, when I was running away. I will embroider around each one of them with red feather-stitching, to blend them in as a part of the pattern. And so we will all be together. (534).

That the novel's conclusion coincides with the completion of this sartorial item is fitting, since it provides a potent material image with which to close Grace's story. The disparate threads of her past are here woven into a patchwork quilt, which is doubly significant because, as she remarks, 'this is the first one I have ever done for myself' (533). The shift from stitching for her benefactors to the luxury of making for herself evidences the change in Grace's fortunes and the elevation of her status from a prisoner to a free woman. Taken from the gowns of the women who have haunted her narrative, the sartorial fragments of cloth that make up the patchwork quilt are also freighted with memory. They preserve the moments of Grace's past in a kind of sartorial diary, one that she might return to and re-read in private. The swatches of cloth cut from the various gowns function here as an index to history. Proffering a material record of her life and its various stages, the scraps of fabric also serve as surrogates for the women who have shaped Grace's story. Surrounded by the blood red border that she stitches, the women are resurrected within the parameters of the quilt. Here, Atwood draws on cloth's capacity to both forge and preserve connection, memory and emotion. Highlighting the strange facility of clothes to transition into their owners, the quilt acquires a lively resonance that promises the prospect of material reunion.

In addition to staging it as a challenge to the subject-object divide, the novel figures the patchwork quilt as a narratological tool that is central to the telling of the tale. Indeed, Atwood relies on this sartorial motif as a structural, formal and metaphorical device in *Alias Grace*. Patchwork quilts, as Jennifer Murray points out, underpin the novel's composition, 'from the typographical layout of the pages to the details of its narrative organization' (2001: 70). Each of the book's sections is named after a patchwork design and prefaced with an image of the quilt in question. These sartorial epigraphs provide a visual clue as to what is to come in the following section, while aligning the novel as a whole with the textile metaphor (Wilson S. R. 2003: 127). Positioned alongside other more literary epigraphs featuring poetic fragments and quotations from press reports, the images of the patchwork quilt designs also force a comparison between the sartorial and the literary. The processes of writing and reading neo-Victorian fiction are thus paralleled with the depiction of patchworking: both seek to fashion a new yarn from existing threads and fragments.

In *Alias Grace*, then, patchwork is depicted as a meditative process aligned with self-reflexivity and storytelling; as a gendered cultural and creative practice, it entails a sense of revision and reconfiguration. The patchwork motif may therefore be taken as representative of the creative appropriation inherent in neo-Victorianism. Atwood's authorial and historiographical practice is here paralleled with the depiction of Grace fashioning a quilt from various garments. Both of these systems of formation are propelled by a distinct desire to create a coherent, unified whole from a series of textu(r)al fragments. Unlike the quilt, however, which is a whole formed of many sartorial parts, the novel lacks a clearly defined outcome and therefore frustrates the contemporary reader's desire for narrative closure. Neither Jordan nor the reader learn the absolute truth about the murders of Nancy and Mr Kinnear. Opposing any defined and teleological conclusion, the novel therefore tacitly endorses the conceptual link between neo-Victorianism and postmodernism, appearing to reject and challenge the totalizing master narrative expected of the Victorian realist text. Beyond issues of fragmentation and uncertainty, however, the dress-patchwork does appear to hold out the possibility of accessing the truth of the tale. The assortment of garments offers a tantalizing glimpse into Grace's past, while the collated fabrics seem to contain, embedded within them, the truth of what occurred between each of the three women. In one of the first essays to examine the patchwork quilt motif in *Alias Grace*, Margaret Rogerson aptly acknowledges its equivocality, asking whether the quilt should be taken as a confessional object and an admission of Grace's guilt (1998: 21), but the focalizing of the narrative onto the quilt itself shifts the focus from Grace to the reader. What is at stake here is whether the *reader* has the skill to disentangle, or to 'unpick' the yarn of Grace's tale, to piece together the patchwork scraps of fiction that make up the novel, and to correctly read the material clues that are stitched into the fabric of her narrative.

To conclude, in Margaret Atwood's *Alias Grace* and Colm Tóibín's *The Master*, dresses, like human protagonists, have their own trajectories, vitalities and vibrant energies. Garments permeate and vivify the fictional diegeses of the novels, while their lively and affective interactions with other characters can be read as potent expressions of Bennett's 'thing-power' (2004: 349). Building upon the spiritual and narrative force that repeatedly imbued old and cast-off nineteenth-century literary clothes, Tóibín's and Atwood's neo-Victorian novels re-imagine fictional garments that are both highly symbolic and vitally active. Victorian dresses (re)appear in these twenty-first-century narratives as actants that are both haunted and haunting. In so doing, the contemporary texts play with and adapt nineteenth-century anxieties around the agentic potential of old clothes to fashion a narrative in which the material culture of the past becomes a mechanism for ghostly returns.

While new materialism has been mostly employed in relation to techno-garments in the fashion world and sartorial disguises in Victorian novels, it is also a suitable theoretical framework for analysing the haunting power of dress in neo-Victorian cultural productions. As a critical concept, it proves the importance and centrality of material culture in our perception of and relation to the past. It also calls into question the processes and procedures by which a historical period might be (re-)framed, (re-)imagined and (re-)materialized in the present. Woolson's dynamic dresses in *The Master* and the lively gowns in *Alias Grace* proffer a provocative image that expresses the agency of non-human things. Not only does this suggest that a dead individual's garments are their ghostly or uncanny doubles but it also shows that in becoming separate and other from the body, dress takes on a curious vitality of its own. These agentic sartorial items, like the neo-Victorian texts from which they originate, enact a tension between presence and absence, past and present, life and death. Evincing a notable engagement with the merging of human and non-human subjectivities, which is a central facet of new materialism, *The Master* and *Alias Grace* also present garments that actively shape both the narrative and the bodies with which they interact. These dresses exhibit agency both because they disrupt the novel, forging, negotiating and concealing characters' identities, and because they are expressive and bear (meta)fictional witness to the past. Migrating beyond Gordon's historical biography about James and Woolson to the pages of numerous contemporary texts, the 'drowned dresses' in Tóibín's novel become narrative agents that re-envision and re-materialize the complex relationship between these two nineteenth-century writers. Similarly, in Atwood's novel, dresses and the patchwork quilt made of gowns are intimately entwined with processes of storytelling and self-fashioning. The narrative qualities of dress which both novels underscore thus ultimately encourages an engagement with dress as an affective and aesthetic memory prompt, one that can be read and deciphered to reveal clues about a past wearer. Above all, both novels demonstrate the ways in which material objects, especially clothes, retain and transmit the stories of those long since dead. Chapter 3, 'Gloves' extends the focus on vibrant matter to consider the agency and vitality of gloves as tools of queer desire in Sarah Waters's neo-Victorian trilogy.

3

Gloves

In 'Hands that Mould the Imagination', a 2003 article written for *The Guardian*, the Welsh novelist Sarah Waters identifies the indelible traces of earlier nineteenth-century works that she finds impressed upon her own contemporary fictions. Drawing striking parallels between the 'fetishistic treatment' of hands in Charles Dickens's *Great Expectations* (1860–1), 'the oddly magnified space they occupy within its narrative economy', and the deployment of hands in her own novel, Waters explains:

> A curious thing happened to me while I was writing my second novel, Affinity [*sic*]. It is set in the 1860s, partly in a women's prison, partly in an upper-middle-class home. It's a rather gothic novel, full of twists and reversals, and for the purposes of theme and plot, there's a foregrounding at certain moments of hands – the drawing of attention, for example, to the strong, possibly sinister, hands of at least two female characters. As I was putting the book together, I was dimly aware that the hands I was describing were recalling some other hands to me; and at last I realised whose those were. They were the scarred and powerful hands of Jaggers' housekeeper, Molly, in Great Expectations [*sic*]. (2003: n.p)

Hands, and by extension, gloves, emerge and are granted particular prominence at crucial moments in all three of Sarah Waters's neo-Victorian works. In *Tipping the Velvet*, *Affinity*, and *Fingersmith*, published in 1998, 1999 and 2002, respectively, Victorian gloves evoke and materialize queer desire. Like the dynamic dresses discussed in Chapter 2, gloves assume vibrant, symbolic and vitally active roles in these three contemporary historical fictions. They embellish the texts' overarching and oppositional thematic concerns, underscoring the narrative tensions that emerge between issues of im/materiality, absence and presence, interiority and exteriority. Operating as sartorial substitutes for and surrogates of the female body, gloves work to both disrupt and mediate the sense of touch. What enlivens the gloves in each of these novels are the traces, whether physical or psychical, which are inscribed both on and within them. Protective yet porous and penetrable, the soft kid leather with which gloves were popularly made during the nineteenth century left their surfaces open to inscription and indentation.[1] Gloves were routinely marked both by the wearer and their physical surroundings. Stretched, stained and scuffed, gloves acquired tangible traces of wear. Moulded to the contours of the hand, they also became fully embodied. Functioning as a type of 'second skin' they absorbed the 'oils and smells of the body' (Stallybrass and Jones 2001: 120), and when detached from the hand that routinely wore them, they continued to signify the absent 'other'. To encounter Victorian gloves in the contemporary imaginary, then, is to confront the textural residue of past hands.

This chapter investigates the centrality of gloves and the material, sexual and textu(r)al traces that they leave behind in Waters's three neo-Victorian novels. It aims to show the significance of sartorial matters in these contemporary re-imaginings of the Victorian period in order to examine neo-Victorian fiction's fixation with the persistent traces and fingerprints of the past. Locating the glove as entrenched within cultural memory as an explicitly Victorian item, the chapter argues that it acts as both a marker of Victorian situatedness and a palpable entity capable of transgressing the temporal, spatial and sexual boundaries that exist between the Victorian past and contemporary present. In the sections that follow, I examine the glove's appeal in contemporary culture as an item that is bound to the past, before exploring its (re)appearance in and disturbance of Waters's neo-Victorian texts. It is my contention that since they have an intrinsic association with touch, a transformative ability to adopt an individual's hand shape and, when given or taken as a keepsake, have the capacity to summon the presence of an absent 'other'/lover, gloves are suitable garments for examining the construction and negotiation of non-heteronormative desire in Waters's neo-Victorian trilogy.

Less overtly self-reflexive than *The Master* and *Alias Grace*, Waters's neo-Victorian novels have been described by Kate Mitchell as 'faux-Victorian': texts which employ recognizably Victorian settings, literary and generic conventions that simulate the Victorian past rather than seeking to actively question its construction or veracity (2010: 117). In undertaking such a task, Mitchell argues, Waters constructs 'a genealogy of female homoeroticism' which works to challenge, subvert and extend our sense of established Victorian literary and cultural histories (118). Although not as explicitly metafictional as the texts discussed in Chapter 2, Waters's attempt to re-fashion the past in these novels 'betrays her awareness that both history and fiction consist of plural

---

[1] For a detailed discussion of glove styles, materials, and modes of production between 1600 and 1980, see Cumming (1982).

representations, none of which is objectively, undeniably true. It is only by merging them together that we get a better sense of the "reality" of past ages and, in so doing, detect affinities with the present, which help us rethink our role and identity' (Costantini 2006: 19). In addition to underscoring issues of cultural memory, and the interweaving of history and fiction, *Tipping the Velvet*, *Affinity* and *Fingersmith* are all encoded within complex intertextual networks. They pastiche a number of nineteenth-century sensation and realist fictions and draw, both implicitly and otherwise, upon the works of Victorian writers such as Wilkie Collins, Sheridan Le Fanu, Charles Dickens, Charlotte Brontë and Oscar Wilde, among others. Featuring a range of lower-class, criminal, lesbian and generally 'othered' female protagonists, Waters's neo-Victorian novels demonstrate a keen interest in tracing 'the varied effects of inequality and prejudice (across a range of social markers) and in how that which is deemed "normative" frequently oppresses alternative ways of being' (O'Callaghan 2017: 2). They raise and interrogate Victorian and contemporary concerns around issues of gender, class and sexuality, and self-consciously operate within frameworks drawn from queer and feminist theories. Openly participating in cultural and ideological debates surrounding women, female agency and same-sex desire, Waters's late twentieth- and early twenty-first-century fictions find continuing relevance in contemporary popular and academic discourse. Though they represent well-trodden critical ground, the three novels under study here are yet to be explored together in relation to the purpose and presence of gloves. Hence, in its examination of the role and function of the glove in constructing queer subjectivities, this chapter contributes to existing scholarship by focusing on the novels' notable engagements with Victorian material and sartorial culture.[2] In what follows, I explore the novels' dealings with dress and fashion and their homologous associations with identity, autonomy and same-sex desire, before turning to Waters's deployment of the Victorian glove.

Fashioning identity, agency and desire in Waters's neo-Victorian trilogy

Following the success of her debut novel, *Tipping the Velvet*, the winner of the 1999 Betty Trask award, *Affinity* and *Fingersmith*, which constitute the second and

---

[2] For explorations of sartorial and/or material culture in Waters's novels, see Arias (2017), Boehm (2011), Neal (2011), Spooner (2007) and Yeh (2014).

third books in Sarah Waters's neo-Victorian trilogy, similarly reflect the critical acclaim of her first. *Affinity* won the *Sunday Times* Young Writer of the Year Award and the Somerset Maugham Award for Lesbian and Gay Fiction in 2000 and *Fingersmith* was shortlisted for both the Man Booker Prize and the Orange Prize in 2002.[3] Tied to one another by the communal threads of illicit lesbian love and the setting of the nineteenth-century metropolis, *Tipping the Velvet*, *Affinity* and *Fingersmith* are likewise bound by a notable preoccupation with the role and significance of clothing as a means of fabricating and manipulating identity and desire.

Set in Victorian England during the 1890s, *Tipping the Velvet* documents the tale of the Whitstable-born 'oyster-girl' Nancy Astley (1999: 4), her rise to music hall fame as the male-impersonator Nan King, and her entries into both upper-class sapphic society and working-class socialist circles. In her first-person narrative told in retrospect, Nan reflects upon these multiple journeys, both literal and sexual. Her tale opens with the monotonous daily routines of a life spent working in her parents' oyster parlour, before detailing the development of her burgeoning sexuality and growing lesbian desire for a touring music hall star, Kitty Butler. The story follows Nan as she joins Kitty on the London stage as both collaborator and lover, before the two separate, leading to her transformation into a 'renter' (202), or male-passing sex worker, and then the kept lover of the wealthy socialite and sapphist Diana Lethaby. The novel concludes with Nan's maturation, her transformation into socialist advocate, and the blossoming of a stable and mutually loving relationship with another activist, Florence Banner.

In *Tipping the Velvet*, dress, identity and performance are all closely entwined. Nan, who takes especial 'pleasure in performance, display and disguise' (1999: 126), is fervently attuned to the power of dress and its multiple effects. Chafing at the societal limitations imposed upon women, she playfully manipulates and thereby transgresses her gendered identity by cross-dressing first in public as a male impersonator and then later in private when she chooses to pass as male. These gender performances, whether theatrical or in earnest, provide Nan with a degree of agency, freedom and control in an otherwise circumscribed and disempowered existence, while simultaneously subverting and therefore challenging perceived notions of the gender binary. In her groundbreaking study in which she identifies and explores the cultural and historical preoccupation with cross-dressing, Marjorie Garber suggests that the

---

[3] As a further measure of their critical and financial success, all three of these novels have also been adapted to the stage and screen.

practice's appeal appears to reside in the way it openly questions 'the categories of "female" and "male", whether they are considered essential or constructed, biological or cultural' ([1992] 2011: 10). Drawing the discussion round to the time in which Waters's novel is set, Ann Heilmann argues that cross-dressing assumed a particularly political resonance at the end of the nineteenth century: for the socially informed New Woman, eager for reform and personal and professional fulfilment, cross-dressing 'challenge[d] the patriarchal conflation of biological maleness, socially constructed masculinity and hegemonic power' (2010b: 83). Calling into question ideas of binarity and gender essentialism, and highlighting the political power of dress, Waters employs clothing to signal her heroine's rejection of social and cultural norms and embracement of gender fluidity and non-heteronormative desire.

Nan's engagement with and interest in the transformative potential of dress begins early-on in the novel when she first sees Kitty Butler's performance at a local music hall. Struck by Kitty's appearance and the spectacle of her costume, Nan describes her as 'a kind of perfect West-End swell. She wore a suit – a handsome gentleman's suit, cut to her size and lined at the cuffs and the flaps with flashing silk. There was a rose in her lapel, and lavender gloves at her pocket' (1999: 12). The qualifying phrase 'kind of' preceding the adjectival 'perfect West-End swell' characterizes the thrilling ambiguity of Kitty's appearance which flickers between male and female, and which incites Nan's curiosity. Compounding her sense of confusion and delight are Kitty's bodily performance and the careful tailoring of her clothes which highlight, rather than conceal, her feminized figure. Nan explains:

> She looked, I suppose, like a very pretty boy, for her face was a perfect oval, and her eyes were large and dark at the lashes, and her lips were rosy and full. Her figure, too, was boy-like and slender – yet rounded, vaguely but unmistakably, at the bosom, the stomach, and the hips, in a way no real boy's ever was; and her shoes, I noticed after a moment, had two-inch heels to them. But she strode like a boy, and stood like one, with her feet far apart and her hands thrust carelessly into her trouser pockets, and her head at an arrogant angle, at the very front of the stage. (13)

Because 'typically' feminine and masculine traits are blended in Kitty's sartorial ensemble, her appearance ultimately serves to invert established Victorian gender conventions. This troubling of cultural perceptions calls attention to the material and social apparatuses by which gender is constructed. Kitty's clothes and shoes, her conscious exterior performance of recognizably 'masculine' behaviours, all signify the set of culturally constituted acts that Judith Butler claims forge, maintain and simultaneously destabilize gender identity ([1990] 2007: 191).[4] Thus, dress in this novel is both a site of gender transgression and a tool with which Waters actively challenges conventional perceptions of gender. It also functions as a narrative stimulus: watching Kitty's cross-dressed performance 'serves as a catalyst for Nancy's own longings to adopt a male persona' (Renk 2020: 119), while the ambiguous clothes and confident gender-bending performance impels her desire.

If dress in *Tipping the Velvet* can be read as an instrument of manipulation, one that both reinforces and rejects the female body and its gendered and social trappings, in *Fingersmith* and *Affinity* clothing is utilized as a tool with which the female characters must cultivate particularly feminized and therefore socially acceptable bodies. Narrated by their two autodiegetic narrators, *Fingersmith* and *Affinity* delineate the twinned storylines of Maud Lilly and Susan (Sue) Trinder during the early 1860s and Margaret Prior and Selina Dawes in the 1870s, respectively. Divided into three sections, the opening pages of *Fingersmith* and the book's first section, are entirely recounted from the first-person perspective of Sue Trinder, a lower-class thief and orphan. Under the protection of her adoptive mother Mrs Sucksby, Sue lives at 'Lant Street, in the Borough, near to the Thames' (2003: 3), until Richard Rivers, a villain known ironically as 'Gentleman', arrives with a plot to steal an heiress's fortune.[5] Encouraged by Mrs Sucksby and the rest of the thieves, and promised 3,000 pounds of the heiress, Maud Lilly's inheritance, Sue agrees to Gentleman's proposal to befriend, defraud and commit Maud to an insane asylum. She envisions her success within the heist in terms of material and sartorial capital when she later boasts that she will 'come back dressed in a velvet gown … "With gloves up to here, and a hat with a veil on, and a bag full of silver coin…"' (2003: 31). Before she can return clothed in velvet, however, Sue must first transform herself from a petty thief into a respectable lady's maid. Concealing her identity in a plain brown dress without decoration, Gentleman attempts to impose on Sue an equally unobtrusive surname before settling on 'Smith'. He says: 'We need a name that will hide you, not bring you to everyone's notice. We need a name" – he thought it over – "an untraceable name, yet one we shall remember … Brown? To match your dress?"' (39; ellipsis in original).

---

[4] Much academic criticism has tended to read Waters's treatment of gender in *Tipping the Velvet* in relation to Judith Butler's theory of gender performativity.
[5] 'Gentleman' passes as such because of his handsome clothes and jewellery that Sue recognizes as 'snide' but nevertheless 'damn fine counterfeits' (2003: 19).

Gentleman's careless collocation of Sue's name with the clothes that she is wearing indicates the significant role of dress in fashioning notions of identity and selfhood in the novel while foreshadowing the duplicitous nature of the plot. Indeed in the novel's second section, which is told from the perspective of Maud, the reader learns of the double deception at the heart of the thieves' plan. Together, Maud and Gentleman who is working in conjunction with Mrs Sucksby, trick Sue into inadvertently dressing as Maud and taking her place in the Insane Asylum. *Fingersmith*'s chiastic narrative structure thus unpairs Sue and Maud, offering alternative and mismatched versions of the same story. A novel of narrative doubles, *Fingersmith* presents twinned storylines and doubled characters with suspiciously similar and often interchangeable names including Maud Lilly, Marianne Lilly, Mr Christopher Lilly, Susan/Sue Trinder, Sue Smith and Mrs Sucksby. This literary device feeds into the plot of mistaken identity, assumed madness and misperception.

Like *Tipping the Velvet*, *Fingersmith*'s plot relies on the performative and transformative nature of dress. The initial trick depends upon Sue's ability to accurately perform her role as an experienced lady's maid, a ploy which Maud, already privy to Gentleman's plans, has no trouble discerning, while the logic of the novel's later storyline appears to, as Ya-ju Yeh suggests, revolve entirely around the role of clothing (2014: 164). It is the exchange of garments that allow for Sue's unintentional performance as lady and Maud's more knowing pretence as maid that brings together and facilitates the novel's final scheme. When Maud insists on dressing Sue in a 'queer' gown of 'orange velvet, with fringes and a wide skirt', she is delighted to find that they look alike: '"Why, look here in the glass", she said at last. "We might be sisters!" She had tugged my old brown dress off me and put the queer orange one over my head' (102). Her excitement is compounded when another maid mistakes Sue for Maud, demonstrating the metamorphic capacity of dress and its significant role in the novel as a marker of identity. At the conclusion of the first section, when Sue is forcibly removed to the madhouse in Maud's place, she becomes suddenly cognizant of the plan when she notes, apparently for the first time, the significance of her sartorial appearance: 'I gazed at my sleeve of silk, and at my own arm, that had got plump and smooth with careful feeding; and then at the bag at my feet, with its letters in brass – the *M*, and the *L*. It was in that second that I guessed, at last, the filthy trick' (174; original emphases). In this novel, then, the sartorial is both a sensationalist, narrative stratagem and a structural device: items of clothing stitch together the two main female protagonists' trajectories and respective storylines.

As in *Fingersmith*, dress acts as a material conduit between *Affinity*'s two main female protagonists and operates, both literally and metaphorically, by weaving together their separate narratives. Written in the form of a dialogic epistolary novel, Waters prioritizes the first-person narrative of Margaret Prior: a bereaved, middle-class woman, whose journal entries narrate the majority of the novel. Preceding her first diary entry, we learn that Margaret attempts suicide by overdosing on 'morphia' (2000: 255) following the death of her father and the sudden marriage between her brother and her most intimate friend, Helen. Margaret's new diary, which begins in September 1874, opens with an account of her first visit to Millbank Prison as a 'Lady Visitor', a role that tasks her with using her social standing to influence the female prisoners she meets there. It is in her new role as Lady Visitor, that Margaret first meets the once-celebrated 'Trance Medium', Selina Dawes (31). Stitched into *Affinity*'s narrative alongside Margaret's story are Selina's own diary entries. Written a year before Margaret's tale, Selina's analeptic narrative provides the backstory to her life as a spirit medium before her imprisonment in Millbank Prison for the reported crime of '*Fraud & Assault*' (27; original emphasis). Her documented 'crime', as Mark Llewellyn points out, largely ignores the specifically sexual undertones of her private séances which are the real cause for her imprisonment (2004: 203). Selina's cryptic journal entries and the culmination of the plot will later reveal the true nature of her séances, which are a cover for more salacious transgressions: Selina, together with her maid and lover, Ruth Vigers, who disguises herself as Peter Quick, Selina's 'spirit control' (136), conducts fraudulent female-only séances for profit and sexual opportunity.

In *Affinity*, the clothed bodies of Margaret, Selina and Ruth work to display their situatedness within their fictional Victorian class and social systems, as well as locating them within the novel's wider symbolic frame. The first items of clothing mentioned in detail are Margaret's grey dress and coat. That her clothes are grey indicates her protracted state of mourning, a particular that is further corroborated by her mournful wish 'that Pa was with me now' (7),[6] and perhaps also signifies her passivity – a trait that will enable the novel's later narrative workings. Writing of the chromatic tones deployed in sensation fiction, Harriet Blodgett asserts that the colour grey signals tedium and mundanity, as well as submissive femininity (2001: 144). Deeply affected by the events preceding the novel, the muted tones in which Margaret is dressed might here invoke a

---

[6] During the period of half-mourning, black clothes gave way to lighter shades of grey, mauve and violet. I discuss mourning dress, especially widows' veils, in further detail in Chapter 4.

comparable reading in their materialization of her grief and apathy. Beyond their emblematic function, however, the grey clothes have further narrative currency because of the fraught status they occupy in Margaret's storytelling process. Writing of her first visit to Millbank prison, Margaret wonders how her late father, an historian, might have begun the tale: 'he might begin it at seven this morning, when Ellis first brought me my grey suit and my coat – no, of course he would not start the story there, with a lady and her servant, and petticoats and loose hair' (7). As Marie-Luise Kohlke points out, 'women's private sphere, their fashions, hairstyles, and mundane affairs' are here 'designated irrelevant to history' (2004: 157). Yet Margaret's narrative brims with allusions to feminine apparel which become sites of sexual and symbolic significance, and which take on actively agentic roles throughout. Deciding instead to commence her narrative at 'the gate of Millbank, the point that every visitor must pass when they arrive to make their tour of the gaols' (7), Margaret's clothes appear to intrude upon her story once more. Before she is able to enter the prison, she explains that: 'I am obliged to pause a little to fuss with my skirts, which are plain, but wide, and have caught upon some piece of jutting iron or brick' (8). Just as these disruptive skirts physically impede Margaret's entry into the prison, they similarly slow the reader's ingress into the story. Emphasizing the notability of dress, such discrete sartorial moments lie at the heart of Waters's wider engagements with Victorian material culture.

If Margaret's diary begins with the suggestive imagery of 'a lady and her servant, and petticoats and loose hair' (7), then it culminates with her equally evocative discovery of a 'mud-brown gown, from Millbank, and a maid's black frock, with its apron of white ... tangled together, like sleeping lovers' (341). These discarded garments materialize Selina Dawes and Ruth Vigers's deception and present an apt metaphor for their secret relationship. Buried in Vigers's tin trunk for Margaret to unearth, the dresses become second-selves or ghostly emanations of the women they once adorned and represented. When Margaret attempts to 'pull the prison dress free' from its amorous embrace with the maid's dress, it becomes animated by Selina's love for Ruth, and she writes: 'it clung to the dark fabric of the other and would not come' (341). The desire that apparently animates Selina and Ruth Vigers's cast-off clothing evolves from the highly sexualized, all-female spiritualist séances that they conduct together and that lead to Selina's downfall. At the time in which the novel is set, Spiritualism, which had begun to gain momentum in the 1850s, had reached its zenith. According to Deborah Lutz, Spiritualism 'found power in the materiality of death'; ghosts were often '"materialized"', manifested through contact with everyday material things such as 'knocking or "rapping" on walls, tables, or other furniture' (2015a: 123), as is Peter Quick in *Affinity*. Waters capitalizes on the material aspect of the spiritualist context in her novel in order to fabricate Selina and Vigers's fraudulent and erotic séances through emphasis on feminine apparel. In the sessions, Vigers who masquerades as Peter Quick demands that lady visitors 'remove certain articles of clothing' when s/he visits them (145), and from within her cabinet, which is 'only a pair of heavy curtains ... hung before a screen, across a hollow in the wall' (151), Selina is half-dressed and provocatively bound and gagged. Margaret is told that 'a band of silk would be placed across her eyes and another put over her mouth, and… she would have them put "a little velvet collar" about her throat' (2000: 152–3). It is this same velvet collar which later becomes a material intermediary between the two women when Margaret finds it placed strategically within her diary and fastens it about her own neck in erotic sympathy with Selina. Believing that it is Selina herself who has sent the collar via supernatural means, Margaret feels it 'grip, as my heart pulses, as if she holds the thread to which it is fastened' (294). Her fervent, sensory apprehension of the velvet band manifests Selina's bodily proximity and control.

Equally provocative is Selina's portrayal of Peter Quick and his apparent control over *her*. To Margaret, she describes this as 'like losing her self, like having her own self pulled from her, as if a self could be a gown, or gloves' (166). Not only does this quotation contain a veiled clue as to Ruth Vigers's repeated adoption of another's identity through items of clothing, but its reference to the removal of garments also implicitly signals the secret sexual relationship that exists between Selina and Vigers. As these examples indicate, clothing forms a vital part of the novel's erotic economy. On this point, Catherine Spooner has aptly argued that garments are indeed 'central to Waters' story of spiritualism, crime and illicit desire' (2007: 351–2), while Monica Germaná argues that dress plays a significant role in the development of same-sex desire in *Fingersmith*, in which 'the acts of dressing and undressing facilitate the development of a sexual relationship between Maud and Sue' (2013: 114).

Tipping the Velvet appears to follow a similar trajectory in which the intimate and socially sanctioned acts of un/dressing prove crucial to the formation of forbidden desire. When Nan first becomes Kitty's 'dresser', assisting her with costume changes in between acts and managing her wardrobe, she admits that she 'adored being able to serve her like this':

> I would brush and fold her suit with trembling fingers, and secretly press its various materials – the starched linen of the shirt, the silk of the waistcoat and

the stockings, the wool of the jacket and trousers – to my cheek. Each item came to me warm from her body, and with its own particular scent; each seemed charged with a kind of strange power, and tingled or glowed (or so I imagined) beneath my hand. (1999: 36)

Enlivened by the lingering imprint of Kitty's body, the clothes enable Nan to figuratively caress her flesh. These worn articles of clothing, still warm from their direct contact with Kitty's skin, become sites of sensory pleasure and open up a private space for the articulation of same-sex desire. Referring to her 'fierce dreamings' Nan explains how 'I took my memories of her, and turned them to my own improper advantage!': 'I was used to standing close to her, to fasten her collar-studs or brush her lapels; now, in my reveries, I did what I longed to do then – I leaned to place my lips upon the edges of her hair; I slid my hands beneath her coat, to where her breasts pressed warm against her stiff gent's shirt' (41). Through this penetrative sartorial imagery, Waters realizes Nan's unspoken desires; she affiliates dress and body and supplements the novel's ostensible fascination with the divide between 'public' and 'private', interiority and exteriority.

While the female-female dressing trope apparent in each of Waters's three neo-Victorian narratives certainly recalls the eroticism of the illicit lesbian plots through dress, the later two novels mostly evade the anticipatory removal of clothes expected by the trajectory of female same-sex desire. Like *Fingersmith*, *Affinity* chooses to subvert the quasi-erotic dressing rituals observed between a lady and her maid in favour of more violent female-female dressing practices. Indeed, what becomes apparent in each of these novels is that the disciplinary power exercised by the insane asylum, Briar House, and Millbank prison, is not merely confined to the incarceration of women's bodies behind bars, and in Maud's case locked doors, but also extends to the corporeal confinement of female bodies within sartorial restraints.[7] Both Sue and Selina in *Fingersmith* and *Affinity* are clothed in the restrictive uniforms of the madhouse and Millbank prison, respectively. Just as it is in *Alias Grace*, dress is here used to actively curtail their physical freedom and autonomy and also to obscure their identities. In a Foucauldian sense, dress plays a central role in the surveillance, control and discipline of the female inhabitants.[8] Regulating and reforming their bodies, dress has both correctional and punitory functions. In *Affinity*, Selina, along

---

[7] Several critics have already drawn attention to the influence of Foucault's concept of the panopticon on Waters's carceral spaces in *Affinity*. See Kaplan (2007) and Armitt and Gamble (2006).
[8] I am referring here to Michel Foucault's notion of the docile body in *Discipline and Punish* ([1975] 1995).

with the other inmates of Millbank, is dressed in a 'mud-coloured gown' which characterizes her inhabitance of the 'grim-earthed place' for which the prison is named (26–7). The pathetic fallacy Waters invokes in her description of the prisoners' clothes, renders them indivisible from one another and from their physical surroundings in a way that doubles their incarceration both within the confines of the prison and within the constraints of their uniform. Extending this sartorial restriction further, Waters specifically references the 'strait-jackets' used to subdue and restrain the female inmates. Following a tour of the prison, Margaret is shown into the 'chain room' by two of the female prison matrons, Miss Ridley and Miss Haxby (179), where the latter tells her:

> 'Our main form of restraint … is the jacket. See, here.' She [Miss Haxby] stepped to a closet and drew out two heavy, canvas items, so rough and shapeless I thought at first they must be sacks. She passed one to Miss Ridley, and held the other one up against herself, as if trying out a gown before a glass. Then I saw that the thing was indeed a crude kind of over-dress – only, with straps about the sleeves and waist instead of braid or bows. (2000: 180)

In a subsequent scene, after Margaret is made to dress for her mother's dinner party, she suffers a nervous episode in which she imagines herself to be similarly imprisoned inside her clothes. Much like the straitjackets in Millbank prison, she imagines that her own gown 'had me gripped like a fist, so that the more I wriggled to undo it, the tighter it grew – at last, *There is a screw at my back*, I thought, *& they are tightening it!*' (257; original emphasis). Through the metaphor of the prison jacket, Margaret draws parallels between her own domestic situation and that of the prisoners, with whom she feels a particular affinity: were it not for her social status, the reader later learns, Margaret would have been jailed for her suicide attempt (256).

The regulatory and carceral implications of dress are likewise emphasized in *Fingersmith* when Sue is forcibly clothed in 'madhouse things' which serve to have an alienating effect upon her sense of identity (2003: 407). Accustomed to the relative finery of her clothes at Briar, Sue catalogues the ill-fitting and outlandish garments that she is given in the asylum, explaining how 'the corset had hooks instead of laces, and was too big for me … The gown was meant to be a tartan, but the colours had run. The stockings were short, like a boy's. The shoes were of india-rubber' (407). In wearing such clothes, Sue feels that all trace of her former identity has been erased. Glancing into a mirror, she realizes with horror that: 'I looked … like a lunatic. My hair was still sewn to my head, but had grown or worked loose from its stitches, and stood out in tufts. … The tartan gown hung on me like a laundry bag' (432–3). In fact, the only item of non-prison clothing that Sue is allowed to keep is Maud's glove, which she reveals she had earlier tucked into her bodice as a keepsake. The glove's function is less than comforting, however, because it serves both as a reminder of Maud's duplicity and the revenge that Sue longs to enact, as well as an incriminating marker of Sue's new, false identity, for the glove has Maud's name sewn into its lining. Taken as proof of her madness – ' "Here's your own name, *Maud,*" they said' (406; original emphasis) – the asylum nurses allow Sue to keep the old glove, which she wears above her heart beneath the tartan gown.

If the glove is taken as a marker of Sue's identity and a sign of her madness, then it also operates as a tool of restriction for Maud. Told in analepsis in the second half of the novel, Maud Lilly arrives at her uncle's house, Briar, and is imprisoned both in her room and within the restrictive 'strait gowns' and kid gloves that her uncle dictates she wear (2003: 183). In a scene that doubles with Sue's own forced dressing in the madhouse, Maud's body is encased in clothes by the housekeeper. Maud narrates the events as follows: ' "You must wear this, to give you the figure of a lady". She has taken the stiff buff dress from me, and all the linen beneath. Now she laces me tight in a girlish corset that grips me harder than the gown' (2003: 189). Dressed to suit her uncle's requirements and obliged to act as an amanuensis for his pornographic book collection, Maud's body becomes an extension of his own. She is especially plagued by Christopher Lilly's compulsive insistence that she wear 'white skin gloves' which the housekeeper 'stitches at the wrists' (189). Aligned with the restrictive corset which 'grips' Maud's body, the gloves with which Mr Lilly fetters his niece function as a form of literal and metaphorical incarceration. On leaving Briar, for instance, Maud reflects on her childhood with her uncle and measures out her life as a prisoner through the synecdoche of gloved time, asking: 'How many gloves, have I outgrown or outworn?' (287).

The restriction the white gloves impose upon Maud in the novel mirrors the process by which Victorian women would often attempt to mould the shape of their fingers by wearing tightly fitting and tapered gloves. According to Ariel Beaujot, 'for the Victorians, the glove was a conforming and contorting device, similar to the corset' (2012: 38). However, in Waters's novel, the hands prove to be of more crucial significance. The encasing of Maud's hands is deeply symbolic and problematic: though the corset might contain her waist, it is the gloves that cut off both her creativity and sexuality. Not only do they keep her hands soft and clean for the safe handling of her uncle's pornographic books, but they simultaneously 'keep her from further mischief', that is, from experiencing onanistic pleasure or from sexual contact with Sue (2003: 201). Maud's is figured as a contaminating, untrustworthy touch, one that must be sheathed and stifled by gloves. For Kathleen A. Miller, Maud

> becomes a *fingersmith*, skilled at the adept use of her hands, yet powerless to use them for her own purposes and for her own pleasure. And although Maud's sight will save her uncle's, and her hands will be his hands (208), the white gloves, both literally and figuratively, will act as a barrier, preventing the heroine from leaving her fingerprints on her surrounding world, including the traditions of Victorian bibliography and pornography. (2008, para 1; original emphasis)

That Maud is denied sexual and authorial autonomy, at least initially, is important because it coincides with contemporary concerns surrounding women and their bodily and reproductive independence. From a contemporary, feminist perspective, Maud's sartorial incarceration speaks to the various manifestations of patriarchy in our own, supposedly liberated, twenty-first-century society; her physical and sexual restriction chimes with the media's continued objectification and control of women's bodies in the present, as well as with contemporary concerns surrounding women's sexual freedoms. In mandating that Maud wear gloves, Waters speaks to such concerns, as well as appearing to insist upon the traditional function of the Victorian glove. Gloves serve to whiten, soften and regulate Maud's hands in *Fingersmith*; as a result, they work to sublimate her desires and reinforce prevailing gender ideologies, as well as bolstering hierarchies of social class. Yet, as the following sections will demonstrate, Waters also appropriates and overturns the social, gendered and heterocentric function of the Victorian glove. In *Fingersmith* gloves subvert class hierarchies since, as we later learn, Maud is not a real lady having been swapped at birth with Sue. They are also the sartorial tools by which the female protagonists' societal and sexual identities are fashioned. The remainder of this chapter examines the centrality of gloves in these three novels, but before turning to this analysis I want first to show how the remediated glove in neo-Victorian fiction can be read against and in dialogue with Victorian discourses surrounding the affectual and emotional functions of women's gloves.

'The impress of her hand': Victorian gloves

Currently kept in storage and available for study only by appointment at the V&A's Clothworkers' Centre in Blythe House, London,[9] are a pair of short,

---

[9] The Clothworkers' Centre is currently undergoing a process of relocation. The new V&A East Storehouse will open in Stratford's Queen Elizabeth Olympic Park in 2024.

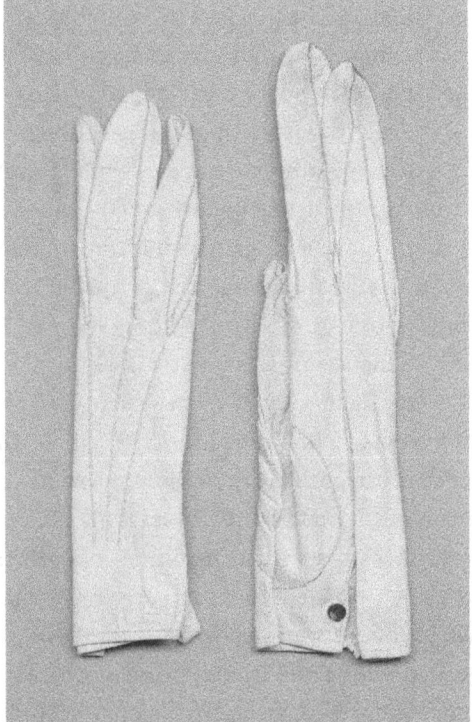

Figure 3.1 Pair of gloves, made by C. Courvoisier. France, *c.* 1887. © Victoria and Albert Museum.

white kidskin gloves with a stud button at the wrist (T15:1-2.2008) (Figure 3.1). Labelled as 'unknown', indicating that their pasts are only partially identifiable since their origins and previous owners cannot be definitively traced, this pair of nineteenth-century gloves convey a vivid sense of the past. Believed to have been made around 1887 in France by the glover C. Courvoisier, there is some conjecture over who the gloves may have belonged to. They were donated to the V&A by an Edward Nugée, who claims that all of the items he bequeathed the museum are associated with the wedding of Elizabeth Wroughton Richards to the Reverend Andrew Nugée on 8 August 1854. The digitized inscription accompanying the gloves online maintains, by contrast, that 'these gloves are much more likely to be connected to the couple's son, Francis Edward Nugée's (1855–1930) wedding in 1887, when he married Edith Isabel Alston (1859–1958)' ('Pair of Gloves' 2021). In addition, the gloves are mismatched: printed in faded blue ink on the inside of one glove is an '8½' sign, while on the other resides a barely visible '7'. These markings indicate the sizes of these Courvoisier gloves, meaning that either the wearer had two different sized hands or, more likely, that they were donated to the museum oddly paired.

Beyond their uncertain provenance and strange pairing, what marks these gloves as interesting is their well-worn appearance; although the kid leather is largely unblemished and still relatively clean and white, the gloves are wrinkled and creased, the fingers crushed together, through years kept compressed in storage, while many of the outer seams have split from incessant use. The V&A's online description of these gloves focuses on the 'crumpled' leather and the gloves' ripped seams, offering a productive way of reading the past in the present: 'the stitching along many of the seams has burst. Gloves of the late 19th century were often worn extremely tight, with glove-stretchers used to stretch the leather enough to enable the hands to be slipped inside' ('Pair of Gloves' 2021). Such wear and tear, rather than categorizing these gloves as ruined and beyond repair, points instead to their history and to the passage of time. From these gloves arise a series of interconnected questions that direct my readings of nineteenth-century gloves and their neo-Victorian counterpoints: what indications of a past life can be read in the tears and split seams of these gloves? What traces can be found imprinted within the leather? And how might these small and seemingly insignificant sartorial items provide a material link to the hands they once adorned? As Deborah Lutz finds in *Relics of Death in Victorian Literature and Culture*, 'the possessions of one gone for good can seem to be embedded with little histories of intimacy, with the touch of the dead one's hands or body' (2015a: 53). Indeed, a closer examination of the pair yields further instances in which the glove's past is mapped onto the kidskin. Only fully visible when held open by the curator, the leather across the palm of the glove is scored with crease lines that usurp the features of the hand and point to the physicality of a past body which the gloves have since outlived. Patches of slight discolouration on the fingertips are evidence of a material and embodied existence; these stains and splashes are the residue of a temporally and spatially distant body and its encounters with the material world. Taken together, the creases, broken stitches and blemishes on the gloves' surfaces reveal cumulative and entangled histories and narratives.

That gloves are imbued with narrative and deeply encoded with a collective sense of history materializes most clearly in S. William Beck's *Gloves: Their Annals and Associations* (1883). One of the earliest studies to recognize the striking symbolic, linguistic and cultural meanings that have been attached to gloves throughout history, it sets out to impress upon readers the importance of gloves in past societies. Beck aims to 'narrate the numerous customs and practices in what we may call glove ritual, and, tracing the past history of gloves' attempts to 'make up what we may call a volume of glove lore' (x). Historically given as tokens or pledges of love, loyalty and protection, or cast down as a challenge and signal of dispute, gloves have been frequently assigned both sentimental and material currency. In spite of this, their study is typically marginalized in dress history and academic commentary more widely (Foley 2015: 35). Part of the glove's apparent neglect in scholarly discourse appears to be contingent upon its relegation as an accessory or accompaniment to other more central items of clothing. Yet, by seeking to accentuate the glove's sartorial consequence within the context of the nineteenth century, this chapter echoes Liza Foley's desire to 'recognise them as deeply significant items of dress' (36). Worn habitually during the period, both inside and outside of the home, gloves were considered foundational pieces of clothing that often bore a remarkably intimate relationship to the wearer. Designed to fit snugly about the hand and therefore worn close to the skin, gloves not only acted as protective intermediaries between the body and the outside world, but they also reflected an individual's personal, aesthetic tastes, along with their economic status and social standing.

The apparently intertwined issues of class and the etiquette of glove wearing appear to have been central concerns of Victorian social commentators. As prominent indicators of both rank and position during the period, gloves were accompanied by a set of rules and regulations that wearers in polite society strictly observed. Valerie Cumming affirms that 'the etiquette of glove wearing was an important feature of nineteenth-century life' (1982: 55). Increased social mobility during this period ensured that individuals needed to both look and act their assigned parts, particularly when it came to sartorial considerations, and various nineteenth-century etiquette manuals and fashion magazines capitalized on this pursuit of respectability. Charles William Day's *Hints on Etiquette and the Usages of Society* (1843) and Florence Hartley's *The Ladies' Book of Etiquette and Manual of Politeness* (1872), are notable examples of nineteenth-century prescriptive literature that contain many glove-related guidelines, including the correct wearing and washing of gloves. The former is particularly strict in its adherence to the social codes surrounding glove wearing in its appeal to readers to: 'always wear your gloves in church or in a theatre' (67), while reminding them that 'Ladies should never dine with their gloves on – unless their hands are not fit to be seen' (1843: 45).

Though gloves were regularly worn by both men and women throughout the nineteenth century, as with the other items of clothing examined in this study their significance for female wearers was consistently over-stated. A prevalent theme in much of the contemporary literature on the etiquette of glove wearing is that women, especially, should take particular care over the appearance and quality of their gloves. Published in 1892, an article which appeared in *Bow Bells* outlined the importance and implications of neat gloves for the female wearer, emphasizing that:

> The hands being one of the most observed portions of the human frame, the consideration of the glove becomes an important item in the cares of the toilet. With well-fitting gloves and boots, the former unobtrusive in colour, and a fashionable arrangement of the hair, a woman need be less particular about the rest of her garmenture than if these essentials were open to reproach. ('Gloves': 264).

Hartley concurs, explaining in 1872 that a 'shabby or ill fitting boot or glove will ruin the most elaborate walking dress' (26). As these excerpts attest, gloves were conceived of as central articles of clothing; they were items that could complete, rectify or remedy a sartorial ensemble assuming they were clean, well-fitting, and purchased in the correct colour: 'the colours of gloves should always be "neutral", such as café au lait brown, brownish grays, and real grays', or white and cream ('Gloves' 1892: 264).

Crucial to its cultural cachet was the glove's capacity to regulate and reinforce hierarchies of gender, race and class. Social acceptability was often epidermally inscribed. As Beaujot claims, hands, and consequently gloves, were a fulcrum of nineteenth-century anxieties pertaining to such issues (48). Noting the racist and racially driven emphasis upon whiteness in the period, she demonstrates how pale, delicate hands were considered the epitome of middle-class femininity in particular, and an indicator of social respectability in the period. Clean, close-fitting gloves which covered and concealed non-white and work-worn fingers were therefore considered essential for subscribing to and perpetuating a sense of ideal Victorian womanhood, as well as for facilitating appropriate class performance and racial identification (Beaujot 2012: 38). Simon Gatrell likewise codifies gloves according to class in his critical survey of dress in Thomas Hardy's literary oeuvre but extends this focus to explore their inherently eroticized connotations. For the working classes, he suggests, gloves were a 'necessary form of protection', but for 'the middle classes in town and country gloves could strongly be eroticized, for they were the only item of clothing that could be removed with propriety in public to reveal the wearer's naked skin' (2011: 87). This sexualized relationship was even more pronounced for the female wearer since 'a lady of refinement regarded her hand as a part of her body which was not lightly to be displayed to members of the other sex' (Cunnington [1937] 1990: 23). As a result, her glove was often associated with the erotic and the sexual. Daniel R. Shafer's 1877 treatise, *Secrets of Life Unveiled, or Book of Fate*, cements this view in his inclusion of a section on 'Glove Flirtations', in which he maintains that women's gloves could be used as a tool for feminine seduction (231–4). Gatrell also goes on to argue that 'the relationship between glove and ungloved hand could come to be a synecdoche for the sexual relationship between clothes and naked body' (87). I would add that the relationship between the gloved and ungloved hand can also be conceived of as a euphemism for the sexualized relationship that lies, not only between clothes and the naked body but also between lovers.

Extending the 'sexual implications of a single glove' in their enlightening article on Renaissance gloves, Peter Stallybrass and Ann Rosalind Jones contend that in the 1700s, a single glove became 'a vagina' (2001: 127). Included in the special issue on 'Things' edited by Bill Brown and published in *Critical Inquiry*, their article examines the literal and symbolic function of gloves in the literature and art of the period. Adopting the sexualized metaphor of the glove, they argue that the seventeenth-century female body 'materialized as stretchable skin, the man as phallic finger' (128). Though their focus remains on the sixteenth and seventeenth centuries, much of Stallybrass and Jones's theorizing can be applied to the literature and culture of the nineteenth century. For instance, Richard Carlile's *Every Woman's Book* refers repeatedly to prophylactics as 'gloves' (1828), while Émile Zola's 1883 novel, *Au Bonheur des Dames* [*The Ladies' Delight*], which revolves around the titular department store in Paris, features female shoppers who are seduced by the implicitly eroticized glove department (El-Rayess 2014: 125). Picking up on these same distinctions in her recent study on the role of touch in eighteenth- and nineteenth-century literature, Kimberley Cox traces gloves' sensual histories and reads them as a sexual stimulant in the period, inciting touch, and encouraging erotic communication (143).

Yet to be explored, however, is the emblematic function of the empty or cast-off Victorian glove. Gloves that were lost, discarded or bestowed as keepsakes were significantly gendered feminine in contemporary print culture. In turn, the retrieval and possession of a cast-off glove by chiefly male protagonists, was often stimulated by unrequited love or unfulfilled desire for romantic, (hetero) sexual congress. George Egerton's 'A Little Grey Glove' (1893), details just such an attachment in its focus on the erotics of a woman's glove as a material substitute for her body. 'Her Glove' a seven-stanza poem published in the *Supplement to the Hampshire Telegraph and Sussex Chronicle* in 1884, adopts a similar focus. After being rejected by his fiancée, who unexpectedly ends their relationship, the male poetic speaker finds her glove 'on the ground, where she threw it / When she gave me back my ring and my love' (5). Admitting that she would be 'indignant' if she 'Knew I'd found and was keeping her glove', the poetic speaker cannot bear to part with it, noting 'how much intertwisted "Love" and "glove" are'. In the remainder of the poem, he caresses the sartorial item; his fingers linger over its material form which 'still keeps… /The shape of her fair slender hand', and he notes its slight defects such as a missing button and a tear in the fabric. Like the C. Courvoisier gloves which bear the external marks of a past life, the gloves' imperfections facilitate an affective and imagined reunion between the man and his absent lover. His palpable despair at having lost his love is alleviated in the final lines of the poem, in which the speaker situates the glove as a sartorial replacement for the woman, declaring: 'If I can't have the hand it protected, / At least I have stolen her glove' (5).

H. K's 'A Glove's Confession', published in 1878 in *The London Journal* advances a similar scenario. Like 'Her Glove', this poetic offering dwells upon a single, forgotten glove and its potent intimacy with a woman's body. In the first stanza, a male speaker seizes the fallen glove of the woman he desires: 'A glove that she alone could wear, / Of dainty shape and size – / The impress of her hand still there / Enhanced to me the prize' (223). Reiterating the uniqueness of the woman's glove tailored to fit her hand, the man conjures its capacity to carry her trace and her trace alone. He also renders the glove vibrant and lively when he personifies it, imagining that it comes alive to talk to him. Through this tactual and communicative contact, the male narrator envisions a sense of ownership over the woman in which possession of her glove is equated with a kind of possession of her body: 'And by this captured glove I swear / Its mistress shall be mine!' (223). Finally, a comparably sensuous longing prompts the male protagonist of the aptly named A. Kidd's poem, 'The Glove' (1878), to claim another forgotten glove. But while the poet employs typical love imagery in his address to the lady's glove in this poem, the erotic implications of the final lines – 'O lady, grant me leave the glove to keep – / The casket that contained a gem so rare; / … That I, awaking from love-laden sleep, / May say, "The gem itself to-day I wear"' (1878: 315) – are unmistakeable.

As these poetic renderings attest, gloves were highly personal tokens that metonymically recalled the body from which they were drawn. As intimate and often deeply eroticized garments, worn close to the skin and invested with an individual's trace, they became highly personal keepsakes, gifts or tokens of affection, sexual attraction and fidelity in the period. Liza Foley explains their enduring significance in the following evocative terms: 'As prosthetic extensions, intimate tokens, or private interior spaces, gloves become enhanced by their capacity to evoke a sense of touch that is embodied, but contains an absence' (2015: 36). As such, gloves, whether Victorian or neo-Victorian, tread the borders between absence and presence and facilitate moments of imagined unity between parted lovers. In drawing upon these sartorial histories, I suggest that Sarah Waters's neo-Victorian fictions ostensibly recognize the intricate literary and cultural contexts in which Victorian women's gloves operated. *Tipping the Velvet*, *Affinity* and *Fingersmith* all openly draw upon such gendered and classed depictions of the nineteenth-century glove but tend to subvert their heterosexual conceptualizations. Waters thus mobilizes the glove as a strategic material tool. Intervening in cultural and sartorial history, her three neo-Victorian novels reimagine the Victorian glove as a lively and symbolic marker of lesbian desire.

Neo-Victorian gloves: Touch, materiality and queer desire

In spite of a wealth of criticism on Waters's three neo-Victorian novels, *Tipping the Velvet*, *Fingersmith* and *Affinity* are yet to be considered together in relation to the residual presence of Victorian gloves. This is perhaps surprising given that the texts are each deeply preoccupied with, yet typically forbidden to, touch. Waters's notable interest in and engagement with tactile sensation has, however, surfaced in several recently published academic works. Drawing upon Sara Ahmed's notion of 'queer orientation' (2006), which is informed by Maurice Merleau-Ponty's phenomenological theory of bodily perception and sensory experience ([1945] 2002), Rosario Arias examines moments of heightened hapticity in Waters's neo-Victorian trilogy. She focuses especially on moments of queer phenomenology and concludes by demonstrating how reading neo-Victorian literature through the lens of touch has particular implications for the way in which we, as readers, engage with the past: 'The tactile experience in contemporary novels set in the Victorian past seems to flatten out the distance, to narrow the time and space existing between the Victorian dead (past) and the contemporary present, thus inviting the reader in the present to "inhabit" and "embody" the past' (2017: 45). For Arias, it is our increasingly digitized society that informs and reflects this neo-Victorian drive towards tactility (52). Drawing on this analysis in her study on touch in eighteenth- and nineteenth-century literature and culture, Cox aptly adds that the way in which authors of neo-Victorian and Steampunk fiction employ the sense of touch is similar to the instances of 'manual intercourse' she identifies in the literature that such fiction seeks to revise and rewrite (2022: 184). Following these perceptive readings, I adopt a different approach in the subsequent sections, concentrating on the ways in which gloves, intimately embedded with the physical trace of past hands, mediate and disrupt tactual encounters and become affective agents of queer desire. Rather than focusing solely on the moments in which the protagonists caress or touch one another, I concentrate on the moments in which gloves are adopted or removed. I situate the glove as a site of encounter and action and pay attention to the manifold ways in which it facilitates, animates and troubles moments of affectual and erotic physical correspondence.

Hands, gloves and glove imagery proliferate throughout the neo-Victorian novels under study here. In all three of these texts, gloves appear as practical, sexual and symbolic objects. In *Affinity* and *Tipping the Velvet*, the word 'glove' abounds, while the importance of the glove as pivotal sartorial item in *Fingersmith* is foregrounded not only within the pages of the novel but also on the book cover of the Virago edition. Christopher Louttit's assertion that the analysis of neo-Victorian book covers augments our readings of the texts themselves, can be usefully employed here to explore Waters's covers in further detail (2014: 106). Printed book covers are a phenomenon that appear to have originated in the early nineteenth century (Genette [1997] 2001: 23). The paratext marks the outer elements at the entrance of the text and serves to direct or dictate the reception of the book to its readers. If, as Genette suggests, the peripheral elements of the novel function as a way of drawing out the main themes inside the text (2001: 2), then it follows that the issues and concerns in Waters's three neo-Victorian novels are made explicit by localizing suggestive imagery in her front covers. Engaging with the licentious space of the music hall, the pornographic book trade and the sexualized séance, respectively, *Tipping the Velvet*, *Fingersmith* and *Affinity* all signal a particular preoccupation with the commercial, material and sexual worlds that their nineteenth-century protagonists inhabit. That their interest is tied up in such issues is initially apparent in each of the text's peritexts.

Reprinted by Virago Press *Tipping the Velvet*, *Affinity* and *Fingersmith* all feature cover photography by Jeff Cottenden that specifically foregrounds the matters and material objects that permeate each text. In the same way that Selina Dawes is alleged to commune with the dead, the cover photograph of the 2000 Virago edition of *Affinity* mediates hidden messages to the viewer: it reveals the novel's preoccupation with issues of touch, the erotic and spectrality. Cottenden's cover photograph directs the viewer's gaze into the lap of an anonymous woman whose hands cradle a spray of purple violets, thus materializing the moment in which Margaret Prior first gazes at Selina Dawes through the inspection flap – or 'the eye' (2000: 23; original emphasis) as the female prisoners call it – in Millbank prison. Drawn to the peephole in the prison door, Margaret narrates Selina's movements in her cell:

> Her hands opened, she raised them to her cheek, and I caught a flash of colour against the pink of her work-roughened palms. She had a flower there, between her fingers – a violet, with a drooping stem. As I watched, she put the flower to her lips, and breathed upon it, and the purple of the petals gave a quiver and seemed to glow … But I didn't wonder, then, about how a violet might, in that grim-earthed place, have found its way into those pale hands. I only thought, suddenly and horribly, What can her *crime* have been? (2000: 27; original emphasis)

Like this passage, the vignette-style cover image contrasts pale hands and purple flowers before fading into the backdrop of encroaching black. The circular black framing functions as a recreation of Margaret's own field of vision afforded by 'the eye' and serves also to situate the neo-Victorian reader as a kind of voyeur, granted a forbidden glimpse of the past. Although the woman in the picture is not wearing gloves, her pale hands, which mirror the faintly suggestive V-shape of her lap, are the central focus of the image. The violet clasped loosely in her fingers is also suffused with erotic and spectral meaning; violets are associated with both lesbianism and, in Victorian floriography, refer to spirituality and resurrection (O'Callaghan 2017: 55; Maxwell 2017: 72).

Motifs of the glove and hand abound in the ensuing narrative. Though denied the pleasure of touching one another, Selina and Margaret are able to communicate via a complex set of exchanges and gestures that foreground hands, fingers and gloves. Following an early encounter in which Selina has handled Margaret's journal and written her a secret note inside of it, Margaret fetishistically writes: 'I took my glove off, and placed my naked palm upon the binding, and the leather seemed warm, still, from the grip of her rough fingers' (2000: 116). Like the inscription that Selina has made within the book, her trace is similarly recorded on its leather surface. The journal consequently becomes a material conduit that transmits the warmth of Selina's 'rough fingers' to Margaret's ungloved hand, thus enabling the two to figuratively touch. Running her hands across the book's surface, Margaret effectively caresses Selina's flesh. Her use of the erotically charged word 'naked' to describe her ungloved fingers is especially potent: recalling the synecdoche of the glove and the undressed body, this instance prefigures the dramatic moment in the novel when Margaret and Selina eventually touch. Writing of the climactic scene, Margaret offers this account: Selina 'reached and took my hand. She turned my fingers and eased back my glove, and held my wrist a little way before her mouth' (308). If, to borrow from Stallybrass and Jones, the glove is a metaphor for a vagina (2001: 127), then the implied eroticism of Margaret's half-removed glove and the proximity of Selina's mouth and hands doubles as a pseudo-consummation scene.

Since their physical separation often limits their interactions, Selina sends Margaret spectral 'tokens', about which the latter writes, '[they] come only as a subtle alteration to the details of my room – I return to it and find an ornament taken up and set down crooked, the door to my closet ajar and my dresses with marks of fingers on the velvet and the silk' (285). Margaret's intoxication with Selina means that she believes such gestures to have come directly from the spirit world, but she later learns that these carefully curated material displays are constructed by the Prior's maid, Ruth Vigers, who acts on Selina's behalf. Although the lingering fingerprints on Margaret's intimate possessions seem to point to Selina's spectral proximity, they actually imply the psychological hold that both Selina and Vigers appear to have over her. This manipulation is later acknowledged by Margaret in terms that draw specifically on textile production. Written shortly after Selina's duplicity is revealed and finding herself ensnared in the plot that has freed Selina from Millbank Prison, the final, potentially suicidal, line of Margaret's journal draws on the process of spinning and lingers on the sense of touch. She writes: 'Your twisting is done – you have the last thread of my heart. I wonder: when the thread grows slack, will you feel it?' (2000: 351).

That gloves are also pivotal objects in *Fingersmith* is clear from their prominence on the front cover of the 2003 Virago edition. Like the 2002 edition of *Affinity*, the *Fingersmith* cover implies hidden meanings in relation to hands and gloves. In this image, a pair of white gloves rest upon a book whose possibly pornographic title is hidden from view. Occupying a paradoxical position from the outset, the gloves act as a barrier, protecting the reader's eyes from the title of the novel, while simultaneously tempting us to move them aside, to read the cover and to touch and turn the pages of the pornographic text. Parallels can be drawn here between such practices and the modern-day obsession with reading about, touching and experiencing the Victorian past. What is most notable, however, is the agency implicit in the image. The empty gloves recall the presence of past hands. Like the C. Courvoisier gloves held in the V&A's collection, the creases and wrinkles left in the empty gloves on the book's cover suggest an absent inhabitant, while the relative gloom of the novel's cover contrasts with the whiteness of the gloves, which look like disembodied hands.

Noting the significance of the white gloves on the front cover of the book in their essay on visual and material culture in neo-Victorianism, Nadine Boehm-Schnitker and Susanne Gruss posit that they are 'symbolic not only of Maud's imprisonment by her uncle, but – as a love token – also evoking the lesbians' love and appealing to the readers' urge to "touch" and "feel" the nineteenth century' (2011: 4). The gloves also have a further implication for the two lesbian lovers in light of the book's title, which alludes to both a kind of petty thief and also to female masturbation and lesbian sex. Gloves, then, are not only indicative of Maud's internment at Briar but they also play a central role in the sexual politics at work within the novel. Since the shape of the glove cannot be divorced from the realities of the hand, it blurs the distinction between body and dress, subject and object. The intimacy that arises in this merging of boundaries between the glove and the naked hand becomes increasingly present in the instances in which Maud is un-gloved in *Fingersmith*. Sue and Maud's growing desire appears to originate in and coalesce around the erotic moment when Maud first allows Sue to remove her gloves for her. Sue narrates: '"Let me do it," I said, undoing the button at her wrist; and though at first she wouldn't let me touch her bare hands, in time – since I said I would be gentle – she began to let me' (93). The sexual charge generated by the removal of Maud's gloves is amplified in a later scene in which Mr Lilly educates Maud on the pornography he has had her catalogue. It can be no coincidence that his first instruction is: 'Take off your gloves' (198). Maud then explains how 'He turns and takes a book from his shelves, then hands it to me, pressing my fingers hard about it. ... The book is called *The Curtain Drawn Up, or the Education of Laura*. I sit alone, and turn the cover; and understand at last the matter I have read, that has provoked applause from gentlemen' (2003: 199). Waters's intertextual reference to *The Curtain Drawn Up* (1818) provides a succinct metaphor for Maud's own dawning sexual understanding, as well for the removal of her gloves, which connote the removal of other more intimate garments. Maud's new sexual knowledge is literalized in the syntax of the final sentence in the quotation: the medial break as she turns the book's cover without her gloves mirrors the revelation of the book's contents. Similarly, the handling of pornographic texts with bare hands further marks Maud's sexual maturation and ultimate corruption via the suggestive and symbolic removal of her white gloves which no longer bar her from knowledge.

In a comparably suggestive scene, Gentleman strips Maud's glove from her hand and kisses her naked palm. Initially viewed through Sue's eyes, this gesture is performatively and purposefully coded with heterosexual and erotic meaning. As she watches the pair, Sue reports that Gentleman 'lifted one of her

[Maud's] weak hands and slowly drew the glove half from it; and then he kissed her naked palm … I saw her sag still closer to him, then give a shiver. Her skirt rose even higher, and showed the tops of her stockings, the white of her thigh' (117–18). Maud's naked hand, lifted skirts, and pale thighs render this scene intensely sexual. Read through the doubled perspective necessitated by the novel's dual structure (see Gamble 2013), however, the removal of Maud's glove by Gentleman indicates only the collusive agreement into which both parties have entered. The episode also hints at sexual and moral violation. Jealously misinterpreted by Sue as libidinal desire, Maud's response to the removal of her glove only becomes clear in the second half of the novel when she reports: 'He pushes my glove a little way along my hand, he parts his lips, he touches my palm with the point of his tongue; and I shudder, with weakness, with fear and distaste – with dismay, to know Sue stands and watches, in satisfaction, thinking me his' (276–7). This same action, performed for Sue's benefit, takes on a deeply unsettling cast when read in light of Maud's feeling and Gentleman's intentions.

Departing from the focus on hands and gloves, *Tipping the Velvet* features a pair of pink dancing shoes in its book cover in accordance with the novel's music hall context. Although they do not grace the front cover, gloves surface repeatedly in Waters's first novel. Their appearance in the text's diegesis often signals scenes of activity: the pulling on or removal of gloves tends to both precede and follow moments of movement and action in which the protagonists enter and leave the narratorial frame. Gloves therefore play a key role in the pacing, temporality and rhythm of the novel. They are central to the text's world-building process; they not only operate as markers of historicity and as signs of social respectability but they also contain implicit hints about sexuality embedded within them. These moments in *Tipping the Velvet* in which gloves generate a sexual charge are slightly more contained though no less evocative than Waters's later neo-Victorian texts. In her first encounter with Kitty, for instance, Nan takes care to mention that Kitty has a pair of 'lavender gloves at her pocket' (1999: 12), the colour of which signals lesbian desire (O'Callaghan 2017: 55), and which also fortuitously match her own gloves that are adorned with lavender bows. When Nan visits Kitty backstage for the first time, it is these same gloves that play a central part in facilitating their first tactual encounter. Nan explains that 'she held out her hand to me, and I lifted my own in response – then remembered my glove – my glove with the lavender bows upon it, to match my pretty hat – and quickly drew it off and offered her my naked fingers' (33). The eroticism of Nan's 'naked fingers' foreshadows the pair's blossoming physical relationship. After Kitty kisses Nan's hands, the latter's physical reaction is recounted in terms that call upon sexual release: 'I put my glove back on. My fingers seemed to tingle against the cloth' (34). In a later portion of the novel, gloves take on an even more overtly sexual role when Diana Lethaby strips off her clothes yet leaves her white kid gloves in place (242). Documenting the removal of successive pieces of clothing, Waters appropriates Roland Barthes's notion of the striptease, in which gloves, considered typical sexual props ([1957] 2000: 85), partially cover Diana's body, drawing attention to and exaggerating her hands and fingers, and thus functioning fetishistically in the novel. When at last she removes the gloves after the two have made love, the moment is even more firmly encoded with connotations of sexual gratification. Nan notes the pale flesh of Diana's hands and aligns them with the whiteness of the gloves in a way that doubles the sexual function of the garment (245). Together, these examples show how Waters appropriates and overturns the traditional heteronormative transmission and function of women's gloves. As sartorial objects that intervene in processes of queer touch, the gloves are suffused with erotic energy. The sensuality of gloves is a recurrent theme in each of the three novels stemming not only from their facilitative function but also, as the next section discusses, from the material traces left both on and within them.

Material traces of the past

In his three-volume work *Time and Narrative* (1985), the hermeneutic phenomenologist Paul Ricoeur outlines a distinctive approach to examining the enmeshment of time, history and narrative. Drawing attention to the confluence of history and fiction in particular, he suggests that the two are interwoven precisely because of 'the borrowings each mode of narrative makes from the other mode' (1990: 101). Ricoeur stresses that in order to fully explain the ways in which fiction and history overlap 'we must enlarge the space of reading to include everything written, historiography as well as literature' (1990: 101). As this study attests, written dress, as well as the object-oriented study of clothes, present additional pertinent spaces of reading insofar as sartorial things document the events, experiences and emotions of the past. The preservative potential of fabric, its capacity to retain and recover the physical traces and psychical resonances of past bodies, make it a powerful mediator between the Victorian period and our own contemporary present. Forging threads of connection between that time and this, clothes contribute to our present-day understandings of and interest in the fabric(ation) of the past.

In order to achieve a full discussion of the way in which history and fiction are connected, Ricoeur deploys the theoretical notion of the 'trace', which finds its most lucid exposition in his essay 'Narrated Time' (1984). Asking 'what, actually, is a trace?', he contends that it is 'a vestige left by the passage of a human being or of an animal. A trace is *left*, a trace *remains*. We speak thus of *remnants* of the past as of remnants of a dinner, or of the relics of a saint or the ruins of an ancient monument' (1991: 345; original emphases). In this conceptualization, the trace occurs as an enduring material, tangible presence that opens itself to interpretative potentialities. Like a relic or ruin, it is a physical thing existing in the present moment that gestures towards the historic past. Sitting at the juncture between past and present, it therefore assumes a striking sense of duality. 'As a physical entity, the trace is something of the present', Ricoeur explains, 'Traces of the past exist now: they are remnants to the extent that they are *still* there, while the past context of the trace – people, institution, actions, passions – no longer exists' (1991: 345; original emphasis). For this reason, the trace has proved to be an especially apt theoretical tool with which to examine neo-Victorian literature and culture. Rosario Arias has productively identified the significance of the trace as outlined by Ricoeur and Emmanuel Levinas in examining the interplay between past and present in neo-Victorianism, arguing that the spectral notion of 'revisitation' that presides over the genre links to the idea of the passage of the trace (2014: 113). More recently, Arias and Patricia Pulham have found Paul Ricoeur's concept particularly suggestive for a reading of neo-Victorian material culture. They posit that the notion of the trace is 'especially apt for critically engaging with the field of neo-Victorian studies as the impact of the Victorians persists and continues to resurface in today's culture' (2019: 214). The way in which that past makes itself known is through its material relics. Since Victorian gloves surface repeatedly in Waters's neo-Victorian works and are recurrently marked with the vestiges of absent wearers, Ricoeur's notion of the trace lends itself to a productive reading of Victorian sartorial culture and its legibility in contemporary culture.

As with the dresses discussed in the previous chapter, gloves take on a peculiarly sentient life that borders on the uncanny in Waters's neo-Victorian oeuvre. What enlivens the gloves in these cases are the traces that are left both on and within them. Unlike the gowns in *Alias Grace* and *The Master*, which appear to act of their own accord, these gloves are apparently animated by and as a direct result of their intrinsic association with their past wearers. In *Fingersmith*, the lively, uncanny function of the glove is invoked precisely when Sue, imprisoned in the Insane Asylum, mistakes Maud's glove for a hand. Originally taken as a keepsake and hidden inside Sue's bodice over her heart (2003: 171), Maud's glove acts as a kind of talisman in reverse:

> I saw something, pale upon the floor. It looked like a crumpled white hand, and it gave me a start, at first; then I saw what it was. It had fallen out of my bosom when the nurse had got the gown off me, and been kicked out of sight. There was the mark of a shoe upon it, and one of its buttons was crushed. It was that glove of Maud's, that I had taken that morning from her things and meant to hold on to, as a keepsake of her. I picked it up and turned it over and over in my hands. If I had thought myself funked, a minute before – well, that funking was nothing to what I felt now, looking at that glove, thinking of Maud, and of the awful trick that she and Gentleman had played me. (2003: 401)

Not unlike the autonomous glove in H. K's 'Her Glove' which recalls the contours of the lover's hand, the verisimilitude of the glove's shape here presents a striking doubling of Maud's hand, both of which return to trouble Sue as a symbol of the former's duplicity. The reappearance of the glove raises the spectre of Sue's own delusion and, at the same time, materializes the return of her half-repressed desire, conjuring Maud's physical body and acting as a potent reminder of their previous sexual encounters. The returned glove thus elicits a strong emotional response from Sue. Here, Waters clearly aligns the sense of touch with issues of interiority and emotion. Touching and feeling are brought together in this passage, emphasizing the mutual correlation that exists between sensorial and psychological feeling. Eve Kosofsky Sedgwick notes this close connection which she finds is bound up in the word 'touching': 'the same double meaning, tactile plus emotional, is already there in the single word "touching"; equally it's internal to the word "feeling"' (2003: 17). Indeed, it is only when Sue is holding Maud's glove – her body's double – that she experiences an affective sensation and feels herself to be truly 'funked' (401).

Margaret in *Affinity* is likewise affected by the unnervingly lifelike 'waxen hands of "Peter Quick"' (2000: 132). On seeing a sign for the newly formed British National Association of Spiritualists, Margaret is struck by the possibility that Selina has entered the same building before. Tracing what she imagines are Selina's past footsteps, Margaret enters the reading room to find the 'plaster casts, and waxen moulds, of faces and fingers, feet and arms' of spirits on display (129), but her attention is captured by 'the grossest thing of all. It was the mould of a hand, the hand of a man – a hand of wax, yet hardly a hand as the word has meaning, more some awful tumescence – five bloated fingers and a swollen, vein-ridged wrist, that glistened, where the gas-light caught it, as if moist' (2000: 130). Though made from wax, the mould which is supposedly taken from Selina's spirit control, Peter Quick, is monstrously authentic. Like Maud's glove in *Fingersmith*, the wax mould is an obvious analogue of the human hand and despite its separation from its owner, Margaret imagines it functioning metonymically when she later writes: 'I remembered the cabinet, and the yellow wax mould of Peter Quick's hand. ... I imagined I might turn and see the hand jerk, might see it pressed to the glass of the cabinet with one gross finger crooked and *beckoning* to me!' (154; original emphasis).[10] On 2 November 1874, Margaret again imagines Peter Quick's agentic wax hand as alive and overtly eroticized when she visits Selina's cell and sees a trace of wax on the floor. The physical residue of the wax leads her to envision Peter Quick's phallic fingers possessing Selina both spectrally and sexually: 'The swollen fingers of Peter Quick's fist – I saw them, I saw them! – were uncurling, and flexing. Now the hand was inching its way across the shelf ... Then it was Peter Quick and it embraced her' (188).

Though seemingly lifelike and autonomous, Margaret later realizes that the wax mould is not a hand. On closer inspection, she remarks that 'it seemed solid to me, last time I looked at it ... I have been used to thinking of it as a hand, and very solid; more properly, however, it is a kind of *glove*' (229; original emphasis). Attesting to the ability of gloves to retain the physical trace of a past wearer, the hollow interior of Peter Quick's waxen glove exhibits the uncanny traces and textures of visceral flesh and thus aligns itself to Quick's spectral, masculinized body. Although she cannot touch the waxen glove, Margaret writes of it in deeply haptic terms:

> I saw then how the wax ended, neatly, at the bone of the wrist. I saw how absolutely hollow it was. Inside it, marked out very clearly upon the yellowing surface of the wax, are the creases and whorls of a palm, the dents of knuckles ...
> It might have been cast there a moment before, and still be cooling from the closeness of the fingers that had dropped it. (2000: 229)

While the empty and autonomous glove is detached from Peter Quick's spirit body, it still signifies his malignant presence through its visible links with his corporeal self.

Of course, the visible traces of hyper-masculinity that remain both on and in the monstrous wax glove are evidence not of Peter Quick, but of Ruth Vigers

---

[10] In Freud's collection of uncanny things, 'a hand detached from the arm' is considered especially *unheimlich* when it is 'credited... with independent activity' ([1919] 2003: 150).

whose hand has provided the model for the waxen glove. Reading Vigers's depiction in *Affinity* as modelled on the 'nineteenth-century stereotype of the "mannish" lesbian', Alan Robinson argues that 'her manly vigour, resulting from her manual labour, is evident in the macabre cast of her hand' (2011: 143). Additionally, the permutation of Vigers's hand into the mould of Peter Quick's hints at the blurring of gender boundaries which Vigers has traversed during her cross-dressing role as the spirit control. Such masquerade functions as a type of erasure which encodes Vigers within the realms of Terry Castle's 'apparitional lesbian', that is, the 'phantasmagorical association between ghosts and lesbians' in literature since the eighteenth century (1993: 60).[11] Castle contends that 'to try to write the literary history of lesbianism is to confront, from the start, something ghostly: an impalpability, a misting over, an evaporation, or "whiting out" of possibility' (28). Although Waters's late-twentieth-century text is engaged in the weaving of the lesbian narrative back into history, it nevertheless appropriates the metaphor of an apparitional lesbian. Vigers – whom Selina compares to 'a ghost' (119) – has, as a result of her lower social standing and plainness, been overlooked by Margaret as a contender for Selina's affections. Tellingly, after Ruth and Selina have escaped at the end of the tale, stealing the clothes that Margaret has purchased for the latter, Margaret cannot even recall Vigers's features (340). If the physical trace of Vigers remains present and visible both on and in Peter Quick's waxen glove, then Margaret fails to see her own maid's physicality reflected in the cast. Margaret's 'un-seeing' and her inability to touch the glove which is encased in glass are precisely what erases Vigers's presence from the narrative and so she haunts the peripheries of the text as a type of ghostly visitor.

Equally disposed to bear the indentations, marks and traces of the hand are Maud's white kidskin gloves in *Fingersmith*. Though typically conceived of as a barrier between her body and her physical surroundings, the animal skin gloves function as permeable boundaries throughout the novel. Noting as much in her essay on deception and reading in the novel, Sarah Gamble states that the kidskin gloves that Maud wears are 'both pale and absorbent, and thus vulnerable to stains and splashes' which, she posits, 'showcase rather than disguise the corrupting substances with which they come into contact, such as ink, blood, and food' (2013: 48). Gamble's remark refers to the symbolic moment in *Fingersmith*, when, unable to eat at Mr Lilly's table without dropping her knife and fork, Maud's uncle removes her cutlery and she says, 'I must eat with my

---

[11] Many neo-Victorian critics have noted the influence of Castle's 'apparitional lesbian' in *Affinity*. See Llewellyn (2004).

fingers. The dishes he prefers being all bloody meats, and hearts, and calves' feet, my kid-skin gloves grow crimson – as if reverting to the substance they were made from' (196). The blood seeping into the kidskin is reminiscent of menstrual blood and Maud's maturation, even as it connotes a sense of regression and decline. By noting the Victorian propensity to have gloves made from goat and sheepskin in the period, Waters also draws further parallels between the glove and the physical body.

Stained gloves are also present in *Affinity* and *Tipping the Velvet*. When Margaret enters the Reading Room of the British National Association of Spiritualists in the former, the only other woman present is wearing 'soiled' white gloves (2000: 128). The repeated references to the woman's dirty gloves reiterate that the spiritualist reading rooms are no place for a respectable lady and augur the damaging consequences of Margaret's involvement with Selina Dawes. Likewise, in *Tipping the Velvet*, the traces of Diana Lethaby's past sexual conquests are discernible on her gloves. When Nan and Diana first meet, the former offers this account: Diana 'raised the fingers of her other hand – her left hand – to my cheek. The gloves, I thought, were rather damp about the tips; and they were scented with a scent that made me draw back in confusion and surprise. She laughed. "But how prim you have turned! You are never so dainty, I'm sure, with the gentlemen of Soho"' (1999: 236). Convinced that Diana has failed to see through her male attire, the 'damp' and 'scented' gloves divulge to Nan Diana's sexual orientation. And although this moment reveals Diana's true intentions, as in *Affinity* this gloved moment also foreshadows future trouble.

Of course, the porous nature of the kidskin glove allows for marks to be left not only on its surface but also within it, for fingers leave their traces in gloves. Gloves, above all items of clothing, retain the impression of our bodies when emptied of them, and absorb the 'oils and smells' of the hands (Stallybrass and Jones 2001: 120). In *Affinity*, the trace of Margaret's anxiety is left within her gloves as her hands sweat inside them (2000: 180), while in *Fingersmith*, although Maud is unable to leave her fingerprints on her uncle's pornography (Miller 2008: para. 1) her trace is nonetheless embedded within the gloves that she wears – one of which will become a keepsake for Sue. Indeed, once Maud and Gentleman's deception has been fully realized and Sue is locked in her cell at the asylum, she says: 'I lay with Maud's white glove in my fist, and now and then put the tip of one of its fingers to my mouth, imagining Maud's soft hand inside it; and I bit and bit' (2003: 420). The single glove which is given, or in this case taken, as a keepsake is inscribed with Maud's trace and thus re-embodies and re-members her. Taking her place in the bed beside Sue, the kidskin hide of the glove is metonymically transformed into Maud's hand as Sue bites down on it, exacting an imagined revenge on her lover's body. Invested with affective meaning, Maud's glove acts as a locus of memory. It dissolves the physical separation between her and Sue, thus synecdochally reanimating the erotic remnants of their past sexual encounters. Brokering a sense of material connection, the glove symbolizes Sue's barely contained queer desire and her desire for revenge, signalling the novel's conclusion.

According to Yannis Hamilakis, 'things are extensions of the human body: they can act as sensorial prostheses. This is not meant to devalue their power and agency but rather to foreground and highlight their ability to enable the body to expand its sensorial capabilities' (2013: 113). The glove, in this sense, is an agentive sensorial emissary that can connect and align parted lovers. In this instance, it exceeds the boundaries of the body; surpassing and supplanting Maud, the glove becomes her physical surrogate. But if gloves function in these instances as 'prosthetic extensions' (Foley 2015: 36) of their owners, enabling intensely sensual and phenomenological encounters between individuals who are spatially remote, then Nan in *Tipping the Velvet* engages the glove as a form of prosthesis in a more literal, embodied sense. At the point in her tale when she transforms herself from male impersonator into 'renter' (1999: 202), Nan pads her trousers with 'a glove, neatly folded, to simulate the bulges of a modest little cock' (195). Central to her ability to pass as male, the folded glove becomes a marker of her performance of masculinity. It makes a further appearance when she agrees to become Diana's kept lover and is presented with 'a flat wooden case' containing two pairs of 'gloves – one pair of kid, with covered buttons, the other of doe-skin and fragrant as musk' (305) which she wears beneath trousers that 'bulged at the buttons, where I had rolled one of the scented doe-skin gloves' (306). Thus the glove, employed as a more unstable symbol in this novel, wavers between representing the female body and facilitating a fantasy of sexual crossing. In its occupation as a more literal form of prosthesis in these moments, Waters further contests the Victorian perception of the glove as a feminine tool of social respectability and instead presents it as a marked challenge to gender essentialism and heteronormative conceptions of the body. In so doing, Waters deploys gloves strategically to signal her departure from the conventions of Victorian literary and sartorial history. In her rejection and re-fashioning of the glove, she rejects standard modes of being.

As this chapter has shown, in Waters's *Tipping the Velvet*, *Affinity* and *Fingersmith*, gloves function as potent sexual objects within the texts' diegetic worlds. As central and fetishized items of nineteenth-century clothing, gloves (re)appear in these three neo-Victorian texts and provide visible, perceptible vestiges of Victorian culture. Although gloves had been a central part of dress culture for centuries, in the nineteenth century they took on a specific gendered resonance. Picking up on and playing with this gendered specificity, Waters deploys Victorian gloves as powerful symbols of lesbian desire. In these three novels, gloves become queer tools with which to trouble social and sexual boundaries. As sites of encounter and physical correspondence, gloves function as 'private interior spaces' (Foley 2015: 36) that are imbued with the trace of past hands. In novels about touch, traces and interiority, gloves are suitable sartorial items with which to imagine and examine the growing desire between the female protagonists. In *Tipping the Velvet* gloves are potent sartorial ciphers; their presence precedes and follows moments of sexual encounter. In *Fingersmith* Maud's gloves are inscribed with her trace and when taken as a keepsake by Sue, invoke her presence, while also doubling as her body's surrogate. Likewise, in *Affinity*, the waxen glove of Peter Quick contains the physical trace of Ruth Vigers's hand and thus becomes a signifier of the secret lesbian romance that exists between the Priors' maid and Selina Dawes. Like the garments discussed in Chapter 1, gloves are endowed with a specifically haunting power and thus take on a life and agency of their own in neo-Victorianism. As a result, they repeatedly transgress both past and present and become agentic, metonymically conjuring the bodies of absent lovers. Ultimately, the spectral entity of the glove and its traces provides a means of deciphering the fingerprints of the past in the present. Representing another conduit between past and present, the Victorian veil is a deeply complex literary and sartorial symbol that is re-fashioned and resurrected in a number of neo-Victorian novels. Focusing on John Harwood's *The Ghost Writer* (2004) and Belinda Starling's *The Journal of Dora Damage* (2007), veils, both actual and figurative, are the central concern of the following chapter.

4

Veils

Veils and the practice of veiling have long cultural histories. Originating in Mesopotamia, and initially worn by elite women according to Assyrian sumptuary and patriarchal law (Ahmed 1992: 14), veils have since gathered about them multiple meanings. Historically, culturally and symbolically resonant, the veil is a mutable garment that has functioned variously throughout history: 'it has been in turn the badge of bondage, of modesty, of religious zeal; the symbol of position, of mourning, of marriage; and yet again it has held its place in the feminine wardrobe merely as a dictate of Dame Fashion' (Lester and Oerke 2004: 61). Operating far beyond its material use-value as a covering for the face and hair, the veil is richly emblematic and conceptually and culturally complex. Veils are mysterious, exotic and surprisingly erotic. At the same time, they connote modesty, reverence and virtue; in many Abrahamic and other religions the veil has been frequently imbued with an aura of piety and respect, yet it has also attracted derision and distrust.[1] In more secular terms, veils also encode a sense of the spectral: performing similar work to shrouds, veils imply the 'barrier between the living and the dead, this world and the afterlife' (Spooner 2016: 422).

It is within such intricately woven and contradictory contexts that veils in Victorian and neo-Victorian fiction operate. Veils proliferated in the literature and visual and material culture of the nineteenth century. Worn as everyday items of clothing and to mark religious rites of passage such as confirmation, marriage or for mourning, they assumed a 'uniquely feminine significance' in the period (Gilbert and Gubar [1979] 2000: 468). Associated with both domestic simplicity and spirituality, mundanity and oriental exoticism, Victorian veils represent rich narrative veins from which Victorian and neo-Victorian novelists alike have frequently mined. Disentangling the complex constellation of material meanings that surround the veil, this chapter opens by tracing its various renderings in

---

[1] In contemporary society, the Islamic veil, or *hijab*, retains its religious associations and is also seen as a politically divisive garment. See Almila and Inglis (2018).

Victorian literature and sartorial culture before elucidating the ways and ends to which contemporary novelists revive and recalibrate the veil motif in neo-Victorian fiction. In unravelling the veil's ideologically fraught status in the nineteenth century, the chapter identifies an apparent dislocation between the literary veil, a distinctly fictional invention that is drawn from and embedded within wider gothic and spiritualist narratives, and the garment itself, which was a familiar, ordinary and useful item of Victorian dress. In much Victorian fiction, the veil is divorced from its practical use-function in favour of enacting fantastical plots of disguise and deception, and it is such literary associations that neo-Victorian novelists self-consciously invoke. John Harwood's *The Ghost Writer* (2004) and Belinda Starling's *The Journal of Dora Damage* (2007) deploy veils and veil-like imagery in ways that call upon and convey many of the same impulses set forth by Victorian novelists in their imaginative depictions of veils. Yet rather than simply rehearsing nineteenth-century preoccupations with concealment and dissimulation, these contemporary authors are concerned with issues of revelation; they appropriate the garment's historical ambiguity, its symbolic and conceptual mutability, as a means of exposing the mechanics of rewriting, revealing and reimagining the nineteenth-century material past.

Victorian veils

An analysis of the uses, both functional and social, of Victorian veils reveals a striking disarticulation between literary veils and the actualities of women's dress in the period. Veils in Victorian sartorial culture were ordinary and ubiquitous articles of clothing. Attached to women's bonnets, hats or hair using a plethora of ribbons, strings, cords and pins, veils were primarily made of lace, tulle or gauze. Their primary function was practical. Veils protected the face, hair and headwear from the elements, while fulfilling a secondary and decorative role as a fashionable, though not compulsory, addition to the Victorian woman's ensemble. Remarking upon the 'oriental conceptions' of the veil, the Irish journalist Charlotte O'Conor Eccles explained in 1895, that far from mysterious and exotic, the Victorian veil functioned 'merely as a useful though not indispensable, article of dress, that disguises many an imperfection and sets off many a charm. Of its advantages in keeping hats straight and hair in order nothing need be said' ('Varieties in Veils' 1895: 547–8). Unlike gloves which were worn both indoors and outdoors, the veil was primarily worn outside of the home, enabling women to negotiate the public sphere. In practical terms, veils provided women with protection from inclement weather and the grime and dirt of a progressively industrialized landscape. Acknowledging the 'utilitarian function' of the veil, Amy L. Montz confirms that 'as its function is to shield the face from the sun and wind, the smells and smoke of London, New York and other major industrialised cities, the veil's importance rose in the late-nineteenth century to become a necessary article of clothing' (2011: 110–11).

The veil's growing sartorial significance finds reflection in conduct and ladies' literature of the period. In 1872, Florence Hartley recommended that her female readers wear 'a thick barege veil' when travelling, adding that 'an elastic string run through a tuck made in the middle of the veil, will allow one half to fall over the face, while the other half falls back, covering the bonnet, and protecting it from dust' (31).[2] The *Young Englishwoman*, a weekly magazine launched by the Beetons in 1864, dispensed the following advice to a lady requiring 'a receipt for a roughness over the face': 'Do not go out during cold winds without a thick veil' ('Our Drawing-Room' 1875: 239), and in 1879, *Sylvia's Home Journal* similarly instructed women to 'protect your face by a thin gauze veil' during the summer months ('Our Drawing-Room': 304). Though not governed by the same social strictures as gloves, veils were necessary for conferring a sense of social respectability on the wearer. One article of 1889 suggested, for instance, that 'many women would gladly dispense with veils, but are unable to do so on account of the way in which the hair blows about when unprotected by a bit of gauze or lace' ('Veils': 15). The veil thus facilitated the necessary outward show of tidiness and neatness in dress.

Beyond its important utilitarian purpose, the veil was decorative and the women who wore it were keen participators within the fashion economy. As with other garments in the period, its length, pattern, colour and style were therefore subject to the vagaries of fashion. Produced in varying shades including black, white, grey, beige, pink and green, veil styles vacillated between the long draperies of the 1830s and 1840s, the small 'mask-like' veils fashionable in the late-1850s and early 1860s ('Our Paris News-Letter' 1864: 103), the long loose veils worn from 1870 (Lester and Oerke 2004: 69) and 'large directoire veils' popular at the end of the century which covered the face and were gathered under the chin (Cunnington 1990: 360).[3] Aside from subtle alterations in fabric, texture and form, veils also experienced a number of reversals and revivals in

---

[2] Barege was a sheer fabric made of both silk and wool.
[3] Directoire style clothes refer to the fashions, inspired by neoclassical design, that were popularly worn in late eighteenth-century France.

the period; their uncertain trajectories reflected the arcs and parabolas typical of most other nineteenth-century fashion trends.

The presence, form and function of bridal veils, by contrast, remained relatively fixed and static during the period. Although they were an already established trend in the eighteenth and early nineteenth centuries, having emerged in England during the early modern period (Lester and Oerke 2004: 67), in the Victorian era bridal veils achieved increased and enduring popularity when nineteenth-century notions of ideal femininity, characterized by submission, chastity and devotion, permeated society. Mostly made of delicate white lace, signalling purity, Victorian wedding veils became useful visible signifiers for this ideologically dominant image of womanhood. Coventry Patmore's 1854–62 narrative poem *The Angel in the House* neatly illustrates the circumscribed domestic, emotional and spiritual roles Victorian wives were expected to occupy; roles which were in turn promoted and praised by prominent cultural commentators and authors of Victorian conduct literature such as John Ruskin and Sarah Stickney Ellis, respectively. In addition to these symbolically gendered connotations, nineteenth-century wedding veils were also politically inflected. After the 1840s, upper and middle-class women adopted Honiton lace veils rather than those made of Brussels point lace in an attempt to follow the fashion set by Queen Victoria. Cognizant of her royal influence, Queen Victoria wore the British manufactured lace when she married Prince Albert on 10 February 1840 in a conscious effort to support the waning lace industry in England (Goldthorpe 1989: 15). The prescribed wearing of a white veil during Victorian wedding ceremonies therefore reaffirmed the garment's ideological links with the passive, dutiful Angel in the House, while also playing into class-based hierarchies informed by systems of conspicuous consumption.

Another veil that persisted throughout the period, and which was likewise intimately bound up with issues of class and gender, was the black weeping veil worn by widows during deep mourning. Elaborate mourning customs, including the adoption of mourning dress and the relinquishing of social duties, were an essential part of the process of public grieving in the Victorian period, as various influential studies have shown (see Jalland 1996; Lutz 2015a). Commercialized mourning practices were informed by the rise of the Victorian cult of mourning and the expansion of commodity culture, both of which propagated the construction of mourning warehouses in Europe and America. Mourning warehouses, which capitalized on consumer culture and coincided with the rise of ready-to-wear fashion, appeared in the early part of the Victorian

Figure 4.1 Advertisement for Jay's General Mourning Warehouse in *The Graphic*, Mourning Dress, 1888 © Illustrated London News Ltd/Mary Evans Picture Library.

period. Jay's The London General Mourning Warehouse located on 247 and 249 Regent Street, was one of the first to be established in 1841; its novelty lay largely in its capacity to provide customers with a wide array of mourning paraphernalia. Outlining the benefits of Jay's, an 1843 article published in *The Court and Lady's Magazine* enthused: 'Here may be found every article requisite for Court, Family, and Complimentary Mourning. The double advantage is, that such mourning can there be obtained without trouble, at a moment's notice, and that the cost is much less than at other places' ('The History and Varieties of Mourning': 61). An advertisement for Jay's published in *The Graphic* in 1888 features an elegantly dressed widow wearing full mourning, complete with a weeping veil, black leather gloves, a black parasol and a handkerchief trimmed with crape (Figure 4.1).[4]

---

[4] The commercial success of Jay's prompted the creation of similar establishments: Maison Jay's was soon joined on Regent's Street by Pugh's Mourning Warehouse in 1849, Peter Robinson's Court and General Mourning House and the Argyll General Mourning and Mantle Warehouse (Adburgham

Addressing the subject of widows' mourning wear in the nineteenth century, one contemporary commentator argued that it functioned as the 'materialisation of the poetry of sorrow' (Mariott Watson 1890: 91). The external sign of grief-stricken interiority, women's mourning dress was the symbol of 'viduity, the ocular proof (as it were) that *Her* heart in *His* grave is lying' (Mariott Watson: 91; original emphases). Evoking the expressive, affective and poetic significance of widow's mourning, this example underscores the role of women in the performance of grief: widows were expected to bear the main responsibility for mourning in the period and were subject to the strictest social and sartorial rules. Rebecca Mitchell explains that 'the widow's clothing and demeanour were expected to mirror the role of the dutiful wife she had played before the death of her husband' (2013: 599), and as a result women closely adhered to ever-more complex systems of sartorial and social behaviour in fear of inciting societal censure.

In the first part of the period, women wore mourning for two and a half years, but from around 1870 the duration of mourning decreased to two years or less. As *The Young Englishwoman* assured its readers in 1875: 'Mourning used to be worn much longer than it is now' ('Letters on Politeness and Etiquette': 294). Codified into three distinct sartorial modes, women's mourning dress consisted of deep or full mourning, ordinary mourning and half-mourning. *Myra's Journal* sets out the complexities of each consecutive stage in an 1875 article on the 'The Etiquette of Mourning':

> First six months, paramatta dress, covered with crape from four to six inches below the waist; bodice entirely covered with crape; plain muslin collar and cuffs. The cuffs worn outside the dress. Mantle of widow's silk, trimmed with deep folds of crape or cashmere; shawl edged with crape folds; plain jet brooch, studs, and chain. Bonnet of crape, with deep crape veil; widows cap. Black kid gloves; petticoat of black material quilted silk, alpaca, or cashmere; no shining material, or glossy fabric is admissible for a widow ... After six months, widow's silk is usually worn; this silk is expressly manufactured for the purpose, matching the shade of crape with much exactness ... During the last twelve months the mourning is gradually lightened; black lace and cut jet ornaments can be worn; linen replaces the muslin parures, and in warm weather, half-lined dresses can be worn by young widows with propriety. (1875: 3)

The asyndetic litany of garments, textures and materials mirrors the complicated and ritualistic system of dressing required of women during the period of

1989: 67). Elsewhere in England, Frederick Forster's Mourning Warehouse was established in Leeds in 1849, while Hannington's Mourning Warehouse flourished in Hove.

mourning. In the first stage, deep black and heavily textured materials, such as paramatta cloth, enshrine emotions of grief and sorrow.[5] As mourning progressed, the material and textural lessening of such fabrics mirrored the introduction of half-mourning colours like violet, white and grey. Such sartorial shifts toward lighter fabrics and colours supposedly coincided with the successive phases of grief (Jalland 1996: 302).

During the deepest phase of mourning, widows wore two kinds of veils. Inside the home they adopted 'white crape indoor caps, with falls that fell down their backs' and 'outside they wore black, crape trimmed bonnets, with long crape veils' (Taylor [1983] 2009: 103).[6] The black crape weeping veil signified a 'funeral pall' and was worn by widows to distinguish themselves from those who chose to wear black for formal wear in the period (Hollander 1993: 382). As perhaps the most visible apparatus of mourning, it represented a readable marker of loss and sorrow, and at the same time functioned as an outward indication of respect. Its material presence conveyed a striking sense of absence that gestured toward the decedent, and which also encompassed the wearer's own liminal position. Secluded within its folds, the widow was prohibited from fully entering or enjoying the public and social spheres, while the literal and metaphorical barrier represented by the veil similarly precluded her participation within the marriage market (Taylor 2009: 33). Since it was worn in public, the weeping veil, as the name suggests, afforded grieving women a degree of privacy from inquisitive stares. Its capacity to act as a protective mask enabled women to negotiate the public sphere during mourning, yet the concealing function of the widow's veil is also beset in some fictional accounts by the implication that what it masks is not real feeling or emotion but rather deception. A short humorous poem called 'Widows' Veils' published in *The Mirror* in 1839 playfully acknowledges the duplicitous potential of the veil, asking 'Why does a veil of deepest dye, / Form part of widow's gear? / Its folds can hide a tearful eye / – Or eye that wants a tear!' (426). Similar anxieties around veils, reality and artifice surface in the fiction of the period, especially in the sensation novel and its literary antecedents.

Veils in the Victorian literary imagination are peculiarly melodramatic narrative devices. Reflecting their material function of concealment, veils represent apposite tools with which to manipulate nineteenth-century textual

---

[5] Parramatta was a heavy fabric regularly worn during mourning in the nineteenth century. It was formed of a combination of silk or cotton and worsted.
[6] Crape, a stiff, unreflective silk gauze, was used for mourning veils and as trimmings for mourning dress during the Victorian period. It was popularized by the manufacturing company, Courtaulds (see Taylor 2009).

bodies and to deflect and divert the gaze of both intra- and extra-textual sartorial readers. Invested with powers of disguise and deception, literary veils beguile, confuse and obscure. In gothic and sensation fictions, the veil masks the secrets, sin and shame of the wearer (Gilbert and Gubar 2000: 469). As receptacles for hidden truths and past transgressions, veils arouse suspicion, fear and awe. They litter the narratives of many Victorian novels, often disclosing more to the reader than to the protagonists to whom they belong. Jane Eyre's bridal veil, around which such issues crystallize, is one of the most recognizable veils in Victorian fiction. In Charlotte Brontë's *Jane Eyre* (1847) the eponymous heroine wakes several nights before her wedding day to find 'a woman, tall and large', wearing a white dress that might be a 'gown, sheet, or shroud' in her bedroom (2006: 326). What follows is an evocative interlude in which the spectre, who is Mr Rochester's estranged wife, the 'mad' Bertha Mason, adorns herself in Jane's bridal veil before rending it in two. Recounting the scene to Rochester, Jane later explains how:

> 'she took my veil from its place: she held it up, gazed at it long, and then she threw it over her own head, and turned to the mirror. At that moment I saw the reflection of the visage and features quite distinctly in the dark oblong glass.'
>
> 'And how were they?'
>
> 'Fearful and ghastly to me – oh sir, I never saw a face like it! It was a discoloured face – it was a savage face. I wish I could forget the roll of the red eyes and the fearful blackened inflation of the lineaments! ...
>
> 'Ah! – what did it do?'
>
> 'Sir, it removed my veil from its gaunt head, rent it in two parts, and flinging both on the floor, trampled on them'. (2006: 326–7)

Brontë's deployment of the 'vapoury' and 'wraith-like' veil works along several interwoven narrative lines (317). As Catherine Spooner points out, although it is 'accorded spectral properties', the veil is 'a definitively material object, purchased in London by Rochester at lavish expense, and as such explicitly politicised by Jane, who is uneasy with the conspicuous consumption it represents' (2004: 46). Reading into the novel's gothic overtones, she posits that the veil's destruction by Bertha 'reveals the existence of a secret' (46). Deeply saturated with material meaning and symbolic connotation, the white bridal veil suggests Jane's innocence but also implicitly signals Rochester's attempted bigamy, rendering clear his deception and revealing the shadowy presence of his first wife. In the above exchange, the presence of the torn veil also figuratively presages the unfortunate fate of Jane and Rochester's forthcoming nuptials. Far from symbolizing Jane's metamorphosis from governess to bride, the intricately woven lace veil signifies only Rochester's web of lies.

Long after the veil is disposed of and Jane reverts to 'the square of unembroidered blond' (323), its torn remnants continue to signify: they eloquently bespeak Bertha's textual and literal marginalization, while simultaneously stitching together the stories of the two women. If Bertha's encounter with the veil tacitly reveals the truth about her own marriage to Rochester, then it also establishes parallels between herself and Jane, who recognizes in the shrouded figure 'her own enraged double' (Gilbert and Gubar 2000: 472). This uncanny doubling is heightened when Bertha, adorned in the veil, gazes at herself in the 'dark oblong' mirror – a gesture that Jane will repeat on the day of her own wedding, when she recounts the following: 'I saw a robed and veiled figure, so unlike my usual self that it seemed almost the image of a stranger' (2006: 331). On each of these occasions, veils disrupt the distinction between self and other. While Jane sees Bertha's face 'quite distinctly' through the veil, the layers of blond will later blur her own features, forcing a reconsideration of her sense of self. In her evocative use of veils, Brontë thus engenders a notable concern with what is seen and known and what remains hidden.[7]

The capacity of literary veils to gesture towards hidden things or, conversely, to hide and conceal, intensifies in the sensation fiction of the 1860s which, as many critics have pointed out, *Jane Eyre* seemingly anticipates. Emerging with the publication of Wilkie Collins's *The Woman in White* (1860), sensation fictions feature convoluted plots, sartorial disguises, criminals, dark family secrets and startling unveilings or revelations. In *The Woman in White*, the novel upon which Waters's *Fingersmith* is partly based, white veils play a key role in the narrative, enabling Anne Catherick and Laura Fairlie to effectively switch places and identities. Similarly, in Ellen Wood's sensation novel *East Lynne* (1861), the text's somewhat improbable plot depends upon the capacity of a veil to disguise its wearer and deceive the family she has deserted. Disfigured after a train accident that has killed her illegitimate child, the disgraced Isabel Vane returns to her ex-marital home disguised as a nanny to care for the children whom she has deserted. The veil shields the scars sustained in the accident, and doubles as a disguise, concealing her identity from the prying eyes of her husband and his new wife. Similarly, in Collins's *Armadale* (1864–6), the intricate plot centres

---

[7] This fascination with veils and occlusion is evident in Brontë's later published *Villette* (1853), in which Lucy Snowe is apparently haunted by the ghost of a heavily veiled Roman Catholic nun.

upon the threat posed by a 'neatly dressed woman, wearing a gown and bonnet of black silk' and a 'thick black veil that hung over her face' (1995: 70). Disguise, deception and dissimulation are likewise among the key motivators behind Lady Dedlock's veiled appearances in Charles Dickens's *Bleak House* (1853), while a similarly veiled woman is the focal point of his earlier published short story, 'The Black Veil' (1836), in which a mysterious woman shrouds herself in mourning to conceal her 'shame, and incurable insanity' precipitated by the execution of her son for criminal activity (2000: 11).

The emphasis upon the mutable nature of veils in these literary texts draws upon the semantic associations of the garment and its linguistic links with the otherworld. As Jen Cadwallader explains, 'By the Victorian period, particularly after the publication of Tennyson's *In Memoriam, A. H. H.*, the expressions "beyond the veil" and its variant "behind the curtain"' referred to the 'figurative barrier separating this life from the afterlife' (2011: 120). She also points out how spiritualist literature is replete with '"thinning" and "lifted" veils and curtains' (120). The title of George Eliot's 1859 novella *The Lifted Veil* employs the veil image as just such a metaphor for the division between life and death, while *The Veil Lifted: Modern Developments of Spirit Photography*, a book of essays on psychical photography edited by Andrew Glendinning and published in 1894, assumes a similar titular resonance. Beyond the immediate context of nineteenth-century spiritualism, however, the veil in Victorian fiction also apparently models itself upon the eighteenth-century gothic tradition in which fictional veils functioned as both a boundary and a disguise (Broadwell 1975: 84); were deeply 'suffused with sexuality' (Kosofsky Sedgwick 1981: 256); and worked to indicate the moral parameters within which women's fashions in Europe were being redefined (Spooner 2004: 28). Drawing upon and extending these polyvalent images of the veil, Victorian fictions, whether gothic, spiritualist, realist or sensation, tend to highlight the potential of veils and other screening garments to conceal and disguise. Similar tensions materialize in neo-Victorian fictions which self-consciously invoke and adapt the numerous associations of the veil, both practical and symbolic, in their contemporary returns to the past.

Neo-Victorian veils

Emerging from and intimately entwined with such richly symbolic narrative histories, veils, both actual and metaphoric, figure prominently in neo-Victorian fictions. Although, as discussed above, they primarily signify 'hiddenness' in Victorian literature, and therefore proffer 'an irresistible image for an age of uncertainty about the relationship between appearances and reality' (Mills 2007: 105), veils in neo-Victorian fiction tend to expose and illuminate. As icons of revelation, neo-Victorian veils suggestively parallel the genre's own revelatory impulses, as well as its drives to (re)interpret, (re)discover and (re)vise, to paraphrase Heilmann and Llewellyn (2010: 4). In the contemporary texts at play within this chapter, veils are thus apt metaphors with which to think through the sometimes-knotty process of unveiling the past in neo-Victorianism.

A hermeneutic impulse to uncover and reveal is evident in the two neo-Victorian novels to which I will now turn. Published three years apart, Harwood's *The Ghost Writer* and Starling's *The Journal of Dora Damage* are each animated by a distinct desire to unveil the past. John Harwood's *The Ghost Writer* documents Gerard Freeman's present-day search for the truth about his familial history, a search that signifies wider neo-Victorian fixations with issues of revelation and return. Belinda Starling's *The Journal of Dora Damage*, by contrast, is ostensibly concerned with concealing bodies and books, but Victorian veils feature prominently in the text as paradoxical points of revelation. Crucial to each of the tales is a focus on visuality and materiality: art, artists and creative productions abound in the two works, as do bindings, canvases, veils and other material surfaces that are open to inscription, fabrication and manipulation. In Starling's text, the titular Dora Damage creatively fashions bindings for illicit texts from personal material and sartorial items; in so doing, she erodes the distinction between subject and object, drawing suggestive parallels between the veiling or covering of both bodies and books. In contrast, the women in Harwood's novel are often depicted in ekphrastic terms; their dress choices and sartorial self-fashioning label them as living, breathing works of art, perhaps pointing to the constructed, or artificial, nature of neo-Victorianism. That the artworks they emulate are recognizably Victorian further speaks to the neo-Victorian drive to pastiche and appropriate past visual, material and literary forms.

The *objets d'art* that litter each of these novels enhance their metafictional workings. Visible in the construction of the narratives is a notable sense of meta-ness, often considered a central element of neo-Victorianism. Starling and Harwood self-consciously adopt neo-Victorian metafictional, metahistorical and metacritical strategies. Each text is engaged in an intricate system of display and revelation whereby it consistently and repeatedly draws attention, albeit in slightly different ways, to its fabrication. *The Ghost Writer* foregrounds allusive tendencies in its efforts at highlighting the complex literary and cultural intertexts within which it operates. Starling's novel, equally constructed with reference to a wide network of literary texts, also displays a certain 'intertextual exuberance' (Kohlke 2008a: 200). Both are strongly inflected with tropes drawn from sensation and gothic fictions, but *The Ghost Writer* subverts readerly expectations via its narrative formation, while *The Journal of Dora Damage* self-consciously plays with Victorian (and neo-Victorian) conventions to rewrite issues of female agency and autonomy. As in the texts discussed in Chapter 2, both novels also draw attention to issues of historical accuracy and authenticity by making use of, and manipulating, the textual record: Dora's first-person journal is bookended by the addition of her daughter Lucinda's letter, which serves to validate her tale, while *The Ghost Writer*'s main story arc is set against the backdrop of several interwoven (fictional) Victorian ghost stories.

Recent critical attention on *The Ghost Writer* and *The Journal of Dora Damage* has focused on issues as wide-ranging as trauma and transgenerational haunting, and gender, feminism and pornography, respectively.[8] Ann Heilmann and Mark Llewellyn examine Harwood's and Starling's texts separately in *Neo-Victorianism: The Victorians in the Twenty-First Century, 1999–2009*, but suggest that, in different ways, the novels both carefully negotiate certain aspects of the present. They read Harwood's text in the light of mourning, cultural memory and inheritance; focusing upon the uncanny aspects of the tale, they suggest that Gerard's search for historical origins 'draws our attention to the conflicted nature of our engagement with our own literary and cultural histories' (2010: 64). Starling's novel, discussed in a later chapter, is one among several other neo-Victorian novels that 'problematize[s] nineteenth-century – and, by inference, contemporary – sexual, textual, and scientific inscriptions of the gendered, classed and raced body' (110). Drawing both novels together in her enlightening comparative analysis, Rosario Arias moves beyond these concerns to instead interrogate the overlaps and intersections between dysfunctional family dynamics, disability and affect (2011). This chapter aims to contribute to these rich and varied discussions by addressing the overlooked role and function of dress, fabric and textiles in each of these novels. More specifically, I examine the interplay of veils, both actual and metaphoric, along with veil-like imagery, such as canvases, bindings and skin, in the respective narratives. In doing so, I follow literary theorists such as Michel Serres ([1985] 2008) and Hélène Cixous and Jacques Derrida (2001), all of whom have drawn in various ways on the ideological complexities of the veil and its connection with barriers, canvases, curtains and skin.

---

[8] See Gruss (2014), Muller (2012) and Petković (2015).

Veils in *The Ghost Writer* and *The Journal of Dora Damage* intersect in interesting ways and prove crucial to the structural and thematic plotting of the respective storylines. As reminders and remainders of the nineteenth-century past, these sartorial items take on curiously vital trajectories and signify in ways that work with and against the novels' central narratives. They are as much sartorial articles worn and used by the protagonists as they are strategies or symbols of narrative reconstruction. In the analyses that follow, veils function as significant visual, material and textual nodes that signify the complex narrative plotting of each novel. They sartorially double the shifts and arcs of the neo-Victorian narratives, subtly anticipating and echoing the flourishes and embellishments of each tale. In John Harwood's *The Ghost Writer* veils recur as metonymies for the main protagonist's attempts at revealing familial mysteries. Within their semi-opaque folds, they appear to hold in tension the im/possibility of attaining historical 'truth': the transparency of veils promises revelation, yet their blank opacity frustrates and disrupts processes of seeing and knowing. The opacity of veils and other similarly blank spaces within the novel, such as canvases and letters, also foreground themes of self-delusion, distraction and beguilement, all of which disturb this neo-Victorian return to the past. Belinda Starling's novel likewise deploys the veil motif as a comment on the role of neo-Victorianism in recovering and reimagining the past. In particular, *The Journal of Dora Damage* examines the gendered dimensions of the veil motif. It calls into question the transformative power of the Victorian veil to conceal and disguise and adopts a veil-like structure in its quasi-concealment of the Indian woman whose story remains untold at the centre of its narrative. These veiling strategies are employed by Starling to question the nature of neo-Victorianism and its ostensibly progressive drivers. Both novels thus employ the veil as a comment on the role of neo-Victorianism in recovering and reimagining the material vestiges of the lost Victorian age.

Veils and canvases in *The Ghost Writer*: Revealing the past

John Harwood's *The Ghost Writer* delineates the tale of Gerard Freeman, a young man living in late-twentieth-century Australia who sets out to unveil the secrets and mysteries of his mother's traumatic past in England. In the opening pages of the novel, the reader learns that Gerard's mother, Phyllis, is concealing a secret from her son whose suspicions about her obscure past are initially aroused both by her silence and by the scarcity of material items that promise to reveal her history. 'We had photographs of my father's parents, of his sister and her husband and children,' Gerard realizes uneasily, 'but of my mother nothing before her wedding day, and very little after' (2005: 12). The only clue to her past that Phyllis discloses to her son is the story that she tells him of her childhood in the British countryside: she claims that as a young girl she lived with her grandmother Viola Hatherley in an idyllic house called Staplefield which, it later transpires, is a fiction that Gerard's mother has borrowed from the Victorian ghost stories written by Viola. In actuality, the house that Phyllis grew up in and which is Gerard's familial inheritance, is a Gothicized version of Staplefield called Ferrier's Close. At the novel's climax, Gerard is lured to Ferrier's Close in Hampstead by his mad aunt, Anne Hatherley, who unveils her existence and reveals the truth behind the murderous grudge she bears toward her sister Phyllis, and by extension, Gerard.

Divided into three parts, *The Ghost Writer* weaves together multiple stories. Gerard's contemporary autodiegetic narration is interpolated with the letters that he writes to and receives from his mysterious UK pen pal, Alice Jessell, who is in fact his aunt Anne, and the four short ghost stories written by his great-grandmother Viola Hatherley in the 1890s. The Victorian ghost stories – 'Seraphina', 'The Gift of Flight', 'The Revenant' and 'The Pavilion' – are linked to one another and the central narrative through the recurring motifs of Victorian veils and canvases. They each elide the distinction between history and fiction and blur the boundaries between reality and imagination. Gerard's attempts at decoding these stories thus work in parallel with the aims of the neo-Victorian reader, who simultaneously grapples with such textual fragments. Playing upon the traditions of the gothic, Viola's Victorian ghost stories intersect with Gerard's own narrative when he discovers them at various melodramatic moments in the novel; through his textual encounters with his great-grandmother's tales, Gerard is brought into contact with, and haunted by, the Victorian past which pervades his present moment. Not only do the stories haunt Gerard but they also appear to encroach on his mother's and her sister's own realities too: acknowledging the premonitory quality of her grandmother's tales, for example, Phyllis cryptically reveals on her deathbed that 'one came true' (122). It is this puzzling assertion and Gerard's discovery of a black and white photograph and the first of Viola's nineteenth-century stories hidden in a drawer that compels his decades-long search for the truth.

Gerard's desire to unveil the secrets and mysteries of his family's hidden past is emblematized by the deployment of veils and veil-like garments in the novel which reflect both the text's and wider neo-Victorian genre's desire to bring to light secret pasts and hidden histories. Veils, both actual and metaphoric, proliferate in *The Ghost Writer*. While critics have referred to the novel's intricate intertextual construction as that of a 'web' (Duncker 2014: 269; Gruss 2014: 131; Heilmann and Llewellyn 2010: 55), it might also be likened to a veil. In its interconnection with and emulation of a number of nineteenth-century texts, the novel veils itself, and self-reflexively masquerades as Victorian.[9] Part of the pleasure of reading *The Ghost Writer*, then, lies in the process of seeing through or stripping back its intertextual layers. On a diegetic level, Gerard's own narrative is similarly enfolded within an interwoven fabric of stories, secrets, lies and letters, a veil of fiction through which he must penetrate in order to discern the truth about his mother's past. Before he can do so, however, Gerard must first negotiate his mother's fear which envelops him. In the early part of the novel Phyllis Hatherley's terror of the outside world keeps Gerard veiled 'in a kind of hermetic sphere, socially and culturally obscured' (Llewellyn 2010: 36). Her attempts to conceal the past from her son shield him from the truth, but also paradoxically expose him to danger: as a consequence of his solitary upbringing, Gerard is easily manipulated by Anne Hatherley's sadistic machinations. But while Phyllis's fear simultaneously shrouds Gerard and leaves him thus exposed, it also notably leads to her own concealment in Australia. Referring to her self-marginalization in terms that conjure the veil's contradictory and liminal position, Rosario Arias aptly terms Phyllis 'an in-between character', situated 'between life and death, past and present' (2011: 348). The unspoken terror that torments Phyllis into concealing her existence from her sister and shrouding herself from the world is similarly equated with a kind of veil by Gerard when he remarks: 'I knew that the anxious, haunted look could descend' upon her face at any moment (2005: 5).

The metaphorical veiling of Gerard's mother is echoed by another veiled character in the text. Supposedly confined to a wheelchair following a car crash that proved fatal to both of her parents, Gerard's 'invisible friend Alice Jessell' (2005: 15) corresponds with him via letter from England, and the two strike up a virtual friendship which quickly develops into love and a long-distance 'sexual' relationship through a technique that Alice claims to have taught herself, called 'directed dreaming' (58). Although her presence in the text is materialized through the letters and emails that she writes, Alice remains persistently veiled throughout the narrative: she refuses to send Gerard a photograph of herself, to

---

[9] Heilmann and Llewellyn note the influence of Vernon Lee's fiction and the Jamesian ghost story on Harwood's tale (2010: 37, 254).

talk to him on the telephone or to meet him in person when he travels to London. Her invisibility intensifies when Gerard realizes at the conclusion of the novel that Alice Jessell is a fictional creation of his vengeful aunt, Anne Hatherley. At the text's conclusion, it is revealed that Gerard's correspondent has masqueraded as several different women throughout the course of the novel, thus invoking the metaphor of the veil as a disguise.

As part of this disguise, Alice/Anne provides Gerard with a metaphorically veiled description of her appearance in the early stages of the pair's correspondence. Evidently appropriated from Pre-Raphaelite portraiture and Viola Hatherley's short story 'Seraphina', Alice's portrayal centres on her hair, which she tells Gerard 'was long, and curly (she called it frizzy), and thick, and "a sort of reddy-chestnut-brown colour"', her 'very pale skin, dark brown eyes' and her long dress, 'which is white and musliny and gathered at the waist, with small purple flowers embroidered over the bodice' (27). Gerard connects Alice's red hair, pale skin and white dress with John William Waterhouse's 1888 painting *The Lady of Shalott* (28), but as Heilmann and Llewellyn rightly point out, despite Alice's depiction as the lady at the mirror, it is in fact 'Gerard who is condemned to leading the lady's mirror existence, as he progressively isolates himself in order to spend all his time on weaving his inner life and longings into the tapestry of his letters' (2010: 56–7). Nevertheless, Alice doubles as a resurrected Pre-Raphaelite muse in this scene. Her ekphrastic and sartorial self-construction anchors her to the artistic movement while firmly encoding her within nineteenth-century discourses that recall the beautiful, delicate and ill-fated female muse. Alice's deliberately anachronistic depiction of her clothes – the embroidered bodice and white gathered muslin gown – also strongly evokes Victorian dress.

White muslin, as Madeleine C. Seys writes, 'was fashionable throughout the nineteenth century, and the woman in white muslin became a ubiquitous figure in Victorian popular culture and literature' (2018: 31). Enumerating its manifold implications in the period, she posits that white muslin 'evokes ethereality, innocence, youthfulness, purity and virginity, and blankness, death and ghostliness' (Seys 2018: 31). Alice/Anne, in her adoption of a white muslin gown, self-consciously plays with, subverts and eschews these symbolic meanings. Employing the white gown as a receptacle onto which she projects various symbolic significances, Anne masquerades as the youthful and innocent Alice, while simultaneously facilitating her self-fashioning as an uncanny spectre in a foreshadowing of her veiled and revenant-like return at the novel's climax. The white Victorian-era gown, echoing its complex connotations, is therefore deployed to disorient and deceive. Of course, white muslin is an apt fabric with which to engineer such deception: its ostensible 'association with virginity, purity and honesty' ultimately 'renders it an ideal disguise' in Victorian literature (Seys 2018: 168), and for Alice it is therefore an appropriate garment with which to figuratively veil herself.

Made of lightly woven cotton, muslin's diaphanousness and transparency renders the contours of Alice's body enticingly visible in Gerard's imagination. At the same time, however, its blank ambiguity enshrouds and conceals her. Reflecting upon Alice's self-professed image, Gerard acknowledges 'the impossibility of capturing an individual face in words alone', admitting that 'my imagination of her remained both painfully vivid and tantalisingly blurred' (27). Gerard's words signal both the difficulty of navigating a nineteenth-century sartorial disguise replete with so many dynamic material meanings, and at the same time, they offer a metafictional approximation of the neo-Victorian novel and its capacity to accurately render the nineteenth-century visual and material past. The impossibility of capturing an 'authentic' historical period in detail is here aligned with the incomprehensibility of the white muslin gown which acts as a kind of veil, evoking the plot's underlying themes of exposure and erasure.

That Alice Jessell's image also uncannily imitates nineteenth-century art becomes patent when Gerard later reads Viola's short story 'Seraphina: A Tale' and draws parallels between the eponymous woman in the painting and his pen friend's self-portrayal: 'Seraphina's resemblance to Alice', he admits, 'was disturbing' (2005: 53). Published in *The Chameleon: A Review of Arts and Letters* in June 1898, Viola's short story revolves around Lord Edmund Napier, an aesthete and collector of beautiful women, both actual and represented in art and statuary. In the early pages of the tale, a young Napier deserts his pregnant and penniless mistress who dies by suicide when she falls from Battersea Bridge. Many years later, after her 'face, overlaid by so many others, fade[s] from his memory' (35), Napier is captivated by a woman he sees in the street whose face is concealed behind 'an extraordinary cloud of auburn hair which seemed to swirl and float about her as she moved' (37). Like a veil, the unknown woman's hair disrupts Napier's line of sight – 'he could see nothing of her face' (37) – and simultaneously shields her own – 'such was the abundance of the auburn cloud that he could not tell where her attention was directed' (37). The erotic allure of the unknown woman's veil-like hair captures Napier's interest despite, or perhaps because of, his inability to see her face and he follows her through labyrinthine London streets until she disappears at the entrance of a mysterious shop.[10] Inside, he finds and purchases a painting of a beautiful, naked red-haired woman, named Seraphina, whom he imagines to be the double of the mysterious woman he has followed.

In the remainder of the tale, the canvas becomes a metonym for the woman's naked body; Napier lavishes his attention upon it and, after he has taken her home, sensually unwraps Seraphina, calling 'for a length of the finest velvet' to 'drape her as a reverently and securely as he might' (46). In this sweep of velvet cloth, the short story demonstrates an intertextu(r)al intimacy with Oscar Wilde's Decadent novel *The Picture of Dorian Gray* (1891). Gray, whose aesthetic sensibilities extend to his collection of luxurious, antique textiles, veils the portrait to which he is fatefully connected with 'a large purple satin coverlet heavily embroidered with gold, a splendid piece of late seventeenth-century Venetian work' (2008: 115). Whereas Napier jealously veils Seraphina from the view of others, Dorian's aim is to 'wrap the dreadful thing' and thereby conceal his own grotesque image. The rich fabric, with its funereal connotations, offers a suitable medium with which to veil this portrait, for as Dorian muses, it 'had perhaps served often as a pall for the dead. Now it was to hide something that had a corruption of its own, worse than the corruption of death itself – something that would breed horrors and yet would never die' (115). The preternatural power that imbues Dorian's own image is matched by that of 'Seraphina', and just as Dorian meets his untimely demise through the work of art, eventually Napier dies after being driven mad by the canvas's beauty. Believing that he is about to enter the portrait to sexually possess the woman in the painting, he falls from Battersea Bridge in a hallucinatory trance and is discovered drowned the following morning in an episode that strangely mirrors the earlier fate of his discarded mistress. In this way, as Susanne Gruss contends, all of Viola's stories 'eerily foresee the fate Anne (as "Alice Jessell") has envisioned for Gerard, whom she intends to drive mad and kill' (2014: 131). 'Seraphina' invokes a further and final plot twist, however, which renders its ties with Gerard's own narrative explicit: at the conclusion of the short story, the narrator reveals that the painting is an illusion just as the chimerical Alice will turn out to be. Instead of the red-haired woman, the portrait depicts what might be 'clouds' or 'dense fog', with only the ghostly 'impression of a woman's features' on the upper half of the canvas (2005: 52). The erasure of the beautiful woman's image transforms the canvas into a seemingly blank space onto which Napier has projected his fantasies. In turn, Gerard's letters, and the letters that he receives from Alice,

---

[10] See Hollander for a discussion of hair as drapery in Pre-Raphaelite portraiture (1993: 72–3).

will also be rendered metaphorically blank spaces that similarly harbour his delusional desires.

A number of actual veils intersect with *The Ghost Writer*'s reliance on themes of detection and revelation. A black weeping veil features prominently in Viola Hatherley's 'The Revenant', which is the story published in 1925 that Arias asserts most 'uncannily replicates Gerard's familial narrative' (2011: 347). It depicts the strained relationship between two orphan sisters, Cordelia and Beatrice de Vere, who live with their aunt and uncle in Ashbourn House (another ghostly reiteration of Staplefield) following the death of their father. The tale begins with Cordelia's assertion that the house is allegedly haunted 'by the apparition of a veiled woman in black: the ghost of her own grandmother, Imogen de Vere' (130). Just as the fictional Alice Jessell is veiled from view in Gerard's narrative, Imogen de Vere is perpetually, and literally, veiled in 'The Revenant'; unable to fully recall her grandmother, 'who had died just before her fifth birthday', Cordelia remembers only 'a silent, veiled figure, sitting by the fireside or moving about the garden' (131). The only 'surviving likeness of Imogen de Vere' is a portrait hung on the second-floor landing of the house, which 'showed a woman of great beauty, apparently in her early twenties' wearing 'an emerald green gown, cut high at the neck; her heavy, copper-coloured hair was loosely pinned up, with a few escaped strands curling across her forehead' (133). This canvas harbours a similar hypnotic quality to the portrait of Seraphina in Viola's previous ghost story, and in the remainder of the tale it is the pivot around which Cordelia's growing psychological obsession with her grandmother grows.

In later portions of the text, Cordelia's preoccupation extends beyond the portrait to encompass her grandmother's black veil which is ostensibly worn to protect her skin from the sun, but which contains and sustains a much darker secret. Like the mysterious woman in Dickens's 'The Black Veil', Imogen de Vere wears a black weeping veil to mask a troubling and traumatic past: following her purported affair with an artist named Henry St Clair – whose collection of mysteriously melancholic paintings Cordelia later inherits – Imogen begins to suffer from a painful and undiagnosed skin complaint that she believes her husband has inflicted upon her as punishment for her transgression. Seeking a double refuge both behind the black veil and inside Ashbourn House, Imogen de Vere is thus transformed into a spectral figure both during and after her lifetime. What becomes apparent as the story progresses, however, is that the haunting presence in Ashbourn House is not Imogen's ghost, but rather her black veil which Cordelia first unearths as a child: 'In the bottom drawer of a clothes-press, she [Cordelia] came upon Grandmamma's black veil, neatly laid out all by itself. She lifted it out and pressed the cool material against her face, breathing in camphor, and some other medicinal smell, and a very faint fragrance of perfume' (2005: 131–2). Metaphor renders this quotation redolent of death, remembrance and discovery. The suggestive use of the phrase 'laid out all by itself' recalls the language of burial and refers explicitly to the 'laying out' of the body after death, which in turn imaginatively invokes the death and interment of Imogen de Vere. In an apparent reversal of this burial trope, however, Cordelia's rediscovery of the black veil, which assumes the characteristics of a shroud, doubles as a scene of exhumation. The disinterment of the veil is thus simultaneously equated with the unveiling of Cordelia's grandmother's corpse and the unveiling of her past, and by extension the plot. Here, the veil is permeated with olfactory imagery which works both to summon Imogen's body and to proffer clues as to the story's narrative workings: the scent that clings to the cast-off garment not only conjures the presence of the dead/absent Victorian 'other' but gestures towards the tale's central mystery. The medicinal smell of camphor thus implicitly reveals the details of Imogen's illness, while also portending the burns that Cordelia will later sustain when she wears the veil again.

Shrouding herself within the veil's black folds, Cordelia experiences an uncanny moment of misrecognition when she stares at herself thus adorned in the mirror:

> When she put it on, the front of the veil came right down to her waist, while the back – it went all around, like a headdress – almost touched the floor. She could still see, though dimly, but when she looked in the long mirror her face was quite invisible, and because of the angle it seemed as if the veil was hovering of its own accord. (132)

As in Brontë's *Jane Eyre*, the generative power of the mirror in *The Ghost Writer* combines with the veil's own uncanny capacity to destabilize identity. Both work in tandem to produce an instinctive physical response in the wearer: 'Panic seized her, and she fled into the corridor' (132). Unable to see her own face, Cordelia is instead confronted with the spectral double-image of her dead grandmother. Adding to the uncanniness of this identification is the fact that the veil appears to adopt a potent life of its own. The veil's haunting materiality is made manifest as it hovers 'of its own accord' within the frame of the mirror, and when it later initiates a series of nightmares 'in which she [Cordelia] was pursued and finally cornered by a malevolent, shrouded figure, who appeared in many guises but always became, in the instant before she woke in terror, her grandmother in the act of raising her veil' (132–3). Cordelia's mingled dread and curiosity at seeing Imogen's face mobilizes the significance of the veil and forges a notable connection with the ending of the short story in which she wears the veil again. After witnessing her fiancé's adulterous relationship with her sister, Beatrice, Cordelia accidentally sets fire to the veil and sustains terrible burns to her face. In this way, she will render herself the true double, or mirror image, of Imogen de Vere.

It is perhaps fitting that at the conclusion of *The Ghost Writer*'s central storyline there should be a literal unveiling. Writing of 'the descriptive words for endings' in relation to neo-Victorian fiction, Patricia Duncker states that 'denouement' means '"an explanation", the elaboration of the reasons why', and also 'an "un-knotting", the unravelling of the threads' (2014: 18). At *The Ghost Writer*'s denouement, Gerard finally disentangles the fabric of stories and lies that ensnare him, while the text's final 'reveal' is dramatized by the removal of Anne Hatherley's veil. Upon entering the library in Ferrier's Close, Gerard's story appears to have come full circle when he finds a stash of papers hidden in a cabinet drawer. This secret archive turns out to be the letters that he has faithfully written to Alice over the years, and his horror at the discovery is amplified when a veiled figure appears in the room behind him:

> 'Gerard'. A slow, insinuating whisper at my back. From the shadows at the far end of the room, an indistinct figure, shrouded in flowing white, detached itself from the wall and glided to the door. Draperies swirled; the door closed; a key turned in the lock. As the figure moved towards the circle of light I saw that she was tall and statuesque and veiled like a bride; a long white veil, floating above a great cascading cloud of chestnut hair that flowed on down over her shoulders exactly as it had in so many dreams of Alice. Her arms were entirely concealed by long white gloves, and her gown, too, was white, gathered high at the waist. Small flowers showed beneath the fringes of the veil, between coiling strands of hair; small purple flowers, embroidered across the bodice of her gown. (2005: 366–7)

Attempting to discover his assailant's face through the veil, Gerard experiences a heightened sense of the uncanny when he notes first that 'no trace of features showed through the veil' (367), and then later, with growing unease, that 'through the shrouded layers of material, I caught the outline of something dark and formless; it did not look like a face' (370). Oscillating between occlusion and revelation, the veil both invites and denies access. As a material textual device, it appears to hold in tension the im/possibility of retrieving the past. While the white fabric registers the distinct probability that Gerard might see through its folds and therefore discern the truth about his familial origins, its semi-opacity impedes and therefore precludes visual and epistemological access. Gerard's fear is therefore largely constituted by his inability to see the spectre's face which is equated with the terrifying realization that he might fail to uncover the truth about his familial history.

Frustrating visual and epistemic access is just one of the veil's many functions in this instance. Suspense is encoded within its white folds and the embroidered muslin gown more generally, both of which eerily resonate with Alice's earlier sartorial self-construction and which, therefore, visibly pre-empt the final resolution of the plot. Before the final revealment can take place, however, the garments work to disrupt and trouble the narrative. Harnessing the sartorial significance of white Victorian garments once more, Harwood's evocative depiction distinctly conjures bridal attire while simultaneously deliberately inverting this symbolism and foregrounding the blank, shroud-like qualities of the all-white ensemble. Writing of the symbolism inherent in white clothes in Victorian fiction, Clair Hughes argues that 'white is an absence, a blank sheet waiting to be filled' (2006: 72). Like Gerard's letters and the empty canvas in 'Seraphina', the veil and muslin dress here converge to function as another *tabula rasa* in *The Ghost Writer*. As additional blank spaces within the novel, the garments thus represent the material means by which Anne has symbolically and literally erased her own identity, while also providing sartorial screens onto which she has projected an alternate self.

Masquerading as Alice Jessell (and Abigail Hamish), Anne's alternate selves work in conjunction with the allusive tenor of the text and its redeployment of veils. Here, the white veil and gown forge visible intertextual links with a whole host of veiled literary Victorian women and therefore open up the haunting possibility of textual return. The veiled woman in this episode functions as an uncanny double of her Victorian forebears: she is 'a spectacular version of Miss Havisham, a ghastly parody of the Pre-Raphaelite maiden as a harbinger of death and decay' (Heilmann and Llewellyn 2010: 62); a resemblance which is also apparent to Gerard who stutters accusingly: 'You're – you're Miss Havi- Hamish' (2005: 368). That this first encounter with Anne/Alice takes place in Ferrier's Close, located in Hampstead, also parallels the opening pages of Collins's *The Woman in White*, when Walter Hartwright is accosted by 'a solitary Woman, dressed from head to foot in white garments' on Hampstead Heath (2008: 20). This ghostly apparition, also named Anne, has escaped from an asylum; by thus adorning herself in a white gown and veil Anne Hatherley theatrically stages herself as a contemporary 'Woman in White', implicitly invoking the attendant intertextual connotations of madness, doubles and disguises set forth in Collins's sensation novel. Beyond these two examples, Anne is intertextually encoded within a long genealogical line of other Victorian ghost and sensation stories. She is a reincarnation of the 'mad' Bertha Mason and a double of the woman suffering from insanity in Dickens's 'The Black Veil'. The overt patterning of veiled women thus functions as a form of purposeful sartorial citation which, in metatextual terms, draws attention to *The Ghost Writer*'s pastiche of Victorian forms. In this plurality of veiled women, Harwood signals how the past has come to dominate Gerard's presence, while the palimpsestuous overlay of veils works to playfully deter narrative fulfilment by suspending the moment of revelation.

Unlike in Cordelia's dreams in 'The Revenant', the desire for revelatory fulfilment is here made possible, however, when Anne casts off her veil, and in doing so reveals the truth to Gerard and the reader:

> The veil floated free; the cloud of chestnut hair slipped from her shoulders and fell at her feet with a soft thud. Lamplight gleamed upon a bald, mummified head, skin stretched like crackling over the dome of the skull, with two black holes for nostrils and a single eye burning in a leprous mass of tissue, fixing me, half a life too late, with the enormity of my delusion as I saw that Alice Jessell and Anne Hatherley and Abigail Hamish were one and the same person. (2005: 372)

Like the Medusa whose naked gaze turns men to stone, Anne's stare 'fixes' Gerard with the 'enormity of [his] delusion' and thus signifies the novel's final revelation: in an uncanny doubling of Viola's 'The Revenant', Anne, the reader learns, murdered her fiancé for his adulterous affair with her sister, before attempting to burn Phyllis with a fluoroscope. This act of revenge failed, however, when Anne accidentally burned herself with the machine, leaving Phyllis to flee to Australia. What is perhaps most notable about this theatrical unveiling is that it is not Anne's 'mummified' visage that horrifies Gerard, nor is it the sudden comprehension of Alice's fictionalization, but rather it is the revelation of his own self-deception that causes Gerard's acutely destabilizing sense of self-alienation.

In their astute analysis of the novel's climax, Heilmann and Llewellyn point out that:

> Harwood's text and the narrator's concluding realization of the magnitude of his self-deception might thus reflect something about our own delusions in the faith we place in the neo-Victorian text and in many respects its too-comforting treatment of the spectral. Like the Victorian fraudster mediums pulling out all the stops in the hoax séance, we are complicit in the fakery of the text and its summoning of the haunted and haunting past. (2010: 169)

To put it another way, Harwood's text plays on and subverts readerly expectations. Caught up in the novel's processes of masquerade, disguise and revelation, what is revealed, or unveiled, is not the 'dread pleasures of the pastiche Victorian ghost story' but rather 'the more terrifying technological realities of the modern world' (Heilmann and Llewellyn 2010: 169). In this reflexive moment, Harwood comments on the mechanisms of the neo-Victorian novel which require the reader to suspend their disbelief throughout, only to recognize the sartorial, material and textual manoeuvrings that have taken place throughout. This episode of unveiling therefore reveals the authorial trickery that lies at the heart of the novel, and of the neo-Victorian genre more widely. The un/veiling of Alice/Anne might be read, then, as a kind of sartorial exegesis on contemporary returns to the past, in which revelation is among the genre's key compulsions.

Veils, bindings, skin: Concealing bodies and books in *The Journal of Dora Damage*

If Harwood's *The Ghost Writer* is preoccupied with themes of detection and revelation, then *The Journal of Dora Damage* is ostensibly concerned with the keeping of secrets and the concealing, or veiling, of both bodies and books. Set in 1859, Belinda Starling's posthumously published novel narrates the tale of the eponymous heroine, Dora Damage, a housewife-turned-bookbinder who finds herself inadvertently bound to the Victorian pornographic book trade. Dora's foray into this illegal trading sphere is a consequence of her husband's rheumatism and his resultant debts, which threaten the family and their bookbinding business with bankruptcy and ruin.[11] Upon discovering that her husband's debilitating condition has left him unable to work, Dora quite literally takes matters into her own hands; she pawns domestic material items and touts for business from the villainous bookseller, Charles Diprose, who commissions her to bind sexually explicit texts for a set of wealthy noblemen that style themselves *Les Sauvages Nobles*. The Noble Savages are modelled on the nineteenth-century 'Cannibal Club', 'an offshoot of the Anthropological Society of London with close links to the Royal Geographic Society' (Heilmann and Llewellyn 2010: 131). The fictional members of *Les Sauvages Nobles*, along with their leader the physician and bibliophile Sir Jocelyn Knightley, have a penchant for producing and consuming hardcore pornography which they have Dora bind to their delight and her

---

[11] The Obscene Publications Act of 1857 prevented the legal sale of pornographic material.

increasing disgust. Sir Jocelyn Knightley's wife, Lady Sylvia Knightley, who is the founding member of the 'Ladies' Society for the Assistance of Fugitives from Slavery',[12] similarly takes an interest in the female bookbinder and commands Dora to employ Din Nelson, an ex-enslaved African American from Virginia in her bookbindery workshop. As Dora's desire for Din grows, she attempts to decline Knightley's business, but is left in no doubt of her position by Diprose who tells her: 'Let me put it simply: you have no choice over what you do and do not bind' (2007: 220). In order to guarantee her silence and cooperation, the Noble Savages threaten her daughter, Lucinda, with a clitoridectomy as a 'cure' for her epileptic condition and imply that Dora will be murdered, and her skin turned into the cover for a book. Like the books she binds, then, Dora risks becoming an object of exchange; her actions inadvertently offer both herself and Lucinda up as commodities to those that would consume them. The remainder of the tale depicts Dora's growing independence and love affair with Din, as well as her attempts to extricate herself from the Noble Savages.

While *The Ghost Writer* stages Gerard's quest for familial origins and historical truth, Dora's tale, a *Künstlerroman*, charts her own quest for sexual, creative and economic freedom. In the novel, Starling raises important questions about the place and role of women in the nineteenth century that can be mapped, in various ways, onto the present day. In her capacity as bookbinder for the Noble Savages part of Dora's quest for liberation involves a process by which she learns to navigate not only the domestic sphere, but also the spaces (generally reserved for men) of commerce and consumerism. Oscillating between both domains, she becomes a woman out of place: her presence in the bookbindery shop undermines 'mid-Victorian union restrictions on female employment' (Kohlke 2008a: 196), while her illicit role in the production of pornographic works further disrupts gender conventions and destabilizes the Victorian ideal of the Angel in the House. This 'subversion of the heavily gendered public/private dichotomy' is, for Danijela Petković, 'conveyed most emphatically through the novel's treatment of Victorian pornography, in which issues of gender, race, class and power come together' (2015: 223–4). Central to these issues, and to *The Journal of Dora Damage* more widely, is the body and its adornments.

---

[12] This fictional society is 'probably modelled on the Ladies' London Emancipation Society, the first nationwide women's anti-slavery society, established in 1863', but despite its apparently philanthropic aims, the society 'exploits its free slaves by exhibiting them in the semi-nude for sensual delectation' and therefore emphasizes how 'women, too, can be participants in the commodification of others' (Heilmann and Llewellyn 2010: 132).

Dress and fabric play a key role in the novel. From the rags that Dora wraps around her husband's arthritic hands (2007: 36), to the 'cornflower blue' silk dress that she wore as a young woman and which she uses to bind the first of Diprose's journals (71), dress and fabric constitute significant threads in the narrative: they stitch together past and present, connect bodies and books and thread together the two spheres that Dora inhabits. The public and private realms of the novel are interwoven, bound by fabric. The Damage's home, where Dora cares for her family, and the masculine space of the bookbindery workshop, where she is tasked with providing a 'public face' to 'very private volume[s]', are divided by a single curtain (118). Dora and Lucinda's excursions into the city are depicted through the oft-repeated leitmotif: 'The toes of our boots went in and out of our skirts like pistons' (33, 52, 270), which similarly combines imagery of domesticity with industrialization. Finally, dress functions as a substitute currency both within the confines of the house and outside of it: Dora sells scraps of cloth to the rag-and-bone man and pawns clothes and household items in order to feed her daughter; as will be discussed, she also offers her landlady, Mrs Eeles, a mourning veil in lieu of two month's rent; and is later paid by Knightley for her bookbinding work in fashionable gowns, accessories and other material and sartorial items.

As in *The Ghost Writer*, Starling's *The Journal of Dora Damage* is replete with references to veils and other fabric bindings. In an intertextual allusion to Dickens's *David Copperfield* (1849–50), Dora reveals in an early part of the narrative that Peter, like David, was 'born in the caul' (15), that is in the amniotic membrane – commonly referred to as a 'veil' – attached to the baby's head after birth.[13] Peter is also associated with other screening garments in the novel including curtains and funerary drapery. The opening pages of Dora's first-person narrative centres on her husband's disappearance behind the curtain that divides the Damage's home with their bookbindery shop. Peter's concealment behind the curtain at the sight of the Damage's landlady, Mrs Eeles, reveals to Dora the gravity of their financial situation; she writes, 'I first realised we were in trouble when Peter vanished behind the curtain separating the workshop from the house just as Mrs Eeles came through from the street' (3). After Peter later overdoses on laudanum and dies, he is wrapped in a shroud and the mirrors in the Damages' home are veiled according to custom (283). Dora herself owns,

---

[13] Dickens's *David Copperfield* begins with David's assertion that he was born in a caul (1997: 1). The caul is sold at auction in the novel to protect the carrier from drowning, which was a popular practice according to Lutz (2015a: 82). Ironically, in *The Journal of Dora Damage* Peter's illness makes it appear as though his 'flesh was drowning' (2007: 203).

wears and barters with a black weeping veil, and just as she uses clothes, veils and other screening-garments to cover her own body, she likewise recycles her old gowns and transforms them into a series of covers for pornographic books. On a metaphorical level, the text's protagonists also conceal secrets from one another: in the novel's opening chapters, Dora attempts to hide Peter's illness from his patrons, as well as obscuring her own transgressive presence in the bookbindery workshop and in the delicate, aesthetic designs of the texts she fashions; later in the narrative, Dora and Din must keep their secret romance under wraps; while at the novel's conclusion, Knightley reveals his biracial heritage to Dora, the tell-tale signs of which, his hair, he veils beneath a wig and a hat (2007: 433).

In these instances, *The Journal of Dora Damage* and its deployment of veils most clearly aligns with the Victorian veil as a marker of concealment or 'hiddenness' (Mills 2007: 105). Yet veils also reveal as much as they purport to conceal in Starling's contemporary reworking of mid-Victorian class and gender conventions. In the novel, as in *The Ghost Writer*, a black weeping veil becomes an important literary and material device. Initially, its narrative significance emerges from its value as an object of exchange. When Dora finds herself unable to pay the family's rent in the early pages of the novel, she presents the veil to her landlady, Mrs Eeles, whose penchant for collecting photographs of dead children and for wearing full-mourning attire, lend her, as Kohlke writes, the intertextual air of a 'Miss Havisham in black' (2008a: 8). Dora recounts the exchange as follows:

> 'What have you brought me dearie?' Mrs Eeles asked.
>
> 'Finest crêpe, and I bought it new, too. Only wore it for six months. I was hoping – I was wondering – if this would be of interest to you.'
>
> 'Only one mourning?'
>
> 'Two actually. Overlapping.' I paused. I had presumed that the less wear the better; it had not occurred to me that successive grievings might have a cumulative effect, that sensations might linger, and indeed, one day, provide some sort of thrill.
>
> 'My parents, you know,' I added. ...
>
> She fingered the crêpe thoughtfully, then bent her head to it, and sniffed it noisily. 'Two months, I'll give you for it.' (30)

On a basic level this passage appears to satirize the ritualistic mourning practices of the nineteenth century, apparently exemplifying Caterina Novák's claim that the 'book's frequent allusions to the macabre' imply 'a parodic exaggeration of the sensationalist trope designed to draw attention to itself' (2013: 120–1). Novák dismisses moments such as these as having 'little or no bearing on the plot' beyond 'a clever critique of neo-Victorian fiction's tendency to increase its market value and audience appeal by the inclusion of ever more shocking revelations about the Victorians' (121). Yet this sartorial exchange strongly dialogizes with the novel's wider thematic concerns. Dora's exchange of her crape veil reveals the value placed upon nineteenth-century dress and recalls contemporary debates about the expense of crape, both of which highlight and reinforce her precarious social and financial position.[14] Her obvious discomfort at Mrs Eeles's fetishistic fascination with the veil reflects not only a twenty-first-century disdain for alien Victorian practices but speaks instead to issues pertaining to class. As a working-class woman facing poverty and ruin, Dora, unlike Mrs Eeles, cannot sentimentalize clothes and so this moment functions to reveal the distance and differences between the two women and their polarized positions within the socioeconomic hierarchy.

In more affective terms, the above exchange serves to highlight the mnemonic power of dress. Speaking to the ability of textiles to conjure the presence of the Victorian 'other', the veil here emphasizes the role of things in neo-Victorianism. In this instance, the veil works to reify the entangled relationship between subject and object, human and nonhuman. Rather than a mere indicator of grief, the black weeping veil becomes in and of itself a symbol of resurrection. At the same time, it ostensibly retains and transmits the owner's intimate memories and emotions for consumption, a notion that is explored in further detail in Chapter 5. Like the glove, the veil is a key site of emotional and physical inscription. In her intensely phenomenological and sensorial engagements with a material item that is closely bound up with feelings of grief and loss, Mrs Eeles prompts a confrontation with the porous permeability of fabric. Her actions, while potentially ludicrous, obliquely remind the reader of the importance of material objects and their role in reviving the past, issues that will become prominent at the conclusion of the novel. Through such encounters, this moment appears to suggest that the histories, memories and emotions that accrue to old clothes might be apprehended and re-experienced in the present.

---

[14] The expense of crape and mourning wear more generally was a common theme in much ladies' literature in the period. In July 1871 *The Englishwoman's Domestic Magazine* complained of the cost of crape, proposing the use of 'Albert Crape' as a cheaper alternative to other available materials ('Economy in Mourning', 1871: 299).

If Mrs Eeles fetishizes the black crape mourning veil, for Dora it remains a practical item of clothing. Beyond its exchange-value, the veil, with its perceived capacity to obscure the face and body, functions for Dora at least initially as a point of access to the public sphere. Dora is acutely aware in the novel of her visibility. She is, as Arias confirms, 'hypervisible': 'Her overt-visibility signals her vulnerability, placed as she is in a disadvantageous position' (2011: 355). Conscious of this apparent visibility, particularly when she enters public spaces alone, Dora writes:

> I felt conspicuous on my own. I was stared at with impunity, especially by the men. Women are experts at the cross-gaze; why do men have to look directly? Was I overdressed in my finest, or not smart enough? Did I look like a lady's maid who had done away with her lady, or a prostitute, even? For, unaccompanied, I became a public woman ... Oh, for an escort on to whose arm I could cling, to allay my fellow street-goers' curiosity and render me invisible. (2007: 53)

Anonymity is apparently bestowed by the mourning veil, which promises to provide Dora with a useful disguise when she later follows Din into the city. As a kind of shield, the veil in Victorian fiction facilitated women's movements in the public realm, and like nineteenth-century heroines before her, Dora swathes herself in a black veil to disguise her features. Yet far from enabling her attempt at deception, the veil paradoxically draws attention to her presence. While the weeping veil confers on Dora the status of a widow and therefore a degree of respectability, it by no means renders her invisible. Although it promises to conceal her identity, Dora soon comes to understand that 'people looked at you if you were wearing a veil; their inability to see your eyes offers a false reassurance that you can't see theirs' (271). The agency assigned to Dora by Starling in the novel is therefore complicated by the veil which, rather than promising autonomy, reveals only the power relations within which (neo-)Victorian women are enmeshed. In an apparent rejection of the Victorian novel's insistence upon the veil's transformative and deceptive abilities, this moment offers a lucid comment on the disenfranchised position of women in society. Dora is so entangled within the power structures of the patriarchal gaze that even under a veil she cannot look without being stared at in return. Whereas Anne Hatherley's veil is effective because it obscures her identity from Gerard in *The Ghost Writer*, Dora's disguise is less than successful because of its very conspicuousness.

Pastiching and subverting the Victorian novel's employment of veils, Starling calls attention to the impossibility of nineteenth-century plots of sensational disguise. While she rewrites notions of Victorian femininity and womanhood, granting greater agency to her heroine, this episode points to the still-circumscribed experiences of women across history. Although Kohlke finds that the novel does little to engage with present-day concerns (2008a: 200), the gendered dimensions of seeing and being seen here intersect with contemporary issues of objectification, sexualization and the gendered, classed and race-based harassment and violence to which women are still frequently subject in the private, public and political arenas. Starling's use of the seemingly innocuous veil materializes juxtaposing issues of liberation and oppression, agency and impotency, especially when Dora comes to realize that unlike a man, 'a woman's life could never truly lack visibility, no matter how low or high her rank' (97). Here, Starling's text indicates the proportions of the nineteenth-century interest in visuality, and its anxieties too, as well as contemporary society's own rising awareness, particularly in the age of social media, of the issues of gendered in/visibility.

Just as the black weeping veil covers yet paradoxically draws attention to Dora's body, the cloth bindings that she fashions for various books perform similar work in the novel. As in *Fingersmith* (discussed in Chapter 3), Dora participates in the pornographic economy in *The Journal of Dora Damage*. Her production of pornographic works differs significantly, however, from Maud's own involvement in scribing, reading and eventually producing her own pornographic tales. While Dora reads some of the texts, engaging with them textually and imaginatively, her contribution lies chiefly in the clothing, or veiling, of such books for consumption. An example of this is seen when Charles Diprose writes a letter to Dora urging her to fashion covers for texts from 'silk, skin, fur, feather', and does so in terms that recall the dressing of the female body: 'Just as some colours flatter particular complexions, and some bonnet styles suit certain shapes of head, so too must you consider the colours and styles of your binding according to the nature of the book' (113). In a later letter, he implores her to ignore a set of books' 'gaudiness', asking her 'to dress them with understated elegance, as one would make a lady of an opera-dancer' (123), thus obscuring their overt 'sexuality' and conferring on them a semblance of modesty and respectability. The disguising of such texts might be read as a kind of veiling. Such a connection is elucidated by the feminine connotations of the veil and the novel's continuous feminization of books. Elaine Showalter explains that veiling was closely associated with female sexuality and the female body in the period (1992: 145), and such notions of veiled female sexuality find continuance in Starling's representation of bookbinding. Diprose warns Dora that he 'will command the most plain, unobtrusive binding to act as shackle and protector for the more mischievous literature, to prevent it leaping off the shelf at the less knowledgeable reader' (113). Like the veil, the 'unobtrusive binding' that Diprose requires Dora to fashion for the more transgressive pornographic works, conceals the books' rampant sexuality, protecting the reader, in much the same way that the female body's overt sexuality was veiled in rituals of mourning and marriage (Showalter: 145).

What begins as a purely economic endeavour soon becomes a fulfilling and engaging creative outlet as Dora channels her artistic skills into the fashioning of such texts. Although later deeply troubled by the increasingly racist and misogynistic material that she is required to bind, Dora experiences a sense of sexual and artistic liberation upon consuming and clothing the earlier works. The libidinous pleasure she finds in the reading and dressing of such texts exposes her capacity for creativity and for experiencing sexual desire: traits that her staid and sexually repressed husband, Peter, has failed to discern, much less encourage, in his wife. When choosing how best to illustrate the binding for *The Lustful Turk* (1828), Dora finds she is 'spoilt for imagery to put on the cover of this extraordinary volume' but decides eventually to adorn its cover with 'a beautiful woman, whose finely embroidered robe slipped fetchingly about her shoulders' (159). Endeavouring 'to distil the essence of the book in the cover design' (159), Dora's words and subsequent artistic practices reveal an aesthetic aptitude for illustrative design and intertextually echo the opening lines of Irving Browne's 1897 poem 'How A Bibliomaniac Binds His Books': 'I'd like my favourite books to bind / So that their outward dress / To every bibliomaniac's mind / Their contents should express' (2011: 27, ll. 1–4).

The creative process Dora enacts in covering the texts in clothes and other domestic items simulates the popular nineteenth-century practice of clothing books in household textiles. 'Cottonian' bindings as they were known, functioned as a form of domestic craft in the period, one that showcased female creativity, industry and thrift. Alluding to this process in a romanticized and metafictional aside, Dora remarks that she remembers 'reading somewhere how [William Wordsworth's] sister Dorothy would cut up her old gowns, and use them to bind the early volumes of his poetry. I had never seen one, but I could imagine the pretty faded floral fabric enfolding his pretty floral poems with the colours of Grasmere, and protecting them with a woman's love' (70). The British Library contains a book owned by Robert Southey, autographed by Wordsworth, and apparently covered in a cloth binding by 'Mrs Wordsworth' (shelfmark c61b14). In a similar vein, the Brontë siblings reportedly clothed the miniature books written in their youth with scraps of clothing and other domestic textile items. In her illuminating object-centred study in which she maps the lives of the Brontë siblings through their surviving material artefacts, Deborah Lutz explains how 'they used, for their mini booklets, scraps of anything available that suited their fancy':

> The Brontës felt an intimacy with these closely handled books, made by their own limbs and clothed with materials familiar from the kitchen or the parlor. This closeness of the body and the book was an ordinary feature of daily life in the nineteenth century, a relationship no longer obvious today. One reason for this different relationship was paper's multiple lives. The literary historian Leah Price explains that through a long chain of recycling, clothes that had kept limbs covered became reading matter. (2015b: 30)

Like the 'multiple lives' of paper that Lutz and Price (2009) acknowledge, dress similarly enjoys many reiterations in *The Journal of Dora Damage*. The clothes that have covered, concealed and warmed Dora's body are transformed into coverings for books which are preoccupied with, and document, the uncovering of a succession of other bodies. Dismantling an old blue silk gown to use as the binding for various journals, including her own, Dora recognizes the malleability of dress and its transformative capacities when she notes that 'its purpose was now more than as a dress to a gentlewoman or a poor unfashionable bookseller's betrothed. This was not a dress whose time was over. It was several books whose life had only just begun' (71). Just as the blue silk gown clothed Dora's body in its past life, in its new life it clothes her journal, which she writes in the metafictional prologue, 'conceals the contents of my heart' (2). Dora's words appear to paraphrase Igor Kopytoff's influential claim that commodities, like humans, have trajectories and life histories of their own (1986: 67). Handed down to her by her mother, re-worn, recycled and then finally used to clothe a number of books, the blue silk dress is bound up in a process of handling, touch and re-fashioning and reinforces the novel's equivalence of bodies and books.

Indeed, just as the canvas that depicts Seraphina is embodied in *The Ghost Writer*, books in *The Journal of Dora Damage* are paralleled with the physical female form. Heilmann and Llewellyn argue that 'at its most complex, intertextual, and ironic, neo-Victorianism explores the inscription and textuality of the desire to repossess the Victorian by performing a slippage between the central character and the text' (2010: 109). They go on to add that the 'metonymy of the female body acting as a "cover" (covering) of the text … is most strikingly accomplished in *The Journal of Dora Damage*' (109). The novel's paratext evidences these same concerns. Kohlke writes that 'the book's cover, depicting a make-believe business signage with a woman's laced-up corset, subtitled "Bindings of Any Kind"' hints at risqué sexual practices with sadomasochistic overtones, implicitly conflating the body of the book with the female body of the titular heroine' (2008a: 196). Extending this reading, the word 'wrapper', which in the nineteenth century referred both to a woman's dressing gown and to the paper cover or jacket of a book, indicates that the Victorians themselves accepted the connection as part of everyday life.

The contemporary novel's insistence upon this intimacy between body and book is further underscored at its climax. Here, the metaphoric connection between text and body extends beyond the realms of the purely figurative to the literal when Dora unwittingly fashions a book cover from human skin. Relying on her naivety and threatening Lucinda's safety, Diprose commands Dora to make a cover for one of Sir Jocelyn's anatomy books out of a strange material that he calls ' "Imperial Leather"' (2007: 342). Forced to fashion the cover away from the prying eyes of the other bookbinders, Dora is unable to place the material:

> It was not hard to prepare, but I found the leather strangely unwieldy. It was stiff to work with, and did not take stretching or glue well. Either it had been badly tanned – which would have been surprising, given the previous quality of Diprose's materials – or it was indeed the skin of an exotic animal. I traced my fingers over it. It had a strange beauty, and the light played beguilingly on its uneven surface. (2007: 350)

That the skin turns out to be from a 'Hindoo widow' renders this passage intensely uncanny (388). When Dora later realizes that the words she has 'tooled blind' on the skin are: *'De humanis corporis fabrica*. Literally, on the fabric of the human body' (385; original emphasis), she experiences an abject sensation of horror: 'I felt my supper rise in my throat, my body revolting at myself ... I knew I would never feel clean again, not until I had ripped every inch of skin off my sinful flesh' (386). Her desire to violently remove her own skin in sympathy with the woman whose flesh she has fashioned into a book cover, compounds the unspoken notion that her role as a bookbinder of pornography has made her complicit in the exploitation of other women. Moreover, her realization that she has covered a book in human skin makes apparent the link that exists between veiling bodies and books when she highlights the sexual sartorial overtones of the violation: 'Sir Jocelyn had stripped this woman of more than her clothes' (389). In this moment, the skin of the unknown woman is strangely displaced and doubles as a second skin which clothes the pseudo-body of the text.[15] These complex correspondences between cloth and skin and text and body serve to further disrupt the subject-object divide and draw attention to themes of revelation.

Despite the novel's ostensible concern with concealment, then, its conclusion, like that of *The Ghost Writer*, features a dramatic unveiling. If the marginalized, overlooked and forgotten are the only 'real' ghosts that haunt *The Ghost Writer*, then a similarly occluded figure troubles Starling's novel. What haunts this narrative is the unnarrated plight of the unnamed 'Hindoo widow' (391). Present only in the fragments of her skin which clothe Knightley's medical treatise, the woman is displaced from her own body, the country of her birth and from the novel more generally. If Anne Hatherley's veil calls into question the ability to reimagine the past, the un/veiling of the Indian widow at the end of Starling's novel raises questions about the ethics of narrative revision. The erasure of the unknown woman's story apparently undermines the novel's ostensible concern with the synergistic injustices of colonialism, medical racism and misogyny. Since a victim of each of these social ills is relegated to the peripheries of the text, veiled behind other more visible narratives, Starling's novel might be seen to imitate, rather than alleviate, the exploitative circumstances that it sets out to critique. Notably, the veiling and subsequent quasi-revelation of the woman at the novel's climax does not work to fully reveal the true circumstances of her life and death. Mediated through Sylvia's second-hand account, Dora learns of Sir Jocelyn's hubristic plans 'to rescue a brave and beautiful widow from *sati* – from her husband's funeral pyre – and immortalise her for ever in the greatest scientific and literary work of the century!' (388–9; original emphasis). In this scenario, Starling rehearses and condemns the hypocritical barbarity of colonialism, even as she veils the female victim from view, stifling her voice and denying her any meaningful subjecthood.

This unexpected half-reveal points to a kind of narratorial uncertainty that lies at the heart of Starling's novel. Acknowledging similar contradictions, Novák has aptly argued that the text thus

> invites two utterly different but complementary readings. The first of these would identify with a courageous feminist heroine and relish her triumph over Victorian patriarchy, while willing to discount the novel's inconsistencies as the

---

[15] See Michie for a discussion of the slippage between skin and clothing in the nineteenth century (2014: 450).

forgivable faults of an otherwise commendable first effort. However another, perhaps more knowing reading would be alert to the many double-edged ironies contained in the narrative. (2013: 130)

For Novák, the novel is therefore an absurdly exaggerated parody of the genre that works by mocking its conventions (131). The figurative narrative unveiling can also be read as a self-conscious comment on the construction of the neo-Victorian novel. In its strategic revelation of the Indian woman, *The Journal of Dora Damage* formally reflects the process of unveiling that is central to the neo-Victorian enterprise. This unveiling situates the neo-Victorian novel as an artful arrangement of literary, material and historical traces. Through the selection and manipulation of such traces, the mechanics of unveiling, the novel cultivates critical perspective on the ethical drivers at work within the genre. In closing with the revelation of the Hindu widow, Starling's densely plotted narrative thus calls attention to what is hidden and what is brought into view in history and, by extension, in contemporary returns to the historic past.

In drawing on the trope of the veil in their two neo-Victorian fictions, both Belinda Starling and John Harwood self-consciously invoke an interwoven tissue of symbolic and metaphoric literary associations that can be traced to the nineteenth century and beyond. In their resurrection of Victorian veils, these contemporary novelists knowingly reflect upon Victorian sartorial practices and attitudes to visuality and representation. Appropriating such concerns, their return to and employment of the veil motif reflects the genre's own interrogation of the Victorian period, its ongoing and enduring desires to unveil and reveal. In *The Journal of Dora Damage* and *The Ghost Writer*, the veil induces a consideration of the processes and procedures of writing and reimagining the past. In the latter, veils become an important visual and material paradigm for Gerard's quest to unveil the past and elicit missing information about his ancestral history. Signifying the novel's intertextu(r)al construction, as well as Gerard's dependence upon the Victorian past, veils call into question modes of contemporary representation. In Starling's novel, the familiar invocation of the Victorian veil's concealing function is subverted; veils, at both sartorial and narratological levels, enact practices of revelation. Both garment and genre work to bring to light secret or hidden things. Moving beyond the Victorian veil as a mere fictional device signalling concealment, Starling and Harwood both situate the garment's conceptual and ideological mutability as a resistance to the knowability of the past. As material forms that are variously depicted as elusive and intangible, veils are, in many ways, unreadable. Their contradictory status as both material garment and symbolic literary construct foregrounds the tensions between reality and representation, history and fiction, that are called forth in these two neo-Victorian fictions. Veils in the contemporary texts thus highlight the problematics of perception; they act as symbols for the complexities of reconstructing historical narrative; serve to acknowledge the limits of narrative representation and work to trouble contemporary readers' access to the past. In all, they foster a sense of uncertainty that leads to productive questions about material culture and its role in reviving the past. Similar issues are raised in the following chapter which considers the ways in which jewels and jewellery provide focal points for reimagining materiality, memory and feminine identity in two neo-Victorian rewritings.

5

Jewellery

Published in 1990, A. S. Byatt's Man Booker Prize winning novel, *Possession: A Romance*, documents processes of historical recovery in which the lives of two fictional Victorian poets are recuperated via a panoply of material and textual relics. Like *The Ghost Writer*, *Possession* is a novel about detection, central to which is the exposure, by two twentieth-century academics, of a secret love affair between nineteenth-century writers Randolph Henry Ash (loosely based on Robert Barrett Browning) and Christabel LaMotte (a fictitious compendium of historic female poets including Elizabeth Barrett Browning, Emily Dickinson and Christina Rossetti).[1] In the novel's contemporary narrative strand, Roland Mitchell, a precariously employed postdoctoral scholar researching the works of Ash, discovers an undisturbed collection of draft letters hidden in an old book that had once belonged to the poet. It is this discovery which propels the romance narratives at work in each of the text's temporal storylines: when he later deduces that these are early versions of epistles sent to Christabel LaMotte, Roland seeks the assistance of Maud Bailey, a lecturer in English literature at Lincoln University and an expert on LaMotte, with whom he falls in love. Together, Roland and Maud reassemble Christabel and Ash's love story through the material and textual remnants they uncover. From these historical fragments emerge the contours of the poets' extramarital affair from its epistolary inception to the birth of the couple's illegitimate daughter, from whom, coincidentally, Maud is descended. In this way, *Possession* is concerned with a search for personal, as well as collective, origins.

In the three decades since its publication, Byatt's neo-Victorian novel has attracted an abundance of illuminating scholarship that has paid close and continued attention to the centrality of documentary traces within the tale (Brindle 2013; Hadley 2010; Shiller 1997). Letters, diaries, books and poems are

---

[1] See Brindle (2013: 10) and Kaplan (2007: 8).

the catalysts for, and receptacles of, 'the tiresome and bewitching endlessness of the quest for knowledge' that stimulates the narrative (Byatt 1991: 4). Containing within them 'jewels of information' (1991: 7), literary sources in *Possession* are reservoirs of profound pleasure and scholarly significance, of frustration, desire and satisfaction. The act of reading such literary fragments, by implication, is a gratifying practice through which intra- and extra-textual readers' desires to access the past via textual knowledge, might be encouraged and even perhaps satiated. What is also apparent, but which has so far been relatively neglected in academic commentary, is that *Possession* traces a narrative trajectory in which material remains come to signify in ways that are as, if not more, important than the literary texts. Indeed, the progression of Byatt's novel stages an increasingly object-oriented approach to historical recovery in which the primacy of the written word is repeatedly challenged. Material things – jet jewellery and a hair bracelet, especially – proffer dynamic nodal points that reify and revivify past relationships and which materialize, and therefore make legible, lost histories. These sartorial objects promise richer, more immediate and evocative forms of engagement with the past. In narratological terms, they also work as conduits between past and present, entwining the nineteenth- and twentieth-century stories and negotiating the spatial and temporal distances that separate them. The 'possession' referred to in the book's title, then, might indicate not only readerly desire to possess the historical past through its 'textualized remains' (Hutcheon 1988: 20), but more specifically, a politics of ownership and affect concerning the poets' lost physical artefacts.

Despite the novel's nascent material plot, in its early pages Roland and Maud express an ambivalence, bordering on distrust, for literary tourism and the perceived capacity of material relics to mediate between past and present, between author and reader. After his theft of Ash's secret letters, Roland, shocked by their urgency and emotion, reflects on and reconsiders his previous engagements with the poet's literary oeuvre, claiming that he 'had never been much interested in Randolph Henry Ash's vanished body; he did not spend time visiting his house in Russell Street, or sitting where he had sat on stone garden seats' (20). Maud articulates comparable sentiments when she proposes a visit to Christabel LaMotte's house only to temper her suggestion by asserting: 'I very rarely feel any curiosity about Christabel's life – it's funny – I even feel a sort of squeamishness about things she might have touched, or places she might have been – it's the *language* that matters, isn't it, it's what went on in her mind' (55; original emphasis). Their words reflect a twentieth-century poststructuralist reluctance to engage with the artefacts associated with dead authors, yet the tension that Byatt registers here between literary and more material forms of knowledge governs the proceeding episodes in which Maud and Roland re-evaluate and exhume a jet brooch and hair bracelet, respectively.

Made from organic matter, the jet brooch and the hair bracelet are suffused with vitality in both the nineteenth-century strand and its contemporary counterpoint. Working cross-temporally, the items of jewellery mediate and materialize key points of intersection between Maud and Roland and Ash and Christabel. In a letter to his wife, Ash describes Whitby jet, a gemstone formed of fossilized driftwood, in a lexicon strongly resonant of new materialist thought when he explains that it was 'once alive' (256) and yet still contains 'its own magnetic life in it' (257). Jet takes on a similar scholarly and symbolic vibrancy when Maud and Roland trace the poets' journey to Whitby and visit a jet jewellery shop. It is here that Maud first comes to realize that her own jet brooch, a family heirloom, was likely purchased by Ash for Christabel as a gift and in turn passed down to her. This moment marks something of a tonal shift in which Byatt outlines her protagonists' rising awareness of the interpretative potentialities of things. What was once 'hideous Victorian junk' and something of a 'joke' (260), is re-conceived of as potent and possibly significant. Shifting in the academics' estimation, the jet brooch is transformed into an authentic historical object that apparently holds out the alluring promise of proximity. Increasingly attuned to the immediacy and mediatory potential of material objects, Roland is drawn to the jet jewellery pieces as tangible sites of encounter. We learn that he 'wanted badly to own something, anything, in this strange sooty stuff which Ash had touched and written about' (261). Here, Byatt probes the academics' growing desire for physical, material congress with the Victorian poets, desires that arguably enunciate our own affective investments in the Victorians.[2]

The ensuing disinterment and subsequent mis/interpretation of a letter and a hair bracelet buried with Ash and his wife Ellen further mirrors modern-day desires to pursue intimacy and emotional connection, however illusory, with historic figures via their physical artefacts. The letter is the final and unopened missive sent from Christabel to Ash in which she reveals the existence of their

---

[2] In the concluding chapter of her monograph on keepsake culture in Wilkie Collins's sensation fiction, Sabina Fazli turns to a number of neo-Victorian novels, including Byatt's *Possession*, in order to trace their deployment of various Victorian keepsakes. She too notes the significance of the forgotten jet brooch and the misunderstanding that arises from the disinterred hair bracelet, but she argues that these are moments that ought to be connected to the nineteenth-century sensation genre. In contrast to my own argument, Fazli suggests that through these two keepsake objects, Byatt 'introduces forgotten forms of material remembrance' into the novel, which 'evoke the sensational trope of past relationships and identities reconstructed through keepsake objects' (2019: 241, 242).

surviving daughter, Maia. Believing that Ash never met Maia, nor knew of her existence, Roland and Maud consequently misread the hair bracelet that lies nestled against Christabel's unread letter. Crafted from the entwined locks of Ash and Ellen, it is wound about with a pale blonde strand of hair that they assume is Christabel's own. Yet, as the postscript reveals, the fair lock of hair is in fact Maia's whom Ash, unbeknownst to Christabel, meets in the final pages of the novel. This moment, as Shiller argues, 'calls attention to what is left out of histories' (1997: 547). In a drive towards the instability typical of historiographic metafiction, *Possession* thus demonstrates the difficulties of possessing the past through its textualized relics alone. But if literary traces are shown to be contingent and partial, then the hair bracelet functions as a key material signifier in *Possession*. Byatt venerates this material object and its power to provide tangible, physical evidence of lives past. She appears to argue, both here and in the novel more widely, for the importance of preserving the material remains of the past and suggests the limitations of analyzing textual traces in isolation. *Possession*'s conclusion not only self-consciously debates the extent to which fiction, letters and poetry can provide a complete and accurate reading of the past but attests to the importance of correctly deciphering sartorial items. Worn against and, in the case of the hair bracelet, partaking of the body, these items of jewellery signify the secrets which material objects conceal, carry and convey. They gesture to complex familial networks and recall hidden human histories. Together, the bracelet and brooch offer points at which the material and the textual converge and in their intersections emerge productive sites for analysis that disrupt conventional readings of the novel. Engineering a kind of reconciliation of the literary and the material, then, Byatt encourages a careful reading of sartorial things.

Similar issues are focalized through the two more recently published neo-Victorian novels around which the remainder of this chapter pivots. Like *Possession*, Ronald Frame's *Havisham: A Novel* (2012) and Diana Souhami's *Gwendolen: A Novel* (2014) speculate about dis/possession, inheritance and history. *Havisham* is a contemporary rewriting and narrative extension of Charles Dickens's *Great Expectations* (1860–1); focalized through the perspectives of Catherine Havisham and, in the book's final section, her ward Estella, the novel reorients the focus from the male protagonists of the pre-text and works instead to reclaim and recuperate the female characters' histories. *Gwendolen* performs similar ideological work. It returns to and rewrites George Eliot's *Daniel Deronda* (1876) from the viewpoint of its long-silenced heroine, Gwendolen Harleth. Written in the form of a first-person letter which she addresses to Deronda, the novel recovers and recentres the titular character's voice, while crafting her an imagined afterlife. United via a process of rewriting, these novels draw upon the textual record but profess the profound importance of sartorial objects, especially jewellery, in the (re-)telling of their respective tales. In *Gwendolen*, Souhami invokes the symbolism of the turquoise necklace and the diamond parure accorded emblematic status in Eliot's novel. In the contemporary text, the jewels function for Gwendolen as the narrative stimuli via which her past, and the secrets contained therein, might be (re-) told in the present. In *Havisham*, jewels are intimately entwined with issues of female identity and inheritance. Disrupting male-centred and patriarchal modes of jewellery-giving, the contemporary novel figures jewels as the interlocking links by which matrilineal love and connection are forged and preserved. In the contemporary texts under study here, jewels and jewellery are therefore figured as female-centric and feminist sartorial items in accordance with the novels' wider political and ethical aims.

Yet to receive sustained scholarly attention, both Frame and Souhami's texts are examples of what Peter Widdowson describes as 're-visionary novels': they each ' "write back" to canonic texts of the English tradition – those classics that retain a high profile of admiration and popularity in our literary heritage – and re-write them "against the grain" ' (2006: 501).[3] Although Widdowson does not use the term 'neo-Victorian', his claim that novels which rewrite past texts are engaged in acts of re-vision resonates with the aims of the neo-Victorian genre. 'Re-visionary novels', like the two contemporary historical fictions under study in this chapter, have a clear cultural and political agenda. Widdowson stresses that such texts often

> align themselves with feminist and/or postcolonialist criticism in demanding that past texts' complicity in oppression – either as subliminally inscribed within them or as an effect of their place and function as canonic icons in cultural politics – be revised and re-visioned as part of the process of restoring a voice, a history and an identity to those hitherto exploited, marginalized and silenced by dominant interest and ideologies. (2006: 505–6)

In his discussion of neo-Victorian texts specifically, although he does not use this phrase either, Christian Gutleben has situated Jean Rhys's rewriting, *Wide Sargasso Sea* (1966) (discussed in Chapter 1), at the forefront of this literary

---

[3] O'Callaghan (2020) analyses Frame's novel in her essay on prequels to *Great Expectations*. For a brief discussion of Souhami's *Gwendolen* see Dillane (2020).

movement (2001: 5). Sally Shuttleworth termed this type of writing 'retro-Victorian' when she argued similarly, that with *Wide Sargasso Sea* Jean Rhys had initiated 'a long line of texts which have sought to open up the silent spaces of history or classic literary texts', the impetus for which, she contends, derives from feminist and postcolonial theory and which gives utterance to those 'denied a voice in history' (1998: 256). Also commenting on the genealogical link proffered by Rhys's text, Ann Heilmann and Mark Llewellyn note how it has served as a useful 'model for later writers in thinking about ways of reading – and rewriting – Victorian texts: to fill spaces, to interject interpretation, to insert clues but not to resolve the mystery itself' (2014: 499). Following Rhys, Souhami and Frame rework classic Victorian novels: their contemporary texts take narrative inspiration from two central nineteenth-century hypotexts but transgress the diegetic boundaries of the original novels. They extend, enhance and attempt to fill the lacunae found in Eliot's and Dickens's earlier narratives and thus adapt the Victorian novels' tales to serve their own contemporary feminist aims. In doing so, they each produce new commentaries on the representation of female identity, inheritance and agency in the neo-Victorian novel, while drawing on jewellery as vital, affective sartorial objects.

Focusing on jewels and jewellery in *Havisham* and *Gwendolen*, this chapter aims to show how such objects provide focal points for fresh considerations of femininity, materiality and memory in the neo-Victorian novel. It traces the migration of fictional jewels from the Victorian hypotexts to their contemporary revisions. Examining the peripatetic quality of jewels as they move between texts and bodies, it centres on the ways in which jewellery contains and transmits secrets, arguing that jewellery synecdochally enacts narratives that have been either occluded or submerged. Before unfolding this argument, however, I consider the role and function of jewellery in nineteenth-century sartorial culture, as well as its affective and emotional significance for female wearers during the period.

Ornamenting the Victorian woman

Jewels have a legitimate place in dress. In an artificial second self, a symbolical 'outer husk', such as clothes in a general way are, clasps and brooches are almost indispensable to neatness, as finishing touches. Properly understood, then, the 'jewels' are the last strokes of the brush that the skilled artist gives his picture as he feels what is needed – here a 'cold' touch, there a 'warm' touch. But brilliants –

they are the *last of the last*: the 'high-lights' – the white speck to 'bring out' this or that curve, and draw attention to the main point. Jewellery has a double function: it either adds a point of colour to intensify or to correct – as do coral, amber, opal, lapis, turquoise, gold, and silver; or dew-dropwise, it attracts to and enhances colours already present – as do pearls, and especially diamonds and brilliant paste. Occasionally both functions are combined, as in the case of emeralds, rubies, sapphires and other coloured transparent stones properly used. But at all times the ornaments are *part* of dress, not independent, and are subject to the same laws. (Haweis 1889: 94–5; original emphases)[4]

Mary Eliza Haweis's article 'Jewels and Dress: Or the Philosophy of Jewels', published in 1889, underscores the centrality and significance of jewellery in the formation of the Victorian woman's sartorial frame.[5] More than simply accessories or adjuncts to other more crucial articles of clothing, jewellery in Haweis's words, occupies 'a legitimate place in dress' and is 'subject to the same laws'. Jewels, when worn correctly, add colour, warmth and emphasis; they illuminate, enliven and perfect. Conceived of via an extended conceit of dress as an art form, jewellery lends the 'finishing touches' or the 'last strokes of the brush' to the female ensemble. In this chapter, jewellery performs a similar function; it is the concluding dress element with which this study clothes, embellishes and re-inscribes the Victorian female body.

Jewellery was specifically associated in the nineteenth century with middle- and upper-class female wearers. Although men tended to wear small items of jewellery such as rings, lapel studs or watches, more ostentatious and decorative jewels often remained the preserve of their female counterparts. As a figurative and legal extension of her husband, a bejewelled woman made manifest his wealth, status and success; for this reason, gifts of jewellery were often given by men to women 'in a show of privilege and prerogative' (Arnold 2011: 4–5). In Charles Dickens's *Little Dorrit* (1855–7), the marriage between the financier Mr Merdle and his wife is conceived of in transactional, materialist and ornamental terms: referring to Mrs Merdle metonymically as 'the bosom', the narrator reveals that Mr Merdle's acquisition of his wife's 'bosom' was not for the purposes of romantic attachment, 'it was not a bosom to repose upon, but it was a capital bosom to hang jewels upon. Mr Merdle wanted something to hang jewels upon, and he bought it for the purpose' (2002: 235). Writing

---

[4] The reference to 'outer husks' is derived from the chapter on 'Old Clothes' in Carlyle's *Sartor Resartus*, when Teufelsdröckh encourages the reader 'to do reverence to those Shells and outer Husks of the Body' (2002: 245).
[5] Haweis (1848–1898) was a British author, essayist and scholar.

of this same moment, Jean Arnold argues that since the 'cultural practices of Dickens's reading audience did not allow Mr. Merdle to display his wealth by wearing jewels', Mrs Merdle's bosom therefore neatly fulfils this gendered and 'class-marking function' on his behalf (2011: 1–2). Connecting the popularity of jewellery with the rise of consumer culture and technological advancements, Arnold goes on to demonstrate how jewels functioned as 'prisms of culture' in Victorian literature, reflecting and refracting a host of intersecting sociocultural issues around distinctions of gender, race and class (2011).

Beyond signifying status, wealth and position, women's jewellery functioned as an intensely personal form of artistic, decorative and individual display. According to Haweis, it could articulate character, identity and interiority in the period. 'This is the true object of all decoration –' she opined, 'to express character. It is like literature, like music – like a blend of both – it is actually a language. Give it thoughts and feelings to utter: decoration was never meant to disguise or obliterate, but to announce and interpret, the individual' ('Jewels and Dress' 1889: 98). Figured here in terms that highlight its communicative and interpretive potentialities, jewellery, like other items of dress, signified semiotically in the period. Encoded with complex narratives, jewels signalled individuality, personal taste and emotional feeling. On a collective level, jewellery also evoked and sustained historical, familial and sentimental ties. The site of exchange and social interaction, it forged and preserved connection, materializing human relationships. The popularity of sentimental and mourning jewellery in the Victorian period, along with the craze for fashioning jewellery from hair which became increasingly popular in the 1850s, bespeaks its affective significances. Sentimental jewellery served to express feeling, emotion and affection. Making use of numerous symbols such as flowers, hearts and hands, employing a variety of gemstones, and incorporating miniatures and later photographs, sentimental jewellery solidified significant moments of accord between individuals.[6] Mourning jewellery memorialized, commemorated and immortalized, while simultaneously signifying loss, grief and absence. And hair jewellery combined apparently divergent functions within its silken strands, simultaneously operating as *memento mori*, ornamental object and a token of familial or romantic attachment. (Figure 5.1) For the Victorians hair was a particularly potent material addition to jewellery. In its severance from the body of a loved one, hair continued to signify the absent donor. As Shu-chuan Yan

---

[6] For in-depth discussions of Victorian sentimental jewellery see Bury (1985) and Cooper and Battershill (1972).

Figure 5.1 Victorian mourning brooch containing the hair of a deceased relative © Wellcome Collection (4.0 International CC BY 4.0).

points out, 'unlike the rest of the body, which is subject to decay, hair remains the same after death' (2019: 125). The permanence and physical materiality of hair thus provided an additional touchstone for the absent corporeal body; stimulated by the sense of touch, hair jewellery educed past physical contact and held out the promise of future contact.

Affective, personal and strangely emotive, jewellery enjoyed a vibrantly symbolic life in Victorian sartorial, visual and literary culture. This nineteenth-century fascination with jewels is particularly evident in contemporary print culture where numerous articles historicizing, and therefore legitimizing, the practice of wearing jewellery appeared alongside commercial advertisements and cultural pieces on style and jewel etiquette. In 1864, *Bow Bells* began a short column dedicated to 'Jewellery' by acknowledging that 'the love of jewels and ornaments has been prevalent among all nations, from the earliest ages' (1864: 115). Published several years later, Alice Mullins's article 'Jewellery as an Art' likewise claimed that 'jewellery has been a favourite form of personal decoration from the earliest times', before pointing to the resonances and continuities between antique and Victorian styles: 'We know with what skills the Etruscans and Greeks worked in precious metals, and that a large part of what is good in our modern jewellery is copied from their designs, and those of other early nations' (1896: 237). Driven by developments in technology and informed by new archaeological discoveries, Victorian jewellers often imitated the classical styles of jewellery worn in ancient Greece and Rome. Other historical periods, such as the Renaissance and medieval periods, as well as various geographical regions, including North Africa, also lent inspiration to nineteenth-century designs. Indeed, part of jewellery's allure appears to have been wrapped up in its exoticized associations with distant lands and foreign cultures. For all their assimilation into British culture, jewels 'suggested the glamour of faraway places'

(Daly 2011: 68). In the aforementioned *Bow Bells* article, for instance, the author catalogues precious jewels and their geographical origins, fetishistically writing of women that

> glitter in diamonds from Golconda, sapphires and rubies from Peru, onyxes from Arabia, turquoises from Persia, emeralds from South America, garnets and amethysts from the East, topazes from Ethiopia, changeable opals from Egypt, and last, though not least, among the glittering gems, pearls from the recesses of the deep blue ocean, in the Persian Gulf and the Gulf of Mexico. ('Jewellery' 1864: 115)

A series of international exhibitions held at South Kensington, London, during the early 1870s, likewise evinced a particular interest in sourcing and showcasing jewels and items of jewellery from the far reaches of the empire (Figure 5.2). Like the Great Exhibition of 1851, the South Kensington exhibitions were designed to showcase international industrial and creative endeavour. The Loan Exhibition of 1872 gathered together and displayed a range of jewels, gemstones and items of personal jewellery from India, Colombia, Albania, Malta and Armenia, among other places (Cole 1875: 120–1). Such examples serve to suggest that empire

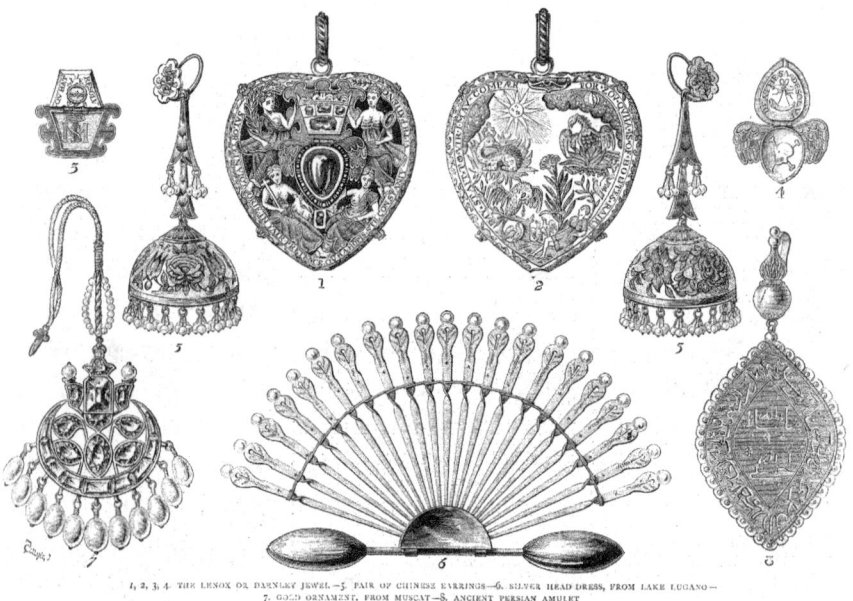

Figure 5.2 Jewellery at the Loan Exhibition, South Kensington Museum, 1872. © Getty Images.

propagated the West's interest in pieces of jewellery from across the globe while proffering unparalleled access to the jewels of other countries and cultures.

Besides designs that were expropriated from other cultures and derived from ancient civilizations, common jewellery motifs in the period included flowers, eyes and serpents. In addition, coral, jet, diamonds, opals and turquoises all rose and fell in popularity as the period progressed and were variously designated suitable or unsuitable depending on the wearer and the social situation in which they were worn. Although they did not alter with the same rapidity as styles of dress, changing jewellery designs complemented the shifting silhouettes of fashionable clothing (Flower 1967: 10–11). In an attempt to keep abreast of fluctuating patterns and motifs, journals and ladies' magazines proffered useful pieces of advice for the sartorially aware female reader. One fashion column noted in 1869 that 'necklaces, chains and lockets, or crosses are worn during the day' with 'redingote dresses' that had open collars.[7] In addition, 'Jewels of cut jet or of finely-carved black wood, studded with small pearls or seed diamonds' were considered 'fashionable for the daytime' ('The Fashions' 1869: 205). Florence Hartley warned her readers in 1872 that diamonds (discussed in further detail later in the chapter) and other brilliant pieces of jewellery 'look well, on proper occasions, on married women. But young girls rarely, or never improve their appearance by the use of these dazzling jewels' (299). Not only were there complex rules governing the wearing of jewellery for women, but gem lore held that precious jewels also transmitted different meanings and could communicate a multiplicity of ideas and superstitions. Discussing the eighteenth century in particular, Marcia Pointon describes the 'linguistic richness of gemmology' (1997: 494) with which the Victorians themselves were familiar. Jewellery also held an apotropaic function in the period. As Joseph Rupert Paxton argued in *Jewelry and the Precious Stones*, 'precious stones have in all ages been signalized by myriad forms of imaginative, poetic superstition', many of which are notable for 'possessing numerous mystic virtues both negative and positive – shielding their owners from peril and adversity, and securing them prosperous fortunes' (1856: 3).

Nineteenth-century fictional depictions of jewels and jewellery fervently engage these complex discourses, demonstrating an acute appreciation of the potent linguistic and magical characteristics with which gemstones were often credited. Besides George Eliot and Charles Dickens, authors such as Emily and Charlotte Brontë, Wilkie Collins, Anthony Trollope and Thomas Hardy, regularly

---

[7] Redingote dresses in 1869 were military-style tailored day dresses.

drew on the symbolic, communicative and moralistic resonances of jewellery.[8] Charlotte Gere and Judy Rudoe confirm that much 'Victorian fiction assumes an intimate familiarity with jewel symbolism', the study of which 'prove[s] crucial to our understanding of attitudes to jewellery in the nineteenth century' (2010: 152). In spite of this, Anne Marie Evans has recently suggested that 'work on the role of jewellery in literature is not currently as developed as the focus on fashion and literature has become in the last few years' (2020: 11). Even less attention has been expended upon depictions of jewellery in neo-Victorian literary and cultural productions. Aside from Sabina Fazli's brief discussion of the way in which neo-Victorianism tends to incorporate Victorian mourning jewellery and other mementoes into its sensationalized narratives (2019), and Rosario Arias's more detailed treatment of hair jewellery and sensorial experience in neo-Victorian literature and culture (2020), the study of jewels in contemporary historical fiction remains somewhat provisional. These articles offer invaluable insight into the pivotal role played by jewellery in evoking sensational narrative tropes and contemporary representations of the rituals of mourning, respectively. Thus, in the following sections, I seek to move beyond jewellery's connection to sensation fiction and Victorian death culture and examine instead its various pivotal functions in two texts that rewrite canonical works of the nineteenth century. In these two paradigmatic neo-Victorian novels, jewellery entails a vital significance, whether it fosters a sense of female identity and matrilineal connection, as will be seen in Frame's tale, or signals narrative, truth and freedom of expression, as found in Souhami's novel.

Heirlooms and afterlives: Jewellery in *Great Expectations* and *Havisham*

First published serially in his periodical *All the Year Round* between December 1860 and August 1861, Charles Dickens's *Great Expectations* charts the tale of the orphan Pip (Phillip) Pirrip, his education and upbringing, and his unrequited love for Miss Havisham's ward, Estella. Acting as both a prequel and sequel to this canonic nineteenth-century tale, Ronald Frame's *Havisham* weaves a new story from the strands of the original in which the hypotext's female protagonists

---

[8] Notably, hair jewellery appears in Emily Brontë's *Wuthering Heights* (1847) and Charlotte Brontë's *Villette* (1853), while diamonds take on specific narrative significance in Collins's *The Moonstone* (1868), Trollope's *The Eustace Diamonds* (1871) and Hardy's *Tess of the D'Urbervilles* (1891), among other novels.

are actively centred. Not only does *Havisham* provide Catherine Havisham with a name and a tragic backstory, in which it fully expounds the events that lead to her voluntary incarceration within Satis House, but it also charts the story of the other Havisham heiress, Catherine's adopted daughter, Estella. In its imaginative resuscitation of both women, Frame's novel descends from a long genealogical line of contemporary returns to Dickens's *Great Expectations*, which have since led Kathryn Hughes to suggest that 'Dickens's characters appear to have become untethered from their texts, even from their creator's control' (2010: 391). Miss Havisham, especially, is a case in point; incorporated into the diegeses of several other novels, poems, plays and films, her numerous trans-temporal and trans-medial resurrections appear to have reified Pip's hyperbolic exclamation in *Great Expectations* that 'a thousand Miss Havishams haunted me' (2000: 303). Besides the many filmic and televisual adaptations of Dickens's text,[9] Sue Roe's novel, *Estella: Her Expectations* (1982) creatively appropriates the characters from *Great Expectations*, while Carol Ann Duffy's monologic poem, 'Havisham', published in her collection *Mean Time* in 1993, proffers a lyrical reimagining of the figure of Miss Havisham.[10] Written in the first-person, it presents a poetic invocation of feminist rage.

As well as intriguing writers of fiction, film and poetry, Miss Havisham has proven to be a source of inspiration for contemporary fashion designers. In 2011 Prabal Gurung credited Miss Havisham as the muse for his catwalk collection. Georgina Chapman and Keren Craig, the founders and head designers of the high-end fashion brand Marchesa, also cited Dickens's female character as the stimulus for their own 2011 ready-to-wear collection. Craig referenced 'the idea that she [Miss Havisham] had been in her wedding dress and jilted at the altar, and the wedding dress slowly disintegrating' ('Marchesa's Miss Havisham Makeover', 2011) as the key starting points for their collection. On the catwalk, Gurung and Marchesa both featured opulent gowns made of lace, tulle and satin, embroidered with jet and gemstones. Drawing on but also departing from Miss Havisham's bleached and faded appearance in *Great Expectations*, the designers dressed their models in provocative tones of red and black, as well as gold, silver, white and cream. These fashionable returns to Miss Havisham bespeak both the generative capacities and enduring iterability of Dickens's characters, as well as the visually and materially potent symbolism enacted as a result of her unusual attire.

---

[9] See Regis and Wynne (2012).
[10] For detailed discussions of these works see Letissier (2012) and O'Callaghan (2020).

Indeed, when Pip first encounters Miss Havisham in an early section of *Great Expectations*, he declares that she is 'the strangest lady I have ever seen, or shall see' (2000: 48). Her peculiar appearance, eccentric sartorial choices and the disarray of her garments most clearly mark her oddity:

> She was dressed in rich materials – satins, and lace, and silks – all of white. Her shoes were white. And she had a long white veil dependent from her hair, and she had bridal flowers in her hair, but her hair was white. Some bright jewels sparkled on her neck and on her hands, and some other jewels lay sparkling on the table. Dresses, less splendid than the dress she wore, and half-packed trunks, were scattered about. She had not quite finished dressing, for she had but one shoe on – the other was on the table near her hand – her veil was but half arranged, her watch and chain were not put on, and some lace for her bosom lay with those trinkets, and with her handkerchief, and gloves, and some flowers, and a Prayer-Book, all confusedly heaped about the looking glass. (48–9)

Strangely and improperly attired, the disordered and unconventional Miss Havisham is transformed into Gothicized spectacle when Pip, on closer inspection, remarks that 'everything within my view which ought to be white, had been white long ago, and had lost its lustre, and was faded and yellow' (49). Miss Havisham's 'faded' garments parallel her body which has 'withered like the dress' until she resembles a kind of 'ghastly waxwork' or living 'skeleton' (49). This visually rich image of the shrivelled bride encased within her decaying wedding dress is one that has evidently precipitated the enduring interest in Dickens's eccentric female character. For Amber Regis and Deborah Wynne, it is her 'uniqueness' that has engendered the many visual reproductions of the character in filmic and televisual adaptations: 'brides are not typically represented as grey-haired and corpse-like, forever inhabiting and exhibiting their bridal condition' they contend (2012: 39). Apparently evidencing their claim, *The Telegraph* announced in February 2022 that a new six-part series based on Charles Dickens's *Great Expectations* would feature the Oscar-winning actor Olivia Colman as Miss Havisham. The latest in a long line of adaptations, the new BBC series speaks to the novel's continuing popularity, as well as underlining its seemingly endless capacity to be rewritten and reworked in the contemporary cultural consciousness, while the *Telegraph*'s focus on the character of Miss Havisham figures her as central to both the novel and its subsequent adaptations.

Such incessant returns to and resurrections of Miss Havisham are not only enabled by her dramatically Gothicized sartoriality but also by the gaps and silences that permeate her story in the pre-text. Much of what the other characters, and by extension the reader, learn of her in *Great Expectations* is rumour and gossip. Her truncated history is mediated to Pip through Herbert Pocket who recounts fragments of her biographical history. For Georges Letissier, Herbert Pocket's account functions as a 'hypodiegetic' narrative which offers only 'peripheral perspectives' on Miss Havisham (2012: 32). We learn that she had been 'a spoilt child. Her mother died when she was a baby, and her father denied her nothing. Her father was a county gentleman down in your part of the world, and was a brewer' (Dickens 2000: 153). After the death of her father, Herbert tells Pip that Miss Havisham fell in love with a man who 'practised on her affection in that systematic way, that he got great sums of money from her' (155). Joining forces with her half-brother in an attempt to defraud her, Mr Compeyson promises to marry but later jilts Miss Havisham on the day of the wedding, leading to her self-imposed exile (155). Confronted with this patchy tale, Pip asks 'is that all the story' and is told in return that it is 'all I know of it; and indeed I only know so much, through piecing it out for myself' (156). Retrieving this expository plot from the background of Pip's *bildungsroman*, Frame's novel represents an alternative attempt to piece together a broader and more complex version of Miss Havisham's life. An 'allographic expansion', *Havisham* 'return[s] to a closed narrative world and time of a classic text and give[s] a different slant on already told events' (Parey 2018: 4). It retrospectively develops Miss Havisham's storyline, offering her the opportunity to set the record straight. As she says longingly to Pip in *Great Expectations*, ' "If you knew all my story" … "you would have some compassion for me and a better understanding of me"' (2000: 338–9).

In his contemporary rewriting, Frame pays heed to Miss Havisham's desire for empathy and understanding. In allowing her to tell her own story he also fulfils her need for narrative authority. For the most part, *Havisham*'s main story arc traces the contours of Dickens's tale but fills in the lacunae of the original: Catherine is a wealthy heiress jilted at the altar by her fiancé Charles Compeyson, who is in league with her half-brother Arthur, and her decline into misery and madness results in her entombment in Satis House with her adopted daughter, Estella. As in *Great Expectations*, the orphan, Pip, is invited to play at Satis House and falls in love with Estella during his visits, but in *Havisham* his story is relegated to the peripheries of the text and Frame instead focuses on recuperating the stories of the two Havisham women. In doing so, Frame tacitly acknowledges that Pip's narrative has traditionally overshadowed the female storyline. Presenting the hypertext as a challenge to the primacy of the original, Frame authenticates Catherine Havisham's first-person narrative by setting it in direct opposition to Pip's own in *Great Expectations*. In the contemporary novel, *Great Expectations* is provocatively figured as a fabulation, a fantastical story written by Pip about the two women, which Catherine recognizes as a form of betrayal (312). Ruminating on the story he might tell of them, Catherine realizes in a metafictional aside that 'our lives are fictions. How others interpret us. What we allow others to do with us. What we make of ourselves' (312). Extending this moment of metacommentary, the novel's conclusion turns to the aftermath of Catherine's death. After she has died of heart failure and the burns she accidentally inflicts upon herself while trying to apologize to Pip, the narrative, distanced through the third-person, turns once more to Pip's plans to write a story. We are told that 'he has the shape of a story in his head, and trims his details to fit. There are different versions of the story, though. One story with – he believes – three viewpoints. Estella's. His. The madwoman's' (357). The dismissive use of the phrase 'madwoman' coupled with Pip's metafictionally staged creative licence in which he 'trims' the 'details' of the story 'to fit' his fictional purposes, works to challenge the authority of the nineteenth-century novel. By resurrecting Miss Havisham and providing her with a voice, Frame therefore opposes Dickens's master narrative in his contemporary retelling of the tale.

Claire O'Callaghan's valuable recent analysis of neo-Victorian prequels to *Great Expectations* complicates such a reading. She argues that by returning to and reimagining the tale of Miss Havisham's misery and madness, contemporary revisions of *Great Expectations*, like Frame's novel, work to reinscribe the pain and violence wrought against nineteenth-century women (2020: 97). While Miss Havisham cannot be rescued from her eventual fate, in centring her story Frame's novel appears, nevertheless, to participate in the neo-Victorian desire to 'do honor to the dead and silenced' (Shiller 1997: 546). It calls attention to gendered forms of violence and, in doing so, re-imagines the realities and lived experiences of Victorian women and their encounters with patriarchal power dynamics. As O'Callaghan aptly acknowledges, the routing of the narrative through Catherine's first-person perspective forces 'us to access first-hand the way that romance fraud functions as a form of emotional violence' (91). In this way, the novel serves to illuminate present-day issues of domestic, financial and emotional abuse. Frame also works to actively establish Miss Havisham's voice. In *Havisham*, the majority of the novel is narrated from Catherine's first-person, autodiegetic perspective, thus forging a sense of readerly identification with the character and allowing her ownership over her own tale. For Heilmann and Llewellyn, 'story-telling, listening (bearing witness), and writing are acts of catharsis which redeem the past and … bring about a profound transformation of the protagonists' lives' (2010: 37). By recounting the events of her life in analepsis, Catherine's story takes on a rehabilitative function in which she addresses and rectifies the injustices of the past. Moreover, the novel's diversity of form, its short, fragmented vignettes, signal the blanks, opacities and gaps in the original story, even as the tale works to redress such omissions.

That *Havisham* is committed to reclaiming female identity, agency and narrative autonomy is clear both in the title, which acknowledges Catherine and Estella without focusing on the marital status of either character, and in the text's opening pages when Catherine meditates on the significance of her famous surname. Here, and elsewhere in the novel, Catherine reclaims it as her own. She states that 'it was the first word I remember *seeing*. H A V I S H A M. Painted in green letters on the sooty brick of the brewhouse wall. Fat letters. Each one had its own character' (2013: 5; original emphasis). She anthropomorphizes each letter in turn, referring to 'Comfortable spreading "H". Angular, proud "A"'. Welcoming, open "V"' (5), and it is clear that these familiar letters are reassuring reminders both of her wealth, status and position, and also of her family. They might even function as a substitute family in the place of her mother and father who are both largely absent in the narrative. A similar scene occurs, of course, in the opening paragraph of *Great Expectations* when Pip reads the epitaphs of his dead parents and explains that 'as I never saw my father or my mother ... my first fancies regarding what they were like, were unreasonably derived from their tombstones' (2000: 3). Pip personifies the engraved letters on each tombstone in terms of the bodily characteristics that they might represent. He reveals that 'the shape of the letters on my father's gave me an odd idea that he was a square, stout, dark man, with curly black hair. From the character and turn of the inscription, "*Also Georgiana Wife of the Above*", I drew a childish conclusion that my mother was freckled and sickly' (2000: 3; original emphasis). With a nod to this moment in *Great Expectations*, Frame's text signals both its investment in and inheritance of the hypotext and its departure from it. *Havisham* implicitly identifies its filial links with Dickens's nineteenth-century novel and, at the same time, points to issues of family and loss as thematic motifs that tie in with ideas of female inheritance, identity and autonomy.

For Catherine, the Havisham name is also synonymous with wealth and position, and it is through these central thematic concerns that the neo-Victorian novel initially evinces a specific interest in jewellery, presenting it as a marker of both female identity and class status, and a symbol of social, familial and affective ties. As an adored only child and heiress to a brewery, Catherine is surrounded by expensive things that assert her affluence and help facilitate her entry into the higher echelons of society. She receives and catalogues a number of precious jewels over the course of the novel, including 'a fire-opal pendant, a bracelet of amethysts, a pearl halter, a gold rope necklace hung with rubies, white and pink diamond earrings, a rare yellow diamond on a ring', jewels that she will later bestow on Estella (2013: 40). For Catherine, these jewels and her fine dresses are 'the tools, the *emblems*, of an education' which provide her with 'a veneer of accomplishment' and serve to ready her for the marriage market (62; original emphasis). Here, Frame demonstrates an acute awareness of nineteenth-century discourses surrounding jewellery. During the period, jewels carried specifically sexual objectives. They implied courtship, love and marriage. As decorative objects of display, they enhanced a woman's beauty and allure, signalling the often transactional traditions of the marriage market.

Besides constructing an aura of material authenticity and historicity, Frame's employment of jewellery in this way also showcases Catherine as a beautiful and desirable young woman. In *Gender and Jewelry: A Feminist Analysis*, Rebecca Ross Russell reminds us that jewellery 'is defined by its connection and interaction with the body' (2009: 1). By retrieving the jewels that haphazardly litter Miss Havisham's dressing table in *Great Expectations* and instead adorning her with them in *Havisham*, Frame works to reinscribe the Victorian female body. He re-fashions Miss Havisham, literally and figuratively reclaiming and reworking her sartorial and sexual identity as a process of recuperation. Later in the text, even after she is jilted and closes the brewery, Catherine's jewels continue to signify; they extend to her a sense of comfort and reassurance, acting as the material reminders of her family's former reputation. Although she herself has aged, she notes with delight that the 'radiance' of the rings on her fingers 'reminded whoever saw them of the Havisham money that had bought them, and the respect formerly owing to us' (297). The agency of the jewels appears to lie in this apparent capacity to forge and reinforce a tangible and enduring sense of familial and individual identity for Catherine.

In *Great Expectations*, by contrast, Miss Havisham's identity is seemingly bound to a piece of jewellery that is entirely absent from the narrative: a wedding ring. Abandoned while in the process of dressing for her wedding, Miss Havisham is subsequently refused the symbol of fidelity that marks a marriage and therefore occupies the liminal position between bride and wife. Theorizing the emotional effect of material objects, Stephanie Downes, Sally Holloway and Sarah Randles posit that 'things may change or alter affective states, consciously or unconsciously, permanently or temporarily, literally … or metaphorically (like a wedding ring)' (2018: 11). In the case of Miss Havisham, it follows that the loss or lack of such an object might be just as meaningful. Like the ring whose circular shape is an emblem of eternity (Pointon 1997: 499), Dickens's Miss Havisham is trapped in an endless cycle of repetition: she continually re-lives and remembers the moments leading up to her wedding day. Since she might therefore be defined by the absence of a wedding ring, Miss Havisham can be interpreted in relation to Freudian and Lacanian theories of castration, loss and symbolic lack. Yet rather than a phallocentric return to the castration complex, the missing wedding ring might be read in terms of female sexuality and reproductivity instead. If the ring signifies the vagina (Doniger 2017: 15), then Miss Havisham's bare finger metonymically represents her empty marital bed and childless state. This perhaps explains her desire to adopt Estella whose name, as Catherine pointedly remarks in *Havisham*, means '"*star*"' (2013: 268; original emphasis), and who functions in both novels as her substitute jewel.

On this point, Hilary M. Schor and Sharon Marcus have each acknowledged Estella's conflation with jewellery in *Great Expectations*. For Schor, Estella is 'a child who is abandoned and bought, a jewel who is brought up to display the jewels of others' (2004: 161). In *Between Women: Friendship, Desire and Marriage in Victorian England*, Marcus extends this reading when she points out that Dickens

> rarely describes Estella's beauty directly but instead materializes her charms in terms of accessories easily transferred from one body to another, such as the 'beautiful jewels' that represent Miss Havisham's investment in Estella as a lapidary object of desire. Like jewelry, Estella is hard, brilliant, and coveted, and Pip identifies Estella as gemlike, her beauty full of 'glitter and colour'. (2009: 180)

When Pip first encounters Estella in *Great Expectations*, his metafictional description of their meeting is also permeated with jewellery imagery. Reflecting upon their initial encounter he warns: 'Pause you who read this, and think for a moment of the long chain of iron or gold ... that would never have bound you, but for the formation of the first link on one memorable day' (2000: 61). The chain of iron or gold refers to both the convict's leg iron and to jewellery, and the two are entwined. As Wendy Doniger writes, 'like the link of a chain, any form of circular jewelry may fetter the wearer to the giver' (2017: 3), and although Estella and Pip never marry, Pip is bound to her as a result of Miss Havisham's machinations and his own adoration.

Pip refers to Estella in further terms that recall jewellery imagery when he recounts how she materializes from a dark passage in Satis house with her light shining 'like a star' and is beckoned over by Miss Havisham who 'took up a jewel from the table, and tried its effect upon her fair young bosom and against her pretty brown hair. "Your own, one day, my dear, and you will use it well"' (2000: 50). Echoing, and at the same time troubling, conventional modes of inheritance, Miss Havisham gifts Estella her jewels while she is still alive to complement Estella's beauty and to demonstrate the Havisham wealth. As literal markers of Estella's financial inheritance, the jewels also embody Miss Havisham's 'revenge on all the male sex' (151), which she intends to pass onto Estella along with the gems themselves. She intends for Estella to use the jewels to attract and subsequently disappoint suitors. Far from being decorative ornaments, then, the jewels function as sartorial extensions and expressions of Miss Havisham's rage.

In Frame's neo-Victorian rewriting, Catherine Havisham similarly objectifies Estella, amplifying her association with jewellery. Congratulating herself on the outcome of Estella's education and refined upbringing, Catherine utilizes the conceit of a faceted diamond when she notes with pride that Estella 'was learning how to sparkle and how to cast an allure' (2013: 295). Estella's transformation from a felon's daughter to a bejewelled heiress strongly echoes the transformative potential of the jewel, which Marcia Pointon explains can be figured through the following analogy: '"gem" ... suggests a raw mineralogical element, "jewel" implies a complex intertwining of nature and artifice, the absorption of the geological into the cultural' (2009: 47). Like a jewel, Estella is moulded and forged under Catherine's tutelage. Mechanically produced and commodified, she becomes an appropriate ornament for Satis House and a suitable tool to carry out Catherine's revenge. As Catherine herself acknowledges: 'This was what the Havisham fortune was *for*. Estella was its creation' (2013: 320; original emphasis). She further likens her adopted daughter to gemstones when she teases Pip by asking him to compare Estella with her jewels: '"Does she suit diamonds better, Pip? Or rubies?" I would hold the stones against her. "Or fire opals?" Estella's eyes would catch the gleam of my jewels' (296). In a later chapter, this imagery is conjured again when Catherine states: 'I showed Estella a necklace, a heavy gold chain with an opal pendant. It had been one of my father's gifts to me. Her eyes lit up with interest. "Put it on." She did so. The necklace complemented her beauty, perfectly served it' (301). In these moments, the boundaries between subject and object are contested as Estella is repeatedly imbued with the properties of her adoptive mother's jewels. Her cold, impervious beauty and intransigent personality are aligned with the precious gemstones and recall the many extratextual superstitions that clung to certain jewels in the Victorian period. Opals, in particular, were considered unlucky in popular nineteenth-century discourse: Haweis declares that 'There is no stone so revengeful when ill-treated' (103). The opals repeatedly paralleled with Estella in the above quotations materialize Catherine Havisham's desire for vengeance and imply the future effects of her actions.

Complicating the notion of the revenge plot, however, are the intimate and affective moments in which both Catherine and Estella engage with items of jewellery in the contemporary novel. Whereas, in *Great Expectations*, the Havisham jewels do not develop beyond their role as plot devices that exemplify Miss Havisham's wealth and desire for retribution, in *Havisham* jewels proliferate as markers of not only female identity and allure but also emotional, matrilineal inheritance. Strikingly, Frame refigures the jewels as emotive objects that facilitate connection and forgiveness between mother and daughter. The intergenerational transmission of jewels from Catherine to Estella begins in the novel with Catherine's own relationship with her deceased mother, Antoinette.[11] Although Antoinette is almost entirely erased from the novel because she dies giving birth to Catherine before the novel begins, her jewellery remains intact and physically present. Her existence in the narrative is therefore directly alluded to through the jewels which act as her sartorial proxies. The bequeathing of jewels from mother to daughter originates, then, with Catherine's own mother whose jewels are handed down to her daughter posthumously. The young Catherine recalls how, on her birthday, her father 'passed over to me, item by item, my mother's jewels':

> My mother had inherited some of the pieces, and I was aware of the quiet dignity of their age. They weighed me to my chair, they slowed me slightly when I walked – not because they were heavy, but because they came to me complicated by their history – and it wasn't at all an oppressive sensation. I felt that I'd been granted an intimate contact with my mother. We were sharing this occasion of my wearing a necklace or a bracelet, and somehow my increased pleasure was being transmitted to her, through time and space. This experience was being recreated in another dimension; by wearing the necklace or bracelet, I was helping to close a circle. (2013: 40)

Enfolded within an intimate system of handling and handing-down, the Havisham jewels are deeply interwoven with issues of exchange, female inheritance and emotional investment in the quoted passage. The point at which the agency of the jewels is invoked is in their personification by Catherine who refers to the old-fashioned ornaments in anthropomorphic

---

[11] Frame's decision to name Catherine's mother 'Antoinette' forges intertextual links with Rhys's germinal rewriting, *Wide Sargasso Sea*, in which she re-christens Bertha 'Antoinette'.

terms. She acknowledges the 'quiet dignity of their age' and uses the past tense verbs 'weighed' and 'slowed' to describe the jewels' complicated histories and allegiances to the past. By ascribing to the heirlooms a kind of dormant vitality, Catherine prefigures the metaphorical revivification of Antoinette Havisham which becomes possible through mutual contact with the jewels. Through her affectual and tactual interaction with the ornaments that her mother has also touched and worn, Catherine supposes that they have been 'granted an intimate contact'. Like the glove, which retains a trace imprinted within it, jewellery is permeated with emotion and memory in this neo-Victorian rewriting and conjures the presence of the absent (m)other. Just as the contemporary neo-Victorian novel returns to and re-fashions the past, the process of inheritance and remembrance as routed through jewellery is here presented as inherently cyclical. Catherine draws on two items of jewellery that are circular in shape, the bracelet and necklace, and highlights their mechanisms of closing to describe how wearing her mother's jewels closes the family circle. Not only does this passage point back to the origin of the jewels in *Great Expectations* but it also foreshadows the system of inheritance that will later inform Catherine and Estella's relationship in the contemporary text.

Originally bestowed upon Estella as a means of facilitating Catherine Havisham's revenge, the Havisham jewels come to signify genuine motherly love, forgiveness and reclamation at the novel's conclusion. The jewels thus initiate the plot's redemptive arc, becoming the material means by which both women connect and communicate with their lost mothers. In the final section of the novel which is focalized through the third person perspective of Estella, who has made an ill-fated marriage to Bentley Drummle, Frame pauses to focus attention on her actions as she adorns herself in the Havisham jewels:

> Estella puts on one of the necklaces. Pink diamonds and fire rubies. This was one of Antoinette Havisham's favourites. She picks up the hand mirror, engraved on the back with a baroque 'H' outsized for the taste of the day. The necklace's heavy gold filigree is likewise rather too fussy, but (she wonders to herself) the stones could be reset, couldn't they, into a simpler arrangement. (356)

Here, the interconnection between the Havisham women is rendered clear. The necklace that has encircled and adorned both Antoinette and Catherine's bodies forges a literal and emotional connection with Estella in the present. Mirroring Catherine's before her, Estella's actions are conciliatory, suggesting a growing sense of filial accord, while her plans to re-fashion the jewels speak to their shifting status within the novel's diegetic world.

This apparent shift in the jewels' function and meaning materializes most notably in the final pages of the neo-Victorian novel in which Estella imagines that she confronts her dead adoptive mother through contact with the inherited jewels. Ten years on from the conclusion of *Great Expectations* when Estella is a wife and mother, 'she turns one of the rings on her fingers. A Havisham ring' and, as she does so, is reminded of Catherine: 'She thinks often of that woman, and of her childhood in that big gaunt house. She feels bitterness towards her, and she feels pity too, and she becomes exhausted trying to balance her feelings. It's as if the woman is still around' (2013: 358). Bearing a striking resemblance to the moment of illusory connection forged between Catherine and her own mother, the Havisham ring connotes a sense of unity and togetherness; it appears to summon its erstwhile owner and, in doing so, draws the two women together. Crucial to this moment of imagined correspondence are the cyclical turning of the ring and the sense of touch Estella imparts, both of which stimulate remembrance. Although this item of jewellery functions outside of the context of mourning, it operates here as a tool and locus of memory, encoding intense feelings of loss, sorrow, guilt and anger. Such tactile transactions engender a further, surprising sense of connection in which the heirloom not only conjures Catherine's presence but brings forth her voice too. Estella imagines she can hear the following words spoken directly by her surrogate mother: 'Death might have stolen the breath from old Havisham's daughter, but he hadn't concluded her narrative. "I only ever wanted to protect you, Estella mine, nothing else; I didn't wish anyone to harm you. *This* is love"' (358–9; original emphasis). In allowing Catherine the final word, Frame stages a further and final act of redemption in which the ring, a Havisham heirloom, is presented as a memorial to female love, forgiveness and emancipation. The circulation of the jewels between the female protagonists in the contemporary text also reflects the transmission of female-centred history. Just as Frame's novel works to write Miss Havisham's story back into the historical record, the jewels function as enduring symbols of solidarity, connection and female lineage; in *Havisham*, they foster powerful intimacies between giver and receiver, mother and daughter.

As if to reinforce the value of material and sartorial items in the novel's reconstruction of the past, *Havisham*'s final lines linger over 'the contents of Satis House' which we learn are 'scattered about several counties, sold at auctions or already in the hands of pawn-brokers or debt-collectors' (359). This dispersal of the house and its contents represents narrative closure even as the Havisham things display sentient tendencies: 'They were restless, and some supposed that the objects were trying to summon back their grander past. To others, it was if a ghostly spirit haunted them. To others still, the items might have been trying to pass on a lesson: that the former owners of these things had suffered for them, and had also loved and laughed' (359). Existing beyond the realms of human apprehension and use, the objects that littered Satis House are set in motion. No longer arrested and held in stasis by Miss Havisham's design, they become animate and energetic actants. That the finale of the tale should hinge upon the renewed trajectories of these material things reinforces the strange symmetry that exists between subjects and objects, human and non-human entities. Inhabiting a transitional space, where the dead and the living are inextricably bound, these things recall and convey a powerful sense of the past. Invested with emotional meaning these little objects signal memory, inheritance and identity. In Diana Souhami's *Gwendolen*, which rewrites George Eliot's *Daniel Deronda*, jewellery undertakes a comparably emancipatory task.

'Talisman' turquoises and 'poisoned' diamonds in *Daniel Deronda* and *Gwendolen*

In the opening pages of George Eliot's final novel, *Daniel Deronda*, Gwendolen Harleth, watched by Eliot's eponymous male protagonist, recklessly gambles and loses a large sum of money at a roulette-table in Leubronn.[12] After she returns to her room, Gwendolen receives a letter that acquaints her with her family's financial ruin and, to pay for her passage home, secretly pawns an Etruscan-style necklace formed of 'three central turquoises' that had once adorned a gold chain belonging to her deceased father (2003: 13). Before she departs for England, however, the necklace which is wrapped in what she correctly assumes to be Daniel Deronda's cambric handkerchief and accompanied by an anonymous note urging her not to '*risk the loss of it*' again, is returned to her room, exciting in her a mixture of emotions and emphasizing the cruciality of jewellery in *Daniel Deronda* (14; original emphasis). Functioning variously as repositories of financial value; material markers of wealth, status, class and morality; and items of symbolic, emotional and affective meaning, jewellery abounds in Eliot's final novel and has elicited considerable critical attention.[13]

---

[12] *Daniel Deronda* was first published in *Blackwood's Edinburgh Magazine* in a series of eight instalments between February and September 1876.
[13] See Arnold (2011), Brooks (1993), Jacob (2016), Dunagen Osborne (2010), Wynne (2008) and Zimmerman (1977).

What is perhaps most notable about the turquoise necklace is its capacity to incite a range of sensorial and affectual responses that remain fluid and unfixed, altering with surprising rapidity across the course of Eliot's narrative. Indeed, the sentimental value of the turquoise necklace shifts dramatically as the story progresses. At the novel's commencement it is the ornament, we are told, that Gwendolen 'could most conveniently part with' having 'never known her father' (2003: 13–14). Emotionally unattached to this piece of jewellery, Gwendolen views it merely as an object of exchange, an alienable possession and instrument of financial assistance. For Margueritte Murphy, it is Gwendolen's careless disregard for, and active 'devalorization' of, her father that incites Deronda's censure (2006: 191). Yet the novel also lends itself to an alternative reading in which the power of jewellery takes centre stage. Although the narrator suggests that the practice of pawning small items of jewellery is typical of a gambling town, it raises, somewhat disapprovingly, the disjunction between the 'romantic superstition' inherent in playing roulette and 'the most prosaic rationalism as to human sentiments which stand in the way of raising needful money' (14). Like most Victorians, then, Eliot appears to believe in and abide by the deeply symbolic, communicative and emotional power of jewellery. Transmuted into a mere object of exchange, Gwendolen clearly disavows the necklace's linguistic, familial and affective value, and it is this indifference that seemingly shocks Deronda whose actions in returning the necklace are accurately read by Gwendolen as a kind of rebuke. Interestingly though, if there is no superstitious feeling directed towards the necklace before she parts with it, upon its immediate return Gwendolen experiences a peculiar feeling of premonition: 'Something – she never quite knew what – revealed to her before she opened the packet that it contained the necklace she had just parted with' (14). Whereas the necklace meant little to her before, in its recovered state Gwendolen encodes it with Deronda's disapproval, reading it as a form of reprimand for her actions. From this point onwards, her complex emotional investment in the necklace develops. At first a source of shame, later the necklace is significant because it takes on instructive and moral sensibilities. The first suggestion we receive of its changed status is when Gwendolen returns home to Offendene and offers her mother the meagre contents of her jewellery box as capital, but self-consciously holds back the turquoise chain, a gesture that surprises Gwendolen herself who remains unsure as to why she must retain it. As the narrator explains: 'But the movement of mind which led her to keep the necklace, to fold it up in the handkerchief, and rise to put it in her *nécessaire*, where she had first placed it when it had been returned to her, was more peculiar, and what would be called less reasonable.

It came from that streak of superstition in her' (229; original emphasis). In this moment Gwendolen is affectively attuned, perhaps for the first time, to the power and signification with which Victorian gems are imbued.

For Deborah Wynne, who reads Gwendolen's ambiguous feelings towards the turquoise chain in *Daniel Deronda* in light of property ownership and her own 'equivocal social identity', it is through this necklace in particular that 'Eliot shows that the world of objects can be a fluid one, where meanings and emotional attachments, as well as objects themselves, are subject to change' (2008: 16). More generally, Gwendolen's connection with the jewels expresses the issue of her own commodification in the novel. Likewise tracing the necklace's fluctuating narrative importance, Katherine Dunagen Osborne argues that in this novel and Eliot's earlier published *Middlemarch* (1871-2), nineteenth-century heirlooms function beyond the traditions of family inheritance and instead become vital to the female protagonists' interior subjectivities, forming 'emotional epicenters or psychic landmarks' within the texts (2010: 466). She shows how, after Deronda redeems it for her, Gwendolen assigns her own unique meanings to the turquoise chain besides those allocated to it as a family heirloom. She reads this item of jewellery not as the sign of Gwendolen's connection to the past and her family history but as a marker of her emotional development, suggesting that Gwendolen sees Deronda as a kind of sympathetic saviour (490). As a material link or lifeline forged between the two characters, the stones which adorn the necklace also become particularly meaningful. Returning to the pivotal moment in which the turquoise necklace is pawned and redeemed, Dunagen Osoborne argues that Eliot's initial disapproval is prompted by Gwendolen's 'lack of awareness of the striking emotional properties of the turquoise' (479). For the Victorians, turquoises were believed to have magical properties; they were 'both "*protective* and *sympathetic*"', qualities that Dunagen Osborne aptly points out, Gwendolen ostensibly lacks (479; original emphases).

Diamonds likewise play an emblematic role in the novel's diegetic world, proving crucial to both the plotting of the tale and the negotiation of its thematic concerns. Since they are heirlooms belonging to the Grandcourt family, they initially enter the text as agents of hereditary status. Before Gwendolen agrees to marry Henleigh Grandcourt and become the possessor of these ancestral diamonds, however, she meets his current mistress, Lydia Glasher, who explains that should Gwendolen accept Grandcourt's proposal, Lydia and her illegitimate children would lose all chance of respectability. In spite of this warning, Gwendolen marries Grandcourt and receives a jewel casket on her wedding night which contains the Grandcourt family diamonds along with a threatening note from Lydia Glasher who had them in her possession. Lydia's enforced relinquishing of the jewels to Gwendolen can be read as a metaphoric renunciation of her claims on Grandcourt, yet her accompanying note 'bequeaths her curse' (Wynne 2010: 116). Lydia's 'curse' and Gwendolen's guilt manifest themselves in the form of the 'poisoned' diamonds which haunt both *Daniel Deronda* and, later, *Gwendolen* (Souhami 2014: 104, 128). What corrupts the jewels in Eliot's text is their troubling transmission between Lydia and Gwendolen. According to Arnold, 'as a family heirloom' the Grandcourt family diamonds 'should rightly pass from one Lady Grandcourt to the next. Their temporary ownership by Lydia Glasher – presumably with the expectation that she would be the next Lady Grandcourt – taints the honor they should confer' and 'equates the new bride with a kept mistress and consequently signals the loss of her [Gwendolen's] moral inheritance' (2011: 23). Jewels thus serve as indices of morality in *Daniel Deronda*: they are tokens of Gwendolen's guilt and redemption. In this sense, the diamond parure and the turquoise necklace are diametrically opposed in the original novel. Arnold goes as far as to suggest that 'turquoise and diamonds are jewels that actually represent opposed cultural values within the text, ultimately confronting one another on Gwendolen's body' (2011: 21). The turquoise necklace is a marker of moral rectitude and symbolizes, for Gwendolen, Deronda's empathetic guidance; the diamonds, on the other hand, are the material and visual tokens of her remorse and shame. As the visible markers of both her burgeoning morality and her culpability, the two dramatically collide in the text.

Handed down like a family heirloom, jewellery and its associated symbolism likewise adorns Diana Souhami's contemporary novel, *Gwendolen*. In this neo-Victorian rewriting, Souhami ostensibly fulfils F. R Leavis's memorable desire to republish Eliot's *Daniel Deronda*, erasing what he referred to as the 'insufferably boring' parts of the book – that is, Deronda's search for the truth about his Jewish heritage – and renaming the remainder 'Gwendolen Harleth' (Leavis 1982: 10). Initially, Souhami mirrors the events of the original novel. Attuned to the hypotext, she layers entire sections of Eliot's prose onto Gwendolen's narrative and closely traces the original story arc. While much of the early plot remains the same, *Gwendolen* serves as both an expansion of and corrective to Eliot's novel. It moves beyond the parameters of its predecessor's narrative, providing Gwendolen with a liberating future and thereby challenging the unspecified and slightly ambiguous life that Eliot mandates for her heroine in the pre-text. At the end of *Daniel Deronda*, Gwendolen, 'withered' by 'grief', claims in vague, and somewhat hopeless terms that she means 'to live' (2003: 671, 672). Remarking upon the apparent bleakness of Gwendolen's final words, Priyanka Anne Jacob explains that they 'are in the future tense, pointing to her potential to become something better than she was – but the novel does not linger to see her through this hoped-for renewal, if it ever comes' (2016: 868). Resisting the uncertainty of Eliot's conclusion, then, *Gwendolen* instead provides what Oliver Lovesey has called 'a feminist sequel to *Daniel Deronda* with Gwendolen escaping the inevitability of marriage as vocation for women, gaining personal agency, and literally taking her new freedom on the road to North Africa with two gay male friends' (2017: 233). In this it seems that Souhami's Gwendolen does not live by the mantra set forth by Deronda's mother in *Daniel Deronda* that 'a woman's heart must be of such size and no larger, else it must be pressed small, like Chinese feet' (Eliot 2003: 523). Signalling the novel's investment in feminist thought, Souhami meaningfully prefaces *Gwendolen* with the above quotation. Not only does this adornment constitute, as Gutleben argues, 'a claim of lineage, an assertion of kinship, of genealogy' between pre-text and rewriting (2001: 17–18), but it draws upon and enhances the tentative proto-feminist strands of the original.

If Souhami's novel revolves around Gwendolen's attachment to Deronda, it nevertheless proffers a feminist opportunity for introspection and reputational reparation. Through a first-person narrative that encourages empathetic identification, Gwendolen attempts like Catherine in *Havisham*, to set the record straight. Her desire to exercise narrative authority is brought to the fore when Gwendolen confronts the fictional George Eliot who makes several appearances in the story's diegetic world. Gwendolen, initially unnerved by Eliot's penetrating gaze and questions, which make her feel 'as if I were a work of fiction, a creation of her pen' (253), later summons up the courage to repudiate the author's omniscience. In a metafictional exchange with Eliot, Gwendolen declares that she is not the 'flawed victim' of her imagination and accuses the author of 'contriving a version of me then condemning her own creation' (256). Souhami thus mobilizes the biofictional mode in order to retrospectively castigate the author's treatment of her fictional creation. Fionnuala Dillane suggests that such 'privileging of the creative fiction over its creator' is typical in biofictional renderings of Eliot (2020: 22). Writing of Patricia Duncker's *Sophie and the Sibyl* (2015) together with Souhami's *Gwendolen*, Dillane explains that 'in both novels there is an overt critique of George Eliot's unsympathetic representation of the very modern Gwendolen Harleth, while the novelist is presented in caricature. George Eliot is set up as a rival to her daring and beautiful heroine' (2020: 23). Souhami seems to move beyond the idea of Eliot as a mere rival, however, when she seeks instead to disentangle Gwendolen's story from Eliot's imaginative control in the concluding section of the novel. In an aside that echoes the representation of Pip's story in *Havisham*, Gwendolen openly disavows the pretext: in her letter to Deronda she declares that she has not read Eliot's latest novel, which is based on the two of them, because she believes that Eliot has 'freely invented and omitted' the facts (293).

In a further act of defiance, Souhami employs the first-person narrative form to express the sexual and psychological trauma that Gwendolen endures at the hands of Grandcourt. While her intimate autodiegetic narration discloses Gwendolen's 'true' feelings for Deronda, the quasi-epistolary format also provides a revelation of Grandcourt's cruelty and a critique of nineteenth-century patriarchal norms. Whereas in Eliot's novel Grandcourt's implied emotional and physical abuse remain largely unspoken, in Souhami's Gwendolen's voice fills the silences within the original text. In a metafictional moment, she tells Deronda that 'what happened ... I have down the years hinted at but told no one', before revealing the details of her suffering (2014: 94). By giving voice to historical issues of psychological and sexual abuse, Souhami's narrative chimes with contemporary concerns. Armelle Parey has convincingly argued that as much as rewritings deal with the past, they are also 'testimonies to the contemporary world whose preoccupations often find their way into new texts' (2006: para. 18). Gwendolen's acknowledgement of Grandcourt's repeated violations is thus couched within twenty-first-century discourse: she acknowledges that, 'what Grandcourt had done to me, would do to me, was not illegal. I was his wife. I had no right or power to refuse him. Consent was immaterial' (2014: 95). Souhami's narrative dovetails with contemporary concerns around issues of consent, harassment and sexual assault. As late as 1991, marital rape was made illegal, and, in the wake of recent social media movements such as #MeToo and #TimesUp, which delineate how women have been routinely harassed, abused and silenced, Gwendolen's words can be read as a significant commentary on misogyny within contemporary and Victorian societies. In its attempt at 'redressing certain wrongs and restoring a suppressed, apocryphal script', Souhami's novel might be read as a gesture of 're-righting', to borrow Chantel Zabus's suggestive phrasing (2001: 191).

Divided into three sections, *Gwendolen*'s narrative structure formally reflects the faceted surface of the 'poisoned diamonds' that populate *Daniel Deronda* and which reappear in the contemporary text. The first section of the novel is entitled 'Grandcourt' and like the original, it recounts Henleigh Miller Grandcourt's acquisition of Gwendolen and the reciprocal exchange of wealth and status conferred by the diamond engagement ring. The second section is headed under the name 'Deronda' and the final section fittingly closes with 'Gwendolen'.

The three sections of the narrative encapsulate the three important figures in the original text's love triangle, as well as echoing the parure of diamonds that Gwendolen receives as payment, or perhaps penance, for her hasty marriage to Grandcourt; that is, the three pieces of jewellery designed to be worn on three separate parts of the body: the wrist, the neck and the head/hair. Souhami also notably stages the reappearance of the turquoise necklace as thematic motif in the novel, yet in its contemporary reiteration the necklace becomes a material means through which issues of narrative, history and memory are routed. The retrospective nature of the neo-Victorian novel here combines with and expedites the memorializing function of jewellery. During the course of the novel, Gwendolen assiduously returns to and re-examines the events of her past which are invoked by the jewels. The turquoise necklace and diamond parure thus operate outside of the functions they held in the pre-text; they are more than plot devices, or simply material manifestations of Gwendolen's guilt or moral dependence upon Deronda. Rather, in *Gwendolen* they are material memories.

In the hypertext, Gwendolen recounts her story through repeated obsessional references to what she calls the 'talisman turquoise necklace' (2014: 190). Worn against the heroine's body while she scribes her letter to Deronda, the turquoise chain sustains and invigorates her; jewels are here figured as an important part of Gwendolen's narrative and history, and aid in her remembrance of the past. This enhanced investment in the turquoise necklace suggests the intensity of Gwendolen's emotional devotion to Deronda and simultaneously recalls the historically inflected concept of Victorian keepsake culture. It was in the nineteenth century that 'small personal articles that were variously called mementos, tokens, keepsakes, remembrancers, and even relics' became central to everyday life. Indeed, the Victorians were 'uniquely conscious of the memento as a specific cultural form' (Barnett 2013: 58). As a keepsake, the turquoise necklace highlights the interdependence of materiality and memory. This re-imagined jewel becomes the physical locus through which Gwendolen engages with, responds to and re-examines her relationship to the past. As a material object that offers itself as a discursive space, it also enables and facilitates an imagined and imaginative form of narrative communication.

That jewels constitute a form of linguistic communication is also evident in Eliot's original text. When she receives the rescued necklace from Deronda in the hypotext, Gwendolen reads into his actions, and assigns the sartorial item specific non-verbal meaning. Increasingly convinced of their mutual affinity, she wears the turquoise necklace around her wrist as a secret message to Deronda during a visit to Topping Abbey with her husband. Wound 'clumsily' about her wrist, the necklace is 'necessarily conspicuous' (2003: 3698). Its enhanced sentimental value is mirrored by its altered state in which it is worn as a cumbersome bracelet. Although Gwendolen is attuned to the power of this necklace, neither Deronda nor Grandcourt seem to understand her affective dependence upon it. Grandcourt does, however, recognize the impropriety of the gesture. Realizing that her actions are an attempt to convey something unspoken yet meaningful to Deronda, he says: 'I suppose there is some understanding between you and Deronda about that thing you have on your wrist. If you have anything to say to him, say it. But don't carry on a telegraphing which other people are supposed not to see. It's damnably vulgar' (371). Thus, in Eliot's novel the exchange of jewels metaphorizes human interaction and communication. Souhami engages this same strategy in order to make the texts speak to one another across temporal and textual divides. In *Gwendolen*, however, the communicative nature of the turquoise necklace is extended. Through this necklace, Gwendolen's 'real' feelings are exposed to the reader. It is a necklace imbued with talismanic potency that facilitates and orients her narrative. An explicit expression of Gwendolen's abiding love for Deronda, she wears it continuously throughout the novel: 'I still wore the turquoise necklace as my talisman. I could not discard the hope I had invested in it' (2014: 174).

This in itself is significant. After Gwendolen covertly wears the turquoise necklace to Topping Abbey in *Daniel Deronda*, Eliot curiously makes no further mention of it in the remainder of the novel. Drawing attention to this notable absence, Dunagen Osborne explains that 'when Deronda abdicates his position as Gwendolen's sympathetic redeemer and protective saviour, the turquoise necklace necessarily loses its charged meaning and thus its presence in the narrative' (2010: 490). She goes on to suggest that, although the necklace's secrets will disappear with Gwendolen, 'the thing will most likely live on' (490) and 'could have a future as dauntingly and thrillingly open as Gwendolen's' (491). In Souhami's novel, the turquoise necklace is resurrected and appears to have the afterlife that Dunagen Osborne prophesizes. Unlike in Eliot's novel, however, it does not fade from the pages of *Gwendolen* after its role as a plot device has been realized. Rather, it retains its 'talismanic' properties, becoming a potent reminder of Deronda, a tangible link between the two texts, and an intimate keepsake for Gwendolen with which she anchors herself and her story to the past. Referring to the hope she has invested in the ornament she explains that it 'became the symbol for my tryst with you, like a rose, a locket or a ring … I wear it now' (2014: 11). Like the protagonists in Byatt's *Possession*, Souhami's Gwendolen recognizes the power of sartorial objects to mediate and materialize memory, and to give shape and form to the historic past.

The textual reimagining of the 'talisman turquoise necklace' in this manner, imbues it with the properties of the souvenir as defined by Susan Stewart in her foundational work *On Longing* (1984):

> We might say that this capacity of objects to serve as traces of authentic experience is, in fact, exemplified by the souvenir. The souvenir distinguishes experiences. We do not need or desire souvenirs of events that are repeatable. Rather we need and desire souvenirs of events that are reportable, events whose materiality has escaped us, events that thereby exist only through the invention of narrative. Through narrative the souvenir substitutes a context of perpetual consumption for its context of origin. It represents not the lived experience of its maker but the 'secondhand' experience of its possessor/owner. (1993: 135)

The concept of the souvenir explicates the preservative impulse with which the jewels are saturated in Souhami's text. As a witness to the past, the presence of the necklace signifies Gwendolen's experience and, at the same time, holds out the assurance of re-experience, promising to reconstruct the past for consumption in the present. If souvenirs, as Stewart attests, mark 'the transformation of materiality into meaning' (1993: 140), then the return to these jewels in the present text speaks to the inadequacy of language alone. As in Byatt's novel, Souhami gestures to the narrative significance of sartorial objects in creating and conveying meaning. In a similar vein, Bill Brown in his recently published *Other Things* (2015), draws upon what he calls 'the logic of "souvenirism"', as a means of referring to 'the dynamic by which objects retroprojectively create the event – the eventfulness of the event – they are meant to record and recall' (274). In this context, the jewels are tasked with the retrospective construction of past events. They are the mediational means by which Gwendolen can work through and record her traumatic history.

On this point, the revisioning and reconstruction of Gwendolen's traumatic past occurs through a series of specific recollections involving the diamonds. Tracing the contours of the original tale, Souhami mirrors the pivotal scene in *Daniel Deronda*, in which Gwendolen, upon receiving the parure of diamonds from Lydia experiences a hysterical episode that Peter Brooks reads as symbolizing 'an unhappy Victorian wedding night' (1993: 247). In the hypotext, this moment closes with the scattered diamonds intended to be read as the external, material signs of Gwendolen's interior crisis. In *Gwendolen*, by contrast, this moment is extended, exposing Grandcourt's cruelty and making explicit Gwendolen's violation. Recalling the gaps and silences of the original novel, Souhami draws on the symbolic and communicative power of jewellery to decrypt the trauma of Gwendolen's wedding night. Since the parure of diamonds is designed to be worn around the neck and wrists it represents physical restraint and can be read in light of Derren Gilhooley's words when he aptly argues that 'violence is implicit in jewellery's very mechanisms of fastening, piercing, clasping and buckling … Sexuality is ever present, not merely with jewellery functioning as a prism to focus nebulous sexual allure, but in the penetration of pin into cloth … the coupling mechanisms of a clasp' (1997: 2–3). The sexual violence inherent in the function and form of jewellery is made manifest in Souhami's novel when Grandcourt's rape of Gwendolen, in which she is 'pinioned' and 'stabbed' (94–5), is echoed by the symbolic violation that follows. Immediately after the assault, Grandcourt insists on personally adorning Gwendolen in the diamonds. Told in analepsis, she describes the episode as follows: ' "you will want someone to fasten them", he said. He took them from their case. His hands crawled at my neck, my hair, my ears, breasts. I sat with my eyes closed' (2014: 98). These same actions undertaken by Grandcourt in *Daniel Deronda* are equally intrusive. In the pretext, despite Gwendolen's reluctance to wear the diamonds to Brackenshaw Castle, Grandcourt forces them upon her (2003: 353). Though, in the Victorian period, diamonds were considered 'the badge of marital status, their adamantine hardness meaning "endurance" for the enduring quality of love' (Gere and Rudoe 2010: 154), in *Daniel Deronda* they signal only Grandcourt's patriarchal desire for ownership and control. Souhami's novel internalizes and expands this unsettling symbolism. The scene in which Grandcourt adorns Gwendolen in the jewels serves to instantiate the explicit sexual violence of the previous pages. The scene thus recalls and amplifies the brutality of his actions, while the presence of the diamonds on Gwendolen's body emblematizes her victimization and Grandcourt's cruelty. In her deployment of the diamonds in this manner, Souhami explicates what Eliot's text can only gesture towards.

Constituting a second and symbolic violation, the physical restraint of Gwendolen with the diamonds also metonymically stages their imperial heritage. Following Elaine Freedgood's methodology in which she traces 'the fugitive meanings' of objects beyond the borders of the Victorian novel (2006: 4), the diamonds in both *Daniel Deronda* and *Gwendolen* can be read as colonial objects that reflect Britain's abuse of other lands and its plunder of their riches, practices that were ratified, and therefore excused, by imperial ideology. Suzanne Daly summarizes diamonds' colonial inflections when she explains that in the Victorian cultural consciousness, they were primarily associated with the Southern Indian mines of Golconda, until their discovery in Brazil and Borneo in 1725 and in South Africa around 1870 (2011: 61). Given their colonial beginnings, all diamonds are heavily implicated in what Pointon has called 'a post-colonial politics of geography, race and class and above all of slavery'; she notes that the diamond mines were all 'worked by slaves… under systems of bodily surveillance' (2009: 43–4). While neither Eliot's nor Souhami's novel makes this historical link explicit, both of the texts' diegetic worlds are largely dependent upon the colonial context of the nineteenth century. Carolyn Lesjak reads Gwendolen's narrative in *Daniel Deronda* as 'a microcosm of the larger system of imperialism, a system which Eliot implicitly criticizes through the trope of empire she uses to describe Gwendolen's relationship with Grandcourt' (2006: 114). Likewise, Julia Kuehn notes that Eliot's novel was written at an 'important moment in British colonial history' and therefore reflects 'the historical question of Britain's contact with foreign nations and cultures' (2014: 24). Following Eliot, Souhami's novel works to 'expose antisemitic biases' (Dillane 2020: 23), while also tacitly alluding to empire when the titular heroine travels to North Africa. The presence of the diamonds in each of the two novels serves to further draw together issues pertaining to empire. Grandcourt's conquest and subsequent sexual and psychological possession of Gwendolen, which Eliot suggestively refers to as his 'empire of fear' in *Daniel Deronda* (2003: 352), metaphorically implies the imperial trajectory of the diamonds, especially when he uses the jewels as agents of his control. Although they largely signal familial inheritance and social respectability, as well as domesticity and power dynamics within marriage, the jewels are for the knowledgeable reader at least, besieged by their imperial histories. Dunagen Osborne contends that during the time in which Eliot was writing *Daniel Deronda*, 'diamonds were enjoying a resurgence in popularity following the discovery of South African diamonds in 1867', but she also acknowledges that, for a Victorian readership, they would have likely been tainted by the violence of colonialism (2010: 484).[14] On symbolic and literal levels, then, the mediated jewels are reflective of the 're-visionary' aims of the novel in which they reappear. Their presence and functions, which exceed their roles in the hypotexts, educe fresh readings. Bridging the gap between past and present, Victorian and neo-Victorian novel, while also highlighting the divide between them, the jewels function as both potent ciphers of continuity and rupture.

---

[14] Popular novels such as Collins's *The Moonstone* (1868) had already begun the process of reflecting upon the exploitation of other lands as signalled through the expropriation of the titular Moonstone, which was based upon the Koh-i-noor diamond.

Of all the material items with which Souhami and Frame attempt to recover, express and reify a sense of the submerged past in *Gwendolen* and *Havisham*, the reappearance of jewellery is perhaps the most significant. Jewels are imbricated in complex social, symbolic and cultural systems. During the nineteenth century, they were deeply suffused with gendered, linguistic and historical meaning. Since they proffered 'the promise of permanence' (Mullins 1896: 240), jewels functioned as archives of memory, preserving frameworks of narrative and emotion. Gwendolen's turquoise necklace and diamond parure, and the jewels passed between Antoinette, Catherine and Estella Havisham, thus represent pivotal, abiding objects with which to resurrect, reimagine and recount the heroines' respective stories in the present. In recognizing the recuperative and subversive potential of these rewritings, this chapter has read the reappearance of jewels as feminist symbols of inheritance and identity. As persistent remnants of the lost Victorian age, such jewels are potent sartorial items with which to apprehend the past. Functioning as a point of return, the jewels in these two contemporary historical fictions are directly drawn from two canonical nineteenth-century novels. In staging these acts of sartorial appropriation, both novels foreground the thematic motif of inheritance, a theme which is itself inherited from the tradition of Victorian realist and sensation fictions. In such fiction, Vincent Pecora argues, 'questions of inheritance, and of the family romance that often attends them' are commonplace; the 'Dickensian narrative of inheritance and family romance, was time and again concerned with the problem of inherited property and, by metaphoric extension, inherited custom, morals, and sensibility' (2008: 179). Frame and Souhami's neo-Victorian novels inherit jewels and their associated meanings from Dickens and Eliot's pre-texts both of which centre around themes of inheritance and dis/possession. However, the contemporary novels undertake to disrupt the trajectory of these inheritances by revising the original texts and reorienting the ways in which jewellery functions in each. Acting as material metaphors for memory and matrilineal love, these literary depictions of jewellery prove vital for enhancing contemporary discussions of female embodiment and identity. More specifically, the study of jewellery in these two texts enriches our understanding of the neo-Victorian novel and its revisionist impulses, as well as proffering a lens through which to achieve extended readings of the nineteenth-century texts on which they are based.

Returning to such jewels and re-examining them in relation to their neo-Victorian remediations is vital as it highlights their affective sedimentation. Their passage along generations of protagonists is mirrored by the figurative transmission of jewels across textual generations, and as the jewels are conveyed from one text to the next, their emotional, narratorial and affectual power deepens. The reappearance of such symbolic jewels in these neo-Victorian novels speaks to the role of sartorial objects in highlighting the continuities and resonances between past and present. Their transmission across intra- and extra-textual generations of women allows them to convey the unspoken secrets of the past, and in doing so, the jewels open up a dialogue between hypotext and hypertext. Just as items of jewellery interweave the two storylines that make up *Possession*'s narrative composition, in Frame and Souhami's novels, jewels materialize familial, historical and textual connections. That the jewels are given new life in these contemporary rewritings is a strategy that closely reflects the neo-Victorianism genre's processes of re-fashioning and revision.

6

Conclusion

The sentimental and symbolic resonances with which jewels and jewellery are imbued in *Possession*, *Havisham* and *Gwendolen* are equally, if fleetingly, evident in Richard Flanagan's biofictional novel *Wanting* (2008). Like the latter two texts, *Wanting* affords the opportunity for compensatory revision. It enters into a powerful dialogue with sartorial objects, engaging them as potent material signs of a collective cultural past. Partaking of postcolonial neo-Victorianism, which 'explore[s] how the dominant culture romanticizes, naturalizes, and authorises narratives and structures of empire as it struggles to come to terms with their continuances in the present' (Ho 2013: 11), Flanagan's novel offers a retelling of European colonial settlement in nineteenth-century Australia. Documenting the country's fraught history of colonial violence and Aboriginal dispossession, the novel centres upon the formation and subsequent destruction of a penal colony in Van Diemen's Land (now Tasmania). Issues of cultural displacement are dramatized through the story of the orphaned Aboriginal child, Mathinna (*c*. 1835–52), around whom one of the novel's main narrative strands revolves. Surrounding this marginalized nineteenth-century figure is a cast of well-known historical subjects, including the Arctic explorer John Franklin and his wife Lady Jane, both of whom adopt Mathinna, as well as the famous author Charles Dickens and his mistress the burgeoning actress Ellen Ternan who occupy the novel's intersecting storyline. In this neo-Victorian rendering of Mathinna's life, Flanagan's indictment of England's exploitative colonial empire is metaphorically enacted through dress.

It is Mathinna's impassioned dancing and distinctive mode of dress, both of which are in the manner of the Wybalenna people, that first attracts the Franklins' attention. We learn in an early passage that Mathinna is conspicuous because she is wearing 'a long necklace of some beauty around her neck and a large white kangaroo skin over one shoulder' (2016: 49). Though mentioned only briefly, each of these sartorial elements is illustrative of Mathinna's culture and community. Both come to her laden with a lingering sense of historical, cultural and familial connection: the white kangaroo skin is the remaining relic of her father, an Aboriginal chief named Towterer, whose death at the beginning of the novel is hastened by the 'Protector's' (George Augustus Robinson) misguided medical interventions; likewise, the necklace which the narrator remarks is 'made out of hundreds of tiny, vivid green seashells, threaded on several yards of possum sinew, then wrapped around her neck a number of times' (2016: 51), is a gift from Mathinna's deceased mother, Wongerneep. Since the crafting of such necklaces represents a vital and enduring cultural tradition amongst Indigenous women, Mathinna's 'beautiful shell necklace connects her to her people' (Lanone 2020: 238). It is in these small and contained yet evocative sartorial objects that Mathinna's powerful sense of cultural belonging is most clearly rendered and her ties to her homeland are first materialized.

For the Western colonizers, however, unwilling to acknowledge and understand Mathinna's attachment to such things, these sartorial items fail to signify. Misreading the kangaroo skin as nothing more than the inappropriate costume of the Aboriginal people, the Protector refuses to allow Mathinna to leave Flinders Island wearing it. Disregarding its familial consequence, he insists that she shed the skin hunted by her father, warning her that it would be 'impossible to arrive at Government House dressed as a savage' (110). The removal of the kangaroo skin, and later, the necklace, which are Mathinna's last physical links with her parents, become emblematic of wider colonial practices that sought to enforce estrangement and alienation amongst the island's original inhabitants. These instances also become a pattern for the novel's later treatment of sartorial culture when Mathinna is taken into the Franklins' home and forced to dress in Western fashions. Troublingly, Mathinna's removal to Hobart Island and her subsequent Westernization is figured by Lady Jane as a kind of social, educational and sartorial 'experiment' (2016: 195). Symbolic of the ills wrought by empire in its attempts to colonize Tasmania, Mathinna becomes Flanagan's 'representative figure for Tasmanian Aboriginals' (Ho Lai-Ming 2012: 22). Crucially, it is her body and its adornments that become the microcosmic sites upon which such issues are most clearly inscribed.

Although Lady Jane, experiencing a moment of maternal longing, wants at first 'to dress that little girl up and tie ribbons in her hair' (118), her attempts to subdue, 'educate' and colonize Mathinna manifest in violently restrictive sartorial terms. This recalls the punitory and correctional capacities of clothes discussed in Chapters 2 and 3, which are employed to reform and regulate female bodies; here, dress is similarly employed to control and suppress, yet its primarily gendered dimensions give way to overtly racial and cultural concerns. After Mathinna is presented to her new guardian barefoot, her 'splayed and very brown feet' visible beneath 'a dark grey serge dress of a type that attracts the word sensible' (116), Lady Jane declares that 'she will be shod and she will be civilised' (117), thus exposing the moral hypocrisies at the heart of the British Empire. The drive to clothe Mathinna in Western dress arises from, and is informed by, nineteenth-century Eurocentric discourse in which dress was regarded as a tool of social and moral edification. In his 1862 book *Colonial Sketches: or, Five Years in South Australia with Hints to Capitalists and Emigrants*, the English writer Robert Harrison notes, for instance, 'the influence of dress as an agent of civilization' (76). For British settlers like Harrison, native dress amplified the necessity of a 'civilizing', read colonial, presence and reinforced xenophobic ideologies pertaining to issues of racial and moral inferiority; Western clothing, on the other hand, was aligned with civility, superiority and social and cultural advancement. It is to such views that Lady Jane appears to subscribe in her insistence that Mathinna wear shoes and a 'red dress that Lady Jane had herself worn as a child, and which she had given Mathinna as a present on the first anniversary of her arrival. Button-shouldered and short-sleeved, belted with a black velvet band, the red dress' we learn 'was made of the lightest silk and cut in the simple high-waisted style popular in the wake of the French Revolution' (130). From this detailed sartorial depiction, the reader is to infer Mathinna's cultural displacement. And although she appears initially eager to exchange her kangaroo skin and shell necklace for the red dress, symbolizing her partial willingness to assimilate, its presence in the narrative gestures towards a growing sense of cultural dislocation. Unlike Antoinette's red dress in *Wide Sargasso Sea* (discussed in Chapter 1), Mathinna's gown does not recall her home or establish a sense of belonging but comes instead to represent only her isolation and disaffection. As one of the central material markers of her 'enforced acculturation' (Lanone 2020: 239), the red dress signals her literal and metaphorical separation from her homeland and heritage. Likewise, 'the beautiful court shoes and party shoes' that shackle her feet and make her feel 'as if her body had been blindfolded' (2016: 119) operate in tandem with the red dress as the visible emblems of empire in this text. Together, they deny Mathinna the traditions of her culture and distort her sense of identity. Though less obviously agentic than the previously discussed items of clothing, the power of dress in Flanagan's novel appears to lie in its contradictory capacity to construct and disrupt both a sense of individual and collective identity and to forge and yet simultaneously reject a sense of belonging.

Towards the novel's conclusion when the Franklins desert Mathinna and leave her behind at St John's Orphanage, the red dress and the shell necklace make another deeply symbolic appearance in the narrative; it is through these two opposing sartorial items that her ambivalent status is made resolutely clear. Here, Mathinna exists between cultures. Abandoned by the Franklins who return to England without her, and unable to assimilate back into Wybalenna culture, which has all but been destroyed by the British colonizers, the red dress and shell necklace serve as the opposing markers of her, now liminal, position. *Wanting* extends this imagery further by tracing the red dress's degeneration from beautiful, elegant garment into murderous and 'filthy red scarf' (247). As the story follows the disintegrating dress it enacts a peculiar slippage between dress and body in which the declining fabric, its increasingly coarse and tattered appearance, is aligned with Mathinna's own interior deterioration, figured through her decline into alcoholism and prostitution. Eventually, the remaining fabric of the red dress is 'twisted' into a 'greasy loop… an inescapable garotte' by Walter Talba Bruney, another Aborigine and Mathinna's drinking companion, and it is this sartorial item that he uses to strangle her to death (247). This is a profound image of destruction that reflects the obliteration of the Aboriginal people, both directly and indirectly, by the European colonizers. In her evocative reading of this same moment, Catherine Lanone explains that the red dress becomes a 'red relic' that both 'seduces' and 'smothers; it becomes a stifling grip, a stranglehold', as well as 'a metatextual sign of her [Mathinna's] "tattered" story' (2020: 238). In its degenerating state, the red dress appears to exert a kind of homicidal agency. It is a material manifestation of imperialism, and a reminder and mediator of colonial violence. It also serves a significant narratological function in its memorializing and self-reflective ability to raise and interrogate past injustices while simultaneously shedding new light on the contemporary novel's cultural and political moment: the publication of *Wanting* in 2008 was coincident with Australia's national apology to the 'Stolen Generation' (see Lanone 2020: 233). The presence of the red dress in both the narrative itself and the history of the novel's construction reveals the way in which clothes can actively participate in and stage ethical and political interventions in the historical past.

The novel's direct confrontation of empire through the sartorial reflects Flanagan's own deeply affectual experiences with a material object in his early twenties. In a 2008 interview with Random House Books, the author recalls the pivotal moment when, looking through a number of colonial watercolour paintings in a Hobart Museum, he first came across Thomas Bock's 1842 painting

Mathinna.¹ Describing his affective encounter with the painting, Flanagan explains,

> I thought it was very beautiful and inexplicably moving. It showed a small Aboriginal girl in a beautiful red silk dress, bound with a black velvet band. 'It's Mathinna', the curator told me. And he told me her story, of an Aboriginal child adopted in the 1830s by the famous Arctic explorer Sir John Franklin and his wife Lady Jane. It was a strange and, for me, immensely moving tale. ('What led you to write Wanting?' 2008)²

Flanagan situates this pictorial rendition of Mathinna as central to his own imaginative project. While Bock's painting only appears momentarily in the novel before Lady Jane throws it overboard on her return voyage to England, the image of the red dress as the origin of narrative endures. It gives rise to Flanagan's novel, becoming the catalyst for his storytelling process. It is the central material motif that stitches together past and present. Utilizing the narrative quality of sartorial things, Flanagan's authorial engagement with the red dress forges a connection between materiality, memory and narrative. The red dress thus becomes a metaphor for the way in which sartorial culture both holds and gives rise to historical fiction. It is the material means with which Mathinna, as forgotten and disregarded figure, is re-fashioned and written back into the historical record.

In accordance with the other focal novels discussed in this book, Flanagan's *Wanting* demonstrates that dress does not simply reflect the nineteenth-century material past; rather, it plays a vital and active role in its shaping and construction. As in the other neo-Victorian fictions analyzed throughout this study, sartorial culture emerges as a central component of the novel's complex processes of re-fashioning and revision in which the lost Victorian age is materialized in the present. *Victorian Dress in Contemporary Historical Fiction* has explored contemporary representations of the Victorian period through the lens of neo-Victorian revision. Focusing on an area yet to receive prominent critical attention, it has argued that dress and fabric are central to the imaginative recreation and rewriting of the Victorian material past. Clothes, as the previous chapters attest, hold within them histories and narratives of encounter. They are the sites of dynamic activity, emotional intensity and temporal and historical

---

¹ After his conviction and transportation to Tasmania in the early nineteenth century, Thomas Bock (1790–1855) established himself as a professional portraitist, specializing in painting Aborigines.
² An image of Bock's *Mathinna* can be viewed on the Tasmanian Museum and Art Gallery's website: https://www.tmag.tas.gov.au/whats_on/newsselect/2018articles/tasmanias_colonial_past_in_focus

connectivity. In the contemporary and nineteenth-century novels examined in this study, they assume a variety of functions that enhance and enliven the texts' fictional diegetic worlds.

At its most basic level, literary depictions of dress embellish the pages of the neo-Victorian novel and proffer a sense of historical authenticity to contemporary returns to the past. Although these items of dress are simulacral – fictional copies of real Victorian garments – they nevertheless proffer a creative and imaginative means of engaging with the past's social, emotional and historical complexities. At the same time, however, neo-Victorian garments function as more than mere historical markers: they provide, and sometimes deny, fictional figures with a sense of protection, a means of self-expression and aesthetic pleasure; they construct, convey and negotiate gender, class and race; signal economic status and political power and provide simulative strategies for immersing the reader in the past by highlighting the intricate affective and experiential aspects of cloth and fabric. Most significantly, perhaps, dress constitutes the body in neo-Victorian fiction. Contemporary representations of Victorian dress allow modern-day readers a means of resurrecting and thus accessing the material textual body. In the neo-Victorian novels examined in the preceding chapters, garments function particularly as material sites that revive and recover the female body, thus rendering it both present and legible.

Of course, the legibility of neo-Victorian women's bodies depends upon the capacity of garments to function as alternative 'texts' that can be read alongside and against the central narrative. Just as the Victorians deciphered the sociocultural cues inherent in dress in the period, I have suggested that clothing in the neo-Victorian novel can be read to reveal the genre's key thematic, narrative and structural mechanisms. Whether real or imagined, dress proves vital to neo-Victorian renderings of nineteenth-century material culture. As Margaret Stetz affirms, 'whatever human beings put on their bodies is a matter of both individual and social significance; how characters (even imaginary ones) are clothed is as crucial and revealing as the actions they take' (2009b: 62). The same is true for clothes that are disconnected from the body. In Chapter 2, for instance, I showed how clothes which exude a certain independence and agency of their own in Colm Tóibín's *The Master* and Margaret Atwood's *Alias Grace* augment intra- and extra-textual readers' understanding by conveying important unspoken signals about character, narrative and plot.

As much as they can be read as highly revealing social and cultural ciphers, clothes can also be decrypted in relation to past individual wearers because dress retains the persistent physical and psychical resonances of absent bodies. On this point, Adam Geczy and Vicki Karaminas indicate that 'much has been written about how clothing acts as a vessel that contains memories embedded in its fabric. Stains, shapes, and sweat that belong to the wearers past but are contained in the present. Cloth preserves the past as evidence of human interaction and is a powerful trigger for social and cultural memories' (2019: 27). I have argued that the cast-off gowns discussed in Chapter 2 and the empty gloves analyzed in Chapter 3 contain the memories, emotions and desires of past wearers woven into them. In these instances, fabric retains the physical and literal traces of the body. Worn against the skin – and often acting as a type of second skin or corporeal double – items of clothing are therefore intimately linked to notions of touch. Indeed, in all of the novels examined in this study, the sense of touch stimulates the act of remembrance and also repeatedly conjures the presence of an absent lover/'other'. As discussed in Chapters 4 and 5, sartorial objects become repositories that retain human emotions; gestures of giving, receiving and wearing, all of which involve haptic correspondence, are central to garments' affective and agentive abilities to retain and transmit memories, secrets and stories across transgenerational divides. In the books examined here, then, neo-Victorian authors draw upon dress, fashion and other textile forms as material routes to the nineteenth century.

A feeling of uneasiness appears to trail some of the literary depictions of dress uncovered here, however. There is a sense that the stories that dress contains, the past(s) it narrates, may not always be conveyed completely or read correctly. In both *Alias Grace* and *Possession*, discussed in Chapters 2 and 5, sartorial items such as a patchwork quilt made from the fabric swatches cut from women's gowns, and certain items of jewellery, hold close their secrets, often refusing to fully divulge them. In narrative terms, this reaffirms the neo-Victorian genre's conceptual ties with postmodernism and, at the same time, aligns with Victorian social fears about the deliberate manipulation and subsequent misreading of sartorial signs. In these instances, the contemporary novels tend to play with issues of readability. They urge us to pay close attention to historical dress, both literally and literarily, encouraging a careful handling and reading of clothes in ways that offer us an indicative means of re-reading nineteenth-century dress and its implications in the present moment. In undertaking such readings, this study has thus sought to offer new ways of thinking about the construction of the past. Neo-Victorian clothes, as each of the preceding chapters attest, sit at the nexus of history, narrative and memory. Since 'textiles form an archive of our intimate existence' (Hunt 2014: 208), they preserve the stories of the past and proffer an affectual link with the present. References to clothes in neo-Victorian novels operate, then, not merely as incidental detail or textual ornamentation, but as sensuous, affective and highly intentional literary devices.

In its exploration of the contemporary re-mediations of Victorian-era clothing, this book has traced the continuing influence of nineteenth-century material culture in our own modern-day society. In doing so it argues that an interrogation of these textu(r)al figurations is as significant for Victorian studies as it is for contemporary cultural research. The sartorial things we value from the first industrial age have accrued symbolic, affective and cultural meanings which are not always apparent when we study them simply as artefacts of their own era. Thinking about what Victorian material items mean now provides a means of interpreting the genealogy of our culture and acknowledging the crucial role the nineteenth century has played in shaping it. By returning to the sartorial items of the Victorian period and imbuing them with memory, agency and narrative, we accord the material things of the past a special significance. In this vein, dress and fabric might be taken as significant intergenerational threads that keep the links between Victorian and neo-Victorian cultures alive.

References

Adburgham, A. (1989), *Shops and Shopping, 1800–1914*, London: Barrie and Jenkins.

Ahmed, L. (1992), *Women and Gender in Islam: Historical Roots of a Modern Debate*, New Haven: Yale University Press.

Ahmed, S. (2006), *Queer Phenomenology: Orientations, Objects, Others*, Durham: Duke University Press.

Ahmed, S. (2010), 'Orientations Matter', in D. Coole and S. Frost (eds), *New Materialisms: Ontology, Agency, and Politics*, 234–57. Durham: Duke University Press.

Aindow, R. (2010), *Dress and Identity in British Literary Culture 1870–1914*, Farnham: Ashgate.

Almila, A., and D. Inglis (eds) (2018), *The Routledge International Handbook to Veils and Veiling Practices*, London: Routledge.

Arias, R. (2005), 'Talking with the Dead: Revisiting the Victorian Past and the Occult in Margaret Atwood's *Alias Grace* and Sarah Waters's *Affinity*', *Estudios Ingleses de la Universidad Complutense* 13: 85–105. Available online: http://revistas.ucm.es/index.php/EIUC/article/view/EIUC0505110085A/7855 (accessed 13 September 2021).

Arias, R. (2011), '(In)Visible Disability in Neo-Victorian Families', in M. L. Kohlke and C. Gutleben (eds), *Neo-Victorian Families: Gender, Sexual and Cultural Politics*, 343–64. Amsterdam: Rodopi.

Arias, R. (2014), 'Traces and Vestiges of the Victorian Past in Contemporary Fiction', in. N. Boehm-Schnitker and S. Gruss (eds), *Neo-Victorian Literature and Culture: Immersions and Revisitations*, 111–22, Abingdon: Routledge.

Arias, R. (2015), 'Neo-Sensation Fiction or "Appealing to the Nerves": Sensation and Perception in Neo-Victorian Fiction', *Rivista di Studi Vittoriani*, 40: 13–30.

Arias, R. (2017), 'Queer Phenomenology and Tactility in Sarah Waters's Neo-Victorian Fiction', *Revista Canaria De Estudios Ingleses*, 74 (2): 41–54.

Arias, R. (2020), 'Sensoriality and Hair Jewellery in Neo-Victorian Fiction and Culture', *Lectora*, 26: 83–97. Available online: https://revistes.ub.edu/index.php/lectora/article/view/32518 (accessed 12 September 2022).

Arias, R., and P. Pulham (2010), 'Introduction', in R. Arias and P. Pulham (eds), *Haunting and Spectrality in Neo-Victorian Fiction: Possessing the Past*, xi–xxvi, Basingstoke: Palgrave Macmillan.

Arias, R., and P. Pulham (2019), 'Introduction: Material Traces in Neo-Victorianism', *Victoriographies*, 9 (3): 213–21. Available online: https://euppublishing.com/doi/abs/10.3366/vic.2019.0350?journalCode=vic (accessed 17 May 2022).

Armitt, L., and S. Gamble (2006), 'The Haunted Geometries of Sarah Waters's *Affinity*', *Textual Practice*, 20 (1): 141–59. Available online: https://doi.org/10.1080/09502360600559837 (accessed 4 September 2022).

Arnold, J. (2011), *Victorian Jewelry, Identity, and the Novel: Prisms of Culture*, Farnham: Ashgate.

Atwood, M. ([1996] 1997), *Alias Grace*, London: Virago Press.

Atwood, M. (1998), 'In Search of Alias Grace: On Writing Canadian Historical Fiction', *American Historical Review*, 103 (5): 1503–16. Available online: https://www.jstor.org/stable/2649966 (accessed 19 August 2022).

Bann, J. (2009), 'Ghostly Hands and Ghostly Agency: The Changing Figure of the Nineteenth-Century Specter', *Victorian Studies*, 51 (4): 663–86. Available online: https://muse.jhu.edu/article/366919 (accessed 20 May 2022).

Barad, K. (2007), *Meeting the Universe Halfway: Quantum Physics and the Entanglement of Matter and Meaning*, Durham: Duke University Press.

Bärbel Tischleder, B. (2014), *The Literary Life of Things: Case Studies in American Fiction*, Frankfurt: Campus Verlag.

Barnett, T. (2013), *Sacred Objects: Pieces of the Past in Nineteenth-Century America*, Chicago: University of Chicago Press.

Barthes, R. ([1968] 1986), *The Rustle of Language*, trans. R. Howard, New York: Hill and Wang.

Barthes, R. ([1983] 1990), *The Fashion System*, trans. M. Ward and R. Howard, Berkeley: University of California Press.

Barthes, R. ([1957] 2000), *Mythologies*, trans. A. Lavers, London: Vintage.

Bayles Kortsch, C. (2009), *Dress Culture in Late Victorian Women's Fiction: Literacy, Textiles, and Activism*, Farnham: Routledge.

Beaujot, A. (2012), *Victorian Fashion Accessories*, London: Berg.

Beck, S. W. (1883), *Gloves: Their Annals and Associations: A Chapter of Trade and Social History*, London: Hamilton, Adams.

Bennett, J. (2004), 'The Force of Things: Steps Toward an Ecology of Matter', *Political Theory*, 32 (3): 347–72. Available online: https://www.jstor.org/stable/4148158 (accessed 10 August 2022).

Bennett, J. (2010a), *Vibrant Matter: A Political Ecology of Things*, Durham: Duke University Press.

Bennett, J. (2010b), 'A Vitalist Stopover on the Way to a New Materialism', in D. Coole and S. Frost (eds), *New Materialisms: Ontology, Agency, and Politics*, 47–69. Durham: Duke University Press.

Bennett, J. (2012), 'Systems and Things: A Response to Graham Harman and Timothy Morton', *New Literary History*, 43: 225–33.

Blodgett, H. (2001), 'The Greying of *Lady Audley's Secret*', *Papers on Language and Literature*, 37 (2): 132–46.

Boehm, K. (2011), 'Historiography and the Material Imagination in the Novels of Sarah Waters', *Studies in the Novel*, 43 (2): 237–57. Available online: https://www.jstor.org/stable/pdf/41228679.pdf (accessed 12 December 2022).

Boehm, K. (2012), 'Introduction: Bodies and Things', in K. Boehm (ed.), *Bodies and Things in Nineteenth-Century Literature and Culture*, 1–17, London: Palgrave Macmillan.

Boehm-Schnitker, N., and S. Gruss (2011), 'Introduction: Spectacles and Things – Visual and Material Culture and/in Neo-Victorianism', *Neo-Victorian Studies*, 4 (2): 1–23. Available online: http://neovictorianstudies.com/ (accessed 12 January 2020).

Boehm-Schnitker, N., and S. Gruss (2014), 'Introduction: Fashioning the Neo-Victorian – Neo-Victorian Fashions', in N. Boehm-Schnitker and S. Gruss (eds), *Neo-Victorian Literature and Culture: Immersions and Revisitations*, 1–19, Abingdon: Routledge.

Boscagli, M. (2014), *Stuff Theory: Everyday Objects, Radical Materialism*, London: Bloomsbury.

Braidotti, R. (1994), *Nomadic Subjects: Embodiment and Sexual Difference in Contemporary Feminist Theory*, Columbia: Columbia University Press.

Breward, C. (1999), *The Hidden Consumer: Masculinities, Fashion, and City Life 1860–1914*, Manchester: Manchester University Press.

Brindle, K. (2013), *Epistolary Encounters in Neo-Victorian Fiction: Diaries and Letters*, Basingstoke: Palgrave Macmillan.

Broadwell, E. (1975), 'The Veil Image in Ann Radcliffe's *The Italian*', *South Atlantic Bulletin*, 40 (4): 76–87. Available online: https://www.jstor.org/stable/3199122 (accessed 31 July 2022).

Brontë, C. ([1853] 1999), *Villette*, Hertfordshire: Wordsworth Classics.

Brontë, C. ([1847] 2006), *Jane Eyre*, London: Penguin Classics.

Brooks, P. (1993), *Body Work: Objects of Desire in Modern Narrative*, Cambridge: Harvard University Press.

Brown, B. (2001), 'Thing Theory', *Critical Inquiry*, 28 (1): 1–22. Available online: https://www.jstor.org/stable/1344258?seq=1 (accessed 20 February 2022).

Brown, B. (2015), *Other Things*, Chicago: University of Chicago Press.

Browne, I. ([1897] 2011), *In the Track of the Book-Worm*, New York: Roycroft.

Bury, S. (1985), *An Introduction to Sentimental Jewellery*, Maryland: Stemmer House.

Butler, J. ([1990] 2007), *Gender Trouble: Feminism and Subversion of Identity*, London: Routledge.

Byatt, A. S. ([1990] 1991), *Possession: A Romance*, London: Vintage.

Byatt, A. S. (2000), *The Biographer's Tale*, London: Chatto and Windus.

Cadwallader, J. (2011), 'The Three Veils: Death, Mourning, and the Afterlife in *The Secret Garden*', in J. Horne and J. Sutliff Sanders (eds), *Frances Hodgson Burnett's The Secret Garden: A Children's Classic at 100*, 119–36. Plymouth: Scarecrow Press.

Carlile, R. (1828), *Every Woman's Book, Or, What Is Love?: Containing Most Important Instructions for the Prudent Regulation of the Principle of Love and the Number of a Family*, London: R. Carlile.

Carlyle, T. ([1836] 2002), *Sartor Resartus: The Life and Times of Herr Teufelsdröckh*, Edinburgh: Canongate Classic.

Carruthers, J., N. Dakkak and R. Spence, (eds) (2019), *Anticipatory Materialisms in Literature and Philosophy, 1790–1930*, London: Palgrave Macmillan.

Castle, T. (1993), *The Apparitional Lesbian: Female Homosexuality and Modern Culture*, New York: Columbia University Press.

Cixous, H., and J. Derrida (2001), *Veils*, trans. G. Bennington, Stanford: Stanford University Press.

Cooper, D., and N. Battershill (1972), *Victorian Sentimental Jewellery*. Newton Abbot: David & Charles.

Cole, H. (1875), *A Special Report on the Annual International Exhibitions of the Years 1871, 1872, 1873, and 1874*, London: George E. Eyre and William Spottiswoode. Available online: https://archive.org/details/gri_33125010838270/page/n5/mode/2up (accessed 23 February 2022).

Colella, S. (2010), 'Olfactory Ghosts: Michel Faber's *The Crimson Petal and the White*', in R. Arias and P. Pulham (eds), *Haunting and Spectrality in Neo-Victorian Fiction: Possessing the Past*, 85–110, Basingstoke: Palgrave Macmillan.

Collins, W. ([1864–6] 1995), *Armadale*, London: Penguin Books.

Collins, W. ([1868] 1999), *The Moonstone*, Ware: Wordsworth Editions.

Collins, W. ([1860] 2008), *The Woman in White*, New York: Bantum Classic.

Coole, D., and S. Frost (2010), 'Introducing the New Materialisms', in D. Coole and S. Frost (eds), *New Materialisms: Ontology, Agency, and Politics*, 1–43. Durham: Duke University Press.

Costantini, M. (2006), '"Faux-Victorian Melodrama" in the New Millennium: The Case of Sarah Waters', *Critical Survey*, 18 (1): 17–39. Available online: https://www.jstor.org/stable/41556147#metadata_info_tab_contents (accessed 1 August 2022).

Cox, K. (2022), *Touch, Sexuality, and Hands in British Literature, 1740–1901*, Abingdon: Routledge.

Cumming, V. (1982), *Gloves*, London: Batsford.

Cunnington, C. W. ([1937] 1990), *English Women's Clothing in the Nineteenth Century*, New York: Dover Publications.

Daly, S. (2011), *The Empire Inside: Indian Commodities in Victorian Domestic Novels*, Ann Arbor: University of Michigan Press.

Davies, H. (2012), *Gender and Ventriloquism in Victorian and Neo-Victorian Fiction: Passionate Puppets*, London: Palgrave Macmillan.

Day, C. W. (1843), *Hints on Etiquette and the Usages of Society: With a Glance at Bad Habits*, Boston: Otis, Broaders.

Dickens, C. ([1836–7] 1995), 'Meditations in Monmouth-Street', in D. Walder (ed.), *Sketches by Boz*, 96–104, London: Penguin Classics.
Dickens, C. ([1853] 1996), *Bleak House*, London: Penguin Books.
Dickens, C. ([1849–50] 1997), *David Copperfield*, Oxford: Oxford University Press.
Dickens, C. ([1836] 2000), 'The Black Veil', in D. S. Davies (ed.), *Short Stories from the Nineteenth Century*, 2–12. London: Wordsworth Classics.
Dickens, C. ([1860–1] 2000), *Great Expectations*, Hertfordshire: Wordsworth Editions.
Dickens, C. ([1855–7] 2002), *Little Dorrit*, London: Wordsworth Editions.
Dillane, F. (2020), 'George Eliot's Precarious Afterlives', *19: Interdisciplinary Studies in the Long Nineteenth Century*, 29: 1–26. Available online: https://19.bbk.ac.uk/article/id/1981/ (accessed 31 July 2022).
Doniger, W. (2017), *The Ring of Truth and Other Myths of Sex and Jewelry*, Oxford: Oxford University Press.
Dove, D., and S. E. Maier (2022), 'Stuff and Things: Introducing Neo-Victorian Materialities', in B. Ayres, S. Maier, and D. Dove (eds), *Neo-Victorian Things: Re-Imagining Nineteenth-Century Material Cultures in Literature and Film*, 1–21, London: Palgrave Macmillan.
Downes, S., S. Holloway and S. Randles (2018), 'A Feeling for Things, Past and Present', In S. Downes, S. Holloway, and S. Randles (eds), *Feeling Things: Objects and Emotions through History*, 8–23, Oxford: Oxford University Press.
'Dress' (1862), *Chambers's Journal of Popular Literature, Science and Arts*, 442, 395–8.
'Dress' (1865), *Blackwood's Edinburgh Magazine*, 425–38.
Duffy, C. A. (1993), *Mean Time*, London: Picador.
Dunagen Osborne, K. (2010), 'Inherited Emotions: George Eliot and the Politics of Heirlooms', *Nineteenth-Century Literature*, 64 (4): 465–93. Available online: https://www.jstor.org/stable/10.1525/ncl.2010.64.4.465 (accessed 12 June 2022).
Duncker, P. ([1999] 2011), *James Miranda Barry*, London: Bloomsbury.
Duncker, P. (2014), 'On Writing Neo-Victorian Fiction', *English: Journal of the English Association*, 63 (243): 253–74. Available online: https://doi.org/10.1093/english/efu019 (accessed 3 October 2021).
Duncker, P. (2015), *Sophie and the Sibyl*, London: Bloomsbury.
'Economy in Mourning' (1871), *The Englishwoman's Domestic Magazine*, 298–9.
Egan, G., (ed.) (2020), *Fashion and Authorship: Literary Production and Cultural Style from the Eighteenth to the Twenty-First Century*, London: Palgrave Macmillan.
Egerton, G. (ed.) (1893), 'A Little Grey Glove', in *Keynotes*, 91–115, London: Elkin Matthews and John Lane.
Eliot, G. ([1859] 1999), *The Lifted Veil and Brother Jacob*, Oxford: Oxford World Classics.
Eliot, G. ([1876] 2003), *Daniel Deronda*, Hertfordshire: Wordsworth Editions.
El-Rayess, M. (2014), *Henry James and the Culture of Consumption*, Cambridge: Cambridge University Press.

Ernst, R. A. (2018), 'Vital Disguises: Sartorial Insurrection and the Female Body in *Bleak House*', *Texas Studies in Literature and Language*, 60 (4): 496–518. Available online: https:// DOI: 10.7560/TSLL60405 (accessed 24 April 2022).

Evans, C. (2003), *Fashion at the Edge: Spectacle, Modernity and Deathliness*, London: Yale University Press.

Evans, A. M. (2020), 'Decorating the Body: An Introduction', *Lectora*, 26: 9-14. Available online: https://revistes.ub.edu/index.php/lectora/article/view/32504/32457 (accessed 22 August 2022).

Ewing, B. (2014), *The Petticoat Men*, London: Head of Zeus.

'Fashion' (1869), *Bow Bells: A Magazine of General Literature and Art for Family*, 10 (245): 246.

'Fashion', *OED Online*, Oxford University Press. Available online: https://www.oed.com/view/Entry/68389?rskey=HE8zIz&result=1&isAdvanced=false (accessed 27 July 2022).

Fazli, S. (2019), *Sensational Things: Souvenirs, Keepsakes, and Mementos in Wilkie Collins's Fiction*, Heidelberg: Universitätsverlag Winter.

Feldman-Barrett, C. (2013), 'Time Machine Fashion: Neo-Victorian Style in Twenty-First Century Subcultures', *Australasian Journal of Victorian Studies*, 18 (3): 72–83. Available online: https://openjournals.library.sydney.edu.au/index.php/AJVS/article/view/9385/9284 (accessed 15 April 2021).

Foley, L. (2015), 'Gloves "Of the Very Thin Sort": Gifting Limerick Gloves in the Late Eighteenth and Early Nineteenth Centuries', in C. Nicklas and A. Pollen (eds), *Dress History: New Directions in Theory and Practice*, 33–49, London: Bloomsbury.

'Foolish Fashions' (1868), *All the Year Round*, 20 (479): 65–8.

Foucault, M. ([1975] 1995), *Discipline and Punish*, London: Vintage Books.

Fowles, J. ([1969] 2004), *The French Lieutenant's Woman*, London: Vintage.

Flanagan, R. ([2008] 2016), *Wanting*, London: Vintage.

Flower, M. (1967), *Victorian Jewellery*, London: Cassell & Company.

Flugel, J. C. (1940), *The Psychology of Clothes*, 2nd edn, London: Hogarth Press. Available online: https://archive.org/details/in.ernet.dli.2015.34079/page/n7/mode/2up (accessed 10 January 2022).

Frame, R. ([2012] 2013), *Havisham: A Novel*, London: Faber and Faber.

Freedgood, E. (2006), *The Ideas in Things: Fugitive Meaning in the Victorian Novel*, Chicago: University of Chicago Press.

Freud, S. ([1919] 2003), *The Uncanny*, trans. D. McLintock, London: Penguin Group.

Gallagher, C., and S. Greenblatt (2000), *Practicing New Historicism*, Chicago: University of Chicago Press.

Gamble, S. (2013), '"I know everything. I know nothing": (Re)Reading *Fingersmith*'s Deceptive Doubles', in K. Mitchell (ed.), *Sarah Waters: Contemporary Critical Perspectives*, 42–56, London: Bloomsbury.

Garber, M. ([1992] 2011), *Vested Interests: Cross-Dressing and Cultural Anxiety*, Abingdon: Routledge.

Gatrell, S. (2011), *Thomas Hardy: Writing Dress*, Oxford: Peter Lang.

Geczy, A., and V. Karaminas (2019), 'Time and Memory', in A. Geczy and V. Karaminas (eds), *The End of Fashion: Clothing and Dress in the Age of Globalization*, London: Bloomsbury.

Genette, G. ([1997] 2001), *Paratexts: Thresholds of Interpretation*, Cambridge: Cambridge University Press.

Gere, C., and J. Rudoe (2010), *Jewellery in the Age of Queen Victoria: A Mirror to the World*, London: British Museum Press.

Germaná, M. (2013), 'The Death of the Lady: Haunted Garments and (Re-)Possession in *The Little Stranger*', in K. Mitchell (ed.), *Sarah Waters: Contemporary Critical Perspectives*, 114–28, London: Bloomsbury.

Gilbert, S. M., and S. Gubar ([1979] 2000), *The Madwoman in the Attic: The Woman Writer and the Nineteenth-Century Literary Imagination*, 2nd edn, New Haven: Yale University Press.

Gilhooley, D. (1997), 'Unclasped', in D. Gilhooley and S. Costin (eds), *Unclasped: Contemporary British Jewellery*, 1–7, London: Black Dog Publishing.

Glendinning, A. (ed.) (1894), *The Veil Lifted: Modern Developments of Spirit Photography*, London: Whittaker.

'Gloves' (1892), *Bow Bells: A Magazine of General Literature and Art for Family*, 19 (245): 264.

Goldthorpe, C. (1989), *From Queen to Empress: Victorian Dress 1837–1877*. New York: Metropolitan Museum of Art.

Gordon, L. ([1998] 1999), *A Private Life of Henry James: Two Women and His Art*, London: Random House.

Gruss, S. (2014), 'Spectres of the Past: Reading the Phantom of Family Trauma in Neo-Victorian Fiction', in N. Boehm-Schnitker and S. Gruss (eds), *Neo-Victorian Literature and Culture: Immersions and Revisitations*, 123–36. Abingdon: Routledge.

Gutleben, C. (2001), *Nostalgic Postmodernism: The Victorian Tradition and the Contemporary British Novel*, Amsterdam: Rodopi.

Hadley, L. (2010), *Neo-Victorian Fiction and Historical Narrative: The Victorians and Us*, Basingstoke: Palgrave Macmillan.

Hamilakis, Y. (2013), *Archaeology and the Senses: Human Experience, Memory, and Affect*, Cambridge: Cambridge University Press.

Hannah, D. (2007), 'The Private Life, the Public Stage: Henry James in Recent Fiction', *Journal of Modern Literature*, 30 (3): 70–94. Available online: https://muse.jhu.edu/article/219887 (accessed 3 May 2022).

Hardy, T. ([1891] 2008), *Tess of the D'Urbervilles*, London: Penguin Classics.

Hardy, T. ([1886] 2012), *The Mayor of Casterbridge*, London: HarperCollins.

Hartley, F. (1872), *The Ladies' Book of Etiquette, and Manual of Politeness: A Complete Hand Book for the Use of the Lady in Polite Society*, Boston: Lee & Shepard. Available online: https://archive.org/details/ladiesbooketiqu00hartgoog/page/n6/mode/2up (accessed 16 August 2022).

Harrison, R. (1862), *Colonial Sketches: or, Five Years in South Australia with Hints to Captialists and Emigrants*, London: Hall, Virtue. Available online: https://archive.org/details/colonialsketche01harrgoog/page/n4/mode/2up (accessed 9 October 2022).

Harwood, J. ([2004] 2005), *The Ghost Writer*, London: Vintage.

Haweis, M. E. (1889), 'Jewels and Dress: Or the Philosophy of Jewels', *Contemporary Review*, 56, 84–105. *British Periodicals* (accessed 2 June 2021).

Heilmann, A. (2010a), 'The Haunting of Henry James: Jealous Ghosts, Affinities, and *The Others*', in R. Arias and P. Pulham (eds), *Haunting and Spectrality in Neo-Victorian Fiction: Possessing the Past*, 111–30. Basingstoke: Palgrave Macmillan.

Heilmann, A. (2010b), '(Un)Masking Desire: Cross-Dressing and the Crisis of Gender in New Woman Fiction', *Journal of Victorian Culture*, 5 (1): 83–111. Available online: https://www.tandfonline.com/doi/abs/10.3366/jvc.2000.5.1.83 (accessed 3 March 2022).

Heilmann, A. (2018), *Neo-Victorian Biographilia & James Miranda Barry: A Study in Transgender & Transgenre*, London: Palgrave Macmillan.

Heilmann, A., and M. Llewellyn (2010), *Neo-Victorianism: The Victorians in the Twenty-First-Century, 1999–2009*, Basingstoke: Palgrave Macmillan.

Heilmann, A., and M. Llewellyn (2014), 'On the Neo-Victorian, Now and Then', in H. F Tucker (ed.), *A New Companion to Victorian Literature and Culture*, 493–506. Chichester: John Wiley & Sons.

'Her Glove' (1884), *Supplement to the Hampshire Telegraph and Sussex Chronicle*, 5.

H.K. (1878), 'A Glove's Confession', *The London Journal, and Weekly Record of Literature, Science, and Art*, 68 (1756): 222–3.

Ho, E. (2013), *Neo-Victorianism and the Memory of Empire*, London: Bloomsbury.

Ho Lai-Ming, T. (2012), 'Cannibalised Girlhood in Richard Flanagan's *Wanting*', *Neo-Victorian Studies*, 5 (1): 14–37. Available online: https://neovictorianstudies.com (accessed 16 September 2022).

Hollander, A. (1993), *Seeing Through Clothes*, California: University of California Press.

Hollinghurst, A. (2005), *The Line of Beauty*, London: Picador.

Hughes, C. (2001), *Henry James and the Art of Dress*, London: Palgrave Macmillan.

Hughes, C. ([2005] 2006), *Dressed in Fiction*, Oxford: Berg.

Hughes, K. (2010), 'Victorians Beyond the Academy: Dickens World and Dickens's World', *Journal of Victorian Culture*, 15 (3): 388–93. Available online: https://academic.oup.com/jvc/article-abstract/15/3/388/4102401 (accessed 3 May 2022).

Hunt, C. (2014), 'Worn Clothes and Textiles as Archives of Memory', *Critical Studies in Fashion & Beauty*, 5 (1): 207–33. Available online: https://www.ingentaconnect.com/content/intellect/csfb/2014/00000005/00000002/art00002 (accessed 16 October 2022).

Hutcheon, L. (1988), *A Poetics of Postmodernism: History, Theory, Fiction*, London: Routledge.

Hutchison, H. (2012), *Brief Lives: Henry James*, London: Hersperus Press.

Ingersoll, E. G. (2001), 'Engendering Metafiction: Textuality and Closure in Margaret Atwood's *Alias Grace*', *American Review of Canadian Studies*, 31 (3): 385–401. Available online: https://doi.org/10.1080/02722010109481600 (accessed 19 August 2022).

Jacob, P. A. (2016), 'The Relic and the Ruin: Equivocal Objects and the Presence of the Past in *Daniel Deronda*', *Victorian Literature and Culture*, 44 (4): 855–74. Available online: http://dx.doi.org/10.1017/S1060150316000243 (accessed 20 April 2022).

Jalland, P. (1996), *Death in the Victorian Family*, Oxford: Oxford University Press.

James, H. (1868), 'The Romance of Certain Old Clothes', *The Atlantic Monthly: A Magazine of Literature, Science, Art, and Politics*, 21: 209–20.

Jameson, F. (1991), *Postmodernism: Or, the Cultural Logic of Late Capitalism*, London: Verso.

'Jewellery' (1864), *Bow Bells: A Magazine of General Literature and Art for Family*, 5: 115.

Jones, A. M., and R. N. Mitchell (eds) (2016), *Drawing on the Victorians: The Palimpsest of Victorian and Neo-Victorian Graphic Texts*, Ohio: Ohio University Press.

Jones, A. R., and P. Stallybrass (2000), *Renaissance Clothing and the Materials of Memory*, Cambridge: Cambridge University Press.

Joslin, K., and D. Wardrop, (eds) (2015), *Crossings in Text and Textile*, Durham: University of New Hampshire Press.

Kaplan, C. (2007), *Victoriana: Histories, Fictions, Criticism*, New York: Columbia University Press.

Kaplan, F. (1999), *Henry James: The Imagination of Genius, a Biography*, Baltimore: John Hopkins University Press.

Kersten, D. (2013), 'Henry James and the Death of the Biographer: A Comparative and Interdisciplinary Approach to the Writing of Lives', in G. Ipsen, T. Matthews and D. Obravodić (eds), *Provocation and Negotiation: Essays in Comparative Criticism*, 219–32. Amsterdam: Rodopi.

Kidd, A. (1878), 'The Glove', *The Graphic*: 315.

Kohlke, M. L. (2004), 'Into History Through the Back Door: The "Past Historic" in *Nights at the Circus* and *Affinity*', *Women: A Cultural Review*, 15 (2): 153–66. Available online: https://doi.org/10.1080/0957404042000234015 (accessed 25 June 2022).

Kohlke, M. L. (2008a), 'De Corporis et Libri Fabrica: Review of Belinda Starling, *The Journal of Dora Damage*', *Neo-Victorian Studies*, 1 (1): 196–202. Available online: https://www.neovictorianstudies.com (accessed 18 August 2021).

Kohlke, M. L. (2008b), 'Introduction: Speculations in and on the Neo-Victorian Encounter', *Neo-Victorian Studies*, 1 (1): 1–18. Available online: https://www.neovictorianstudies.com (accessed January 2021).

Kohlke, M. L. (2013), 'Neo-Victorian Biofiction and the Special/Spectral Case of Barbara Chase-Riboud's Hottentot Venus', *Australasian Journal of Victorian Studies*,

18 (3): 4–21. Available online: https://openjournals.library.sydney.edu.au/index.php/AJVS/article/viewFile/9382/9281 (accessed 1 May 2021).

Kohlke, M. L. (2014), 'Mining the Neo-Victorian Vein: Prospecting for Gold, Buried Treasure and Uncertain Metal', in N. Boehm-Schnitker and S. Gruss (eds), *Neo-Victorian Literature and Culture: Immersions and Revisitations*, 21–37, Abingdon: Routledge.

Kohlke, M. L., and C. Gutleben (2010), 'Introduction: Bearing After-Witness to the Nineteenth-Century', in M. L. Kohlke and C. Gutleben (eds), *Neo-Victorian Tropes of Trauma: The Politics of Bearing after-Witness to Nineteenth-Century Suffering*, 1–34, Amsterdam: Brill.

Kontou, T. (2009), *Spiritualism and Women's Writing: From the Fin de Siècle to the Neo-Victorian*, Basingstoke: Palgrave Macmillan.

Kopytoff, I. (1986), 'The Cultural Biography of Things: Commoditization as Process', in A. Appadurai (ed.), *The Social Life of Things: Commodities in Cultural Perspective*, 64–91. Cambridge: Cambridge University Press.

Kosofsky Sedgwick, E. (1981), 'The Character in the Veil: Imagery of the Surface in the Gothic Novel', *PMLA*, 29 (2): 255–70. Available online: https://www.jstor.org/stable/461992 (accessed 16 September 2022).

Kosofsky Sedgwick, E. (2003), *Touching Feeling: Affect, Pedagogy, Performativity*, Durham: Duke University Press.

Kuehn, J. (2014), *A Female Poetics of Empire: From Eliot to Woolf*, Abingdon: Routledge.

Kuhn, C. (2005), *Self-Fashioning in Margaret Atwood's Fiction: Dress, Culture, and Identity*, New York: Peter Lang.

Kuhn, C., and C. Carlson (2007), 'Introduction', in C. Kuhn and C. Carlson (eds), *Styling Texts: Dress and Fashion in Literature*, 1–13, New York: Cambria Press.

Lanone, C. (2020), 'Biofiction Goes Global: Richard Flanagan's *Wanting*, Dickens, and the Lost Child', in M. L. Kohlke and C. Gutleben (eds), *Neo-Victorian Biofiction: Reimagining Nineteenth-Century Historical Subjects*, 232–61. Amsterdam: Brill/Rodopi.

Latour, B. (1996), 'On Actor-Network Theory: A Few Clarifications', *Soziale Welt*, 47 (4): 369–81.

Leavis, F. R. (1982), 'Gwendolen Harleth', *The London Review of Books*, 4 (1): 10–12.

Le Fanu, S. ([1871] 1982), *The Rose and the Key*, New York: Dover.

Lesjak, C. (2006), *Working Fictions: A Genealogy of the Victorian Novel*, Durham: Duke University Press.

Lester, K., and B. V. Oerke (2004), *Accessories of Dress: An Illustrated Encyclopedia*, New York: Dover Publication.

Letissier, G. (2012), 'The Havisham Affair or the Afterlife of a Memorable Fixture', *Études anglaises*, 1 (65): 30–42. Available online: https://www.cairn-int.info/journal-etudes-anglaises-2012-1-page-30.htm (accessed 1 July 2022).

'Letters on Politeness and Etiquette' (1875), *The Young Englishwoman*: 290–4.

Llewellyn, M. (2004), '"Queer? I should say it is criminal!" Sarah Waters' *Affinity* 1999', *Journal of Gender Studies*, 13 (3): 203–14.

Llewellyn, M. (2008), 'What Is Neo-Victorian Studies?', *Neo-Victorian Studies*, 1 (1): 164–85. Available online: https://www.neovictorianstudies.com (accessed 14 January 2022).

Llewellyn, M. (2010), 'Spectrality, S(p)ecularity, and Textuality: Or, Some Reflections in the Glass', in R. Arias and P. Pulham (eds), *Haunting and Spectrality in Neo-Victorian Fiction: Possessing the Past*, 23–42, Basingstoke: Palgrave Macmillan.

Lodge, D. (2004), *Author, Author! A Novel*, London: Secker and Warburg.

Lodge, D. (2006), 'The Year of Henry James; or, Timing is All: The Story of a Novel', in D. Lodge (ed.), *The Year of Henry James The Story of a Novel*, 1–103. London: Penguin.

Louttit, C. (2014), 'The Way We Read Victorian Fiction Now: Penguin and Neo-Victorian Book Design', *Neo-Victorian Studies*, 7 (1): 104–28. Available online: https://neovictorianstudies.com (accessed 8 February 2022).

Lovesey, O. (2017), *Postcolonial George Eliot*, Basingstoke: Palgrave Macmillan.

Lutz, D. (2015a), *Relics of Death in Victorian Literature and Culture*, Cambridge: Cambridge University Press.

Lutz, D. (2015b), *The Brontë Cabinet: Three Lives in Nine Objects*, London: W. W. Norton.

'Marchesa's Miss Havisham Makeover', [video], YouTube (AP 18 February 2011, uploaded 24 February 2011), https://www.youtube.com/watch?v=RC-A4MRh3wI

Marcus, S. (2009), *Between Women: Friendship, Desire and Marriage in Victorian England*, Princeton: Princeton University Press.

Marriott Watson, R. (1890), 'Suits of Woe', *The National Observer*, 5 (108): 91.

Maxwell, C. (2017), *Scents and Sensibility: Perfume in Victorian Literary Culture*, Oxford: Oxford University Press.

McCorristine, S. (2010), *Spectres of the Self: Thinking about Ghosts and Ghost-Seeing in England, 1750–1920*, Cambridge: Cambridge University Press.

Merleau-Ponty, M. ([1945] 2002), *Phenomenology of Perception*, trans. C. Smith, Abingdon: Routledge.

Michie, H. (2014), 'Permeable Protections: The Working Life of Victorian Skin', in H. F. Tucker (ed.), *A New Companion to Victorian Literature and Culture*, 449–61. Chichester: John Wiley and Sons.

Mida, I., and A. Kim (2015), *The Dress Detective: A Practical Guide to Object-Based Research in Fashion*, London: Bloomsbury.

Miller, K. A. (2008), 'Sarah Waters's *Fingersmith*: Leaving Women's Fingerprints on Victorian Pornography', *Nineteenth-Century Gender Studies*, 4 (1). Available online: https://www.ncgsjournal.com/issue41/PDFs/miller.pdf (accessed 1 January 2023).

Mills, K. (2007), *Approaching Apocalypse: Unveiling Revelation in Victorian Writing*, Danvers: Rosemont Publishing.

Mitchell, K. (2010), *History and Cultural Memory in Neo-Victorian Fiction: Victorian Afterimages*, Basingstoke: Palgrave Macmillan.

Mitchell, R. (2013), 'Death Becomes Her: On the Progressive Potential of Victorian Mourning', *Victorian Literature and Culture*, 41 (4): 595–620. Available online: https://www.cambridge.org/core/journals/victorian-literature-and-culture/article/death-becomes-her-on-the-progressive-potential-of-victorian-mourning/885E3 9E1FA71993179B99F0961ABF484 (accessed 20 January 2022).

Montz, A. L. (2011), '"In Which Parasols Prove Useful": Neo-Victorian Rewriting of Victorian Materiality', *Neo-Victorian Studies*, 4 (11): 100–18. Available online: https://www.neovictorianstudies.com (accessed 10 January 2021).

Montz, A. L. (2019), 'Unbinding the Victorian Girl: Corsetry and Neo-Victorian Young Adult Literature', *Children's Literature Association Quarterly*, 44 (1): 88–101. Available online: https://doi.org/10.1353/chq.2019.0005 (accessed 14 December 2021).

Muller, N. (2012), 'Sexual F(r)ictions: Pornography in Neo-Victorian Women's Fiction', in K. Cooper and E. Short (eds), *The Female Figure in Contemporary Historical Fiction*, 153–33. Basingstoke: Palgrave Macmillan.

Mullins, A. (1896), 'Jewellery as an Art', *The Magazine of Art*, 236–41.

Munteán, L., L. Plate and A. Smelik (2017), 'Things to Remember: Introduction to Materializing Memory in Art and Popular Culture', in L. Munteán, L. Plate and A. Smelik (eds), *Materializing Memory in Art and Popular Culture*, Abingdon: Routledge.

Murphy, M. (2006), 'The Ethic of the Gift in George Eliot's *Daniel Deronda*', *Victorian Literature and Culture*, 34 (1): 189–207.

Murray, J. (2001), 'Historical Figures and Paradoxical Patterns: The Quilting Metaphor in Margaret Atwood's *Alias Grace*', *Studies in Canadian Literature / Études en littérature canadienne*, 26 (1): 65–83. Available online: https://journals.lib.unb.ca/index.php/SCL/article/view/12873/13929 (accessed 2 June 2022).

Nead, L. (2013), 'The Layering of Pleasure: Women, Fashionable Dress and Visual Culture in the Mid-Nineteenth Century', *Nineteenth-Century Contexts*, 35 (5): 489–509. Available online: https://doi.org/10.1080/08905495.2013.854978 (accessed 14 July 2022).

Neal, A. (2011), '(Neo-)Victorian Impersonations: Vesta Tilley and *Tipping the Velvet*', *Neo-Victorian Studies Journal*, 4 (1), 55–76. Available online: http://neovictorianstudies.com/ (accessed 2 February 2022).

Novák, C. (2013), 'Those Very 'Other' Victorians: Interrogating Neo-Victorian Feminism in *The Journal of Dora Damage*', *Neo-Victorian Studies*, 6 (2): 114–36. Available online: https://www.neovictorianstudies.com (accessed 16 January 2022).

Novick. S. M. (2007), *Henry James: The Mature Master*, New York: Random House.

O'Callaghan, C. (2017), *Sarah Waters: Gender and Sexual Politics*, London: Bloomsbury Academic.

O'Callaghan, C. (2020), '"Awaiting the death blow": Gendered Violence and Miss Havisham's Afterlives', in E. Bell (ed.), *Dickens After Dickens*, 83–100. York: White Rose University Press.

O'Conor Eccles, C. (1895), 'Varieties in Veils', *The Windsor Magazine: An Illustrated Monthly for Men and Women*: 547–51.

Oliphant, M. ([1876] 2002), *Phoebe Junior: A Last Chronicle of Carlingford*, Peterborough: Broadview Press.

'Olivia Colman to star in BBC adaptation of Great Expectations' (2022), *The Telegraph*, https://www.telegraph.co.uk/news/2022/02/18/olivia-colman-star-bbc-adaptation-great-expectations/ (accessed 29 March 2023).

Oulanne, L. (2021), *Materiality in Modernist Short Fiction: Lived Things*, London: Routledge.

'Our Drawing-Room' (1875), *Beeton's Young Englishwoman: A Volume of Pure Literature, New Fashions, and Pretty Needlework Designs*, London: Ward, Lock, and Tyler. Available online: https://archive.org/details/youngenglishwom00beetgoog/page/n8/mode/2up (accessed 1 August 2022).

'Our Drawing-Room' (1879), *Sylvia's Home Journal for Home Reading and Home Use or Tales, Stories, Fashions, and Needlework*, London: Ward, Lock, and Co. Available online: https://archive.org/details/sylviashomejour00unkngoog/page/n6/mode/2up (accessed 1 August 2022).

'Our Paris News-Letter' (1864), *The Englishwoman's Domestic Magazine*: 103.

'Pair of Gloves' (2021), V&A Collections. Available online: http://collections.vam.ac.uk/item/O146175/pair-of-gloves-c-courvoisier/ (accessed 10 October 2022).

Parey, A. (2006), 'Jane Eyre, Past and Present', *La Revue LISA / LISA e-journal*, iv (4): 1–8. Available online: https://journals.openedition.org/lisa/1741?lang=en (accessed 2 December 2021).

Parey, A. (2018), 'Introduction: Narrative Expansions – The Story So Far', in A. Parey (ed.), *Prequels, Coquels and Sequels in Contemporary Anglophone Fiction*, London: Routledge.

Patmore, C. ([1854–62] 1866), *The Angel in the House*, 4th edn, London: Macmillan.

Paxton, J. R. (1856), *Jewelry and the Precious Stones*, Philadelphia: John Penington & Son.

Pecora, V. (2008), 'Inheritances, Gifts, and Expectations', *Law and Literature*, 20 (2): 177–96. Available online: https://www.jstor.org/stable/10.1525/lal.2008.20.2.177 (accessed 17 October 2022).

Petković, D. (2015), '"The Public Face of this Private Volume": Feminism, Pornography and the Subversion of the Gendered Public/Private Dichotomy in *Journal of Dora Damage*', in S. Šnircová and M. Kostić (eds), *Growing Up a Woman: The Private/Public Divide in the Narratives of Female Development*, 223–42. Newcastle: Cambridge Scholars Publishing.

Pointon, M. (1997), 'Intriguing Jewellery: Royal Bodies and Luxurious Consumption', *Textual Practice*, 11 (3): 493–516. Available online: https://doi.org/10.1080/09502369708582292 (accessed 24 September 2022).

Pointon, M. (2009), *Brilliant Effects: A Cultural History of Gem Stones and Jewellery*, London: Yale University Press.

Price, L. (2009), 'Getting the Reading out of It: Paper Recycling in Mayhew's London', in I. Ferris and P. Keen (eds), *Bookish Histories: Books, Literature and Commercial Modernity, 1700–1900*, 148–64. Basingstoke: Palgrave Macmillan.

Primorac, A. (2018), *Neo-Victorianism on Screen: Postfeminism and Contemporary Adaptations of Victorian Women*, London: Palgrave Macmillan.

Prown, J. (1982), 'Mind in Matter: An Introduction to Material Culture Theory and Method', *Winterthur Portfolio*, 17 (1): 1–19.

Pulham, P. (2012), 'Neo-Victorian Gothic and Spectral Sexuality in Colm Tóibín's *The Master*', in M. L. Kohlke and C. Gutleben (eds), *Neo-Victorian Gothic: Horror, Violence, and Degeneration in the Re-Imagined Nineteenth Century*, 147–66. Amsterdam: Rodopi.

Pykett, L. (2003), 'The Material Turn in Victorian Studies', *Literature Compass*, 1: 1–5. Available online: https://onlinelibrary.wiley.com/doi/pdf/10.1111/j.1741-4113.2004.00020.x (accessed 10 February 2023).

Regis, A., and D. Wynne (2012), 'Miss Havisham's Dress: Materialising Dickens in Film Adaptations of *Great Expectations*', *Neo-Victorian Studies*, 5 (2): 35–58. Available online: https://www.neovictorianstudies.com (accessed 13 March 2022).

Renk, K. (2020), *Women Writing the Neo-Victorian Novel: Erotic 'Victorians'*, London: Palgrave Macmillan.

Rhys, J. ([1966] 2000), *Wide Sargasso Sea*, London: Penguin Books.

Ricoeur, P. (1990), *Time and Narrative*, 3 vols, Chicago: University of Chicago Press.

Ricoeur, P. ([1984] 1991), 'Narrated Time', in M. Valdés (ed.), *A Ricoeur Reader: Reflections and Imaginations*, 338–55, Toronto: Toronto University Press.

Rigby, E. (1847), 'The Art of Dress', *Quarterly Review*, 79: 372–99.

Roberts, H. E. (1977), 'The Exquisite Slave: The Role of Clothes in the Making of the Victorian Woman', *Signs*, 2 (3): 554–69. Available online: https://www.jstor.org/stable/3173265 (accessed 20 May 2022).

Robinson, A. (2011), *Narrating the Past: Historiography, Memory and the Contemporary Novel*, Basingstoke: Palgrave Macmillan.

Roe, S. (1982), *Estella: Her Expectations*, Brighton: Harvester.

Rogerson, M. (1998), 'Reading the Patchworks in *Alias Grace*', *The Journal of Commonwealth Literature*, 1 (33): 5–22.

Russell, R. R. (2009), *Gender and Jewelry: A Feminist Analysis*, Scotts Valley: CreateSpace.

Sampson, E. (2021), *Worn: Footwear, Attachment and the Affects of Wear*, London: Bloomsbury.

Schaffer, T. (2000), *The Forgotten Female Aesthetes: Literary Culture in Late-Victorian England*, Charlottesville: University Press of Virginia.

Scherzinger, K. (2008), 'Staging Henry James: Representing the Author in Colm Tóibín's *The Master* and David Lodge's *Author, Author! A Novel*', *Henry James Review*, 29 (2), 181–96. Available online: https://doi.org/10.1353/hjr.0.0009 (accessed 19 August 2021).

Schor, H. M. (2004), *Dickens and the Daughter of the House*, Cambridge: Cambridge University Press.

Schouwenburg, H. (2015), 'Back to the Future? History, Material Culture, and New Materialism', *International Journal for History, Culture and Modernity*, 3 (1): 59–72.

Seigworth, G. J., and M. Gregg (2010), 'An Inventory of Shimmers', in M. Gregg and G. J. Seigworth (eds), *The Affect Theory Reader*, 1–25, Durham: Duke University Press.

Serres, M. ([1985] 2008), *The Five Senses: A Philosophy of Mingled Senses*, trans. M. Sankey and P. Cowley. London: Continuum.

Serres, M., and B. Latour ([1990] 1995), *Conversations on Science, Culture, and Time*, trans. R. Lapidus, Ann Arbor: University of Michigan Press.

Seys, M. C. (2018), *Fashion and Narrative in Victorian Popular Literature: Double Threads*, Abingdon. Routledge.

Shafer, D. (1877), *Secrets of Life Unveiled, Or Book of Fate*, Baltimore: Shafer.

Shannon, B. (2006), *The Cut of His Coat: Men, Dress, and Consumer Culture in Britain 1860–1914*, Athens: Ohio University Press.

Shiller, D. (1997), 'The Redemptive Past in the Neo-Victorian Novel', *Studies in the Novel*, 29 (4): 538–60. Available online: https://www.jstor.org/stable/29533234?seq=1 (accessed 21 January 2022).

Showalter, E. (1992). *Sexual Anarchy: Gender and Culture at the Fin de Siècle*, London: Virago Press.

Shuttleworth, S. (1998), 'Natural History: The Retro-Victorian Novel', in E. S. Shaffer (ed.), *The Third Culture: Literature and Science*, 253–68, Berlin: De Gruyter.

Sloan, C. (2016), 'Possessing Dresses: Fashion and Female Community in *The Woman in White*', *Victorian Literature and Culture*, 44: 801–16. Available online: https://doi:10.1017/S106015031600022X (accessed 5 June 2022).

Smelik, A. (2018), 'New materialism: A Theoretical Framework for Fashion in the Age of Technological Innovation', *International Journal of Fashion Studies*, 5 (1): 33–54. Available online: https://doi:10.1386/infs.5.1.33_1 (accessed 9 December 2021).

Souhami, D. (2014), *Gwendolen: A Novel*, London: Quercus.

Spooner, C. (2004), *Fashioning Gothic Bodies*, Manchester: Manchester University Press.

Spooner, C. (2007), ' "Spiritual Garments": Fashioning the Victorian Séance in Sarah Waters' Affinity', in C. Kuhn and C. Carlson (eds), *Styling Texts: Dress and Fashion in Literature*, 351–69, New York: Cambria Press.

Spooner, C. (2016), 'Masks, Veils, Disguises', in W. Hughes, D. Punter and A. Smith (eds), *The Encyclopedia of the Gothic*, 421–4, Chichester: John Wiley and Sons.

Stallybrass, P. (1999), 'Worn Worlds: Clothes, Mourning, and the Life of Things', in D. Ben-Amos and L. Weissberg (eds), *Cultural Memory and the Construction of Identity*, 27–44, Detroit: Wayne State University Press.

Stallybrass, P., and A. R. Jones (2001), 'Fetishizing the Glove in Renaissance Europe', *Critical Inquiry*, 28 (1), 114–32. https://www.jstor.org/stable/1344263 (accessed 7 February 2023).

Starling, B. (2007), *The Journal of Dora Damage*, London: Bloomsbury.

Steele, V. (2001), *The Corset: A Cultural History*, New Haven: Yale University Press.

Stephen, C. (1868), 'Thoughtfulness in Dress', *Cornhill Magazine*, 18 (105): 281–98.

Stetz, M. (2009a), '"Would You Like Some Victorian Dressing with That?"'. *Romanticism and Victorianism on the Net*, 55. Available online: https://www.erudit.org/fr/revues/ravon/2009-n55-ravon3697/039557ar/ (accessed 4 January 2022).

Stetz, M. (2009b), '"A Language Spoken Everywhere": Fashion Studies and English Studies', *Working with English: Medieval and Modern Language, Literature, and Drama*, 5 (1): 62–72.

Stetz, M. (2017), 'Looking at Victorian Fashion: Not a Laughing Matter', in M. L. Kohlke and C. Gutleben (eds), *Neo-Victorian Humour: Comic Subversions and Unlaughter in Contemporary Historical Re-Visions*, 147–69, Amsterdam: Brill/Rodopi.

Stewart, S. ([1984] 1993), *On Longing: Narratives of the Miniature, the Gigantic, the Souvenir, the Collection*, Durham: Duke University Press.

Stickney Ellis, S. (1839), *The Women of England, Their Social Duties, and Domestic Habits*, 11th edn, London: Fisher, Son. Available online: https://archive.org/details/womenofenglandth00ellirich/page/n5/mode/2up (accessed 10 June 2022).

Summers, L. (2001), *Bound to Please: A History of the Victorian Corset*, London: Berg.

Taylor, L. (2002), *The Study of Dress History*, Manchester: Manchester University Press.

Taylor, L. ([1983] 2009), *Mourning Dress: A Costume and Social History*, 2nd edn, London: Routledge.

Tennant, E. (2002), *Felony: The Private History of 'The Aspern Papers'*, London: Vintage.

'The Etiquette of Mourning' (1875), *Myra's Journal of Dress and Fashion*: 3.

'The Fashions' (1869), *The Englishwoman's Domestic Magazine*, vi: 205.

'The History and Varieties of Mourning' (1843), *The Court and Lady's Magazine, Monthly Critic and Museum*: 159–61.

Tilley, C. (2006), 'Theoretical Perspectives: Introduction', in C. Tilley, W. Keane, S. Küchler, M. Rowlands, and P. Spyer (eds), *Handbook of Material Culture*, 7–11, London: Sage.

Tóibín, C. (2004), *The Master*, London: Picador.

Toussaint, L., and A. Smelik (2017), 'Memory and Materiality in Hussein Chalayan's Techno-Fashion', in L. Munteán, L. Plate, and A. Smelik (eds), *Materializing Memory in Art and Popular Culture*, 89–105, Abingdon: Routledge.

Trollope, A. ([1871] 2011), *The Eustace Diamonds*, Oxford: Oxford University Press.

Veblen, T. ([1899] 2007), *The Theory of the Leisure Class*, (ed.) M. Banta, Oxford: Oxford University Press.
'Veils' (1889), *The London Journal, and Weekly Record of Literature, Science, and Art*: 15.
Waal, A., and U. Kluwick (2022), 'Victorian Materialisms: Approaching Nineteenth-Century Matter', *European Journal of English Studies*, 26 (1): 1–13. Available online: https://www.tandfonline.com/doi/full/10.1080/13825577.2022.2044143 (accessed 7 May 2022).
Wallace, D. (2005), *The Woman's Historical Novel: British Women Writers, 1900–2000*, Basingstoke: Palgrave Macmillan.
Waters, S. ([1998] 1999), *Tipping the Velvet*, London: Virago Press.
Waters, S. ([1999] 2000), *Affinity*, London: Virago Press.
Waters, S. ([2002] 2003), *Fingersmith*, London: Virago Press.
Waters, S. (2003), 'Hands That Mould the Imagination', *The Guardian*, https://www.theguardian.com/books/2003/mar/01/featuresreviews.guardianreview37 (accessed 29 March 2023).
'What led you to write Wanting? – Richard Flanagan talks about his new book Wanting', [video], YouTube (Random House Books AU, uploaded 21 October 2008), https://www.youtube.com/watch?v=CU8HBveze3A (accessed 26 March 2023).
Widdowson, P. (2006), '"Writing back": Contemporary Re-Visionary Fiction', *Textual Practice*, 20 (3): 491–507. Available online: https://doi.org/10.1080/09502360600828984 (accessed 22 April 2022).
'Widows' Veils' (1839), *The Mirror of Literature, Amusement, and Instruction*, 34 (984): 426.
Wilde, O. ([1891] 2008), *The Picture of Dorian Gray*, London: Penguin Classics.
Wilson, E. (2003), *Adorned in Dreams: Fashion and Modernity*, London: Virago.
Wilson, S. R. (2003), 'Quilting as Narrative Art: Metafictional Construction in *Alias Grace*', in S. Wilson (ed.), *Margaret Atwood's Textual Assassinations: Recent Poetry and Fiction*, 121–34. Columbus: Ohio State University.
Wood, E. ([1861] 2005), *East Lynne*, Oxford: Oxford University Press.
Wynne, D. (2008), 'Equivocal Objects: The Problem of Women's Property in Daniel Deronda', *19: Interdisciplinary Studies in the Long Nineteenth Century*, 6: 1–21. Available online: https://doi.org/10.16995/ntn.473 (accessed 15 July 2022).
Wynne, D. (2010), *Women and Personal Property in the Victorian Novel*, Farnham: Ashgate.
Yan, S. (2019), 'The Art of Working in Hair: Hair Jewellery and Ornamental Handiwork in Victorian Britain', *The Journal of Modern Craft* 12 (2): 123–39. Available online: https://doi.org/10.1080/17496772.2019.1620429 (accessed 15 May 2022).
Yeh, Y. (2014), 'Between Reality and Contrivance: Body Performance and Class Imagination in Sarah Waters' *Fingersmith*', *Humanitas Taiwanica*, 81: 149–72.

Yoder, E. M. (2014), 'Sad Rags: Tales of Enchanted Dresses', *Sewanee Review*, 122 (3): 478–83. Available online: https://doi.org/10.1353/sew.2014.0076 (accessed 25 July 2022).

Zabus, C. (2001), 'Subversive Scribes: Rewriting in the 20th Century', *Anglistica*, 5: 191–207.

Zimmerman, B. S. (1977), '"Radiant as a Diamond": George Eliot, Jewelry and the Female Role', *Criticism*, 19 (3), 212–22. Available online: https://www.jstor.org/stable/23103202 (accessed 12 February 2023).

Index

affect 2–3, 5, 9, 15, 20–4, 35–8, 62–3, 84, 86, 93, 104, 126, 136–7, 140, 142–3, 151–2, 155–6, 158–60, 165, 169–70, 174–8
agency
    female 3–4, 14, 27, 41, 47–8, 67–8, 110, 127–8, 140, 151, 162
    of things 3, 21, 23, 25–6, 30–1, 33–7, 40, 45, 49, 62–3, 88, 97–8, 152, 155, 174, 176, 178
    see also, Bennet, Jane; new materialism
Angel in the House 102, 123
animate 26, 29, 34–5, 37, 48–9, 57, 73, 86, 92, 158
    see also, agency, of things
Arias, Rosario 9, 24, 50, 67 n.2, 85, 92, 110, 113, 117, 127, 146
Arias, Rosario and Patricia Pulham 7, 9, 19, 32 n.3, 92
Arnold, Jean 141–2, 158 n.13, 161
art 4, 20, 33, 45, 83, 109, 115–16, 141, 143
assemblage 21, 35, 50, 60
    see also, Bennett, Jane
Atwood, Margaret 26, 32, 37–8, 49–56, 59–63, 176
    Alias Grace 26, 32, 37–38, 49, 50–2, 56–8, 60–3, 66, 75, 92, 176–7
authenticity 15, 37, 51, 53, 94, 110, 115, 137, 149, 152, 176

Barthes, Roland 2, 13, 91
Bayles Kortsch, Christine 14, 56
Bennett, Jane 21, 23, 33–6, 48, 58–60, 62
    see also, new materialism; thing power
biofiction 26, 37, 50, 56, 162, 171
Blackwood's Edinburgh Magazine 4, 158 n.12
Boehm, Katharina 22, 67 n.2
Boehm-Schnitker, Nadine and Susanne Gruss 9–10, 19, 89
Bow Bells 32, 82, 143–4

bracelet 27, 136–8, 152, 155–6, 165
    see also, hair jewellery; jewellery
Brontë, Charlotte 67, 106–7, 118, 129–30, 145, 146 n.8
    Jane Eyre 106–7, 118
brooch 27, 104, 137–8, 140, 143
    see also, jewellery
Brown, Bill 20, 35, 83, 166
    see also, thing theory
Byatt, A.S. 20–1, 27, 135–8, 165–6
    Possession 27, 135–8, 165, 170–1, 177
    The Biographer's Tale 20–1

Carlyle, Thomas 16, 29–31, 48–9, 59
    Sartor Resartus 16, 29–30, 49, 59, 141 n.4
class 7, 12, 16–17, 29, 52–3, 67–8, 70, 72, 78, 81–2, 102, 123, 125–6, 141–2, 151, 158, 168, 176
Collins, Wilkie 36, 67, 107, 120, 137 n.2, 145, 146 n.8, 168 n.14
    Armadale 107
    The Moonstone 146 n.8, 168 n.14
    The Woman in White 36, 107, 120
colonialism 28, 44, 132, 139, 167–8, 171–4
    see also, imperialism; postcolonialism
commodity culture 12, 16, 20, 54, 102
conspicuous consumption 12, 16, 102, 106
    see also, Veblen, Thorstein
Coole, Diana and Samantha Frost, 'Introducing the New Materialisms' 21, 33, 35
    see also, new materialism
corset 5–6, 19, 76–7, 131
costume 19, 36, 43–4, 51, 69, 74
    see also, disguise
crinoline 5–6, 52–3
cross-dressing 10 n.4, 19, 68–70, 95
cultural memory 7, 15, 66–7, 110
    see also, memory

Dickens, Charles 22, 30–2, 36, 48, 65, 67, 108, 117, 121, 124, 138, 140–2, 145–51, 153, 169, 171
  Bleak House 36, 108
  David Copperfield 124
  Great Expectations 65, 138, 146–53, 155–7
  Little Dorrit 141
  'Meditations in Monmouth Street' 30–31
  'The Black Veil' 108, 117, 121
diamonds 139, 141, 144–5, 146 n.8, 152, 154, 156, 160–1, 163–4, 166–9
  see also, gemstones; jewellery
disguise 36, 43, 51, 62, 68, 72, 100, 106–8, 111, 114–15, 120, 122, 127–8, 142
dress history 3, 15–16, 19, 81
  see also, history
Dunagen Osborne, Katherine 158 n.13, 160, 165, 168
Duncker, Patricia 19, 113, 119, 162

Eliot, George 108, 138–40, 145, 158–65, 167–9
  Daniel Deronda 138, 158, 160–3, 165–8
emotion 13, 15, 20, 22–4, 28, 30, 35–6, 38, 48–9, 61, 78, 91, 93, 102, 105, 126, 136–7, 140, 142, 152, 155–6, 158–60, 163–4, 169–70, 175–7
empire 28, 144, 168, 171–4
Englishwoman's Domestic Magazine, The 17–18, 126 n.14
entanglement 2–3, 11, 21, 29, 34–7, 46–7, 49, 60, 80, 126–7
  see also, new materialism

fashion 3–6, 9–20, 24, 26, 28, 31–3, 37, 54, 62, 67, 81, 99, 101–2, 108, 145, 147, 172, 177
  see also, fashionable; re-fashion
fashionable 4, 10, 29, 33, 53, 100–1, 124, 145, 147
  see also, fashion; re-fashion
femininity 5, 14, 17, 53–5, 72, 82, 102, 128, 140
  see also, gender
feminism 27, 33, 67, 78, 110, 132, 139–40, 147, 162, 169

Flanagan, Richard 28, 171–5
  Wanting 28, 171, 174–5
Foley, Liza 81, 84, 97–8
Frame, Ronald 27, 138, 139–40, 146–7, 149–52, 154–7, 169–70
  Havisham 27, 138–40, 146–7, 149–53, 155, 157–8, 162–3, 169, 171
Freedgood, Elaine 20, 167
Freud, Sigmund 45, 94 n.10, 153
  see also, uncanny

Gatrell, Simon 18, 26 n.9, 82–3
gemstones 84, 137, 142, 144–5, 147, 154, 160
  see also, diamonds; jewellery
gender 14, 16–17, 19, 27, 29, 52–3, 61, 67–70, 78, 82–3, 85, 95, 97–8, 102, 110–11, 123, 125, 128, 142, 150, 169, 173, 176
  see also, femininity; masculinity
Gilbert, Sandra and Susan Gubar, *The Madwoman in the Attic* 99, 106–7
gloves 3, 26–7, 52, 63, 65–7, 69–70, 74, 77–98, 100–1, 103, 148, 177
  see also, kidskin
Godey's Lady's Book 17, 54
Gordon, Lyndall 39–40, 42 n.10, 48–9, 63
gothic 49, 65, 100, 106, 108, 110, 112, 148
gowns 1, 3, 17–18, 26, 32, 39, 41, 44, 46, 48–9, 51–2, 58, 60, 62–3, 77, 92, 124–5, 129, 147, 177
Gruss, Susanne 110 n.8, 113, 116

hair jewellery 142–3, 146
  see also, bracelet; jewellery
Hamilakis, Yannis 47, 97
haptic 11, 85, 94, 177
  see also, touch
Hardy, Thomas 18, 82, 145, 146 n.8
  Tess of the D'Urbervilles 146 n.8
  The Mayor of Casterbridge 18
Hartley, Florence 81–2, 101, 145
Harwood, John 27, 98, 100, 109–11, 120–2, 133
  The Ghost Writer 27, 98, 100, 109–13, 117–24, 125, 127, 130, 132–3, 135
haunting 30, 32 n.3, 38, 40, 42, 45–6, 50, 57, 62, 98, 110, 117–118, 120–1
Heilmann, Ann 19, 42, 69

Heilmann, Ann, and Mark Llewellyn, *Neo-Victorianism* 7, 11, 109–10, 113–14, 120–2, 123 n. 12, 130, 150
history 8–9, 11–12, 15, 24, 37, 50, 60, 66–7, 80–1, 85, 91–2, 97, 99, 109, 112, 120, 128, 133–4, 138, 140, 149, 157, 160, 164, 166, 168, 171, 174, 177
historiography 8, 55, 61, 91
historiographic metafiction 8, 38, 138
    see also, Hutcheon, Linda
homoeroticism 26, 43, 44–5, 66
homosexuality 43, 45
    see also, lesbian; sexuality
Hughes, Clair 13, 18, 41–2, 120
Hutcheon, Linda 8, 38, 136
    see also, historiographic metafiction

identity 3–5, 12, 18, 25, 27–8, 35, 42, 47, 51, 53, 67–8, 70–1, 74, 76–7, 107, 118, 120, 127, 134, 139–40, 142, 146, 151–2, 155, 158, 160, 169, 173
    sexual 44, 152
imperialism 20, 167, 168, 174
    see also, colonialism
industrialization 20, 22, 101, 124, 144, 178
intertextuality 7, 11, 67, 89, 109, 113, 120–1, 124–5, 129–30, 155 n.11

James, Henry 37–40, 42, 45
    'The Romance of Certain Old Clothes' 40, 42
jewellery 3, 26–7, 134, 136–46, 151–61, 164, 166–7, 169–71, 177
    see also, bracelet; brooch; hair jewellery; necklace
jet 27, 104, 136–7, 145, 147
    see also, mourning

Kaplan, Cora 7, 19, 24, 75 n.7, 135, n.1
kidskin 79–80, 95–7
    see also, gloves
Kohlke, Marie-Luise 7, 9, 37, 73, 110, 123, 125, 128, 131
Kosofsky Sedgwick, Eve 93, 108
Kuhn, Cynthia 52, 56–7, 59 n.13, 60

Lanone, Catherine 172–4
Latour, Bruno 34 n.5
lesbian 67–8, 75, 85, 87, 89, 90, 95, 98
    see also, queer
Lester, Katherine, and Bess V. Oerke, *Accessories of Dress* 99, 101–2
Llewellyn, Mark 7, 72, 95 n.11, 113
Lutz, Deborah 31, 73, 80, 102, 124, 130

Marcus, Sharon 54, 153
masculinity 4, 56, 69, 94, 97, 124
    see also, femininity; gender
material culture 10, 12, 31, 55, 62, 73, 89, 92, 99, 134, 176, 178
Material Culture Studies 3, 19, 20, 33
materiality 9, 19, 23–4, 31–2, 34–7, 40, 42, 46, 58, 65, 85, 109, 118, 134, 140, 143, 164, 166, 175
memory 9, 11, 15, 22, 24–5, 28, 30–1, 37–8, 40, 42, 46–8, 50, 59–61, 63, 97, 134, 140, 156–8, 164–5, 169, 175, 177–8
    see also, cultural memory
metafiction 2, 7, 38, 51, 68, 109, 115, 129–30, 150, 153, 162–3
Mitchell, Kate 9, 66
mourning 24, 72, 99, 102–5, 108, 110, 124–7, 129, 142–3, 146, 157
    see also, veils, weeping; widow
muslin 104, 114–15, 120
Myra's Journal of Dress and Fashion 17, 104

narrative 2–3, 5, 7, 9, 11–15, 20, 22–3, 26, 30–2, 35–8, 42, 44, 52–3, 55–6, 61–3, 65, 70–3, 80, 91, 95, 99, 105–6, 108–11, 118, 120–1, 124–5, 132–4, 136, 140, 142, 146, 149, 150–1, 157, 161, 163–6, 169, 171, 174–8
necklace 28, 139, 145, 152, 154–6, 158–61, 164–6, 169, 171–4
    see also, bracelet; jewellery
neo-Victorianism 3, 7–8, 10–11, 16, 19–23, 32, 38, 61, 89, 92, 98, 109, 111, 126, 130, 146, 170–1
new materialism 3, 20–2, 26, 32–7, 40, 62–3, 137
needlework, *see*, sewing
Novák, Caterina 125–6, 132–3

O'Callaghan, Claire 67, 87, 90, 139 n.3, 147 n.10, 150
olfactory 24–5, 48, 118
    see also, smell

patchwork 50, 50 n.12, 52, 56, 60–3, 177
patriarchy 1, 14, 51, 55, 69, 78, 99, 127, 132, 139, 150, 163, 167
performance 19, 44, 68–71, 82, 97, 104
 see also, performativity
performativity 51, 70–1, 89
 see also, performance
phenomenology 1, 9, 24, 33 n.4, 44, 85, 97, 126
Pointon, Marcia 145, 153–4, 168
postcolonialism 140, 168, 171
 see also, colonialism; imperialism
postmodernism 8, 38, 61, 177
Pre-Raphaelites 114, 116 n.10, 120

Queen Victoria 102
queer 19, 43, 63, 65, 67, 85–6, 91, 97–8
 see also, homosexuality; lesbian

race 7, 82, 123, 128, 142, 168, 176
realist fiction 3, 61, 67, 108, 169
recycling 10, 125, 130
re-fashioning 3, 9–10, 15, 25, 32, 51, 55, 66, 97–8, 130, 152, 156, 170, 175
 see also, fashion; fashionable; self-fashioning
Rhys, Jean 8, 139, 140
 Wide Sargasso Sea 25, 139–40, 155 n.11
Ricoeur, Paul 92

self-fashioning 9, 53, 63, 109, 114
 see also, fashion; fashionable; re-fashioning
sensation fiction 3, 67, 71–2, 105–8, 110, 120–1, 128, 137 n.2, 146, 169
senses, the 24, 29, 46–8, 59, 65, 85, 88, 93, 143, 157, 177
 see also, touch; smell
Serres, Michel 11, 25, 110
sewing 16, 55–7
sexuality 3, 5, 7, 14, 43–5, 67–8, 77, 90, 108, 128–9, 153, 167
 see also, homosexuality; lesbian
Seys, Madeleine C. 14, 114–15
Shiller, Dana 8, 135, 138, 150
silk 1–2, 43, 53, 69, 71, 74, 88, 101 n.2, 104, 105 n.5, 105 n.6, 108, 124, 128, 130, 148, 173, 175

skin 45, 59, 66, 75, 77, 81–4, 110, 117, 122–3, 128, 131–2, 171–3, 177
smell 24–5, 47, 48 n.11, 66, 118
 see also, olfactory
Souhami, Diana 26–7, 138–9, 140, 146, 158, 161–70
 Gwendolen 26–7, 138–40, 158, 161–69, 171
spiritualism 1, 73–4, 93, 96, 100, 108
Spooner, Catherine 29, 30 n.1, 67 n.2, 74, 99, 106, 108
Stallybrass, Peter and Ann Rosalind Jones 37, 66, 83, 88, 96
Starling, Belinda 27, 98, 100, 109–10, 122–5, 127–8, 132–3
 The Journal of Dora Damage 27, 98, 100, 109–11, 122–5, 128, 130, 133
Stetz, Margaret 6, 19, 176
Stickney Ellis, Sarah 17, 102
storytelling 13–14, 55–6, 61, 63, 73, 175
supernatural 51, 56, 60, 74
 see also, haunting

Taylor, Lou 13, 105
temporality 5, 10, 11, 13, 25, 48, 66, 80, 90, 135–7, 147, 165, 175
 see also, time
textiles 9, 11, 14, 54, 61, 88, 110, 116, 126, 129–30, 177
texts and 3, 9, 12, 14–15
texture 3–4, 14, 66, 94, 101, 104–5
thing power, *see* Bennett, Jane
thing theory 3, 20–1, 33
 see also, Brown, Bill
time 11, 15, 24–5, 53, 77, 80, 91, 130
 see also, temporality
Tóibín, Colm 26, 32, 37–8, 40, 42–3, 45, 48–50, 56–8, 62–3, 176
 The Master 26, 32, 37–9, 42–6, 50, 56, 58, 62–3, 66, 92, 176
touch 24–6, 45–6, 57, 65–6, 78, 80, 83, 85–91, 93–5, 98, 130, 136–7, 143, 156–7, 177
 see also, haptic; senses, the
trace, the, *see* Ricoeur, Paul
trauma 7, 110–11, 117, 163, 166

uncanny 2, 24, 30, 40–1, 45, 49, 62, 92, 94, 107, 110, 114, 118–21, 131
undressing 44–5, 74, 87

Veblen, Thorstein 16
　see also, conspicuous consumption
veils 1, 3, 19, 26–7, 70, 98–102, 105–22, 124–9, 132–4, 148
　bridal 41, 102, 106, 120, 148
　weeping 105 n.6, 102–3, 105, 117, 124–8
　see also, mourning; widow
velvet 1–2, 70–1, 74, 88, 116, 173, 175

Waters, Sarah 1, 19, 23, 26–7, 53, 63, 65–70, 72–8, 85–6, 89–93, 95–8, 107
　Affinity 1, 23, 26, 53, 65, 67–8, 70, 72, 74–5, 85–6, 88, 93, 95, 96–8

Fingersmith 26, 53, 65, 67–8, 70–2, 74–6, 78, 85–6, 88–9, 92, 94–8, 107, 128
Tipping the Velvet 19, 26, 65, 67–8, 70–1, 74, 85–6, 90, 96–8
wealth 4, 141–2, 149, 151, 154–5, 158, 163
widow 72 n.6, 102–5, 127, 131–3
　see also, mourning; veils, weeping
Wilde, Oscar 67, 116
　The Picture of Dorian Gray 116
written dress 13, 21, 23–4, 91
　see also, Barthes, Roland
Wynne, Deborah 158 n.13, 160–1

Young Englishwoman, The 17, 101, 104

www.ingramcontent.com/pod-product-compliance
Lightning Source LLC
Chambersburg PA
CBHW052116300426
44116CB00010B/1691